King's Gambit

Mark Nelson

HADLEY
RILLE
BOOKS

KING'S GAMBIT
Copyright © 2013 by Mark Nelson

Cover art © Tom Vandenberg

Map of Perspa © Ginger Prewitt

ISBN-13 978-0-9849670-1-8

Edited by Terri-Lynne DeFino

Published by
Hadley Rille Books
Eric T. Reynolds, Publisher
PO Box 25466
Overland Park, KS 66225
USA
www.hadleyrillebooks.com
contact@hadleyrillebooks.com

For my parents, the two biggest heroes in my life.

Acknowledgments

This book represents, I hope, the best sort of interaction between editor and author. From draft to draft *King's Gambit* was subject to close scrutiny, encouragement, cajoling and outright criticism that is essential if a story is going to be the best it can be and still remain true to its original vision. Terri-Lynne Defino embodies all the qualities a developing author needs: passion and compassion, honesty and skill, a great ear and a sharp pair of eyes. She catches me when I get lazy and applauds me when I get it right. I'm proud of the work here from both of us.

Once again, extra eyes helped in this novel's evolution. Jessica Carter, Kekoa and Grace Gabriel, Jeff Charbonneau, Kathy and Ken Johnson, and my other colleagues at Zillah High School, Kim and Rich Ross, my parents, Joey Barat, my wife, my kids and the folks who were kind enough to purchase and read my first book; I owe all of you so much more than mere thanks. The support and response from my audience has been one of the most interesting and exciting experiences of my life. I feel blest interacting with such positive and inspiring people.

Special recognition should go to Eric T. Reynolds and the rest of the HRB family. Since meeting everyone last May, I feel like I am connected to a great group of professionals dedicated to producing quality, lasting stories. And a special thanks to the owners and staff of The Northtown Coffee Shop in Selah, Washington for good brews, friendly service and a great atmosphere for writing and editing.

And to my sister-authors at Heroines of Fantasy, thank you for letting me contribute to the blog. Getting mentioned in the same breath with all of you is an honor.

Happy Reading!
Mark Nelson
Spring 2013

Chapter 1: Eleni Caralon

JANUARY'S CHILL MADE the library a cold place to work. Eleni Caralon paused her writing, put down her quill and blew on tired, frigid fingers. She raised her eyes from her work; beyond the circle of light generated by her two small candles, work tables and stacks full of bound volumes receded into shadow. The ceiling of the third floor room loomed as an indefinite weight suspended in the darkness above. She drew in the tantalizing hints of candle wax and dust, the mold of age and weathered tomes. In the brief months of her tenure as the first female scholar at the College in Pevana such tinctures of smell and taste, that intrinsic mixture of wisdom, words and warrant, had become as familiar to her as the outline of her husband Tomais' face.

Eleni blew once more to warm her fingers, and then took up her quill, dipped it into the ink well and continued writing.

Although I feel the passage of time
In the history of words that aren't mine,
It all comes to a purpose in some way;
The words will show me how, someday.
And the story of the sun in our lives
Is written in the language of fine lines
That frame the shapes of our eyes
In a tracery of loyalty divine.
And the mirror then holds the key
For all things that were or will be;
So I must needs pause and spare a glance
To see what sort of words may chance. . .
To come.

Her thoughts ran out as the ink thinned to a barely legible line at the last word, and she put the quill back in the well. She contemplated the piles of papers stacked before her tablet and the changes to her life they represented.

She had known their authors only briefly during those heady days of the Summer Festival last August. The right hand pile held the troubled expressions of Devyn Ambrose, the tack-maker Malom's former horse trainer. They had been found neatly tied by a leather thong and nestled in an oilskin pouch tied to an old cavalry camp desk. Malom gave them to Tomais one day in the early autumn after Eleni's husband had delivered an order of newly cured leather to his establishment. By then everyone in the area knew of Eleni's appointment to the college.

As Eleni read his journal and poetry, she came to understand something of the anger and the angst of those days. For her, such notions of power and faith denied, of threat and loss, existed only on the periphery; things beyond her ken and care at the time. But as Eleni noted the changes in her life and city over the winter, Devyn's words took on added meaning and spurred her on to collect as much local truth, as much of the visceral Pevanese housed in rhyme and story as she could.

She reached out and ran the fingers of her right hand over the topmost page of the left-hand pile, one of the only clean pages in the stack. The others were a collection of rumpled, torn and soiled bits and pieces pasted together with stick-um. They had come to her on a cool day in November, nearly two months ago, when she stopped by to deliver an order of mended shirts for one of the king's cavalry officers quartered at Gania Landare's boarding house. Graciously accepting the offer of a cup of hot tea before leaving, she and Gania sat in the kitchen, quietly talking of the changes that had come to Pevana since the summer. The memory of the sound of Gania's gruff voice made Eleni's lips purse in a small smile.

"And I'll tell you, young mistress," Gania had said, pouring tea from a steaming kettle. "I'm of two minds these days. The King's coin goes far, mind you, and the lot I've got sleeping upstairs are pretty fair spoken—and nice to look at, too, if I do say. What I don't like is the noise. They move with such a clatter in those boots and body armor. I've come to dread the days when they set to drilling. All that stamping and shouting puts me off my thought. I can't imagine what Prince Donari thinks about having so many strangers filling up his city."

"They are soldiers, Gania," Eleni had replied. "I think the noise must come with the trade. I've never found, in all my readings, any accounts of battle described as *quiet*. But at least they pay, for now. Would you rather the king's soldiers with a vocation, or poets and dreams?"

"Yes, well, mistress, I don't hold much stock in books *telling* much of anything. As for noise, well, take young Talyior now. You made some shirts for him last summer I recall. He spent most of his time scribbling and trying to show himself for an artist. And what did his poems get him? Trouble along with fame, that's what! And my house thrown over in the bargain. What did he win, mind you? Set upon by Sevire's bravos at the Finals word had it, the night he took the prize! Him and the other fellow, Ambrose, both gone in the night, forgotten. Now that's silence for you!"

"True, but words have a way of remaining behind. Words last, you know. Long after the poet's voice is silenced, the words can still speak. Words can raze mountains, Gania, mark me, they can topple kings."

"I wouldn't know anything about that, mistress. I'm an honest housekeeper. There are times when I miss the lad, but the coin from these horse-boys is more consistent. You've given me bits to think on, and that reminds me. After I cleaned up the place the night Talyior went off to the palace, I gathered up his bits and pieces. I almost tossed them on the midden pile because I hardly expected him to live past the night. He never came back, but I kept them. Set here and finish your cup and I'll fetch them. If you don't find them useful, they might make a nice blaze with the ink and all."

Eleni had taken those remnants of Talyior's efforts, set them next to Devyn's, and studied their messages that winter. As the chill deepened, her obsession grew, and she felt tied to the lives outlined within; they cast an eldritch magic on her that intensified over time. They set her rooting about the shelved tomes where she came across other small bits of fine paper tucked away in books like long-forgotten book marks. These snatches of verse, all composed in the same fine hand, comprised the middle pile of the three.

The middle pile especially intrigued her, for many of them took the form of questions, the kind a young, perceptive mind would ask about the large questions in life. She picked up the topmost piece of paper, her most recent find and the one she liked the best:

They flout their pillars of reason and sense
Using such to construct a sound defense
Against the strangeness of the new
Against a changing of the view:
A line of crows atop the fence.
Let them caw in futile unison
Waste the gift of Renia's benison
While the young seek their way
To claim the power of their day
And so break the febrile foundation. . .

She replaced the paper on its pile. All three bore a relation that lurked just beyond her candle's glow, but understanding loitered outside of candlelight, lost in shadows that promised everything but as yet delivered nothing.

Changes—understanding them was the key.

She made ready to leave. Her candles had burned down three hourmarks. She suspected dawn an hour off. Gathering her bundles together, she eased them carefully into a bag with a long strap.

Before the events of the summer, it held her sewing kit and extra threads.

Blowing one candle out, Eleni took up the other to light her way down the main stairs, and out of the building. She trailed a finger along musty spines as she moved through the shelves and wondered if

14

those authors felt secure in the answers they found. Were all such collected thoughts affectation, a vain attempt to explain fate? Minuet's arrows were the easy answer merited for children to provide order. Eleni loved words and the books that held them, but suspected they represented only partial answers.

In the end, perhaps fate is change.

History tended to forget beginnings in favor of endings. The truth was: things happened. Lives altered. Fate and change. Change and fate.

A whispered breath of wind extinguished her candle just before she turned to go down the stairs. The sudden darkness forced her to grab the railing, foot poised above the topmost step while she waited for her eyes to adjust. And in the silence of the moment, she heard steps approach down the hall and then voices coming from two shadows at the foot of the stairs.

"My Lord Prelate—" began the right-hand figure.

"You've returned too soon, you fool!" The left-hand shadow hissed. "The time isn't right. You could spoil everything."

A sullen growl responded from the shadow on the right. "What was I to do, my lord? Roderran somehow got wind of me and decided he needed a messenger. How could I refuse?"

Eleni's breath caught in her throat, and her knees threatened to give way. She knew both those voices: Lord Prelate Byrnard Casan, and Jaryd Corvale. The last time she had heard the latter's growl, the Maze burned. Fear ripped through her veins, but she managed sidle back a few feet from the stairway to listen.

"I expect you to follow orders, idiot! Donari has a long memory. You should have come with Roderran, not ahead of him."

"He gave me letters, to you, my lord. I had to take them."

"Letters? What nonsense! Letters can fall into the wrong hands."

"But they did not, my lord. I have them right—"

"Incompetence!" the Prelate fumed. "The vanguard is here in this compliant, if decadent, city. Spring is only a season away and he sends me letters. Give them to me. No, not here, you fool! Come into my chambers."

Both shadows faded away into the darkness. Eleni knelt to gather her wits and courage. A moment later a door opened, spewing a shaft of light that gave shape to the hallway's dimensions. She froze, afraid but compelled. The light slowly faded as the door swung to until the barest sliver remained. She knew those rooms; Casan and Corvale were likely seated around the Prelate's desk in the inner office.

She settled her books and papers more snugly in her bag and crept down the stairs. Her heartbeat throbbed as she neared the half-open door, the urge to run rising like a clench in her throat. She paused at the door, fingers lightly touching the wall, and slipped halfway into the room. Their voices, faint but audible, contested with the pulsing in her ears. She calmed her breathing, listened, paces away from two of the most dangerous men in the kingdom, arrogantly secure in their isolation at that late hour. Glasses tinkled. Liquid poured. Leather creaked.

"Mmmm, very good my lord. The fare on the road south left much to be desired."

"If you had remained in Perspa as I had arranged, then you would have drunk better—much good that it would have done you. Now, let the wine ease your tongue. Speak! What was Roderran's mind ere you left?"

"He was restless, over jovial, to my thinking. The waiting has not suited him. He wanted to accompany the foot when they left in October. The Queen's miscarriage has overset the balance of their marriage."

"Don't be presumptuous," the Prelate growled. "Give me news without the speculation, you fool."

"My lord bade me listen and observe." Corvale's sullen tone transported her back to that rainy night from the summer; that cold and contemptuous voice, the face twisted in a mix of fear and derision despite having the point of Senden Arolli's sword pressed against his larynx.

"The Queen's misfortune happened in August!" The Prelate's waspish disgust snapped her thoughts in two. "What of it?"

"The palace maids say he hasn't slept with her since."

"I see," said the Prelate. "And he has turned to?"

"Just about every other female in the place."

"He always was a rake." The Prelate laughed, a mirthless chuckle that chilled Eleni's skin. "Especially when he was looking forward to a campaign. And the queen?"

"She has removed every one of Roderran's conquests that she can discover. The maids say the atmosphere in the palace is horrendous. She rages. He rampages. She despairs. He grows increasingly uninterested. I think he would set her aside if he could though it leaves him heirless on the eve of coming south."

"What did I tell you about speculation?"

"I beg my lord's forgiveness, but you asked for news that might impact affairs here. Surely you must see what that portends?"

"I see it, fool! I don't need you to instruct me on Perspan dynastic policy. No king may leave the realm without an heir at least expectant in the royal womb. He's behaving stupidly, neglecting her for invasion plans. She's had time to heal. He's ignoring her, risking insult to her father—a third of whose troops are quartered here now. He's leaving too early. He's leaving my hands tied. He's leaving—"

"—Donari as his only possible heir."

The Prelate heaved a breath "Which is unfortunate."

"For Donari." Corvale chuckled.

Their words, the implications struck Eleni like winter's first hard wind. Whatever King Roderran's behavior in the capital, or his intentions in coming to Pevana, Prince Donari was her patron. *Unfortunate.* She had to get word to him.

Easing back through the door to the center of the passageway, Eleni held her breath until she came to the main doors. She did not even pause to tie a scarf around her ears against the cold, and spared one glance back down the hallway.

The office door remained nearly closed. *Safe.* Clutching her bag of papers, she squeezed through the main door, shut it quickly against the draft, and ran like fear for home.

The predawn sky began to splatter a cold rain that grew in intensity, pushed along by a chill northern wind, drenching her by the time she reached her front door. She struggled with the latch. When she finally managed to open it, a bracing gust threatened to tear the handle from her hand. She stumbled inside, closed the door and leaned back against it with a quivering, dripping sigh.

She listened for sound of her husband. Her noisy entrance had not awakened Tomais, or he wasn't there. She slumped a little. The wind and rain beat against the windows with increasing fervor. Words on pages, words overheard. The weather was not the only thing changing; she could feel it down to her shivering bones.

"Tomais! Tomais?"

No answering call. Had he worked through the night in his workshop? Or was he already gone for the day? Pushing off the door, Eleni stripped off her wet cloak, let her bag slip to the floor, and sat down at the kitchen table, cradling her tumbled thoughts with fingers of ice.

It will be a cold, wet day of worry. Damn it all.

Chapter 2: Gallina

RAIN DRIPPED DOWN THE BACK of Devyn's neck as he urged his mount through the stream and up the last slope to where the gates of the mining town called Gallina still stood open despite the late hour. After a half-year spent on the road playing at inns, tupping maids, and spending Prince Donari's gold, the constant presence of King's Theology priests all along the coast never ceased to gall the good times as efficiently as the weather did.

They moved inland, hoping to avoid both, but a late winter storm had trapped them in a hillside cave. The aftermath resulted in nearly a month of wet, frustrating travel, plagued by paths cut by streams in spate, mud that sucked at hoof and boot. They had been forced to endure more than a few cheerless camps, shivering under poor cover, waiting out the worst of it. Once he and Talyior set out from their cave, Devyn's first intention had been to cross the hills to the head of the valley that ran down to the coastal city of Teirne, the first of the independent city states, but whenever they stopped they heard variations of the same thing: rumors of northern war preparations, pushy priests, and more rain.

Devyn took note of the signs. *More than our fame has followed us. Doors, paths. The north is closed. I couldn't go back to Pevana now even if I wanted to. Too many changes.*

He reined in his mount before the gate to allow Talyior to catch up. Underneath his friend's soggy hat, Devyn noted the concern for the canvas-wrapped guitar bouncing on his shoulder. If water got into the wood, the facing could warp. A pity. Verse set to music had become their stock and trade. Devyn was doubly happy that his own flute was safely stowed away from the damp at the bottom of his saddle bag.

Talyior drew even with him and Devyn turned his horse so that, side by side, they rode underneath the wooden arch and into Gallina, a hardscrabble mining town allegianced to Desopolis, the largest of all the southern city-states.

Devyn asked directions to the nearest inn from the two gate guards. It turned out to be the only one in the place; a two story affair that sported its own stables and fronted the square. Devyn dismounted and checked the weight of his purse. He doubted they would meet with much call for their show in such a poor-looking place, but he knew he still had enough for a day or two in a warm bed for both of them.

He was too tired to haggle with the bearded, balding innkeeper over the price. After a desultory meal and an hour's warmth by the fire, they headed up to their room. Devyn lay on his bed while Talyior sat in a chair quietly strumming away the journey's effect on guitar strings seemingly no worse for the torrential rains.

"How did we come to this?" Talyior asked.

"A series of unfortunate events, as I recall," Devyn replied, his mood just on the edge of testy. He still felt a chill around his heart that the fire could not leach away. "One too many innkeeper's daughters for you, I think. That last one back on the coast, remember."

"She had dark hair. Reminded me of Demona."

"She also had a young man attached to her, or didn't you notice?"

Talyior strummed, an off-note this time. "Nope. I never do, never have, probably never will."

"You are hopeless."

"Probably, but I just spent a month without, wet, and wandering. Right now I'd settle for just forgetting everything and sleeping dreamless."

Devyn turned to face his friend. "Can you? Forget her? Tal, it has been half a year."

Talyior did not return the look. He placed his fingers intently on the strings, strummed and sang quietly:

* * *

And it was rain on a Wednesday
That washed the name of my lover
From the sands of a Tuesday
Where we lay down together
For a time.
But as the rain smoothed away the grains
I lost hold of her name
And try as I might I just can't remember...

He let the strings fade to silence. "I don't know," he said. "When I think about forgetting, I just remember more." He leaned his guitar against the chair, took the candle over to his bed, settled himself on the covers and blew them both into darkness.

The weak sun burning through the late-winter haze woke Devyn up first and, leaving Talyior snoring into his pillow, sent him downstairs in search of breakfast. The innkeeper's wife provided him with a cup of hot tea and a meat roll. Devyn sat at a table outside the inn munching, and warming himself with the tea against the morning chill.

It was market day in the village, and Devyn watched idly as carters from the little upland farms round about brought in what scanty extra produce they had to sell along with the odd wares. There were precious few of them. One held thick woolen sweaters, woven from the last of the summer wool stock. Another bore a collection of earthen ceramics and votive statues. The sight of the Old Ways artifacts drew Devyn's interest. Smells of incense sparked memories of summer flames.

He watched idly as a young mother pushed a barrow full of linen cloth past his table. As she labored, she chatted with a young girl of maybe twelve or thirteen walking alongside.

". . .and it looks like we'll have some sun after all," said the mother.

The girl's piping, musical voice snicked Devyn's interest as the pair drew near. "And we could use a bit of sun, couldn't we, mother? It makes everything look less dreary."

"Yes, dear, watch out for that puddle there. Now, Grayce, let's set these up between old man Harvet's tools and Smithson's statues. It'll be our little joke, a bit of softness between the work and the gods!"

"But won't that be upsetting, mother? Smithson's face always reminds me of Boriman, such a scowl."

The young mother chuckled. "That may be true, missy, but Smithson is a friend of your father's, and besides, even the god Boriman is said to have a sense of humor."

"So, was that thunder last night him laughing?"

"Very likely. I said he had a sense of humor; I didn't say it was soft."

Devyn smiled sadly. Kembril used to delight in telling tales about the mischievous, cranky deity whose adventures usually involved mistaken identity and upset milk pails. Bittersweet memory teased but deigned to take him, and Devyn sipped them away with the sweetness from the tea.

The woman moved on to join the other carters to begin setting up her wares, her voice fading, leaving Devyn alone with his thoughts. Despite Gallina's isolation, he could sense an aspect of community he had missed in the towns and villages he and Talyior had frequented along the coast. He took another sip; the warm liquid softened cynicism's crust grown in him, washed it somewhat away. All through their coastwise adventures Devyn had felt the same pressure building, as though the problems he and Talyior left behind in Pevana followed them. The choice to head south only offered a partial solution. As he sipped, Devyn wondered if they were running *from* something or *to* it.

Folk gathered to inspect the wares on display. Devyn watched idly, nursing the second cup of tea the inn keeper's wife brought to him, uncalled for but appreciated. He even contemplated taking a stroll around the stalls and carts, but the notion died stillborn as he shifted weight to rise. In that moment a dog ran barking into the square from the western entrance, followed by a mounted procession led by several red-clad riders with a broad brimmed red hats.

They thronged in to the square, discommoding the shoppers and breaking the peaceful rhythm of the morning. The people scattered, but the priestly guards quickly positioned themselves so as to hem the people in, blocking their escape. Folk pushed, shouted surprise, anger and dismay. A child began to cry. Devyn's heart sank.

One of the outriders tipped over a stall of garments. Devyn sat up in his chair and tensed when a fractious mount of another one of the guards upset the barrow of linens. The young mother Devyn noted earlier only just managed to sweep her child out of harm's way. When another swung his weapon in a vicious arc, crashing through the ceramic, Old Ways statuettes, he half rose, cursing under his breath as he reached for his missing sword, still upstairs with the snoring Talyior. The commotion in the square brought other folk out, and when the innkeeper and his wife rushed through the door and by his table, he took his moment and slipped back inside.

He found Talyior wide awake, dressed and just finishing tossing his things into a pack, sword already strapped fighting style to his back. He looked up when Devyn entered.

"I've got your stuff already set," he said, setting his pack straps and glancing outside. "If we're lucky, we might be able to use the crowd to get to our horses. Their mounts look like they've ridden awhile. We might be able to outpace them."

Devyn checked the window before moving to the other bed to check his pack. "It is getting ugly out there. This is no passive group. Too many and too well armed. They smell like scouts."

"All the more reason for us to leave—now."

"Look," he said, grabbing Talyior's arm and urging him over to the window where they both knelt down below the sill. "We can't leave until they do, or we need to create enough chaos to make an escape, and I don't want to lose all our stuff."

Devyn felt Talyior's arm tense and guessed his friend understood their predicament.

"Dev, what are you thinking?"

"I'm not sure, but just running away seems wrong." Devyn scanned the scene below, the alarmed townsfolk, the market place in a shambles. Spearmen blocked the four streets and hemmed the mass. There were dark looks on the faces of some of the local men, miners toughened by hard labor.

A glimmer of a plan began to form in his mind, which flowered fully by the time he turned to tell Talyior. He smiled at the pained look on his friend's face; a season's worth of close contact had taught each of them how to read the other.

Devyn set to trussing up his pack. "It's not looking good down there," he said in tight, clipped tones. "Our Priest friends aren't too subtle. I might be able to rustle up something."

"And meanwhile?"

Devyn laughed a little. "Meanwhile, you mean while I'm down there running stupid risks and causing chaos. . ."

"Exactly, you know, making things difficult?"

Devyn tied off his pack flap. "I know you don't approve, but I'm tired of avoiding these fools. They've been all over this region, and you know what's coming after them. We've had a run, my friend, and it has been ripping, but those fellows down there mean more of what we left Pevana for. Lark's over."

Devyn shoved his pack over to Talyior and turned back to the window. Suddenly, their reasons for wending south became problematic. Were they escaping unpleasant memories, or were they taking sides in a conflict likely to consume the whole region? So serious, so quickly. Talyior must have sensed something similar, for he crossed to glance over Devyn's shoulder, and grunt at the scene below.

"Right," he murmured. "Lark's over. What are we doing?"

"I don't know, but we can't stay here."

"Perhaps we can't stay anywhere, without choosing."

"You know how I must choose, T. I don't ask you to choose the same."

Then it was Talyior's turn to chuckle. "Ridiculous," he scoffed. "And I always thought I was the romantic one."

"We could split. You could go home."

"To what? Rugs? My family? Absurd."

"So," began Devyn.

"So," finished Talyior, settling his guitar strap over his shoulders where it gave a musical tang when it bumped the pommel of his sword. "I've got your pack. Go do what you must, but watch yourself. Those spears look vicious. I'll have the horses saddled and ready in minutes." He turned at the door. "What will you do?"

Devyn checked to make sure his sword was loose in its sheath. "Something improvisational," he quipped. "I'm pretty good at inciting riots."

Devyn glanced again out the window; the *brothers* had trapped nearly a hundred townsfolk in the square. The Priests' guards, armed against carters and potters, paced their mounts back and forth. Missionary guards. Devyn sneered. Gallina apparently did not warrant an official military detachment. It was a true backwater. A dozen or so armed men could well dominate the place enough to accomplish the Priests' objectives. Settling his sword, grabbing his hat and cloak, he made his way to the front entrance and out the door to mingle at the back of the crowd.

Devyn sidled up behind the horseman stationed over near the stable. The guard in front of Devyn, at least, would have to go, and several more besides if they were to get away. He put a hand out, ever so gently, to pat the flank of the horse. Perhaps Devyn retained his touch with horses from his days at Malom's, or perhaps luck favored him, but the beast did not flinch or turn its head. He checked the square. All eyes seemed focused on one of the Priests, a sallow-faced fellow with graying temples poking out from under his red hat. When he spoke it was with a cold, commanding voice.

"Brothers and Sisters!" he began. "I bring you glorious news! No longer do you need live in ignorance and fear, subject to failed prayers to fashioned relics and empty pottery." He gestured to the upset table of statuettes, glaring the crowd silent.

Devyn ducked down beneath the guard's horse and deftly undid the belly strap. Keeping low to the ground, he worked his way around the back of the people facing the square and looked for something to use for missiles.

And then he saw the handful of broken Old Ways statuettes.

A group of women huddled together in front of the mess. The Priest admonished the people with empty words masking a sword pointed at the heart of belief. Devyn scowled, bent down and picked up a broken Borimon and hefted the god of mischief once for balance. He grinned as he heaved it high in the air and bent to grab another piece to throw. As the first missile grazed the rump of the head Priest's horse, shattering as it hit the cobble stones of the square, Devyn let loose a well-aimed throw that struck the nearest rider in the back of the head and toppled him from the saddle. The Priest's horse reared in alarm, upsetting and throwing the rider who landed with a sickening crunch on the ground.

The rider in front of the inn's stable urged his horse forward through the press of people and promptly slid off as the unstrapped saddle tipped sideways. Devyn darted into the mob, heading toward the now clear stable entry. People shouted in fear and anger. Miners grappled with guards. The other priest had dismounted and knelt at the side of his fallen comrade, shouting orders to the remaining riders to clear the area. Devyn had to pass right by him on his way to the stables. Talyior appeared in the doorway, mounted and holding the reins of the other horses. Devyn quickened his pace, noticed he still had a statuette in his hand, so he paused to lay the object on the chest of the unconscious priest. He bent down quickly to whisper into the face of his companion.

"Never discount the weight of the Old Ways, brother."

The man stared in disbelief for a second and then grabbed at Devyn's cloak as he rose to leave.

"Guards," the man began, but he never finished his sentence because Devyn, spinning neatly against the pressure of the man's grasp brought his left fist smashing into his face. The man slumped, stunned and bleeding over his companion. One of the guards rode up and thrust his spear. Devyn ducked under the blow, the wind of its passing almost knocking off his hat. Instinct then took over and Devyn drew his sword and in the same motion stepped inside the rider's guard and stabbed him in the groin. He ducked under the horse's nose to avoid the thrust of another rider, slashing at the man's arm as he ran by. He heard a cry and the rattle of the dropped weapon hitting the stones.

Just then Talyior clattered up with their horses. Devyn sheathed his blade and swung himself up in the saddle, turning once to survey the chaos he had caused. The square was a shambles. Every horseman was struggling to control his mount, people ran about in a melee of fear and riot.

"Come on!" Talyior yelled in his ear. He spurred his horse into action and headed down the southern way down and out of the town. Devyn followed, but at the edge of the square he reined back, stood in the stirrups and shouted at the top of his lungs, "Keep to the Old Ways, Brothers!"

He urged his mount after his friend, southwards, leaving blood and remorse behind.

Chapter 3: Pevana: Donari

PRINCE DONARI AVEDUN CURSED as he read the latest missive from King Roderran. In slightly curt yet pompous tones, his exalted cousin informed his *Subject Lord* of his intention to arrive at Pevana's Land Gate within a fortnight:

You will arrange a suitable welcome and rely on the Lord Prelate Casan in all things at need. Our August Presence must be seen as a moment for the historians to record, and it would be appropriate for the folk to gather and cheer our entry under the walls of our city. The people need to see me, cousin, and they need to see you welcoming me, as is your filial duty. I trust I can expect Pevana to do her utmost; now and when things ripen in the spring. Until we meet again, prepare for us, lord.

Roderran II, King of Perspa

Donari fought a strong urge to set light to the paper. He had never been close to his cousin-king, the difference in their ages attested to that, but when he was younger, such times as they had met and interacted there had been at least diffidence and cordiality. And yet, in the years of his rule, Roderran had visited Pevana only once, in the first year of his reign, to attend the funeral of Donari's grandfather.

Since then, nothing.

Until last summer when everything changed: expectations, temple burnings, priestly manipulation. Roderran's interest in the south complicated the prior year's Summer Festival, and the letter just delivered presaged even more upset that Donari definitely did not want. Summer's misadventure had proven, despite his own opinions of himself, that Donari had genuine ideas about rule; and he liked his independence.

Independence is something Roderran cannot abide. Not in me or the southern city states.

He crumpled the letter and left his study, his pace quickening to keep up with his racing thoughts.

Turning the corner to the hall that led to his rooms, he barreled into a maid bearing a stack of folded linen. Maid and linens went down in a tumble. The shock of the collision brought Donari back to his present.

"Anlise, Anlise! I'm so sorry! I didn't see you."

"Please you, my lord! I'm fine. It was my fault. I should have seen you. I'm so sorry! So, so. . ." She bent down to her fallen burden. "I'm so clumsy."

Donari glanced at the scattered linens and smiled.

"A pretty excuse, my dear, and untrue. I am the mindless one here. Let me help you with these." Against Anlise's stuttered protests, he knelt down and began helping collect and refold the abused bedding.

Will Roderran run over us and the south the same way? Can countries be put back to rights as easily as rumpled cloth?

Together they put the pile back to rights. By the time they finished, Donari discovered his ill humor evaporated, replaced by a small dose of self-effacement. Of the two of them, his folds had been the less precise. Donari got back to his feet. At that moment, Cryso came hurrying around the corner and nearly tripped over the scene.

"Ah, Cryso! Just in time. Would you please help Anlise here deliver these? I'm afraid I just ran her over."

"Absolutely, My Lord. It will be my pleasure. Should we consider remodeling the hallways wider?"

"Amusing, and in keeping with the *other* renovations sparked by our Lord Prelate. Perhaps I should send to him for ideas. I will be in my chambers. Send someone to roust Senden, please."

"Very good. I think young Drue is available. I will send him."

"Excellent." He bowed to Anlise. "Again, apologies, my dear. Good night."

The girl bobbed once and backed down the hallway, but Donari noticed a different look had replaced her earlier fluster. The change sent a small chill down Donari's back. As the girl turned the corner and disappeared, that chill turned into a thought. Donari half-raised a hand in question as Cryso made to follow.

"Yes, My Lord?"

"Anlise has been with us for some time, yes?"

"Correct, she came to use near two years ago from House Grimaldi."

"I don't recall seeing her in this wing of the palace much."

"Correct, again. She looked after the rooms where we housed the Lord Prelate and his staff. When the Prelate removed himself to the college library, Anlise was given other duties primarily in this wing. Is there something lax in her work, Lord?"

"No, no, not that I would have noticed." *But is that what I should have noticed? Her face, before she started apologizing, almost angry. And after. Casan. What mischief is this?* The sense that he stood poised on yet another variable swelled. Spying a vase on a side table with the last of the winter's hothouse roses, he gently disengaged the freshest from the arrangement and handed it to Cryso. *Mischief or myth? If it is to be myth, then let it be a good one.*

"Cryso, please give this to Anlise when she has finished."

Cryso smiled as he bowed, balancing the linen pile in the move. "I am sure she will appreciate the gesture."

Donari paced back and forth in front of his fireplace while he waited for Senden. He sipped from his goblet, his mind racing too far ahead of himself to actually taste the vintage.

Even kings can be worked. . .

Last summer's boast, despite all contrary indications, remained deeply true in his core. It had to be. He was Prince Donari Avedun of Pevana. He had to believe he was smarter than his hammer-fisted cousin and the bellicose Lord Prelate; if he was not then the letter he still held in his hand presaged a winter of sorrow to be followed by a tragic spring.

"If I am not equal to the challenge," he said softly to himself, "then both I and my city will be casualties of war by summer next."

He sighed, deeply, taking another sip from his goblet, sat down in an overstuffed chair set in front of the fire. He watched the flames dance, rubbing at his knee, and wondering if the ache was due to the length of his day, or the prospect of having to bend it before Roderran.

The Lord Prelate Casan seethed at the familiar tone of Jaryd Corvale's note outlining an interesting if risky opportunity for another try at Donari; enduring another interview with the detestable, however useful, man was a small price to pay, especially when set against the successes of that afternoon's council session.

Extra northern guards at the city entrance.

Concessions for more billets in the city itself.

Additional monies forthcoming.

Casan savored the memory of a compliant Donari agreeing to his many suggestions concerning the king's arrival. The growing ill humor turning to outright dismay passing over Donari's face stirred Byrnard's loins in a way no woman ever had.

Such a disappointing effort, Donari. I expected more. Alas, you only thought you stopped me last summer. And now you know your peril. I do not lose, and neither does Roderran.

A knock sounded at the door and Corvale entered unbidden, a small effrontery. Casan let him sit and fidget while he reviewed the progress made over the intervening months since the Summer Festival: two new King's Theology temples, appropriate curriculum added to the college canon, and new missionary groups set into motion spreading the word southwards. Last summer's irritations remained mostly as memory now.

And when Roderran arrives, Donari will be more than cowed. There will be an end to the bravado; in fact—He let his glance flick to Corvale—*perhaps to the necessity of the prince himself.*

He put the note down and fixed his raptor's eyes on Corvale until the man stopped fidgeting.

"A bold suggestion."

"Bold, yes, but you like the idea."

"Like? Interesting, rather.   And you think you could use the crowd and chaos of the arrival to effect something?"

"I'm quite positive, my Lord. He will be about the city seeing to things, he or his familiar, that Arolli fellow, especially on the day itself. I'd like to get both of them, for surety."

"Surety?"

Corvale let a grin steal over his face. "Yes, surety, and a little revenge. I need a little chaos after all this protocol and running missives."

"I'm quite sure you do, but do we?"

"With Donari gone, the city will adhere to the King."

"How can the people do otherwise? The King's troops drill in their fields, two of the northern lords are here, and the King himself is coming. The realm has no more need of Donari. Alive, he might serve as a bridge, but dead could work as well."

"So I take him?"

Casan hesitated. Until Roderran produced an heir from his body, Donari stood as his heir. There was danger to the kingdom if they succeeded; danger to themselves if they failed. *I'll turn this city into a brothel for Roderran if I have to. Even a bastard could clinch the thing.*

"Make it look questionable. If there is doubt, once the army moves south, folk won't care. We could say what we want."

"Lie?"

The Lord Prelate fixed Corvale with a sardonic glare. "Since when have we ever professed scruples? When matters of state require a lie, we lie."

Corvale gave a low chuckle. "Excellent, my lord."

Casan smiled in return. "Yes, it could be, provided you are thorough. We have three weeks or so. Take extra care if you must move about the city. I don't want you to become obvious to either Donari or his spy. Keep to the grounds of the college during the day. Take some time and plan this well. Take both of them if you can, but make sure of Donari. Senden Arolli," Casan murmured over his goblet. "He's the one we need to distract. He's too much about."

"I owe him, personally."

"But this is so much more than a *personal* matter, fool! Take him too early, or the Prince, then we risk chaos we cannot control. And control here is our aim." He paused, sipped once, twice, and then smiled like a tabby over a trapped mouse. "So we need to set Senden chasing shadows."

"Should I set someone to talking, then?"

Casan snorted. "No, by all that is rational, no! Leave thinking to me. You get your men practicing at the butts, but away from prying eyes! You may go, but watch yourself!"

Corvale left and Casan finished his wine, contemplating rumors and how to place them. Finally, he rose from his chair and made his way through the library to the doors cut to service the passageway to the new church, humming an old marching song. Softly.

The church, an imposing, lofty structure, the first construction consecrated in The King's Theology, possessed a bell tower begun with stones taken from the burned and demolished Old Ways temples. Eventually, it would rise to dominate the skyline, putting all of Pevana under its watchful eye. Everything about this new building spoke of power and reform. Even now, after a winter's worth of building, Casan considered the hint of smoke still clinging to the lower levels better than incense.

The sight of several dozen in the pews awaiting that evening's service pleased him even more, further cementing his theory that if one were bold enough, audacious enough, people would follow because, in the end, the simple needed someone to lead. In what or where to did not matter, as long as someone pointed out the direction clearly.

Casan advanced to the foot of the rise that held the pulpit and the ornate lamp that served as the signiary of the King's Theology. In the front row pew, hands clasped in fervent prayer, sat one of the newest converts, a young, nubile creature who worked in the palace. Casan looked at her delicate form and smiled.

He reached out his boney, birdlike-taloned hand and lightly touched her hair in a near caress, sketching the grace moves as she reacted to the touch.

"You look troubled, child." He pitched his voice into the role of benevolent guide to salvation.

"My assistants tell me you come here often. How might I assist?"

The girl, attractive despite a pinched sort of intensity, blinked up at him in momentary confusion and awe. Casan noted the early signs of womanhood in the swell of her breasts, and beneath the fear in her eyes he saw the beginnings of the dissembler that all woman became when they reached their flowering.

"My lord Prelate, forgive me, I did not see you. I was—"

"Searching for answers in the light. Yes, I see. I come here often on my own for the same reasons. Aren't we all on the same journey? The light calls us out of our darkness, away from the immolations of plants and appeals to fallen gods. Where better to ask for guidance than in the House of the King's Theology? Let this place be a house of truth for you, my dear. Your presence is most welcome."

"Let us finish our prayers together, my dear," he continued. "I was going to mount to the pulpit, but seeing you here, and the questions in your eyes, I see a better service I can offer."

"My lord, I am not worthy of such attention."

"The Light bathes everyone equally, child, in this place the great and the small cast the same shadow. You seem troubled, speak, perhaps I and the power of the Light can help."

"I'm not sure if I know how, my lord. I work in the palace while my family struggles to keep our holdings afloat. I can sense how they think of me there; a lowly drudge, different. I don't feel the same as them. They laugh at my coming here."

"No one should berate the quest for truth, my dear. I sense that you do not enjoy your duties in the palace?"

"I'm not sure, my lord, the work is easy but dull at times. Gossip rules the maid's quarters. The prince is kind, but. . ." She paused as if saying more would be a betrayal.

"Yes, I see your troubles. Loyalty and obligation sometimes are difficult to reconcile. You want to help your family and your prince, is that it? And these troubled times make you unsure. Allow me to help you."

"Help?"

"Yes, help you to save your loyalty and your obligation to your family. I can ease their fortunes, child. The Light gives me power to do so, but I, too, am worried for Prince Donari. I am afraid there are those who aim at the diadem he wears. I have heard whispers that an attempt on his person might happen. He has made enemies of the richer merchant set like Sevire Anargi. I fear what will come when Roderran arrives. There will be events, attention given to the king, I am afraid for Donari's security in such a pass."

"What can I do, lord? I'm just a maid, and the palace is full of whispers and eyes."

"Listen, watch, give voice to your fears to those with whom you work. Try and get them to see, to watch the palace with new eyes. Donari is not safe. I fear the changes that might come if he were to...fall." He smiled benignly at her before continuing.

"Now, let us finish our devotions . . . ah, forgive me, child. I do not remember your name. My congregates increase daily."

"Anlise, my lord."

"Anlise." He savored her name on his tongue. *Little mouse, you will lead Senden down more holes than he will be able to navigate.* "Finish your prayers, and may the light go with you when you leave."

He sketched a fraudulent benediction over her and composed himself to silent reflection. He remained thus until he felt her rise and leave, a whisper of dress, cloak and commission. He stayed in the pew until her footsteps faded in the distance and surprised himself by actually praying.

*   *   *

Eleni avoided returning to the college grounds for several days after her scare outside the Lord Prelate's office. She spent the first day shuttered up at home, worrying about what to do, afraid to concern Tomais. When he returned home the day she discovered Corvale's return, he had been bubbling with excitement over a flood of new work from a newcome company of lancers. The order would keep him and his assistants busy through March. He swelled with such pride that Eleni could not bring herself to squash his joy. She forced herself to smile and admired her husband's success. She almost believed her own performance.

Almost. She had wanted her words. Words had freed her. Words had given her an opportunity. And now words she overheard coming from an evil voice sent her spiraling into a personal darkness that threatened to ruin the very joy and freedom she cherished. Where Tomais saw opportunity and gain from the military's presence, she saw ruin and despair. *No more innocence. Wealth and words, but where is happiness now?*

How she missed that innocence, now, as she stared at the pile of papers littering her work space in the topmost floor of the library. Tomais had left home at noon, braving the wind and rain to return to his work and oversee his laborers. In his cheerful, expectant countenance Eleni found the courage to return to her studies.

During her research, she found several aged volumes on one of the shelves that contained writings from the times of unrest that attended the organization of Perspan control of the Pevanese region. There were poets in Pevana from its inception, and Eleni found herself intrigued by some of the verse she encountered. The books, stuck behind a phalanx of newer volumes of material dealing with the history of the wine industry, must have lain untouched for a generation. Within the cracking covers she found letters, poems, passages torn from what must have been larger pieces, loosely bound, rarely signed but most definitely Pevanese in origin.

She read all the volumes that afternoon, losing all sense of time and herself in the process. There were love poems, diatribes against the rise of the northern hegemony, fears of lost independence, fears of change, the uncertainty of business, love, parenting and passion. She felt like she was reading a kind of chaotic history text; the kind that those in power would never allow in a real classroom. And as she read she marveled at the sheer diversity; each separate piece took her in a new direction. And yet when she finished the final page of the final volume, staring distractedly at the books before her, she realized that everything she read led to the same understanding: the soul of Pevana.

Eleni sat back, sighed over her discovery. There had been great power in those disparate bits and pieces; a collective unity that spoke of culture and courage. It had all sounded familiar. And then she realized why as her eyes wandered to the piles of Ambrose, Enmbron and the unknown author's writings. She sensed similar themes in their words and her own for that matter. Ambrose had spoken out. Enmbron had explored his emotions and touched something close to the soul of the city. And the cynical, whimsical riddles of the unknown poet teased at other strands. Comprehension surged through her until her scalp tingled. The soul of Pevana was her people's lives and largely entrusted to the care of her poets. They were the caretakers of truth, charged with a sacred duty to record and remember.

She placed the two older volumes in her basket, gently covering them with a pile of her notes. She blew out her candles, glanced up through the high windows and caught a glimpse of the quarter moon, riding high towards midnight, shredding the dregs of the storm clouds in the process. The pale light bathed her face, and she felt a cold chill tingle down her spine.

Moonlight and stormclouds—are they symbols or messages?

She shifted her grip on her basket and her thumb lightly brushed the topmost page of her pile of notes, her most recent discovery. It, too, mentioned the moon. Its lines came to her from memory as she made her way to the stairs.

I waited for wisdom under a full moon's light
But the only thing that came was a chill.
And I realized ice, too, though silver bright

Could never substitute for you
The cold no replacement for truth
And warmth not subject to my will.

The cadence tripped along her thoughts catlike and reassuring, and in that moment she knew beyond any doubt that she, too, was a poet of Pevana. Her sense of conviction steadied her stride as she turned on the landing to descend the last flight of stairs to the library's main floor to come face to face with Jaryd Corvale.

"Your pardon, mistress," he said gruffly. Eleni smelled the wine on his breath; the effect repellant as her memories of him. He gestured at her basket. "Are you a student? Your work keeps you late."

Eleni fought to remain composed. "I am, indeed. I lost track of the time, and am now on my way home to my husband." She clutched her basket tighter and ducked her head, pulling her hood lower over her forehead to hide her face.

"Husband, eh? Well, then, he's either a very lucky man or a squeaker to let his woman spend all hours of the night amongst these dusty shelves." He leaned in; his breath was even worse in such near proximity. Eleni pulled her hood even closer and sidled nearer to the stairs.

"Good even', sir."

"Well, then." He sniffed. "Off with you home, tweets. And good even' to you, as well."

Eleni hurried down the stairs, stumbled as she turned on the final landing. Even in the dark with the library door shut fast behind her, she could feel his eyes following her, assessing, inquisitive. She glanced behind her. Nothing. No one. Only darkness. And yet when she stepped into the night, Eleni ran as if it were possible to outrun fear.

Chapter 4: Pevana: Senden Arolli

SENDEN AROLLI TRUDGED back up the slope from the southern gate toward the neighborhood of the Golden Cup. Frustrated, and tired from a week overseeing Pevana's preparations to receive her king, he needed a drink before heading up to report his progress to Donari. He sent his horse with others to the palace stables, feeling the need to walk and clear his head, and for Senden that meant side streets and alleys. Having to be so official made him feel exposed; dealing with shopkeepers even moreso.

The intermittent winter rains had not helped matters, especially the deluge that attended the beginning of all the work. They made a good start despite the ambivalence of the royal troops quartered in the city, who hindered efforts by keeping to their regular schedule of drill and debauchery. At least once a day through the winter, Senden explored the limits of his tact and diplomacy dealing with representatives of the Dukes of Collum and Sor-Reel, Roderran's nominal commanders. They assailed the Avedun palace with howls of anger and remonstrance when Senden had been forced by expediency to re-direct work gangs from building shelters for the Royal troops to making the building fronts on the main avenue from the land gate to the citadel more presentable.

The two puissant lords disdained the notion of having soldiers build their own shelters, insisted on keeping their troops free to train and turn the fields to the south into a churned up morass of mud and turf. Several times a day the two Dukes sent battalions careening through the muck as best they could in mock charges and set maneuvers. To the commoner, watching from the walls, no doubt the display was fortifying and impressive, but Senden received a different message.

"*We are here in our thousands,*" the clanging, shouting, stomping mass said, "*making you house and feed us while we keep ourselves in fighting trim. And lest you think otherwise, here's another demonstration of what we will do to Pevana should you be silly enough to dispute the fact.*"

Senden stepped up to his ankle in a puddle, adding yet another layer of wet to his already soaked disposition. Cursing under his breath, he squelched on in ill humor.

Foolery and foul besides. But the real foolishness happens after they release the men to their billets.

Hungry, dirty and thirsty, they descended upon the city to monopolize the laundry services, well water and whatever spirits their meager pay allowed them to purchase from the ale and wine shops. And therein lay the bulk of the complaints from merchants in the city, for all too often payment was neglected, insufficient or completely forgotten.

And all of them come to me to complain.

No amount of carefully worded messages to the Lords Collum or Sor-Reel resulted in anything approaching substantial moves to rectify the errors; not even an apology. And so the license continued, complaints piled up, and behavior worsened. Senden took a secret smattering of perverse pleasure in ordering storefronts and buildings gentrified, dooming the troops to wet lodging or crowded billets.

The city has to be made ready for Roderran. Donari does not have a choice, and so neither do I. Renia's Grace! He squinted up into the rain. *But I wish she didn't have quite so many tears!*

The Golden Cup loomed out of the grey like a haven, and Senden quickened his pace. He motioned for a pint and took it to an empty back booth, took a pull from his mug and willed his churning thoughts to stillness. Savoring the slight bite of the hops in the ale on his palate, he sucked the liquid down.

He finished the pint, stared at the dregs in the bottom of the mug and contemplated ordering another. Before he even thought about raising his hand to do so, Saymon himself brought over two mugs, plumped one of them down next to Senden's empty, and settled smoothly into a chair.

"A toast," he said quietly, his voice rolling like beer foam from beneath his beard, "to twice earned ale to take winter's edge away."

"Honor that, my friend." Senden raised his mug and took a pull. "Honor that. Your ale is passing fine. My thanks."

Saymon drank again, his eyes, brown points peering out underneath bushy eyebrows, fixed intently on his guest. "You've always liked my fare," he said gruffly. "And yet it has been near six months since your last visit. A most memorable evening, if memory serves me correct. Six months, and I wonder, what brings the prince's eyes and ears back to the Cup to praise my ale?"

Senden lifted his mug slightly. "Beer. Thirst compels me, Saymon; that is all."

A bushy eyebrow rose quizzically. "All?"

Senden let his next sip linger on his tongue before responding. He glanced casually to take in the room. The place was half-full of patrons intent on their own pots and conversations. He let himself relax and swallow. "Mostly all," he said quietly. "I needed to think. I've been so busy dealing with Roderran's arrival I feel like I've lost track of something."

"Ha!" Saymon grunted, bushy eyebrows joining. "Now there is a new turn. The man who knows everything about everyone in Pevana has questions and doubts. Speak!"

Senden stared at the dissipating bubbles in his cup. "I'm not sure I know what to say," he said quietly. "Since the army's been here and mixed things up, rhythms are all out of balance somehow. The Prince feels it, too. He's been frustrated by the council, the Lord Prelate's actions, and. . ."

It had been here, the night of the Poetry Competition, where Donari set upon action rather than delay and deflection. Now, with the advent of spring, Roderran's arrival, and the army's assemblage, it was again time to act or risk being acted upon.

Six months ago he and Donari found the tools to use for their designs. Now, scanning the common room, Senden saw no such tools.

He drank again to ease the clench building in his stomach. Senden suddenly felt himself trapped into a pattern he could neither ken nor break.

He leaned forward, elbows on the table and ran his free hand through his hair. "I know I'm missing something, Saymon, but this weather has me fogged up."

"Winter and too much work can do that to a man."

Senden waved away the kindness. "No, it is not the tasks or the season. I've always been able to make connections between things. Donari expects me to."

Brimaldi took a pull from his mug. "Well, that *is* your job."

Senden buried his grimace behind a pull from his own mug. "Ouch, that was cheap—and true. Are you so direct with all your customers?"

"Only the ones I like; especially if they are attached to those who make policies that affect my life and business."

Brimaldi's words froze Senden in mid-swallow.

Policies. Life. Business.

"I wonder," he sighed.

"About what?" asked Saymon.

"What I've lost track of."

"And that is?"

"Policy, plans, distractions. I've had a feeling these last few days. So busy. Too busy."

"That's nothing new for you."

"But this feels different, Saymon. Whispers down the halls of the palace. A thousand and one things to see to for the king's arrival. I've hardly had a moment for myself or the prince."

"You sound concerned. What can you do?"

"Much and little, I'm afraid." He tossed off the dregs of his pot. "But if I am right, then I have another task."

"Which is?"

"I'm still not sure. Stop chaos from happening, maybe?"

"Sounds difficult."

Senden rose to leave. "Difficult comes with the job." He fished a coin from his purse and tossed it on the table. "For the ale and the words."

Brimaldi pushed the coin away. "No need. Call it my new policy."

Senden's return route to the citadel took him through the northern skirts of what remained of the Maze. The lower half had been consumed in the flames of August. The clearing created had been cleaned up and then left undeveloped. Now it housed several companies of northern troops and a cavalry command—and the simple grave of the poet Kembril, whose death venerated the ground. Even the Northern troops respected the small wrought-iron barrier the locals erected for its protection. To Senden's mind came images of the flames of that fatal night, and he wondered if the troops appreciated the irony of their billeting.

The notion deepened his sense of unease. Their presence was an insult to the memories of the poor who had once dwelt there; a peaceful place now turned to a training ground for war. Senden felt an urging, a gentle push from the spirit attached to the gravesite, to pull rank on the cavalry troop and order them to move elsewhere, but his better sense prevailed. It would only be a gesture and the time for such things had long passed.

Senden let his swirling thoughts point his way. The straight road to the citadel just would not do. He slipped through shadowed ways to where a side street cut up the hill near the harbor gate. Outside of Gania's boarding house, where the young love-struck poet, Talyior, had once let a room, Senden observed late returning cavalry officers cleaning off their boots and greaves at the common well; more military muck intruding on a place of poetry and civic peace.

The soldiers finished their haphazard cleaning and stumped off to their billets. Senden watched four of them spill through Gania's door, raising hoarse voices loud in calls for food and wine, leaving him alone in the square.

A voice from behind him snapped his attention away from the door.

"They seem to be everywhere these days."

Senden turned and found himself face to face with a young woman, and he knew her despite the gloom and the shadows cast over her features by her hooded cloak. "Good evening to you, Mistress Caralon. What brings you out in such a chill?"

"I was on my way to see Gania, but the soldiers. . ."

"Yes, a loutish lot by any definition, and all over the city, too, and better avoided whenever possible these days. She will be busy with that bunch. Allow me to walk you home."

She almost smiled. "It is not soldiers I fear, sir. I was on my way to see Gania, to see if she knew a way I could reach you."

"Is something wrong? How go your studies?"

Eleni leaned closer, her voice falling to a whisper, reaching out a hand to touch his arm tentatively, almost plaintively. "Jaryd Corvale is back in Pevana. I overheard him talking to the Prelate in the library. I'm afraid something terrible may happen."

"Terrible? What do you mean?"

"I did not hear everything, as I said, because it was late and dark and I was afraid they would see me. But what I did hear made me fear for Donari, for everyone, really. They sounded so smug and evil. And then I nearly ran into Corvale on the stairs this evening. He was awful. I was afraid he might remember me from, from before. I didn't even go home. I had to talk to someone. Gania was my first thought. How could I go to the palace? I feel eyes everywhere now. And what would I say? I don't understand completely. Something is going to happen, and I feel helpless to stop it."

Senden's spine began to tickle as Eleni unburdened herself. Suddenly all the mysteries in the beer foam came clear. The truth had always been there, tucked away behind the harassing pace, waiting for him to slow down enough to see it.

Corvale was back and in touch with Casan; violence and cruelty making plans that he had no knowledge of, until now. His half-formed suspicions flared into full awareness.

"Renia's Grace," he whispered. "They wouldn't."

"I don't understand, what do you mean?" Eleni asked. Senden looked at her, saw the fear, sensed the courage, remembered a balcony conversation.

"And if you understood, what would you do?" he asked.

She stopped, turned to face him, lamplight lending her features a tense, pinched quality.

"If I had the means," she whispered fiercely. "I would do what I could to save what I could."

He gestured onward, and she fell into step beside him. He chose his next words carefully.

"I'm sorry you had to be the one to hear such evil things. You don't deserve it. And yet now I am doubly glad Donari granted you that appointment, Mistress Caralon. I remember telling you Pevana had need of all her poets. I never thought it might come to something so, uncomfortable."

"Then you do think they plan something?"

"Until now, hearing your news, I had only vague thoughts. I've been kept busy and let something slip. I should have seen it. The Prelate has always wanted Donari discredited, perhaps even removed from the chair. That is Casan's style."

"But Donari is our prince."

"Only as long as King Roderran says so."

"But that seems so—"

"Cold? Calculating?" Senden finished for her. "Look at the signs, Eleni. Soldiers everywhere, you said. Donari is prince under the Perspan crown. The power of that crown now dominates this city. The one who wears that crown is coming. I think you are correct. That conversation you heard was no lie. Something terrible is going to happen."

"Corvale sounded so eager."

"Corvale is a killer. They might plot to murder Prince Donari, but dead or discredited, the effect will be the same."

His words added to the chill of the evening as they walked along. He could sense Eleni struggling to come to grips with the truth of her fears. They turned the corner on to the street where Eleni said she lived. She stopped him with a light touch on his arm.

"What can I do?" she asked. "I said if I had the means I would do what I could."

"Could you go back to the library? Keep your eyes and ears open for me?"

"Now? After?"

"Especially now and absolutely after. You still need to live your life, Eleni Caralon. Chase words and let me deal with the rest. Just stay away from the Prelate and avoid Corvale. Watch for anything else out of the ordinary while you study. If something slips, get a note to Saymon Brimaldi at the Golden Cup. Agreed?"

She hesitated, weighing her courage and conviction against fear and trepidation. "Agreed," she whispered. "I'll go back."

She turned to continue on to her door then stiffened momentarily. There, burdened by a load of tack materials under one arm and holding a lantern aloft in the other, stood the tall young man Senden recognized as Tomais, Eleni's husband and *voice* from the summer's competition.

"Eleni!" Tomais exclaimed, "Good timing! I can't seem to reach my keys. Could you?"

"Of course!" she responded, hurrying forward and reaching into her basket for hers. "My dear, this is Senden Arolli, I met him at Demona's during the troubles last summer. He kindly consented to see me home from Gania's. Tomais, Senden. Senden, my husband, Tomais Caralon."

Tomais graced Senden with an infectious, guileless smile. "Good even' and my thanks, sir!" He set down the lamp and switched his bundle of unfinished tack to his other arm so he could offer his handshake.

"Entirely my pleasure, young man," Senden replied warmly. "Your lady wife has quite the reputation as a seamstress, and if what I recall is still true, as the first full-time female scholar in Pevana."

Tomais had a firm grip that tightened somewhat at the mention of Eleni's scholarly status. Senden noted the look of pride and good humor in the young man's eyes as Eleni, fussed after her keys.

"Oh, yes," he chuckled. "Eleni and I have undergone some *times* since last summer. She has found her words, and I have found almost more work with the army's coming than I can handle."

"I can see, that, and good fortune to you. It seems there is profit down at the horse-lines this season. Do they deal fairly with you?"

Tomais raised his chin proudly. "Quite well, sir. They may be Northerners, but they pay well enough. There is a captain who serves as their supply commisariat, and he has been pleased so far with my work that he now recommends me to every incoming troop. These lashings will be for the remounts for the Lord of Sor-reel's guard." He turned his smile to his wife as she held the door. "I'm moving in high company these days!"

"No less than your due, my dear," Eleni said as she shifted out of his way so he could get by.

"At this rate, by summer we could afford to add that other room to the house! Is there food? I'm famished. Could we offer Master Arolli a bite and a cup of something?"

Eleni spared Senden a quick look of entreaty, Senden took the hint and politely declined when Tomais returned from dumping his load in the hall.

"It is enough to have spent a few minutes sharing your wife's company, and I have other duties tonight. Good even' to you, Mistress Caralon, and you, sir. May your good fortune continue."

He bowed them good night and moved off up the street towards the main way up the hill. The once whirling trail of his thoughts now formed arrow straight for the citadel and Donari. Death's chill gathered in the night air.

Chapter 5: Donari, Daggers and Diplomacy

Prince Donari carefully schooled his features as he turned to deal with the Lords of Collum and Sor-reel, both obviously angry, bearing dark countenances and swords sheathed at their hips. The incongruity of two men protected by two-thirds of the realm's fighting men should find need to bear weapons at all times, and here in the heart of the citadel of the city, kept his greeting briefly locked behind his lips. Both men wanted raised levies to begin training foot soldiers for the spring campaign. Donari, rather, wanted to keep as many of his people at home with their families as long as possible. They were undeniably meant for front line fodder. If delaying could grant them even a few months more, it was worth enduring the ill-will of such Lords that would use them.

These men are warriors, have been for all their lives. They rule restive people in the north and east. Doubtless, lives spent largely on campaign would come to have about them certain quirks. But as he drew breath, a deeper thought came to him: *And yet these last few months have taught me that enemies come in all shapes, and from all directions.*

"Well met, my Lords," he said in his affected drawl. "Gentleman, your brows would whither the palace gardens. You need something to make things more pleasant. Cryso! A glass for us, if you please."

"We haven't time for palace niceties, Prince Donari," Collum gruffed. "How dare you send our messages back unanswered! Arrangements were agreed upon nearly a month ago at our last conference! Where are our levies for training?"

Donari studied Gaspire Amdoran's hard face for any trace of family. They were thirdhand cousins, sharing an aunt, a jawline and little else. Donari respected, but did not like him. Lord of the second largest fief in the realm, an intimate of the King and extension of his arm, the man had ruled and fought for a hard twenty-five years.

"Come, Gaspire, let us not wrangle. It's much too cold for that." Donari rose from his seat and moved toward the nearest fireplace. The reception hall had four of them spaced about the walls, and the one closest to the Prince's throne had several chairs and a table for close discussion. A motion at the hall's entrance drew his glance and revealed Senden Arolli looking both damp and in a hurry. Donari waved a hand casually as he took his seat, and in response Senden retreated to the shadows behind the door. "Please," he continued, "take the glass Cryso holds for you and sit down. You, too, my good Reegan. Come, if you two gentleman can keep from tripping on your blades, let us sit and work this out amicably. I find it so much more effective than shouting."

And if I, too, were to adorn myself with steel, what sort of signal would that send?

Reegan Morrel, Lord of Sor-reel, bore a look not nearly as dark as Gaspire's, but that did not reveal much to Donari. As he bowed them over to the chairs near the fire, he thought he noticed a hint of a smile on the man's lips, quickly hidden behind the first tentative sip from his glass.

"Gaspire, you've not touched your wine!" Donari sat with them, raising his own glass. "Drink and take away the venom!"

Gaspire glowered at him, but took his sip nonetheless. "There," he said. "A sip for manners. But what of my claim?"

"Cousin—" Donari began.

"King's representative and Captain, rather!"

"But *cousin*, nonetheless. And a guest in my city."

"On the King's business, which you are hampering, sir!"

"I?" Donari raised a hand to his chest. "How so?"

"You refuse to tally out the reserves we have requested for training." Gaspire's glance included the Lord of Sor-reel, who kept his silence but nodded in agreement. "We need them, now, in order to make them useful."

"It is still the middle of winter! Have you no mercy?"

"The King's intent is to march south with the warmer weather. I need a trained force ready. Would you rather I take them later, untrained, on the war trail? Would that be a mercy? I have no time for niceties, Prince. I want your men."

Donari fought down the bitter retort that rose like bile in his throat. Gaspire was no Byrnard. He was dangerous only as directed by royal orders. He, too, could be played.

"Ah, yes, good reasons, my lord, good reasons," he said smoothly. He took a generous mouthful from his cup, letting the wine linger on his tongue, drawing the pause into a near silence before going on. "But I couldn't possibly spare you the men right now. Doubtless you have heard that Roderran is on his way. Now, I have had to use every available man to make ready the city. King's orders, mind you. He wants storefronts painted and the like? My hands are tied and my ankles shackled, gentlemen. I've only a few days before his column appears at the Land Gate. You must understand."

"I understand that your words are smooth, Donari."

"*Prince*, actually."

"*Cousin*," Gaspire insisted. "My aides tell me you haven't even posted the notices. You are playing at something; don't deny it."

"Prince, you know he speaks the truth," added the Lord of Sorreel. "We can't ignore the obvious."

"My lords, my lords." He sweetened his affected drawl. "Really, now, let's not be so, so, oh what is the word I seek? Contentious? Yes, that's right; contentious."

Gaspire slammed down his cup. "Stop, damn you! I'll not stand impudence!"

"You seem to be standing now." Donari strove to hide his amusement. He raised his hand. "Peace! Cousin, I jest; a sad hold-over from my misspent youth. My dear mother, Renia rest her soul, was forever railing at me to be more serious."

"Your jests are ill done, lord, and will cost you."

"Doubtless, I am sure, but I am still Prince of this city and fief, my lord, and I must do what I must. I apologize for angering you in the matter of men. I quite understand the issues of the timetable you've been set by the King. And yet you wouldn't have me anger Roderran either, would you? Come, sir. What kind of shrift would you expect from the King if he is forced to slink in, cold, wet, and unacknowledged by a festooned processional, replete with cheering, healthy, and *numerous* people?"

Gaspire's anger cooled. Reluctantly. He took a deep breath and expelled it; frustration, resignation, whatever existed in that expelled breath ended in the man grabbing his neglected wine glass and draining it to the dregs.

"Your words are slippery, cousin, but not without merit." He leaned in close. "In the end you will have to do your duty. Your *duty*, sir. Have a mind to it, for Roderran will not be pleased one way or the other."

Donari slumped back in his chair, watching the two lords leave his hall as he drained his own glass. He heard Senden's quiet tread come near. His friend and spy slid into the seat next to his own.

"You walk like you have wet boots."

"Observant. Time to improve Pevana's streets, lord."

"It's late. I assume you've been out all day and night?"

"Your list was extensive."

Donari breathed a quiet laugh. "That's your fault for being so efficient." He motioned toward the empty glasses and half-full bottle. "And you have my thanks and apologies. I assume you were close enough to hear?"

"All of it."

"Thoughts?"

"Strange and unpleasant. Gaspire sounded threatening."

"Yes, Roderran is close enough now for them to stop playing nice. Something's up, my friend. Do you agree?"

"Oh, yes. I've had similar from their underlings. What makes you think they will try something?

"Because last month Gaspire didn't wear his sword in the palace."

Senden shook his head slightly. "Not very polite of him."

"Bold, rather. Came in here making demands for manpower. I think we've run out of time, my friend. What news else?"

"More of the same and more immediate my lord." Senden paused to drink before continuing. "Corvale has returned and has been closeted with the Lord Prelate for at least the last week or so."

Donari frowned at the dregs in his cup. Senden's declaration did not surprise him. Quite the opposite; it fit the pattern of old troubles in a new time. "So," he murmured. "And there is more? From whom do we receive this information?"

"I had words with Eleni Caralon. You gave her entry into the college last summer."

"Ah, yes, our lady-poet. I do remember. Quite lovely."

"And married. To Tomais Caralon, leather-worker and recently the recipient of greatly increased orders from the King's troops."

"Right. She was one of the few things that went well during that chaos. What ever happened to the other two fellows, Enmbron and Ambrose?"

Senden smiled. "They left the city in a hurry after the feast. You remember the troubles we had trying to quiet Sevire Anargi after half his bravos wound up dead or maimed that night? It seems the lads made off with two of Sevire's prized stallions stabled with Malom Banly. The last I heard of them they were plowing their way through wine and women along the coast heading south."

Donari chuckled softly. They had been so helpful in curbing Sevire's arrogance. And now Sevire re-inserted himself in the growing troubles by aiding Roderran's war effort, diverting some of his shipping to transport material and presenting his wheezing flatulence at the Council meetings since November. Suddenly, Donari wished the two impetuous young men were close at hand.

"Yes, I remember them well, indeed," he answered. "So, tell me, what else did you learn from our seamstress turned scholar?"

"Enough to convince me that the Lord Prelate and Corvale plot your murder, my lord."

Again, despite its abruptness, Senden's comment failed to surprise. *Dynastic murder? Has it come to that?* "It does make a sick kind of sense, when you think about how things have gone this winter. Bastards."

"Bastards with an armed force at their disposal and the king's warrant. I do not like the smell of it."

"Absolutely, absolutely. If Amdoran is involved, even worse. We are in a spot then. Advice?"

"We know our enemies, but I wonder if they know the real nature of theirs?"

"All well and good, but this is rather more serious than deflecting the ambitions of men like Sevire Anargi. Roderran needs the city."

"And the way I see it, Casan thinks, once he has Pevana, he might not need you."

And that did stun Donari. He looked up and saw real fear in Senden's eyes for the first time. That, more than any threat to his life or his city, caused him to feel the first pangs of dismay.

"Again, my friend," he said quietly. "Advice?"

"Stay alive, of course," Senden whispered. "Perhaps you should start following our good Gaspire's lead and wear a sword."

"And would that not reveal our suspicions?"

Senden grimaced. "Then keep a dagger about your person then, and strap on that old leather jerkin under your outer clothes. It is that or I cannot leave you unattended; anyone else would raise that suspicion just as surely. And we both agree, I have tasks."

"You have dangers enough, my friend. All right then," Donari told him. "Two daggers to keep you content. Search me out this plot, and I will take proper care. Cryso and I will work something out."

"My lord I have known you for all of your life. Without you Pevana is lost. With you, I harbor hope for both Pevana and the realm. No idealism, just good sense. Look at the fool who rules us. Look at his lackeys who demand our grain and blood. Prince Donari, surely you must see what your life means. To your people. To Pevana itself."

Donari took a deep breath to banish the chill creeping along his skin. He let it go with a sigh. "Go to it, then," he said. "And may Renia help us."

Senden stood and bowed. "May Renia help us to help ourselves, my lord. Good night."

In the silence that descended, Donari replenished his wine, swirling it untasted in his glass. Destiny was a poignant thing, full of irony and half-realized ambition. He could almost hear the otherworldly sound of bones being shaken for another mad tavern game of Perspan politics. As he drained the wine in his glass, the rattling sound ceased and instead became the clatter of bones on stones, casting their lot.

Gaspire Amdoran rode in silence next to Reegan, Lord of Sor-reel, biting back the string of curses that pushed against his calm. His younger cousin's tone and demeanor rankled his sensibilities and teased at the core jealousies Gaspire knew he suppressed. If he could have gotten away with it, he would have run Donari through, silencing that glib tongue with one well-aimed thrust. Uncertainty of how Roderran would respond kept him from it. Too obvious. The note from Casan he kept concealed next his skin suggested something more obscure and untraceable.

A carriage sat idle at the base of the slope where the road leveled off before the Land Gate Square—exactly where he was told it would be. He motioned Sor-reel and the escort to go on, only shaking his head when his fellow lord raised a questioning brow. Drawing rein next to the carriage door, he leaned down as a pale hand motioned him closer.

"How did he receive you?" The Prelate's voice came from within as a disembodied rasp. Gaspire supressed a grimace.

"As you suggested he would: pompous and slippery. He plays the fop, but my cousin is playing at something. The delays and excuses will not work for the king's designs."

"Then you agree? Something must be done."

Amdoran straightened in his saddle. Personal ire aside, he was a military man, not a sentimental fool. Pawns were used and discarded to make way for greater plans, greater men. He knew that—and so did Donari. He reined his horse in a circle.

"Agreed," he growled as his horse danced beneath him. "Do it. How, I do not want to know, but do it."

Kicking his mount into a slow lope, the Lord of Collum left the carriage, the Prelate, and whatever evil he had planned behind him. Gaspire had a war to plan.

Chapter 6: Pevana: Sevire

SEVIRE ANARGI SET THE LEDGER DOWN on his desk and adjusted the folds of the blanket around his shoulders. Despite possessing ample rolls of fat that should have insulated him from the cold, Sevire Anargi hated the chill of winter. Even Pevana's mostly temperate climate left him shivering during the cold snaps of January and February. Warm wine, a fortune in firewood and coal braziers, and his wife's ample charms barely served to succor him through the season. He detested the dull interlude that necessarily attended winter. He huddled in his study, looked balefully for a long moment out the window at the grey sky crouching over the harbor. *Miserable, cold, bored—but this?*

His shipping lay at dock in the harbor, the winter gales limiting trade to small coastal ventures of indeterminate profit. For several months, Sevire had to content himself with counting his money, smiling benignly at partners and competitors, making the rounds of the interminable social gatherings that so delighted his wife, Demona. He hated all of it, and he had to work hard to keep his anger within limits. At least he made sure there were no bruises on Demona; especially so since the unfortunate debacle of the Summer Festival and the odious affair with young Talyior Enmbron.

It had been a crowning disappointment to have that wretch escape the trap Sevire had set. There were ample bruises to go round amongst the servants of house Anargi then! He spent the fall working to restore his name and reputation within the affluent society and trying to live down the embarrassment of that chaotic time; and though he missed gelding the young rake, he took sweet revenge upon the young man's family.

The dockside warehouse burning had been followed by a carefully executed series of *events* that left the once prosperous rug merchant Baylior Enmbron's enterprises in ruins, the family dwelling destroyed, the patriarch and his wife both, sadly, tragic victims of the same blaze.

Memories of that successful plot warmed Sevire's cockles during the grey days of winter; that and having a contrite, biddable Demona recognizing the error of her ways. Truth be told, he had never enjoyed taking her more than during the months just after ending her little dalliance. She took his girth from behind without complaint whenever he wanted. The feeling of power such moments afforded almost took away Sevire's distrust. Almost. Last summer's lessons taught him to never trust anything, especially women and princes.

Prince Donari and his henchman, Senden Arolli, played a considerable role in those upsetting events, and his sense of frustration grew to distracting proportions when he realized he could do nothing about it. He could wheedle seats at city council meetings, he could scold and nag as he wished, but despite all his annoying attempts, Donari remained aloof and distant, an untouchable fly buzzing about on the fringes of all his entanglements. All through the fall Sevire sensed the Prince laughing at him behind his supercilious smile, in the mock-formal bows he gave when taking advantage to partner Demona in dance, or in the sage looks he gave when Sevire attempted to make some point in council.

Sevire found himself hating Prince Donari even more as the winter months dragged. It played upon his mind even as he tupped Demona. It worked to make his lash that much heavier on the flanks of the matched pair that drew his carriage on those rare moments when he felt vigorous enough to take the reins himself. It caused him to all too frequently ruin the ends of his pens when doing accounts.

Then had come word of the King's intention of a campaign in the south that would require men and ships, Sevire's ships. He pulled the Royal warrant from under a pile of papers and re-read the glorious missive and its *earnest request for his aide* in the coming struggle. The letter hinted at gratitude that could reach noble aspirations. All he had to do was place his resources at the King's disposal, to lend his obvious genius for organization and transport to the cause, and there was no end to the speculations.

He understood Roderran could take what he wanted, whenever he wanted and Sevire would have no recourse in the end. And yet, beneath such unpleasant notions, he felt tremors of possibility in the chance to solve the problem of the seemingly untouchable, ever-meddling, ever-pompous Prince Donari.

And now the Prelate's missive, its barely-veiled threats and demands. Promises. Sevire heaved his bulk upright, threw off his blanket from his shoulders. Shuffling towards the door shouting for his steward, he dashed off an answering note while the man fetched his wine.

"Take this to the library and make sure the Prelate gets it."

"Yes, my lord."

"Be quick! Go!"

Sevire Angari watched the man scurry off, revenge warming him from the inside as no wine, woman or blanket ever could.

Chapter 7: Desopolis: Devyn and Talyior

LYVIA TAMORGEN, BASTARD DAUGHTER OF the tyrant Sylvanus of Desopolis, looked up from the pile of fabric she had been fingering, her eye drawn by a disturbance at the city gates. A wagon laden with goods for market trundled in, its wheels making a clatter as it transitioned from the beaten earthen road to the city's cobblestone streets. Behind the wagon, two horsemen jogged in, dusty, disheveled and so obviously at odds with the usual morning market crowd that Lyvia stared. The wagon lurched to a sudden stop in front of them, and the travellers' mounts, upset by the action, whickered and sidestepped in alarm. One of them came quite close to her, and she could see hints of blond hair and a flash of blue eyes under a sagging, wide-brimmed hat. He had something loosely wrapped in leather strapped to his back, and as he passed she thought she heard the musical thrum of guitar strings.

She followed as the press cleared the way ahead. Both men dismounted and walked their horses. Lyvia kept behind and to the left, listening as they spoke, intrigued by their northern accents.

". . .glad we pushed it hard enough to get here just in time to see all these wonderful, southern market stalls," said the blond, raising his voice to be heard above the bustle. "I can't imagine missing this for a, say, slower pace, fewer saddle sores and a chance at a bath."

"Quiet," the dark haired, smaller one on the left said. "You were just as tired of the road as I was, and that last village didn't have a room. At least this way we put a few more miles between us and what we left in Gallina." Despite the dark look, Lyvia noted the smile surely meant to take any sting from the words.

"Apology accepted," the other one responded.

"What apology would that be Talyior, my friend?"

"The one you obviously meant to give, my dear Devyn, but that I could not hear what with your head up your horse's butt."

"I should have left you back up the road to find your bath."

"Why? We are out of money anyway. Besides, I'm not the one whose thoughts reek of horseshit."

"That's right, you are the one who still smells like one of Demona's handkerchiefs."

"Better that than the other."

"That depends," said the one called Devyn, who paused yet again when the wagon in front lurched to a stop, "on which lasts longer, the smell of shit or bad memories."

"That's not fair."

"Anything to stifle you."

Lyvia let them pass out of earshot once the way ahead cleared again. *Talyior. Devyn. Nothern voices. Northern names. Gallina.* She kept them in sight as they moved into the city proper. Everything about them screamed of news and curiosity and long-standing friendship. Even their banter hinted music and poetic rhythm. She held back when the crowd thinned, paced them some distance until they came to Tanli's, a guest house on the slope above the harbor. Lyvia knew the place well, and if what she guessed about the newly arrived Devyn and Talyior were true, there would be music and an interested crowd in the common room that night.

Broke and they sounded tired. A partial rest, perhaps. Time enough to see to a few things, and then it's a back booth tonight!

Devyn awoke refreshed and encouraged. Leaving Talyior asleep, he left their shared room to greet the day properly. Last night's effort had gone well. Tanli's served up good food, good wine and a receptive crowd. Talyior, he noted, had quickly chosen a pretty face in a back booth to sing to. Devyn also noted the size of her escort.

Not quite the usual easy conquest, he thought, *but not a hopeless one*; the young lady in question had returned glance for glance, smile for smile.

60

The city was not quite what he expected. It boasted a fine, natural harbor, distinct from the river's mouth and well-defended by towers at each end of a narrow entrance. Close inshore boasted a generous anchorage and several substantial piers. The city arched around the waterfront, climbing a gentle slope to flatter terrain near the inland walls. White-washed buildings reflected the sun that hung above the northern headland. Devyn took a tentative, relaxing breath and stepped into the street to search out a temple or shrine to Renia.

All Old Ways deities had their representation in larger cities, according to custom, with one or two predominating. Tolimon held sway in Desopolis, and yet after pushing through a crowd at an intersection, he looked up and it was there: a smallish building with an understated copula upheld by slender pillars. These protected a life-sized statue of the weeping goddess. The steps were clean, an alms-box full of vegetables and fruit for the needy graced the topmost, and at the edge of the covered portico an offering bowl perched on its stand. It still held clumps of drying flowers and wheat stalks, offerings awaiting the weekly immolation by the priestly caretakers.

Devyn climbed the steps and gently ran his fingers over the weathered rim. The feel of the stone set off a wave of home-sickness and longing for his own such bowl still in the corral of Malom Banley's horse hostelry in Pevana. A shuffle and quiet cough interrupted his reverie. Devyn turned to see a priest in holy robes with a pair of speculative eyes in a wizened, bewhiskered face watching him curiously from off to the side. Behind him hovered another, younger man, sallow-faced. *Probably an acolyte.*

"Flowers and wheat for Renia, but for Talimon they give silver and gold," the priest said tersely, coming closer.

"What care the form," Devyn responded, "if the offering be made with a pure heart?"

The priest sighed. His breath smelled like oiled fish, his teeth stained yellow; his less than devout manner set Devyn's teeth on edge.

"Ah, a true believer! Is the young master a student of theology then? A pilgrim?"

Devyn smiled ruefully and gave a last caress of the stone bowl. "I'm no pilgrim. I'm not sure what I am at the moment. I was looking for something." He glanced down at the basin. "But I think I left it back home."

"And home is to the north, I assume?"

"Yes, or it was, such as it were. Your altar stone reminded me of other days."

"All days, all ways, are as one to the Goddess. She listens and weeps for all men."

"But her house fell in flames back where I came from; a victim of men's greed."

The priest bowed his head. "Ah, yes, Man has ever been beset by his own weaknesses. It is our charge, to make offerings and prayers so those that falter can still find their way. Perhaps, if the young master were to leave an offering, his unspoken prayers might be heard."

"I've no flowers, father."

The priest reached up a gnarled hand that ended in cracked and dirty nails and took hold of his sleeve. "Ah, but anything, even the smallest coin given with a good will is useful."

Devyn shook off the man's hand and turned to go, disgusted by the man's touch, the sense of *ill* almost physical. He retreated back down the steps, but the priest's avaricious voice followed him.

"Silver and gold will buy you sincerity, my son! A handful of weighty markers will grant you the absolution of Renia's tears! The holy waters!"

Devyn kept the priest in sight as he walked away. "Renia's Grace," he muttered, quickly losing himself in the flow of people setting about their daily tasks, hoping to put the priest's jarring discordance behind. The sights and smells of Desopolis only worked in half-measure, however, and by mid-morning he was back in the room he shared with Talyior, staring at a blank page while his friend snored gently from underneath jumbled covers.

He leaned back in his chair and looked out over a city that should have spoken to him, that should have lent him words and rhythms, that should have validated what he had lost and given up to get there, but nothing of the sort happened. Perhaps he let the priest get to him, but everything Devyn saw afterwards, the folk at work or children at play, seemed to lack awareness. The sour taste of disappointment lingered as a clench upon his tongue.

In Pevana, he watched flames extinguish hope, watched thugs in the pay of the King's Theology attempt to intimidate, confuse and condemn—and yet folk had protested. But in Desopolis there seemed to be a different kind of wasting, one born of apathy, and perhaps innocence. The image of the bloody cleric laying prostrate in Gallina's square returned. And that dark memory fueled his growing despair.

I know what is coming to this sleeping south. I know too well.

Staring out the window, he conjured a gathering darkness that belied the mid-morning sun. And at the core of that darkness, flames.

He let go an exasperated breath, pushed himself away from the window and returned to his pen and paper; and the words suddenly came in a frenzied, angry rush:

Where do you go when the silence reigns?
When the people you thought you knew
Turn away in seeming ignorance?
What appeal can you make?
Would Renia hear?
Would she lend a tear to you
To wash your pain away?

What is the course for the fool to follow
When every question eludes an answer,
When truth recedes like reason after wine—
A distant
Distance.
Made vague and purple in silhouette.

And all is fragmented, broken like
The detritus of your dreams bouncing as

Flotsam in the gutter flowing with
Bitter waters.
Rhythm, light and resonance
Elude you,
Leaving silence in their wake—
A fateful pause
A lost advantage.
You hear rumors in the night of war and decay;
The red tide of menace progressing in its
Carnivorous way
To take the core of what upholds the light.
And pale faces in your dreams mouth silent words at you
A warning, a request?
In such an uncertain time as this,
Can one bear the shadow's kiss?

Devyn stared at the words on the page; they pointed toward. . .something. He tossed his pen down. He expected more, but he felt himself at a crossroads too horribly reminiscent of his trials from last summer.

He closed his eyes, pressing fingers to his lids. Instead of oblivian's darkness he saw the face of his old teacher, Kembril Edri: Cracked lips. Skin bruised and blackened. The old soldier-turned-poet smiled slowly, pieces of skin flaking off, rising like embers. The memory of his mentor's death loosed a rush of emotion that intensified as more pieces of his mentor's face fell away into the darkness. Kembril's lips worked, mouthing silent yet unmistakable words—

Shadows don't kiss.

Devyn gasped, tears starting behind his clenched lids. In his vision Kembril's eyes broke away so that all that was left was the mouth. And as it moved to form words, it too crumbled away.

Go back.

Devyn's eyes flashed open, blinked away moisture to clear his vision.

I fled Pevana, seeking escape and fled Gallina for truth. But there is no truth here. I left it home with my bowl.

Shadows did not kiss; they lurked, covered action, made action possible. Jaryd Corvale had sent his master into the shadows of death without paying the price of the crime. His lie of the last six months came clear to him.

I ran away.

The South would suffer worse than Pevana had, if war came sweeping down with the spring. More lives would be consumed unless something, or someone, blocked its course.

He scanned the words of his poem again, heard the bed creak and the sound of Talyior's footsteps drawing close and made a move to shift a blank page over. Talyior arrested the move with a finger jabbed on the paper.

"Words! About time! I was beginning to wonder."

"I thought you were asleep."

"I was, but the heavy sighs coming from the table woke me."

Devyn grinned. "I think what you heard were your own snores. Sounded like a row of piglets."

"It was a good dream, finally. Let me read this." He swept up the page before Devyn could stop him, settled in the other chair and read. Devyn watched Talyior's first, eager look be replaced at the end by a contemplative frown. Talyior gestured out the window, pushing the page back to him.

"With a view like this, and after the night we just had, I find it hard to see how you could be so dark."

"I went out earlier. Had an encounter with a holy man."

"And it didn't go well."

"Not even close." Devyn gave a brief review of his misadventure, and Talyior chuckled softly.

"You let a priest intrude on your good mood?"

"This wasn't a King's Theology shithead; this was a caretaker of Renia's Temple. Tal, I didn't expect to feel the same kind of slime."

"So he wasn't as pure as you expected. Why does it matter?"

"Because I need the Old Ways to be pure, untainted by the fraud back in Pevana. I needed this place to be, *something*. You didn't kill that man in Gallina. We know what we left behind."

"Maybe we need to give this place a chance."

The sincerity in his friend's voice loosened the tightness around his mood. Devyn took the page, glanced once more at the questions it held, and then folded it away.

"Perhaps you are right, and by *a chance* I guess you mean time to test out the qualities of the local ladies?" He gave his friend a shove. "Or maybe one in particular?"

"Then you saw her, too?"

"I saw *you*. Noted her. Dark hair. Nice eyes. She was in a back booth, right? I was busy trying to keep time. You have an agile neck, my friend, to be able to stretch it at such an angle."

"Jealous?"

"Happy, for you." And Devyn surprised himself by actually meaning it. He leaned his chair back on two legs while Talyior splashed water over his face and hair from the basin by the door.

"I think I could like this place," Talyior said, combing his hair back with his fingers. "And I didn't think I was that obvious. Do you think she'll be back?"

"If you could keep time and sing on key."

"Ha! Amusing. At least you haven't lost your sense of humor. I'm off to explore. Since you've run afoul of religion, I think I will go in search of a sticky bun. Coming?"

"Not just now, but thanks, Tal. I'm glad you feel better about this place. Maybe I over-reacted, but take care all the same."

"Always."

Devyn noticed he left his sword behind when he swept out of the room.

Lyvia Tamorgen checked her appearance one last time before leaving, laughing at herself a little over her sudden attention to detail.

She had grown up accustomed to being the center of attention, bastard status notwithstanding. And yet over the last week she had taken pains to avoid notice as she kept an eye on the two musicians, Devyn Ambrose and Talyior Enmbron. A quiet word with Tanli, the owner and proprietor of the tavern where the northerners boarded and played, helped her blend in without undue notice.

Blend in, but not without notice, after all. The blond caught her eye more than once, or a dozen times. She managed to leave that evening without talking to him, the size of the escort she had been forced to take with her serving nicely in that regard. She always took someone with her when she went about the city at night; one of the restrictions placed on her bastardy freedom by her father's concern. But during the day she allowed herself the run of the place, and not even her father's insistence worked to change her mind.

No one knew Desopolis like Lyvia Tamorgen. That knowledge allowed her to watch Talyior as he went about feeling out the city. The darker one, Devyn, with his somber aspect, did not interest her as much. She sensed a curiosity in Talyior, an eagerness to see and smell and experience her father's city. He often looked like a man who, having tried on exotic new clothing, discovered he liked the way the fabric felt.

Lyvia pushed a loose strand of hair back under her fishing hat. In the week since his arrival, Talyior quickly formed the habit of greeting the morning from the city's main quay. Lyvia counted on him being a creature of habit. In her experience, most men were.

Talyior. She tested the name in her mind and glanced once more at her face in the mirror.

"Talyior," she whispered. "Time to make my acquaintance."

She climbed out the window in her bedroom and down the trellis to the garden below. She retrieved two poles and a small basket of food that she asked Cook to prepare for her and set off down toward the shoreline. The morning sun just began to poke above the northern headland when she reached the edge of the pier.

He was there, sitting on the planks, back against a piling, playing his guitar. Lyvia approached, her boots making little ticking sounds in syncopation with his strumming. She stopped before him, her back to the sun. She watched his eyes open, take in her shoes, pass upward to squint against the sunlight.

"Good morning, glory," he murmured.

"If you are looking for coin," Lyvia said, letting a smile form. "There are better places and more profitable, and if you hope to play the fish into a basket, save your fingers. Fish are deaf. Hooks work best."

Talyior rose quickly, and Lyvia noticed they were nearly the same height. Her smile deepened.

"No, mistress," he said. "I just play to greet the morning. I found the waves peaceful."

"Yes, I'm sure. You play at Tanli's."

Talyior bowed slightly. "Yes, my companion and I have a room there."

"Right, the gloomy fellow with the dark hair. I remember and, from the sound of it, from the North."

"Correct, mistress, on all counts. We are exiles, of a sort, from Pevana. My friend's name is Devyn Ambrose, and I am Talyior Enmbron, ex-patriot poet, at your service. And you are?"

Lyvia laned back, amused, and paused as though weighing the consequences of her next words. *He has no idea.*

"My name is Lyvia," she said. "And I have lived here all my life. Good day to you, Talyior Enmbron from the north. Enjoy your pier. I'm off to fish before the sun puts all of them to sleep."

"Why two poles?"

"So I can catch twice as many fish, of course. Don't they fish where you come from?"

A wistful look came over his face, and she wondered what memory passed there.

"I have a passing acquaintance."

The slight change in his tone intrigued her.

"You sound like a story," she said. "Can you row?"

"Row? A boat?"

"No, a rocking chair. Of course a boat."

"I can," he flustered. "I do."

"Good, come on then. I have a skiff tied at the end of the pier. You don't look like you have anything pressing to attend to. If you behave yourself, and don't sink us, I'll let you use one of my poles."

Talyior laughed, a pleasant sound. "Again, I am at your service, Miss Lyvia . . . Lyvia . . . You never gave your last name."

She laughed in turn, stepping away. "Correct, Mr. Poet, I didn't." She reached the ladder at the end of the pier, tossed the poles in the boat, handed him the bag of food and turned to steady her feet on the rungs before descending. "Lyvia will do, for now."

Talyior handed down his instrument and the food bag and settled himself on the rower's bench while Lyvia shipped the tiller.

"You have me at a disadvantage," he said as he shoved off and settled the oars in their slots.

"I know. I rather like it that way. If you catch the first fish, I may tell you my last name."

"And if I catch two before you?"

"I might tell you my story and let you tell me yours."

"And three?"

She arched an eyebrow around a chuckle. "I might let you buy me dinner at Tanli's tonight. Now, row!"

The way he put his back into his stroke told her everything she needed to know.

They returned to the pier in the early afternoon, four fish dangling in the water from a string tied to the painter. Lyvia felt sun-kissed and contented. She and Talyior had spent nearly six hours on the boat, trading stories punctuated by long, oddly companionable silences that surprised her more than what she gained from Talyior's gushing trust; the silence never seemed forced. He responded to her careful prompts genuinely. When he ran out of words he would fall silent and let the boat's rocking set the pace of their thoughts. She deflected his deferential proddings easily. She could tell right away she was the more adroit. She had always reveled in using her worldliness to keep fools away, but she found his simplicity, despite being a man well-travelled, interesting and sad all at the same time. As the afternoon sun slipped across the sky she found herself slipping likewise into a different way of thinking. The rise and fall of the skiff on the waves knit together a subtle cloth of sense impression and empathy.

Life, or someone, has taken advantage of him, and yet he still smiles. Did I ever have that? He might be foolish, but he is no fool.

A breath of cooler air dispersed Lyvia's thoughts and she returned to the present. She looked at this man, this stranger who held her attention more intently than any other heretofore, and decided he deserved at least some truth. When he found the courage to ask her about the men in her life, she responded without hesitation.

"Many interested but none serious," she quipped. "At least on my part. I've a unique situation in my life. Free but not really. Men have been a disappointment so far."

"So far?"

"Yes, the most recent gave up a month ago after a winter's hard slog. He is the third son from the same family to have a go. Idiot. I think he still might harbor hopes even though I never encouraged him. He was a real catch."

"Upsetting."

"Only if I let it be."

"Does this third son idiot have a name?"

Lyvia hesitated. Talyior put the question lightly, but the memory moved her first to caution. He must have sensed her reluctance, for he raised a hand as if in apology.

"Do you ever let anyone in?"

She looked at him then, noting the set of his jaw, the deeper question in his eyes. "I let you into my boat, didn't I? But if you must know, his name is Sollust Megare. His father owns ships and lives like a lord. His son thought he was doing me a favor by gracing me with his advances."

She let it go at that. *Not yet. Not quite.* "I have a question of my own, since we are talking about the past now. What was her name?"

"Whose name?"

"The name of the woman who hurt you." The thrust of her question pierced his smile, and it faded like sunlight going behind a cloud. A shadow lingered in the frown on his brow.

"I didn't know it was that obvious."

"All men are obvious. Who was she?"

"Her name is Demona. She's married to the richest man in Pevana."

"So, I suppose it didn't end well. I'm sorry. We have disappointment in common, then, Talyior Enmbron." She smiled, pleased to see his shadow pass.

"Time and miles lay between. Wisdom over wealth; that sort of thing. I'm happy enough, I suppose."

"Happiness. Fishing. Small joys, those."

"Well, you let me in the boat. Blame yourself."

Ah! He's good! I should know better than to bandy words with a poet.

Just then the wind freshened and the chop intensified. The boat took an abrupt plunge, breaking the mood and saving her from having to say more. Taylior took the oars when she pointed back toward the pier. They rowed back in silence, tied off and tossed their gear up on the planks. She let him help her up the last ladder rung, and the touch of his hand, roughened by his labor, rasped against her sensibilities like a file.

"You know," she said, taking the fish from him and placing them in the now empty food bag. "You and your friend really are quite good. I rather enjoyed the *show.*"

"Kind words," he said. "We enjoy ourselves, and it helps keep us in wine and stew."

They walked together down the pier to dry land. She stopped them when they came to a place where several streets joined together to form a small square. "I've decided that you need a more affluent audience. I might be able to help you."

"How will you do that? Bribe someone with fish?"

"No," she told him, and turned away. "I'll speak to my father."

"And your father is?" Talyior hurried after her, gesturing to the fish. "I did, after all, catch one fish."

"Ah, true, but it came *after* I had three on the string, and it was the smallest one at that!"

"And you would hold that against me? Quibbling over details? I did all the rowing!"

She laughed. "And you weren't half bad, either." She hesitated, lowering her lashes, alternately pleased with and cursing her own unease. "Why do you really want to know who my father is?"

"Is that not a necessary bit of information if a gentleman wishes to court a lady?"

Ergan, her gargantuan body guard, and a handful of soldiers in palace livery exited onto the square from a side street. Ergan motioned the lot of them her way.

"I need to go now," she said. "Otherwise those fools are liable to arrest you, and that would spoil what has been a wonderful day."

"Arrest me? Why? Who are you? Will I see you again?"

"So many questions! And no time for answers." She gestured to the guard coming their way at a clip. "I will speak to my father and arrange a more suitable audience for you; more lucrative and more interesting. That would be hard to do if you were locked in the city gaol. Now go! The quickest way to Tanli's is up that street."

"But, but. . ." Talyior sputtered.

She leaned in and placed a faintly perch-smelling finger lightly against his lips. The urge to kiss him burgeoned. Ergan and his men were too close. Movement in a doorway, glanced over Talyior's shoulder, proved to be none other than the ill-remembered face of Sollust Megare. Staring. Angry. She grinned, eyes narrowing, and the burgeoning overwhelmed. Moving her finger, she replaced it with an eager, quick kiss he had no opportunity to return.

"Don't hold my parentage against me," she called as she turned away. "And I won't hold your rowing skills against you!"

"Wait," he gasped. "Please! Who *are* you?"

Lyvia looked once at the onrushing mass of uniformed humanity and back again at Talyior.

"I am Lyvia Tamorgen, daughter of Sylvanus Tamorgen, the Tyrant of Desopolis." His reaction brought laughter bubbling up from her core. She gave him a healthy shove. "Now, go!"

She did not watch him dart off but turned back to Ergan and her life, aware the tingling in her lips presaged change.

Chapter 8: Desopolis: Destiny Engaged

LYVIA PACED AHEAD OF HER ESCORT; she rather enjoyed imagining Ergan carrying a string of fish, forced to hold it at arm's length so as keep it from slapping into his trunk-like legs. Each of the other guards sported a pole and tackle, parodies of the spears they normally bore. She allowed herself a small smile as she walked.

Little bastard me, I am free!
There's no end to all the things I can see.
In and out of doors, up and over walls
Cos' no one cares if the bastard falls.
I'm a shadow soul playing secretly
Behind the throne and the tapestry
Little bastard me, that no one knows
Cos'no one cares where the bastard goes.

She hummed the little ditty as she paced up the slope to the palace gates, a little-girl rhyme she composed to assuage her abused hopes. It had faded into the mythology of her life like most childhood memories, sublimated but always there when one's daring drove one to kiss a near stranger in the middle of a public square. As the only child of Sylvanus Tamorgen, Tyrant of Desopolis, she had grown into her maidenhood having the run of the city. Unacknowledged officially despite her father's heart, her bastardy conferred on her a certain freedom that she learned to exploit early.

She told Talyior the truth when she said her life had been a succession of suitors since she turned twelve. None ever held her attention. The most persistent and least interesting of them had been

Sollust Megare. When she pecked Talyior in the square, she hoped to tell the hapless Sollust once and for all to kiss off.

And now, Talyior.

She walked up the sloping street toward the palace, marveling at the notion she could feel so attuned to him after a day bobbing about in a boat, but she did.

And his lips had been . . . very nice.

As she walked underneath the palace gate arch, she laughed at herself a little; she needed to see her father.

I never went to him with my little-girl problems; what does it mean that I go to him with this kiss?

She sobered quickly. This was more than a kiss and jumbled emotions. Talyior had told her much more than he imagined during their time fishing. Broken hearts, flames and northern priests in Pevana. Blood in Gallina. Threats.

Lyvia had grown up knowing the value of information. From her earliest days, she took to sifting palace and city gossip for useful bits. And while officially unofficial, she always found ways to be of service to her father. She found hidey holes that allowed her to spy on council meetings, and some of them had recently dealt with fears of invasion from the north. And that connection ambled along beneath her thoughts as she walked back to the palace. Northern unrest and Perspan ambitions meant trouble for her father, Desopolis and the south entire. She had news to share and questions to ask on several fronts that Ergan, huge lump of devotion that he was, could not answer.

Sylvanus Tamorgen of Desopolis shifted, trying to ease the ache in his backside. He had been in the saddle and on the road making a last, fast tour of the weapons caches in the hill forts north of the city. Rumors of unrest and bloodshed filtered down to him from the mining town of Gallina, and before he left the news from sea-traders along the coast all spoke of increased shipping crowding Pevana's harbor. The six month silence from his spies in that city spoke volumes in itself. Whether they were dead or just forced underground by the flood of Perspan troops, the effect was still the same: southern ignorance of northern plans. He knew they were coming. He had more confidence in his means to counter, at least as much as Desopolis could alone, any thrust south through the passes into the central valley, but a seaborne assault would be much more problematic. If Roderran had the ships, Heliopolis, Teirne, and Eadne could all very well burn, leaving Desopolis isolated.

He reset his aching buttocks in the saddle and spurred ahead of his escort, turning off the road to climb a small rise that pushed the river westwards before finding its final course to the sea. A wide view greeted him when he reached the summit. His domain stretched in all directions: river and hills to the north, rocky peaks to the east and west that separated Desopolis from her nearest neighbors, Heriopolis and little Eadne.

And that is the biggest problem I face, those hills, and the fools who lead the cities behind them. So independent, and in the end, weak.

He stared back north, assessing, considering. Thirty years' experience had shown him that, as long as the north remained distracted by generations of internal strife, the south could slumber in peace, squabble meanly amongst themselves about borders and fishing boundaries and generally ignore the larger, possible dangers. He knew he had been right to spurn the northern demands over the years, but now he saw that he had only delayed payment.

He put the spurs to his mount to descend back to his men awaiting him on the road. Each downward pace limited his perspective.

Those hills. I tried for years to make them see.

But prosperity oftentimes precludes foresight, and Sylvanus had grown grey and bitter with the failures. Wealth was a great producer of complacency.

Reaching the head of the column, he set them off again at a quicker pace. He had seen enough, done what he could, ruled the longest, outwitted and outlived all of them. If they could not see what loomed, it was their problem.

He had survived by learning how to sniff out information and act decisively. And what he smelled as he pounded the dusty miles back toward Desopolis was smoke. Cities would burn when spring let loose Roderran's forces. Troops had been quietly raised, trained and dispersed to avoid prying northern eyes. He made subtle, more easily-defendable changes to city and harbor walls. And yet he knew something more, something dramatic and ambitious was called for in order to avoid or at least soften the pending blow. He had prepared as he could with men, but he also needed Renia's Grace and a pathway to a miracle.

He clattered through the streets toward the palace, ignoring the smattering of cheering folks who noted his entrance; and then he noticed Lyvia waiting in the courtyard. His hip popped with a sound like a chicken getting its neck broken for the pot as he swung his leg over to dismount. *My body gets louder the older I get.* He swept her up in his wake along with Ergan and one or two others and passed on into the entrance hall of the palace. Once inside he quickly divested himself of riding gear, light-cuirass, and greaves, tossing them into the arms of two servants whom he dismissed with a curt nod.

"Give me a moment, Lyv," he muttered out of the side of his mouth. "I need to rinse off this road dust. I'll meet you in your rooms." He did not pause for a reply and stomped off in search of water.

Ten minutes later, his mood lightened symmetrically by the level of brown he left behind him in the tub, Sylvanus approached his daughter's apartment alone, a rarity, and took care to observe how quickly the guard came to attention and responded to his gesture to both knock on and swiftly open the door. Laxity was a disease that started in the small things, those things deemed unimportant by events or attention. If things became ragged and imprecise here, then how bad could things get further removed, say, in the city guard, or the troops stationed in the countryside? The guard's response satisfied Sylvanus in many ways, not the least of which being his daughter's safety.

He paused under the lintel of that smartly opened door to take a deep breath and resettle the freshly cleaned silks on his shoulders. He and Lyvia shared a complicated love. Sylvanus knew he was a good ruler but a bad father.

If he had been an ordinary man, doubtless their lives would have been different. There would have been moments, closeness, and subtle joy. Sadly, perhaps for their relationship, he was no ordinary man. He was Sylvanus of Desopolis who, being titular father to all, could not allow himself to act, at least outwardly, as a real father to one save behind closed doors—like those that snicked quietly shut behind him.

Lyvia rose at his entrance, and he noticed anew how the late afternoon sun on her features reminded him of her mother. He smiled. She returned it. Whatever tension he may have felt in his jumbled impressions faded as she responded to his gentle embrace with surprising pressure.

"So," he murmured into her hair that smelled faintly of a long remembered scent. "I've never known you to greet me in the courtyard, not even when you were little. Care to explain?"

She broke the embrace and glided back to her window bench. Sitting, she faced him again with a face half smile half frown.

"I'm not sure where to start. I'm still trying to piece it all together."

"What happened?" He moved to join her on the bench, leaning back against a side panel. The window seat looked out over the palace garden to the south. It was a well-sighted apartment, despite Lyvia's unofficial status, for it took in the entirety of the lower levels of the city down to the shore and the harbor.

"A week or so ago a pair of musicians, poets, really, arrived. They took rooms at Tanli's where they perform. I have gone several times. They are northerners."

"Ah! That's it. Ergan mentioned them. He thinks they might be spies."

She smiled again. "Ergan means well," she said quietly. "But he sees complicity in everything. I think he's wrong in this case."

"What makes you say that?"

"Because I've listened to them."

"And?"

"And they don't have the look or sound of spies."

Sylvanus scowled. "Surely you have something more than that to go on! By Tolimon's balls, girl, don't take me for a fool. What else?"

"Well," she hesitated. "I spent the day fishing with one of them. His name is Talyior Enmbron, a rug merchant's son, late of Pevana. We talked. He doesn't have a dissembler's style. He's . . . nice."

That last brought the other eyebrow up. He settled himself. "Nice you say? Tell me everything, Lyv. Everything."

"I confess I was interested at first because they were something new," she said. "This place has gotten so predictable. Our people, father, seem half-aware to me. These two looked and sounded like men intent on *seeing* their world. Plus, they were both rather good looking and sounded, oh, I suppose mysterious and smart. I'm not sure. But after spending today with Talyior, I'm convinced there is something—"

"Something?" he asked. "As in what? Special? Dangerous? Useful?"

"He might be all three, especially combined with his friend," she responded quickly. "I got to know him, got him to talk. I wanted to find out why he came here. He and his friend fled northern troubles, and yet he also made me take a look at us. I know you've never taken me into any of your councils, but did you know the walls around here are pretty thin in places? Also, you really should have the trellis outside your chambers trimmed back or removed altogether. It's getting sturdy enough to bear someone heavier than myself. Father, whether you acknowledge me or not, I *am* your daughter. I might not know all your secrets, but I have overheard some of your talks with Ergan and others. I know we are in trouble, and that you need all the information you can get; especially now with warmer weather marching up the peninsula."

Sylvanus hesitated, stunned by her word choice. *And warmer weather marching up means an army marching down.*

"Information, father," she continued. "It's been your lifeblood for as long as I can remember, and I can tell you are worried about the silence from the north. I think I know a little about why. Talyior and his friend, Devyn, were in Pevana during the unrest last summer. In fact, they were part of the chaos, actually. He spoke with true respect about Prince Donari, father, and why would a wandering poet speak with such conviction about his overlord. Talyior spoke about there being a festival, festering troubles, upset merchants, burning Old Ways temples and the like. That is policy. Whose? I smell something here, father. These two poets, good men both, but what they might be able to tell you about Pevana and her Prince, and about Roderran and his plans, might be worth examining."

"You make leaps here, daughter. How can you make such assumptions?"

"Because I am your daughter."

"Granted, point taken, but still, Lyv, a stranger, however 'nice' is just not—"

"He's honest."

"Fine. I agree these two might be worth talking to. I'll have Ergan round them up." He turned to go and felt her hand on his shoulder.

"Perhaps it would be best not to haul them in like criminals," she urged. "I'm sure others have noted their presence and made similar connections to mine. Let me see what I can contrive tonight. They are scheduled to perform again at Tanli's."

"You seem to have kept yourself occupied. What are you not telling me?"

She hesitated then. He pushed a hunch.

"Just what did you mean by *nice?*"

"I kissed him."

"You what?"

"Right on the lips in the square by the pier. I liked it. I *know* he did."

He fixed her with a long, uncomfortable look. He noticed she did not blanch now the truth was out. He felt a mix of pride and exasperation. She was, indeed, his daughter. When she was younger it had been easier to put the larger issues he faced in front of fatherhood, but the challenging, defiant look in her eyes told him those days were likely over. His expression must have given him away, for she reached out and touched his shoulder.

"You look like you swallowed a lemon," she said, laughter in her voice.

He relaxed as though accepting the inevitable. "The bitterness is that we come to this, *now*, when we have so little time."

Her face sobered at that. "Then all the more reason to meet these men, yes?"

"I just did not expect there to be another *reason*."

"It was just a kiss."

"But the look in your eyes just now says it might be more than that."

"And if it is?"

"Go get your boy, bring him and his friend, and we'll deal with it. Do me one favor, though. Take Ergan."

"Well, then, so much for subtlety. Agreed. I take Ergan. Don't worry."

And yet long after Lyvia had left for her mission to Tanli's, Sylvanus found himself pacing back and forth across his sleeping chambers, alone, for he had banished Leonara, his current favorite, to the women's quarters. He was not sure how he felt about Lyvia kissing this Talyior fellow, at mid-day in a public place no less. *Perhaps I don't have the right to question. She's not a child any longer. Where did the years go?* Guilt, however latent, was a strong motivator for introspection. Today his daughter showed him she had a life outside his power, and that was reason enough to spare some attention for these two newcomers to the city; especially the charming, *interesting* Talyior Enmbron.

He stopped his pacing to pour himself a half-measure of wine from the decanter poised on the window sill. He looked out at the night, sipping and mulling her other pertinent comment. Her reference to Pevana sparked a distant memory, a chance encounter in a hallway nearly twenty years ago when he and other leaders of the southern cities had traveled there to negotiate trade terms. He remembered Pevana's current ruler as a somewhat wild-looking youth, a stripling not more than fifteen, still five years removed from the diadem of power. *But he had sharp eyes. A good mind, then, I think.* To have survived Roderran's rule and prospered in such a situation said something for Donari's abilities. Sylvanus knew what he needed to about Roderran. He wondered where the cousin fit into the King's plans.

And that was really why he paced his rooms after midnight, chewing on the dregs of a bad day. For months on end he had been struggling for something, a key, a bit of information, a way through the maze of troubles that invasion presaged. And behold, with a day's innocent fishing and a simple kiss, his daughter might have given him just that. *Ah, but even I know there are no simple kisses. I have to meet Lyvia's poets. And I have to be 'nice.'*

Appearances were vital; especially where they concerned what he had begun to think of as his only recourse . . . ideas that still had not completely crystallized. Yes, appearances were vital, for how else was he to turn what he had to do into the *right* thing to do? He stifled his first thoughts and continued pacing. Two hours later he smiled at the moon, took a last look out his balcony at his slumbering city, took to his bed and slept like an innocent man.

Chapter 9: Desopolis: On the Way to Tanli's

DEVYN LISTENED GOOD-NATUREDLY as Talyior spun out the tale of his day, assuming this to be another of his friend's dalliances, the like of which he had witnessed several times during their journey together. As well as he had come to know Talyior, his friend's willingness to dive into emotions still surprised him, as did the exuberance with which he embraced life despite its many disappointments. It showed in his poetry and song, this personal quest to fill himself up with experience. Each hill vista sparked introspection, each town burst full of promise, each girl was enough, for a time, to replace Demona.

As Talyior gushed about fishing with the newest, most ravishing, amazing, wondrous creature in the world, Devyn found himself smiling, drawn out by a small measure from the dark mood that perplexed him since his experience at Renia's Temple. He was happy for his friend even if this newest infatuation, too, would pass. He knew the pattern: attraction, distraction, competition, or an angry father, suitor or older brother, and then off down the road to a new encounter. Said sequence had followed Taylior down the peninsula, and thus, Devyn as well.

"...and her name is Lyvia Tamorgen, the tyrant's daughter!"

The mention of the girl's name brought Devyn back abruptly to the present.

"What was that?" he asked.

"I said her name was Lyvia, and she wants to help us find a more *affluent* audience!" Talyior paused in his pacing. "Have you heard anything I've said?"

"Right: ravishing girl, been watching our act, good listener, amazing lips. Got it, but..."

"Got it, but what?"

"But are you completely out of your mind? She's the daughter of Sylvanus Tamorgen. If Demona was dangerous, what do you think she'll be? There's fire and then there's fire, my friend. And meddling with the daughter of a tyrant could land both of us in said tyrant's gaol. That's not an audience I'd like to meet, thank you. Give me the uncouth set at places like Tanli's. I'm not that ambitious."

"I forgive you your lack of ambition," Talyior said, a serious look on his face but mirth rising in his voice. "Lyvia might be worth a few risks. You need to pull yourself together, D! Think of the possibilities! Tonight's show could be ripping. You need to loosen up a little and pick one of the girls who keep buying you drinks. So morose! You aren't a priest for Renia's sake, are you?"

Devyn's eyes snapped up at Talyior's last words and a smile teased his lips. Risks notwithstanding, he had wisdom enough to see his friend at least partly right. His troubling dreams, the affair at the temple, Gallina, all had combined to put him off his balance. He had stopped seeing the fun in chaos. Before Talyior had returned from his day with Lyvia, he had been contemplating leaving, following the whispered words of Kembril's spectre and returning to Pevana. But now, looking up into his friend's intense, eager face, he realized that he might still go, but not yet.

"No," he said in a voice that started low but rose to match Talyior's tone. "I'm a poet, not a priest. I'm taking you down tonight, and when I do, you might find yourself sleeping on the roof!"

"If Lyvia is there, I wouldn't mind in the least."

"You are going to get us into real trouble, you know."

"I know. We've lived through it before."

"There are no quick getaways from a place like this. She may have sounded unattached, and she may even have meant that little peck you called a kiss, but she is the daughter of a ruler, and there may be other parties in the mix."

"Perhaps, but somehow I doubt it. She's interesting."

"You need to stop thinking about her breasts and tune your guitar."

"And when was the last time you cleaned the spit out of your flute?"

"Don't be petty or I'll break it over that thick head of yours."

"Oh, no sack action, bad verses and lapsed talent reduce you down to insults? Please!"

"Please nothing. I'm hungry." He rose and gave Talyior a friendly shove toward the door.

"For food only?" Talyior asked over his shoulder as he turned to open the door.

"Yes, damn you!" Devyn growled, pushing him through. "Food and a little action."

"The bitch kissed him! In the square! On the lips! A common tavern player!"

Sollust Megare rolled the litany around in his head as he swilled his way through yet another bottle of his father's best wine.

"Bitchy, bitch, bitch," he slurred between slurps. "Witchy, witch, witch. On the lips, lips, lips. Cunt deserves to be whipped, whipped, whipped."

Sollust knew better than to look at himself in a mirror. His better sense, reduced to a whisper after months of dissolution, told him he had quite gone off, but the wine fueled his anger over Lyvia Tamorgen's rejection of his suit. He had been of better mind then, still somewhat his father's son with money and place to recommend him.

"And the bastard bitch said no." He breathed into the cup, blowing bubbles in the liquid before slurping yet again. "No! To me! Sollust the true son, no bastard, I! And I'd still have her. She said no!" The final *no* began as a whine, changed to a sob, and only ended when he drained the cup dry.

He reached for the bottle, saw three, lunged after the right-hand one and missed, tried again for the middle one and succeeded. He sloshed another measure into his cup and tried to focus his too-fuzzy brain on what he needed to do.

"*Sober up,*" whispered the last thread of his better sense. "*Drink,*" urged his broken heart. "*Get back at the bitch,*" raged his failed hopes. "*Better yet,*" reasoned his cock, "*save her from herself.*"

The idea blossomed for him like a rose tinged with inebriated wisdom.

"Yes, save her. I can do that. She's too young to see how foolish she looks. She needs me to do it for her. Bastard or no, she's the daughter of Sylvanus and should know better."

"*But she did know better,*" whispered his better sense, ever so faint. "*And she told you so, repeatedly.*"

"Stop it!"

Sollust blinked, once, twice, surprised at the sound of his own voice. He waited, wine-soaked stupor growing, for his better sense to respond, but there was silence within and without. He let his head sink down on the table, lips fluttering like butterflies as his broken heart, failed hopes, and strangely tumescent cock settled about his head to whisper plans.

He awoke at sunset more from instinct than design. He tested his head. No whispers. He checked his wine bottles. Empty. He shoved back from the table, nearly over-balanced, then righted himself to move across the room to the washstand.

Sometime during his drunken nap, one of the maids must have refilled the basin. That meant someone had come into the room and seen him, but Sollust had fallen so far into his drink that the thought barely registered. He had been telling himself he did not care so often since Lyvia's final dismissal that he actually believed it. *So what if the maid saw me! But then she might tell father, and that's no good. I haven't time for one of his talks.*

His recent behavior placed him in a difficult position with his family. He still lived at home, barely. Early on, his pursuit of Lyvia had been a point of familial pride. His father actually encouraged him, but when word spread of his failure things began to change. Father turned cooler, less jovial, less willing to over-look Sollust's growing penchant to taverns and late hours. When Sollust's angst over Lyvia turned into obsession, things turned colder still.

He splashed water on his face and hair, slurping some to cool the fire in his throat. Combing his greasy locks back from his face, he broke his rule and stared at his reflection in the mirror. The face that peered back at him retained some of the darkish good looks that had served him well in the beginning, but even he could see the circles under his eyes, their bloodshot whites, the strained, taught nature of the mouth and jaw.

"You have no friends," he whispered to his reflection. "One by one they've fallen away. All you have left is her."

He smiled ruefully. The more craven his behavior regarding Lyvia became the more he came to realize he could not stop. The more he lost of what meager promise he once had, the more he filled up his days with observing Lyvia. He turned disheveled by degrees. He watched and waited as his life bled away. But he was through waiting.

"She fucking kissed him!" he spat at his reflection.

He had watched Lyvia and her most recent dalliance walk away from the pier that afternoon with a mixture of interest and revulsion. He recalled seeing the fellow before at Tanli's soon after he and his partner arrived to take rooms and perform there. He even spent an evening listening to the drivel they called music and poetry and decided they were substanceless strangers. Lyvia came three nights consecutively. From his corner booth he watched her take keen interest in their act. The look he thought he saw on her face as she listened to the taller, blond one made his wine taste bitter, for she had never given him the like despite all his early efforts.

He splashed his face one last time, dried it on the towel, spun on his heel, a bit unsteadily, and left his chambers. He took care to use the servants' stair to the back door so as to avoid his father. The beauty of the sunset was lost on him as he shuffled down the back alley lane that ran passed the kitchen garden and into the gathering gloom.

"The priest will know what to do with those northerners," he muttered as he shuffled along. "And I will save Lyvia from herself."

*   *   *

Lyvia ran a final brush-stroke through her hair by the light of the setting sun before sweeping its fullness together and twisting it into a tight bun, held in place with two diamond studded hair pins. They were her favorites even though she had formed a quick dislike for Sollust Megare, the suitor who had given them to her.

A fool, but he had nice taste in jewelry.

Tanli's would be full tonight. With so many eyes present, she was not sure how she would arrange a private moment with the northern poets. She grinned at her reflection. Her fingers moved of their own accord to her lips. The conjured feel of Talyior's mouth deepened that grin to a fully-fledged smile. Despite her assurances to her father that she knew what she was doing, she knew she fished in deep waters. *But, little bastard me/I am free.* She shrugged away any doubts as she reached for her light shawl. Tonight would bring changes; she would have to trust to chance.

She swept out of her rooms, thankful at that moment that she was not *legitimate* enough to warrant permanent servants. She had grown up on her own and was used to doing things for herself. Right then she did not need some hovering chambermaid getting in her way and taking her out of her rhythm. Lyvia knew she lacked certain of the more refined qualities found in court ladies, but that was mostly by choice. The affected manners of the concubines and their servants seemed tedious and silly; the world outside the palace walls, sewing circles, and gossip drew her more deeply. She had her ear against the wall of the world and found it a much more interesting experience, vastly more so than any of the many suitors who chose to ignore her official status and pursued her through her teens. They were too pompous for their own good. Most of them had never gotten well and truly dirty their whole lives. Their fingers were too clean, their minds too full of genealogy tables, account balances and rote learning. She had no intention of ending up tied to a man unless *she* chose *him*.

She descended the main staircase to find Ergan and two other rather thuggish looking guards awaiting her. She frowned, but they were there on her father's orders and so would have to be tolerated. Ergan fell in step with her as she passed with the other two stumping behind.

"Aren't you big enough?" she asked out of the side of her mouth. "Did you have to choose these two walking statues?"

Ergan smiled; his chiseled physiognomy making it somewhat of an ironic sneer, even if his voice was gentle.

"My lady looks as beautiful as ever—and ready for an interesting evening of wine and song . . . or something to that effect? And, yes, sadly, I did have to choose these two fine young fellows behind us. Your father insisted. He thinks I'm getting too old to handle things alone for you, and something about tonight seems important to him."

She looked at him sidelong as she exited the palace doors.

"Did he talk to you?"

"Not at length."

"But enough?"

"Enough, indeed. So his name is Talyior? Interesting. On to Tanli's then. Carriage?"

She accepted the jibe, but for some reason the idea of a riding procession nettled her. She shook her head.

"No, we walk. And have those two pillars of Tolimon stay back from us. Tonight I want unobtrusive, if that is possible."

"Quite possible," he chuckled, "but not likely. It is Tanli's, after all."

Lyvia decided not to comment and paced the rest of the way in silence; her thoughts punctuated by caution, anticipation, and the heavy, rhythmic thumping of her large attendants.

Chapter 10: Desopolis: Nightmare at Tanli's

DEVYN LOOKED UP from his empty plate and recoiled a little. When he and Talyior sat down to full servings of Tanli's best, the place had looked empty. Now, pushing away from the plate, he discovered the room noisy with diners and workers swilling away the dust with ale and wine. A subtle thrill of unease wriggled down his spine.

He scanned the room looking for the source of his feeling but did not see anything overtly out of place. A group of scraggly-looking fellows in a back corner booth sat busy with goblets and tankards, talking animatedly amongst themselves. One of them, laughing at some jest, did look for an instant at Devyn, but the expression on his face remained unchanged and his friends quickly drew his attention back to their private mirth.

Devyn allowed himself a small smile when Talyior made the same pass after looking up from finishing his last bite. *Not as quick, perhaps, but not slow, either.* He raised an eyebrow in answer to Talyior's questioning glance and gave a slight shake of his head, he scanned the room again. Then a commotion at the door drew his attention. A young woman entered in the company of four mountains. Out of the corner of his eye he saw Talyior stiffen slightly. Devyn recognized her from several nights ago. In fact, looking closer, he recalled having seen her in the audience more than a few occasions in the time they had been at Tanli's. The girl's effect was not universal as most of the patrons kept to their business with plate and pot, but the group in the corner took notice; the one with the darkest hair and straggling beard stared openly.

Devyn gave a curt nod to the door.

"Lyvia, I presume?"

Talyior spared a quick look. "Yes, and well-escorted. I recognize the tall one from this afternoon."

"And obviously well-known by some here." Devyn nodded again toward the group in the back booth.

"In the corner?"

"Yes. In fact, I recognize one of them now. The one on the left is the Priest from the Temple of Renia. Had a *discussion* with him over the question of a donative."

"And the other? His eyes are just about out of his head."

"No idea, but he seems captivated by your mistress Lyvia."

"This could get awkward."

"And maybe a little fun."

Devyn chuckled; the last time he felt this charge of energy was in Gallina, the moment before he hurled his first stone. He watched the proprietor hustle over to greet and seat Lyvia and her party. Tanli took their orders and returned, pausing at their table.

"I see you've finished your meal, and from the looks of the plates it wasn't half-bad." His bald head bobbed up and down, heavy jowls jiggling with each word. "I'll take that as a compliment. I also trust you've seen the room fill up. If you've something special in mind, I say tonight would be the night to try it. And the sooner you start the better, if you get my meaning?"

"We do indeed," Devyn replied, shuffling over to the edge of the booth and rising dramatically. "Come, T, my erstwhile troubadour, it is time to play."

Talyior grabbed the neck of his guitar and started toward the cleared space on one end of the room that served them for a stage. Flourishing his flute, Devyn followed. He felt eyes on his back, and not those of the anticipating crowd. Anticipation, yes, but a darker sort. As he and Talyior settled into the stools stationed for the purpose, he glanced up to find the source exactly where he expected it to be. Leaning closer to his friend, pretending to listen as he tuned a string, he murmured. "Those boys don't look like they appreciate music."

"Agreed." Talyior plucked a string. "Odds they do a bit of drinking first and then try something."

"Evens says you are right. We've rolled the bones at longer odds. Let's play. Maybe our poetic genius will forestall the inevitable."

"How about that Pastoral to Borimon to start?" Talyior grinned. "Give that fake priest from Renia's temple something to think about while he looks for courage in his cup."

"Ah, you are too good to me, friend."

"Always happy to be of service."

He raised his flute to his lips to breathe life into the opening bars. Talyior set fingers to strings and followed and soon closed his eyes as he played, lost in the song. At first the music flowed over Devyn like it normally did when they played, but the tensioned he perceived earlier persisted. In their months of play and travel he had always been the quickest to take the measure of their audiences. While he ran his fingers over the stops of his instrument, he let his eyes run over the crowd. What he observed disturbed him. Some listened in rapt attention. The girl Talyior pointed out called Lyvia fixed on them with such intensity that he almost missed a chord change. The sullen group in the corner fingered their cups and stared. And others about the room held similar, almost expectant expressions. He even recognized a few faces, but of those he did not, most bore a dark cast.

They pushed through several tunes without pausing for comment, but Devyn knew they couldn't keep it up all night. When Talyior gave a last flourish on a song, Devyn looked up at the crowd, inviting them to call out the next tune.

"Something about Borimon's balls!" A voice in the back yelled. Devyn thought it came from one of the dark ones he noticed earlier.

"Do you know the one about Tolimon in the Temple?" shouted another. Suddenly comments and requests came from all over the room with alarming intensity.

"You need real balls to sing about Boriman with a fancy-boy flute!"

"Yeah! The only way he'd reach the high notes would be if he buggered himself with it!"

A tough looking fellow leaning up against the raised serving table slammed an empty mug down. "You guys stink like my horse's hind end!" he announced. That brought another round of comments.

"They do not, I like them!"

"Maybe you ought to clean your ears!"

"How do you know what your horse's rear smells like? Did you shove your head up it?"

"Quiet down, let them play!"

"Tanli! Another pot and more music or we leave without paying!"

The noise changed the tone of the room completely. Things got heated quickly as attention veered away from them as folk turned to take issue with their neighbors. He glanced at the corner booth, saw the priest's sneering smile and understood. *Too quick. Too easy. Staged.* He looked away, noted Tanli, his sweaty face fairly jiggling with fear and concern, waving at him to do something. Then from the back booth came a familiar voice.

"Play a song about Renia. If you've no coin to spare, make a different offering!"

Devyn glanced up, caught the eye of the priest from the temple. *You bastard.* Hesitation meant disaster, so he forced a smile.

"I've the perfect tune for you, good priest," he called back, and struck the first notes of an old favorite Kembril Edri taught him when he was a stripling still haunting the Maze.

Renia's tears wash away all the fetters that keep you chained
Like the dust of your childhood
Gone flowing down the drain.
Renia's tears leave you clean and from trial absolved
Like a puzzle you've spent years trying to solve
When the answers were always there
If you chanced to care.

He heard the comments as a counter rhythm as he played his flute for the bridge.

"Hey, Renia's a northern goddess."

"What's he about?"

"Renia's a slut, my grandfather pissed in her bowl once."

"No she isn't you twit, and your grandpa was a lying cunt."

"Hey, he doesn't sound right."

"What's he mean by *fetters*?"

"There's a statue of her in her temple. Nice tits."

"You'd tup a statue."

"Yeah? Well, I did your wife, a statue moves better!"

Devyn could feel the emotion rising again but did not care. He had no choice but to answer the sneering priest's challenge and brazen the thing out. He lowered his flute, raised his hand for attention in mid-breath and sang as loud and clear as he could:

And Renia's tears are shed for you, my friends
To bathe you in the warmth and the light
The wrong and the right become clearer then
Like truth defended
Hope apprehended
By the strength of the faithful few.
  What can Renia's tears do for you?

He paused. Murmuring. Disgruntled faces met his darting glance. Others nodded in acceptance and agreement. The loudmouth from the bar hefted his mug. Devyn stood, looked an apology at Talyior and took a step backward. Some of the patrons stood up, most of them from that dark-faced set.

"Nice going," Talyior grated.

As Devyn drew breath to respond, an unholy shriek from the priest in the corner booth broke the spell.

"Blasphemy!" the man raged, leaping onto the table and pointing a quivering finger at Devyn. "Blasphemy and treachery and falseness! He mocks the gods! Brothers! He mocks us all!"

"Treachery, brothers!" another from the booth cried. "Who are these frauds anyway? They are spies, I say, SPIES—treason and mockery! Call the watch!"

One or two patrons attempted to shout the crowd down. Devyn saw the priest in the corner point. The tough at the bar heaved his mug in their direction and missed, the crockery shattering against the wall behind. The man next to him stepped over to the closest table, upended it and poured the contents of his glass over the woman sitting there. In an instant the room transformed into a melee of shouting, shoving patrons. Women screeched protests and tried to get out of the way. The group with the priest advanced through the chaos. Chairs and glasses flew through the air like missiles.

Devyn and Talyior backed away, shoulder to shoulder, sizing up the chaos.

"Having fun yet?" Talyior shouted, using his guitar as a club and slamming it down on the head of the first man to reach them. Devyn grimaced at the discordant twang as the instrument shattered.

"This was no accident!" he shouted. He bent his flute on the first thug to reach them. A chair leg clipped his shoulder. A blow numbed his ear. Talyior went down. He actually saw the fist that sent him reeling into darkness.

Lyvia let Ergan and the other two guards form a shield between her and the brawl and move her over behind the serving table. People fighting jammed the way to the door, and the opening itself quickly became crammed with the curious from the street drawn by the uproar inside. She watched with dismay as Talyior and Devyn struggled to keep their feet. A group advanced and swarmed them down to the floor. She wriggled to Ergan's side as he shifted an arm to ward off attempts by others to join their relative safety. The fighting became general. Tanli cowered near the steps that led upstairs. The mass that took down the poets now moved back through the chaos toward the door.

She watched their progress from behind Ergan's shoulder with interest. It just did not fit what went on in the rest of the room. The priest that had started the mess stood near the door, several men next to him shoving fighting pairs out of the way as if keeping a path open.

Then she saw a face that changed her interest to rage and fear.

"Sollust!" she spat. "Ergan, see? I didn't notice him when we came in. This doesn't look or feel right to me. If he's involved, then I know why."

"Stay back, my lady," Ergan growled. "The three of us aren't enough for this lot." Two drunken fools pushed up against the table, grappling each other's throats. Lyvia grabbed a metal serving platter and brained them both to the floor. Talyior's bloody face swam before her, his slack form held upright by two rough looking thugs. Another balanced Devyn's unconscious body on a shoulder as the whole group surged to and out the door. The priest followed them.

Lyvia caught Sollust's eye. The man stared at her for a second in the doorway, hate, desire, victory and fear twisting his face into a disgusting mask. He smiled, bowed briefly and followed the priest. The fighting quickly slackened, further convincing Lyvia that the whole thing must have been planned. But why? She made a promise to herself to push a knife blade through Sollust's smile the next time she saw him.

Turning to Ergan, Lyvia snapped off a quick series of orders. "Send your men to follow them, but I suspect they may be heading for the temple district. You and I will go and collect their things from their room, take them to the palace and let my father know what has happened."

Ergan motioned his guards into action and then set about clearing a path to the stairs, at the foot of which cringed a pale-faced Tanli, who meekly handed over his keys. Lyvia helped Ergan collect what they could of Talyior and Devyn's belongings into a large linen bag. Lyvia paused to drop a small purse on a wobbly table. "My apologies, Tanli," she said in passing. "I hold the two poets blameless in this. Send to the palace tomorrow for more if this doesn't cover your losses." She did not wait to acknowledge the proprietor's mute look of appreciation.

Ergan carried the bag easily slung over his massive shoulder, while he steered Lvyia into a side street that allowed a quicker route to the palace.

"My lady, do you know what you are doing?" he asked quietly as they paced hurriedly along. "What do you think you can do against such a mob without involving the guard or yourself directly? By the time we could act, they will likely be dead. I recognized several of that bunch, ruffians and hired knives all of them."

Lyvia did not answer at first. The sight of Talyior handled so roughly by the mob moved her, and their collected things made such a small bundle. She wanted to know more. When she responded, her words came out in clipped, abrupt sentences.

"Claims made by types like that priest and Sollust aren't worth the energy they used to shout them. Sollust is a fool, a mean-spirited little fool, but he's not a murderer. The priest might be. We have to hurry."

She quickened her pace as much as her dress would allow.

Voices recalled Devyn from the dark dreams he followed. Then light burned away all surreal images, and he squinted in the light of a smelly lamp held close to his face. He coughed, tasted blood, winced and flinched away from the heat and light, and yet he could feel his senses returning quickly as he looked for something on which to orient. The light blinded him momentarily then mercifully left him. His head and vision cleared. He lay bound hand and foot in a darkened, damp-smelling room half-filled with boxes and large burlap sacks, one of which served him for a headrest. A few feet away, a shadowy figure thrust the lamp in Talyior's face. What the lamp-bearer saw satisfied him, for he stepped back and unveiled the light to its fullest.

"Right," the figure growled. "That's done it, then, time for more light and a few words with our visitors."

The man placed the lamp on a box near where Talyior lay, and Devyn saw their captor was the priest he had last seen inciting the charge against them at Tanli's. The room gave him no clues, but he suspected they had been taken bruised, battered and bound to the basement of Renia's temple in Desopolis.

There were others with the priest, for at his words two other lamps were unveiled, revealing a handful of rough looking men, one of them the squint who first shouted them down back at the tavern. Indignation competed with a groan as he struggled to sit up. His movements brought a knife blade against his throat. He forced himself to relax. The priest brought a stool over, placed it between him and Talyior and gave them each a good long look before clearing his throat and spitting.

"Well now," he wheezed in a gravelly voice. "I suppose you are wondering why you are here, Renia's blessing on you both. Don't scoff, you," he said, pointing at Devyn. "I actually do mean it, even though I doubt you and your friend deserve it."

Devyn coughed and spat in his turn. "Who are you?" he muttered around a fat lip.

"I'm Renia's voice in Desopolis, boy! Of course! And you know it, so don't get smart."

"Renia's voice in Desopolis," he mocked. "Who neglects her place and tries to extort money from the pious. I've seen that before from King's Theology priests."

The priest leaned over and slapped Devyn once, hard, and instantly blood spurted from his split lip. The priest settled back on his stool.

"No more sauce. You have a hard face. I have some questions."

Devyn spat blood, some of which dribbled down his chin. For a moment he stared at the priest. *Liar. You aren't Renia's. Whose are you, then, if anyone's?*

"Ask," he said.

"What are you doing in Desopolis?"

"Playing music, sharing poetry. Trying to make a living, which you interrupted."

"Lies," he hissed. "Blasphemy."

Devyn shook his head in frustration and pain. "What do you want? It was a song. Why did you and these others attack us? We are just two travelers trying—"

"That song was a message," the priest interrupted. He leaned forward to spray his next words into Devyn's face. "And I don't want any messages sent here, get it? Only the ones I want sent."

Devyn's mind raced with half-formed possibilities. The priest had not felt or sounded right to him on that first encounter. The crazed fanatic sneering at him now in the lamplight reminded him too much of the man he killed back in Gallina.

"You're mad."

The priest smiled. "What did I tell you about sauce, eh? But never mind that now. Here's what you are, and this is what I will let out when they find you floating in the harbor. You see, you're one of those King's Theology twats, you and your friend. You came here planning to burn a few temples, pick the locks on the gates and let in the Perspan fools. I saw a purpose for you right away, boy, when you simpered up to the temple. Not very polite of you, I must say, and not very devious, either. Refusing to make a donation. It's a wonder you didn't have your bucket of pitch on your back and a lit torch. Oh yes, that will make a great story."

Devyn did not respond immediately. He would have laughed at the absurdity if his lip would have allowed.

"Sollust!" barked the priest.

"Yes, Priest Bandle?"

"What do you think?"

The one called Sollust paused before replying, and in his eyes, despite the weakness of the light, Devyn could see the tint of dissolution mixed with petty cruelty and arrogance. He had the look of a man who kept accounts and manipulated the payback to his own advantage whenever possible.

"Taken separately," Sollust sneered. "They don't look like much. This one," he said, pointing at Devyn, "has too pointy a chin for me, and his cheeky rhymes are irritating. And this one," he continued, turning his malevolence on Talyior. "This one is more my concern. He's been misleading Lyvia. I've watched him since the first time she took notice of him." As he spoke his voice dropped into a darker, evil sounding octave, confirming Devyn's first impression of him. "This one really needs to have his throat cut for getting in my way." He leaned down, bringing his face closer to Talyior's. "She's mine," he finished in a sinister, near-whisper. "And I will gut the man who interferes."

"Trust me, friend," Devyn murmured. "We will gladly take ourselves elsewhere. Just cut us loose, and we are out before the morning mist burns away."

Sollust laughed. "It's not as easy as all that, prick!" he sputtered. "Bandle may be a whoreson bad priest, but he sees things. He says you two don't fit. It is all over the harbor, up and down the quay. Every ale-house since November has heard the same whispers about spies, dying gods, war. Lyvia will need saving, and I think it just might be she needs saving from the likes of you or what you bring with you."

Devyn moaned. This was worse than a nightmare. He rolled on to his side and caught Talyior's eye. They were in the hands of ignorant madmen. The whole scene felt like something out of focus, as if it were a painting composed by a near-sighted idiot. His mind raced, but he could see no way out. Talyior's look communicated he had reached a similar conclusion.

"So!" barked Sollust, giving Talyior a solid kick in the ribs. "Let's deal with these fools."

Bandle reached over and delivered a cross-handed blow to Devyn's face. "Right," he wheezed. "Time to carve you up for the gods." He stood and drew a cruel looking knife. "A couple of you back there come over and hold him down for me. I want to enjoy this." He raised the blade.

But before the blows fell, a crash rang out above their heads, as though a door had been rudely forced, one loud shout of warning followed by the sound of rushing feet. Their captors responded instantly.

"Ho! What's that then?" coughed Bandle. "It's the Watch! Time to scatter, boys!"

Like mice scurrying to find shadows when the pile of rags they had been nesting in gets disturbed, Bandle, Sollust and their crew scrambled off out of sight. Before he left, however, Sollust whipped out a long bladed knife and made a try at slashing Talyior's throat, but the blow never fell because as he lunged forward Devyn kicked out his left leg and caught Sollust on the right knee with a satisfying force that caused Sollust to yelp in pain, drop the knife and hobble off and away, whimpering and cursing with every step.

A moment later a squad of armored soldiers clattered into view led by Lyvia and her massive bodyguard, who with a gesture sent most of them on in pursuit of the kidnappers.

Lyvia, smiling apologetically, cut Talyior's bonds while her bodyguard did the same for Devyn.

"I'm so sorry," she said. "This wasn't what I had in mind when the night started."

Talyior coughed, tried to draw a full breath but only half-succeeded. "I'm sure," he managed finally. "But your timing was still pretty good at the end. They were just getting serious when you showed up. Thank you."

"I had them followed," she responded. "When I told you I wanted to get you to the Palace, I hoped for something a bit less dramatic and bloody."

Devyn saw the look she gave Talyior as she spoke. *Formidable, ware, my friend!* "My lady," he interrupted. "You speak as if you know what is going on. I've suspicions myself, but these men—"

"Are dangerous, I know," she responded. "Sollust is petty, but the other one; he was unexpected, which raises other questions. About you. About us. And other things." She turned to Talyior. "If you weren't quite so bloody I'd kiss you," she whispered. "But that will have to wait. I think it's time you met father."

* * *

Chapter 11: Pevana: A Morning's Assembly

*T*HE GODDESS RENIA *reclined on her couch and let her Otherworld senses sift the threads of the mortal lives humming below, and came aware of the hive activity and intrigue coming from her city of Pevana. Thought she took, having an especial care for that place, and what she glimpsed brought a mixture of wrath and resignation: a man in black loitering near dark corners, questing after rumors, archers practicing their skills in an abandoned warehouse next to the harbor walls, folk mouthing words to a false god led by false priests clothed in gaudy red robes in a place cadged together from her temple remnants. And such was her alarm that she sat upright and sent her will out to touch that of her familiar, Minuet of the Arrows, who came with preternatural swiftness to kneel before her lady.*

"My lady calls and I answer. What task has she for her Minuet?"

"The mortals below disturb my rest," the goddess answered in voice composed of timeless patience and sorrow. "See how they undo my faith? And so quickly?"

And Minuet bowed at the resignation she heard. "For us, a moment, perhaps, my lady, but for them a season. And much can occur in such a time in a mortal life. They change, lady."

"They burn and confiscate my consecrated stones, turn my altars into basins for watering beasts, dare to mutter prayers into the aether with no thought where to direct them. I weep, Minuet, for all that falls below."

"Such is your way, my lady, to succor Man with your water."

"But never as bitter as these I now give." And from her eyes fell three pendulous tears that slid down her immortal, alabaster skin.

Ever-mindful, Minuet took their appearance as a summons to act, and ere those tears could fall she bathed the tips of three of her barbs in each one as they hung suspended. Then Minuet turned and strode to the rim of Renia's perch and waited. The goddess waved a weary hand, a gesture holding all the power and sublimity missing in the forgeries committed below. She blew away heaven's murk so Minuet could be sure of her targets.

With a kite's swiftness Minuet loosed her three barbs; one to fix the courage of a young seamstress scholar as she contended with fear and forces beyond her ability, and the others to pin the fates of two wandering poets, placing them on pathways to heroism and renown.

Life and death, however, still hung in the balance.

Eleni Caralon took one last look in the mirror and confronted her demons, taking herself to task in the process. Since her last misadventure with Jaryd Corvale and talk with Senden Arolli, she managed to find a less obtrusive entrance to the library and attempted to keep up with her studies. Nerves kept her looking up from her work to check her surroundings. Though she had not seen the man in the library since that second night, she had spied Corvale from a distance several times as he rode to and from the practice fields.

He doesn't know me. He won't find me. Tomais and I are safe.

With such thoughts she reassured herself she had done what she could to thwart his designs on Prince Donari and that all would be well. Senden requested she keep to her normal schedule, and by the strongest effort, she had.

She might have succeeded completely if Jaryd Corvale had not shown up at her residence the day before King Roderran was due to arrive. She barely noticed the knock on the door and stopped mid-motion when she heard Tomais's footsteps downstairs move to open it. She heard the whisper of the latch move, the sweep of the sturdy wood, and then. . .

That voice.

"Tomais Caralon?" His words came to Eleni as a whisper of cold air down her back.

"Yes, I am Tomais, what can I do for you?"

"Name's Corvale. I'm newly attached to Lord Gaspire Amdoran's horse. I'm told you make excellent tack."

"A bit late for business, don't you think?"

"Sorry, took awhile to find you. It's a small matter, but I have duties in the morning and I need some tack first thing. Besides—" And there was a mirthless chuckle. "—it's never too late to make money, eh?"

"True, true!" came Tomais' innocent answer. "And I have some pieces here that might serve for something small. What do you need?"

"A new bridle and a spare girth strap. Nothing ornate, mind you. Just something serviceable for now. Will you do it?"

"I'm certain I have what you need. I have to deliver some gear to the company down by the clearing in the morning. I'll bring yours then, too."

Their voices dropped to a murmur and a vague clink of coins passing hands, then the sound of the door closing. Eleni forced herself to swallow her fear as Tomais bounded up the stairs.

"Eleni! Look!" he gushed, tossing one gold and three silver coins onto her work table. "A late order but a handsome price and an easy job! Business has been astounding."

Eleni smiled and fought to make it appear genuine. "Nothing more than you deserve, my dear. Folk like your work because it is good."

She accepted his kiss, and hoped her response did his joy justice. *Oh, have a care, my love! He is evil. Couldn't you hear it in his voice?* But words remained thoughts as his lips parted from hers.

"You are my life," he whispered into her ear, his hand moving to her flat abdomen. "Let's go to the bedroom and see if we can add something else to it."

She put her arms around his neck, matching ardor for ardor. In her upset over the encounter with Jaryd she had lost track of the days, but it was beyond guessing now: she was late. That same upset had kept her from speaking at first suspicion; instead of succumbing, she dove headlong into the passion not even Jaryd Corvale could dampen.

Change, chaos and a child. Fate comes in threes.

A tear tingled the edge of her eye that she hoped he mistook for joy. She let him kiss it away. With it went the rest of her resolve and when he took her to the bedroom she outmatched his intensity with a fire born of more of desperation than desire.

Tomais left Eleni sated and slumbering and set out underneath a drizzly mist with straps and Corvale's stirrup trace over his shoulder. He headed toward the field created from last summer's Maze fire where the Collumese cavalry unit billeted there. Rather than rebuild, the locals pushed away from the space, holding it in reverence for the old poet buried where the great oak had stood. Kembril Edri's grave, surrounded by a wrought iron fence, stood out in its solitary position at one end of the field a mute commentary on the military proceedings that invaded its peace.

Tomais ran a finger along a shapely posthead in passing. In his dealings with this particular troop, he often had occasion to observe their training, usually from the vantage point of the gravesite. The horses would careen about the place in mock charges and complicated maneuvers, but they always stayed well away from the fence itself. Tomais felt as though he stood in an island of calm amid all the equine chaos. Eleni had told him the tale of what happened that night last summer. Tomais knew of Kembril only as a kind derelict. Eleni's tales of the poets at the center of all the troubles, and the poems she brought home to study, forced him to see the connections between those days, those lives, and his own. His present prosperity had grown from that tragedy. He looked down at the simple gravestone and read once again the inscription:

Kembril Edri, Pevana's Poet

May Renia's tears wash away all sadness and want forever...

* * *

A noise disturbed Tomais's reverie. A line of horsemen had formed up on the far side of the field. A single shouted command set them at a walk, another increased the pace to a canter, and still another brought the unbroken line into a full gallop that swept up and around Kembril's gravesite in a flurry of tossed turf and thrashing hooves. He bent his head down to avoid the mess and noticed a little girl had joined him at the fence. A tiny little thing, all dirty blond hair and freckles wrapped in a tattered cloak against the chill wet, crouched against the base of the enclosure, hands pushed through and gripping as if holding on against a current. Tomais knelt down to further shield her from the horses as they made their return pass.

"This is no place for a child," he said mildly, ruffling the girl's hair. "You're like to get stomped on by one of these beasts."

The girl ducked away from his touch and gave him a look that spoke of the Maze. "This didn't used to be a place for horses. It was a place for kids. The old poet wouldn't like all this noise."

"But they are here now, and bigger than both of us. Would you like to tell them to leave?"

"I already did; a month ago when they first arrived. They laughed at me."

"That was not very nice of them."

"*They* are not very nice."

Tomais chuckled softly; the child rewarded him with a reluctant smile. He asked, "What's your name, young mistress?"

"My name is Tasia, and I already know who you are. You are the tack-maker, Tomais Caralon, and you are married to Eleni, the scholar."

"You seem to know an awful lot."

Tasia looked down at the gravestone. "It is what I do now," she said. "I watch things, for the Maze, for the old poet sleeping here, for the Prince Donari."

"So, you've been watching me, have you?"

"When you come here, I have seen you."

"And you don't like the King's soldiers? They have dealt fairly with me, at least."

She quirked an eyebrow. "You are a grown man. I'm just a little girl. They don't deal with me at all. They don't *see* me. And that's good."

"You like not being seen?"

"It's safer." Tasia stood up, her smile replaced by wariness. "You have a customer." She backed away as Jaryd Corvale rode his wild-eyed bay towards them. "Be careful with that one. He's got a dark face."

Tomais resisted the urge to watch her go. If she were as unseen as she claimed, he saw no reason to draw attention to her. "Corvale!" Tomais waved him closer, leaning away when the bay's muzzle snuffled at his chest. "I have your girth strap and bridle!"

"Caralon! You work fast!"

Tomais handed up the strap and bridle. "I found a serviceable piece not long after you left."

Corvale gave the items a casual look, hooked the bridle over his saddlehorn, fished out a coin and tossed it to Tomais. "This for the speed of the work. Good day to you."

He wrenched his horse's head around and spurred off. The bay kicked up a protest, narrowly missing Tomais, who nearly toppled over the fence trying to avoid the blow. He steadied himself, brushed some dirt off his coat, and tried to mistake Corvale's parting laughter. Shaking his head, he looked instead for Tasia. Was she watching? Of course she was. Somewhere.

"You were right, child," he said aloud. "He does have a dark face."

Patting the bars surrounding Kembril's grave, Tomais pocketed the coin from Corvale and started for home, and Eleni, and better thoughts than those he was having.

The weak, early spring sun, rising over the clouds clinging to eastern hills greeted Donari and his escort as they passed through the citadel gates. Folk lined the way to the square that opened on the inner curtain of the Land Gate. Word had come from watchmen on the walls. Roderran's column had been sighted riding over the flats, heading for the river ford. They were several leagues away yet and would be at the gates soon. Donari kept his pace slow as his group descended the hill to the city proper. He wanted to observe the fruits of Senden's labor and avoid having to wait at the gate. He wanted to time it to give the impression of fealty with pride, strength with filial loyalty. Sitting too long in the saddle, in the shadow of the Land Gate arch might stiffen his back, but more importantly it might communicate more subservience than he intended.

Senden smoothly maneuvered his mount alongside Donari's at the crossroads where the Land Gate met the road from the Citadel and the straight way that climbed up from the harbor. They rode stirrup to stirrup, waving and smiling at the folk lining the way.

"My lord is looking resplendent, this morning. Cryso outdid himself."

"Actually, the shirt scratches, but I didn't have the heart to tell him. I guess I earned a little discomfort. It is just what I need to keep my wits about me today."

"For king or murderous intrigue?" Senden asked humorlessly.

"Are they not one in the same?"

"We don't know. . ."

"No, we don't. We know nothing than overheard whispers from evil mouths. It is as if the city has pulled all her curtains and locked all her doors for all the information we have been able to collect."

"Which says more about where this threat comes from than gossip."

"Indeed it does, Senden. Indeed it does. I feel like a target, powerless."

"Not as long as I am here, my lord. I've taken precaution."

"And?"

"I have men in place—watching. Ready. Young Lamice, our best pair of eyes, is on the wall with a bow. Should anything untoward happen, he will be in range to act."

Senden's calm words sent a chill down Donari's spine. "Well, then, at least the day won't be completely tedious. Anything else I should know?"

Senden nodded. "Corvale rode out an hour ago with a squad of cavalry."

"Then why all the preparation?"

"Because I don't trust it, my lord. He rode out too . . . obviously. Shiny bastard. Seemed too *loud* for him."

"As if he wanted to be noticed."

"Exactly."

"And the Lord Prelate?"

"About his business, and more's the suspicion, with Roderran nearly at our gates."

A clutch of citizens to Donari's right cried out as Donari passed, "Prince Donari! My Lord! Here!" And he obliged, reaching down to touch as many outstretched hands as he could. Did they notice the ice of his fingers? The sweat beading his lip and brow? Was this some part of the plot to put an arrow in his back, separating him from Senden?

"Good day to you, friends! Well met! Let's show our King a proper Pevanese greeting, eh?" Waving jauntily, he reined cooly, but quickly, back to Senden's side.

"If a bolt does not come out of the blue to finish me today, I suggest we exact a little payment for the day's discomfort."

"I would expect nothing less, my lord." Senden's tone was light, and yet something of sobriety in it turned Donari's head. The passing vestiges of anger faded; Senden said, "No bolt from the blue will reach you, Donari. Not without passing through me first."

"I know that, Senden. May Renia grant it doesn't come to that."

For that briefest of moments, the shouting crowds, the weak sunlight, the itch of his shirt and the threat of death lifted. *Such a friend, I have. Blessed Renia, such a friend.*

"I would, of course, expect to be avenged, my lord, with all the style you are known for."

Donari shook his head ruefully. "I would and more," he said. "But I charge you with keeping yourself safe along with your prince. I, *we*—" He gestured to the people cheering. "—need you."

They moved on down the length of the Land Gate way. The crowds lining the road and hanging out of upper story windows grew thicker as they neared the great square. The throng pushed against the crossed spears of the guards detailed for the purpose, narrowing the road, and, just before they reached the square proper, checked their progress completely.

They waited as the soldiers struggled to gently push back the folk and clear the way. Then the way ahead cleared, revealing Eleni Caralon for the briefest moment, standing amidst the crowd. The eyes that met his were the deepest blue and spoke to him of love, and words, and worry. She seemed to mouth something, but Donari could not make it out. Then the cry went up on the wall, swelling as the crowd behind took up the call, and she was gone, swallowed by the crowd.

Donari and Senden moved to their appointed places in the center of the square. The winches took up the slack. And the great, iron-bound gate opened.

Eleni gripped Tomais's hand tighter as Prince Donari rode on. He had looked right at her, picking her out of the press, connected by shared knowledge. Tomais did not seem to notice. She could feel his excitement in his firm grip; several of Lord Amordan's cavalrymen would ride in with the king, sporting his handiwork. Eleni stood beside him, a confusion of pride, love and dread; and all of it sauced ill by her lies of omission.

A child unshared. Knowledge ungiven. Loathing for Tomais' involvement with the very people she mistrusted; the people who would hurt him if he ceased being useful. Pride that his work earned him the praise and renown he so well deserved. Fear for her husband. Fear for her Prince. Fear and fear and fear...

Renia, help me. I am lost in this.

The blackness of it all fell about her shoulders, belying the sunburst that bathed the road in light. Folk around them cheered the change and grew festive. Tomais gathered her closer and squeezed them both through to the road. Ahead, the Prince's retinue reached the gate square. Eleni let Tomais lead her close behind the group of leading merchants. Tomais kissed her hand and pointed.

"Isn't this great, Eleni? Look over there near the gate. Those are the bridles I told you about. The ones for Lord Amordan's cavalry!"

"Yes, yes I see, dear," Eleni managed to squeak through a throat constricted tighter than the roadway behind. "I am so proud. And so should you be."

"I am. These are important times, love. I can feel it. My trade. Your studies. Change! I'm glad we are seeing them together."

The tightness in her throat choked off all words. Eleni hid her lapse behind a smile she did not feel. Tomais did not notice. He craned his neck, looking over heads to try to get a glimpse of king or prince or more of his handiwork. Eleni held his hand all the tighter, trying and failing to swallow the words or spit them out.

Change is not always good, husband. Oh. . .

Donari was the only one who remained ahorse when the gates swung open; all the others dismounted or stepped respectfully down from their carriages. All the players in the drama stood present and ready. Sevire Anargi, there among a collection of the major merchant households, eyes darting about the scene, wrapped like an old spider in a massive, gaudily appointed cloak. Despite the heat of his ravishing wife, dutifully at his side, the man looked about to freeze solid.

Further down the line, the Lord Prelate stood chatting with the other northern nobles. Collum, Sor-Reel, Lomillar, Avadar, Hallar and Trenar. All of them tall, martial-looking men in their armor and standards, surcoats decorated with their emblems; all their sigils showing predators real and fanciful like the brutally whimsical Lomillaran griffin and the stealthy Trenaran leopard. And then Donari glanced up at the Pevanese standard, Avedun white with a blue dolphin signifying Pevana's connection to the royal house and its allegiance with the sea. *Predators all. What says that of the lot of us?*

The sun began to burn away the last of the morning tidal mist. The prospect of kneeling loomed bitter.

The gates finished their slow grinding motion and lay back revealing the cobblestones that marked the end of the paved area. The head of the column came into view. Four mounted standard bearers with high pennons paced ahead of the van and halted twenty paces before the gates. They separated to allow a single trumpeter to ride quickly out between them and blow a sharp, lofty fanfare. As the last notes echoed down to silence, a tall man in jet black armor appeared out from the mass of the column. He rode a white horse caparisoned in rich black and gold trappings. A golden crown topped his high helm. Horse and rider passed through the gate and came to a dramatic, rearing halt before the people waiting inside.

Donari shook his head at the show, urged his mount forward, and went to greet his liege-lord and cousin.

Roderran nearly fifty, retained the robust attitudes and tastes of a much younger man, boundless energy and self-confidence, not much of an intellectual. He came to the throne young and took five years to subdue the northern lords to his rule. Five years of personal combats, high-handed diplomacy and outright civil war to secure his reign.

Some considered him hard but not cruel. Remembering the last letter he received from the King, Donari knew better. *He is both. Who else would use faith to divide?*

Donari could see it clearly stamped in the triumphant expression on Roderran's face as he controlled his mount's restive power, sparks springing like fireworks from iron shod hooves striking cobblestones. Roderran spurred forward to meet his cousin. Despite the heavy, stern appearance of his helm, the King's eyes danced with self assurance. His handshake was firm as befitted a meeting between cousins of the blood royal.

"Well! Cousin! Are we well met?" Roderran called out. Their horses sidled apart, and Donari had to raise his voice to be heard above the noise of the crowd.

"Quite impressive, my lord. And welcome to Pevana, at last." He calmed his mount with an effort, for it and Roderran's had taken a keen interest in each other, though Roderran's was taller and fuller in the chest. The similarity between horse and rider struck Donari. As he prepared to finish his greeting, Donari realized that Roderran excelled at making other men look up to him.

"Allow me to accompany you up through the town to your citadel," Donari said, "As in all things in the realm, sire, Pevana is yours to command. Camps have been raised for the horse and foot in your train. We've a banquet laid on for this evening after the council you've requested this afternoon. If I know my servants right, you'll find a flagon of our best to rinse the journey from your palate."

Roderran leaned closer. "I like the sound of that well enough," he said. And then he leaned back in his saddle and shouted, "We are well-pleased with our cousin and lord of Pevana for this most appropriate welcome. People of Pevana! Great days are ahead of us! We come among you at the beginning point of a great adventure!"

The crowd roared. Dutiful approval? Or heartfelt enthusiasm? Donari tried to convince himself that he did not care. His people loved him, despite or because of his somewhat checkered past. Still, he feared he fell short in comparison to his cousin.

Roderran leaned in again and gave him a brotherly cuff on the shoulder. "I see my Northerners are all here, but these others in line there. I trust they are from your leading houses?"

"They are, and will be in council as you—"

"Ah, but I can spare a moment to greet such loyal subjects." With that he dismounted smoothly and waited rather impatiently for his cousin to do the same.

Donari's hesitation grew uncomfortable. The ceremonial cloak was just that—*ceremonial.* Walking in such a crowd would be nigh-impossible. Dismounting gracefully was out of the question. Roderran's smile stiffened. His brow furrowed just enough.

Donari gathered his cloak and legged down. Awkwardly. The garment caught his foot as he tried to swing down from the saddle, and he was stuck with one foot still in a stirrup and the other tangled in brocaded cloth. His horse sidled toward the crowd. Senden's timely intervention saved Donari from real embarrassment as he deftly moved in to sweep up the folds and help his lord finish his dismount. Effortless, as if he had rehearsed the move a thousand times, he reached out and loosed the cloak clasp, rolling up the fabric even as it slipped from Donari's shoulders.

Donari moved to Roderran's side, introduced the Pevanese elite. With each name, Roderran dispensed a nod or gratuitous smile or an innocuous word of fake interest. Despite his lack of respect for some of them, Donari felt embarrassed for his people, even if most of them were too in awe of the king's august presence to recognize the insult.

Donari watched the performance with growing disgust. His mood darkened as they made their way toward the end of the line, wishing the King would dispense with the charade and get on with the real business that awaited the council meeting called for that afternoon.

Roderran finally came to Sevire, who managed to make a decent bow.

"My king," he simpered. "I was so honored to receive your letter. Anything, anything that House Anargi can do. . ." His voice faded to an obsequious stutter, his fat form an animated rag doll with loose, jiggly parts.

"And the realm has need of all you can spare, I'm sure." Roderran moved on, but Sevire sidled alongside, half-pushing, half-obscuring his wife in his eagerness to keep the king's ear. Roderran's face registered disgust as he put up an imperious hand. The motion froze Sevire.

"Enough," he began, but then he paused, attention claimed by something else. A breath of wind eased through the square, fluttering pennons and cloaks, and the last of it lifted a tress of Demona's hair so that it danced over Sevire's shoulder, serpentine, tantalizing. The king put his hand on Sevire's chest and moved him aside to reveal Demona, bathed in sunlight.

Demona gave the king a deep, respectful curtsy and in the motion her cloak folds separated slightly, revealing her magnificent cleavage, looking up at the king with her legendary eyes. Roderran, mesmerized by what he beheld, smiled, recognizing the invitation. The king's smile deepened, and he raised her up with his own hand before kissing hers.

"Enchanting, my dear," Donari heard him murmur. Then Roderran turned back to Sevire and continued, voice returning to its regal tones. "And we are most pleased by our subject Sevire Anargi and his most generous offer of ships and money for our noble cause! Our thanks to House Anargi! Most loyal!"

Donari had to admire his sense of timing. Any longer or with words less to the point would have become noticeably awkward. Roderran moved on, once again in control, to finish greeting the others in line, reached the end of the line and turned to remount his horse. Donari followed, noted the look on Demona's face. *How long before she's in his bed? I wonder what Senden would—*

Donari did not see the crossbow bolt. It passed under his chin to ricochet off the cobble stones, imbedding itself in the right haunch of Roderran's mount. He turned in time to see the arrow shot by Senden's man, Lamice, pierce the would-be assassin's neck. The man toppled, rolled down the roof and fell to the ground. Screams. Shouts of alarm.

Roderran's horse reared in fear and pain, nearly throwing the king from the saddle. Donari rushed forward to grab the halter, calm the beast. Another bolt, from the opposite direction, glanced off the metal carapace covering the horse's cheek. The bolt rebounded deep in Senden's thigh. The horse redoubled its thrashing, toppled the king over its withers and stunned Donari's shoulder with a foreleg. Senden and Donari fell to the ground. Chaos exploded in a mass of rushing feet, wailing women, shouted orders and curses.

The King's household troops rode up to form a shield around Roderran and help him back to his feet. Senden raised himself to a sitting position, grasped the barb with both hands and broke the fletching from the shaft. Blood pulsed, drenching his leg. Donari reached for his neck cloth to use as a tourniquet; the motion brought shooting pain.

"Ah!" He grasped his shoulder. Two figures darted between him and Senden, one bending to his friend, the other to him.

"Ease, my lord." Eleni Caralon's face swam into view. "Tomais will help Senden."

A glance beyond her showed Tomais looping a length of leather around the wound, binding it off and helping Senden to rise. Eleni put her shoulder under Donari's, attempting to help him to his feet. Chaos, everywhere, but in his small circle of existence, calm. Sound muted. Only that of her exertions, the muffled whisper of her soothing voice. Roderran was already a-horse upon another's confiscated steed. Spears and shields and armor; and Eleni's gentle assistance.

"You've much to explain, cousin!" Roderran's furious bark broke through Donari's misplaced serenity. The king and his escort spurred their mounts forward, gathering others as they gained speed, sending folk tumbling out of their way as they clattered up the road toward the citadel.

Eleni let go of Donari's arm when he pulled it gently from her. Her terror when the chaos began became relief the moment she saw him whole, if dazed. He had recovered quickly and now turned toward the gate where a whole troop of horse thundered through, drawn by the turmoil in the square and the perceived attempt on the king's life.

No, not the king; our prince!

The square was now a cacophony of screams, terrified people, kicking horses, and soldiers with pikes advancing from all sides. And above it all, a single voice that turned her blood to ice.

"Clear the way! Ware! Clear!"

Eleni froze in terror as Jaryd Corvale lashed his horse into motion. Time slowed. Their eyes met.

You! It was you that did this!

But her mouth would not work. Eleni could only stare, watch his dark face twisting deeper into hate and frustration as he searched for and found Donari. Like a nightmare unwinding before her eyes, Eleni saw him pull his horse round, dig in his heels, and barrel their way.

"No!" her voice ripped from her throat. She grabbed the prince's arm and yanked him out of that murderous path. They fell together just in time, Donari's body shielding hers. Hooves clattered past, slipping in Senden's blood, skittering and spinning and flailing the air like scythe blades.

Over the safe haven of her prince's shoulder, Eleni saw it all in agonized clarity: Corvale nearly toppling from his saddle, each sinew of the terrified horse lunging to maintain its balance, the passage of that final, flung iron-shod foreleg crunching into the side of Tomais's head, blood splurting from her husband's ears and mouth as he fell. And fell. Forever he fell as her own disembodied voice screamed over and over.

No, no, no, no, no, Tomais! No!

His body landed with a soft thump beside her still in the protection of Donari's now-desperate embrace. Tomais' open eyes did not see her; they were already dim in death before he hit the ground. Seconds claimed eternity. The world fell silent around her.

Eleni tore her eyes from her husband's crumpled body. Donari was trying to help her unresponsive body to its feet. Beyond him, Corvale surveyed his handiwork with a mixture of disappointment and mirth. His gaze came to hers. He touched his fingers to his brow, inclined his head, and spurred his mount out of her line of vision.

Time stopped. Light fled like a candle snuffed. Life narrowed to a point. Then, merciful darkness.

Chapter 12: No Options. . . .

DONARI GOT TO HIS KNEE with some difficulty, rolled his cloak up and used it to cushion Eleni's head. His shoulder throbbed with each move, slowing him, bringing dark spots before his eyes. Sounds came to him vaguely, distant and evasive like truth in a dream. It was all he could do to keep from blacking out, and adding to his discomfort came the thought he had failed. Avarran's face swam into view, and Donari saw the fear and anger at war there.

"My Lord!" Avarran grabbed his shoulders, the action setting off a fresh wave of pain. Donari moaned, took a breath and managed words. "Are you all right?"

Donari shook his head in an attempt to clear it. "The king?"

"Is well away and safe, my prince. I sent others after him. He was well covered by his own men. Are you hurt?"

"My shoulder." He winced. "Throbs like a thunderhead but I'm fine. See to Senden. Clear a space here and send someone sensible to find Cryso and tell him to look after the king."

"Yes, my lord." Avarran's face disappeared. Donari got to his feet and stood over Eleni, shielding her from the disturbed hive of milling townsfolk and soldiers. A swell of northern badges thrust in through the gates, pushing up against his own troops with growing anger. Donari struggled to maintain is protective stance, as well as push and shout men around him forward to form some sort of line.

Control this. If they break ranks. . .

He looked around quickly. None of the northern lords remained in the square. Behind him shields crashed against shields. Avarran shouted orders, tried to quell the growing riot. Donari swallowed, tasted copper and bitterness. Senden limped into view, leaning on a guard, his trail leg bound and dripping blood around the end of the offending barb.

"I'm sorry, my lord prince," he began. Donari waved off his apology.

"Not now, Senden," he said. "No blame. This is my failure."

"I should have seen this."

"*We* did, Senden! But this is more than even Casan could have wished for." He glanced at Eleni's inert form, her face, waxen pale, and thankfully oblivious, and then to the contorted features of her husband pooled in his own blood. "He will pay for this. Pay dearly." He let go a deep breath. "She likely saved my life, Senden, and this is the thanks she gets for her courage."

The tumult at the gates quieted as Avarran succeeded in restoring order. Someone brought horses, helped him mount. Donari scanned the scene with bleak eyes. There were other wounded laying about the square, crushed and trampled by the crowd and the horsemen that rushed to protect the King. Donari slumped in the saddle as he took in the cost of the morning—not the least of which was Roderran's parting venom, and the mistaken belief that he had been the assassin's target, not the Prince of Pevana.

And how can I convince Roderran of that? Casan could not be more pleased if I were dead.

And yet he was Pevana's Prince, at least until Roderran divested him of the rule. He had to do whatever it took to salvage the situation. Donari gathered the reigns and turned his mount. Avarran stood by his stirrup awaiting his orders.

"Hand her up to me." He gestured to Eleni's form, holding up his hand when Avarran would protest. "She saved my life. I will see to hers. Now do as I say."

Avarran motioned to his men, who brought Eleni to their prince and handed her up as easily as a doll into a child's arms. Donari settled her gently, ignoring the pain in his shoulder and telling himself it was less than he deserved.

"Get those wounded to places where they can be looked after," he commanded. "Place guards in every square. Keep our people out of mischief as much as possible. The northern troops have a dark aspect. They need to be soothed into camp. Send men around to the alehouses and ask, don't order, ask that they close their doors for the day. With the disorder this morning has caused, off duty drunkenness could have evil results."

Avarran gestured to Tomais' corpse, now covered by a riding cloak. "And what shall I do with the body, my lord? He was well-known. There may be a strong response."

Donari considered for a moment, shaking his head in pain and sympathy for the young man and his widow. "Clean him up. Take him to the Sisters at Renia's Temple. He will need rites and burial."

"It will be done, my lord." Avarran shook his head. "Such a pity."

"And more's pity to come," Donari muttered, then, "Finish up here and send a report to the Palace. No, don't send. Come yourself. If I survive this interview with any authority at all, you, Senden and I will have things to discuss."

Avarran rushed off to his tasks. Senden, Donari and what was left of his escort moved off, avoiding the handful of wounded and the group dealing with Tomais' corpse. They went slowly towards the citadel and the succor of the Palace like mummers in a funeral march. It began to rain as they neared the Citadel gates. Donari rode beneath the arch, trying and failing to shield Eleni. Renia's grief? Or a final commentary on a truly wretched morning that promised to become a deplorable afternoon?

Reaching the outer courtyard, he handed Eleni's unconscious form down to his attendants and dismounted; the movements accompanied by pain such as he had never known before. Black dots danced before his eyes. He feared he might faint. Leaning his head against his horse's shoulder, he gave himself a moment to let the throbbing subside. The beast ruckled gently and remained, blessedly, at ease. Donari gave it a small pat as he pushed off and turned to go, thankful for even that small mercy.

Cryso ushered him up the steps with a timorous hand to his elbow, as though his Prince were suddenly transformed into a fragile artifact. Donari shook off his light touch.

"I'm all right, Cryso," he said. "I am bruised but not broken. Some rest and a sling will do me, I suspect. Get the physician to look at Senden's thigh. I doubt the barb was poisoned or else he'd be dead by now. Did you see the king?"

Cryso's face blanched. "Yes, my lord. He came through the gates with his escort all a-clatter and frothing-wroth, crying out about assassins and treachery. His men dealt with him. I am told he is in the apartments prepared for him with guards posted. He left word for you to repair to him as soon as you arrived, but perhaps my lord would rather delay somewhat? It would give me time to have you better looked after before the council."

Donari nodded his agreement. He mounted the steps slowly. Senden had already been carried inside. Eleni had been placed on a stretcher beneath a light coverlet. Two pages waited at the palace doors, but Donari waved them ahead. "Put her in the rooms down from my own," he ordered them. "Let the physician look to her after he gets done with us. She has suffered a great loss this morning."

Twenty minutes later, cleaned up, his badly bruised left shoulder wrapped in emollient-soaked bandages that deadened the pain as well as stabilized it, Donari and the two guards approached the guarded hallway where King Roderran awaited. Men bearing the livery of Sor-Reel and Collum started to bar his way as Donari made to enter. Stunned at first, then angered, he kept his voice calm as he used his free hand to gently uncross their spears.

"Gentleman," he whispered. "Let us not add insult to the injuries of this day. The king expects me."

"Orders, my lord," grunted the one from Sor-Reel. "You, sir, and alone. Your guard will wait here."

Donari seethed but suppressed it. Turning would give them satisfaction. "Laudable caution," he said, raising his voice in clipped tones. "One of you, stay and keep these fellows company. The other will return to Senden and tell him what's afoot and take any further directions from him. And now, gentlemen," he addressed the guards, "kindly open that door. Now."

Roderran angrily paced the floor of a sumptuously appointed apartment that once served Donari's grandfather when he was Prince of Pevana. The lords of Sor-Reel and Collum were with him, and the remains of a hurried meal lay savaged on a side-board, a jumble of half-torn chicken pieces and empty wine glasses.

"Leave us," Roderran barked when he noted Donari's entrance. The two other lords left reluctantly. Gaspire of Collum gave Donari a particularly dark look as he passed. Donari ignored them. Roderran came to within a pace of his cousin and stood glowering down at him from his comparatively elevated height.

"What kept you?"

Donari gestured to his bandaged shoulder. "There were injuries. Searches to set in motion."

"Personally?"

"My man was one of those injured. Your men rode others down in their haste to get you away."

"Can you blame them?"

"Not entirely. It was chaos."

"Chaos barely describes it. Treason might be a better word."

"Treason? Perhaps, but not what you—"

"They tried to kill me!" Roderran roared, wine-tainted breath spattering Donari's cheek. "Is this how you rule my province? Are you fit, cousin?"

Donari forced himself to remain calm, wiped spittle off his cheek. "Calm yourself, cousin. The plot was aimed at me, not you."

"You?" Roderran laughed madly. "For what purpose? Who are *you* to need assassinating?"

"Cousin, where is your heir?" Donari asked calmly. "We received word of a plot and have been taking measures. The time and place were elusive, but the target has ever been none other than me."

"You expect me to believe that?"

"What reason would I have to lie?"

"You are a slippery one, cousin. Perhaps it was your own plot gone wrong."

Donari recoiled. "Whatever you may think of me, Roderran, I have been a loyal servant to your crown."

Roderran seemed to calm slightly. He paced a few steps, fingers to chin and head bowed. Donari waited while his cousin deliberated. When he picked his head up, the storm upon the king's face had lifted. "Despite rumor, I have never had reason to believe otherwise, cousin. And if what you say is true, you and pointed others have heard of the Queen's latest failure. If the bitch could carry a child to term, you would not be such an obvious *target.*"

His calm gave Donari courage enough to hazard the truth. "Others may not be so loyal, cousin. I have reason to believe the Lord Prelate was behind this attempt."

The king's eyes narrowed, the storm returned to his face. Donari's blood grew cold. He stood taller, held his cousin's gaze.

"The Lord Prelate is doing faith's business and bringing all my people into the light," Roderran said, his tone as icy as Donari's blood. "And he said you would lay blame at his door."

Of course he did, that old snake. Donari's ire rankled, but he changed tactics. "The only *light* I have seen from Casan and his crew has been fire-red since last summer. The fool has turned my city into an armed camp of religious fanatics."

"You forget yourself. Pevana is *my* city."

"Which you have neglected."

"I have been occupied in the north." Roderran waved his hand as if shooing a dog. "Pevana is *your* charge. You were tasked to keep the peace, to—"

"But if you will only listen, Casan—"

"—does my will, as should you! Leave him. He is beyond you. Now that is an end to it."

Donari steeled himself, composed his features. *So that is how it is, cousin.* Casan was worse than an old snake; he was an important one, and one Roderran counted more so than his cousin and heir, should a choice have to come. Storing the knowledge, Donari let it go. For the moment.

"There is blood in square, *sire*," he said. "*Your* people have suffered not only today, but last summer. Surely you can't allow—"

"What I allow and do not allow is not your concern, Donari." The king's cold voice sent a tremor through the prince. "Impertinence was always the flaw in your side of the family. Know your place or have it be your undoing."

Donari kept his silence now. Roderran's calm was far more frightening than his storm. The wildness lurking behind the set of his cousin's eyes, the tension in his form, chilled.

Renia's tears, he will kill us all and not even look back to see the carnage.

"Why the south, Roderran?" The softness of his tone betrayed his sudden grief, but Donari did not care. Not now. "Why now, after so many years of peace?"

Roderran smiled. "Perhaps I have done with beating northern heads and have a mind to beat some southern ones instead. Say it is my will, rather, both are reason enough for a bold king to act."

"But invasion? The city-states are no threat. The Old Ways are—"

"An inconvenience that I have removed from the north, and will from the south. We will be one people, cousin, and those port cities will become part of *my* realm."

"But there are other ways to go about—"

"Impertinence!" Roderran barked. "The south has made you careless, cousin, soft. Soft and careless just like the rest of the south. Weak! They will see soon enough. And it will please me greatly to watch Sylvanus' ruin."

"Sylvanus of Desopolis?"

"A boil in need of lancing."

Donari's mind whirred. Demanded fealty and trade ties denied when Roderran's father still sat the throne had barely made a ripple in Pevana at the time. A tantrum thrown, and typical of Northern sensibilities—as was a grudge held over through generations of kings. Donari knew better than to broach this subject. Roderran was set on his war; the personal satisfaction was a bonus, not a cause.

Roderran refilled his glass, walked over to the window and leaned against a corner panel. Outside, the rain had swelled into a heavy drizzle. Droplets blown by a slight breeze began to dot the panes and collect into little rivulets. The window faced south. The range of hills Roderran's forces had to cross faded to indistinct grey shapes beneath a veil of cloud and mist. The brief spring sun that graced Roderran's pompous entrance was only a memory. The tension in the room dissipated. Donari joined him at the window.

Roderran gestured. "How long will this last?"

"Could go on all day, maybe several days. It will be worse in the hills there. The roads. . ."

"Yes, quite impassable." The king blew a breath through his lips. "We had a taste of it a week out, and those hills are higher they tell me."

"Higher, rougher, prone to slides."

Roderran gave him a bleak look, nodded resignation. "It might not matter much in the end. We will be some days sorting out this mess anyway. I had hopes of a few weeks, but it looks more like a month." The king's demeanor softened, a look quite at odds with the fury of a few minutes ago. "How is your shoulder?"

"Bruised and sore. I should mend. Perhaps this rain will give me time to before—"

"Mended or not, I'll not leave you behind. Your people will fight with better heart if you lead them. This rain is no boon, but it will give you time enough to heal, time enough to marshal your addition to my forces, and time enough, perhaps, to prove my faith in you." He turned from the window. "And your man, Senden. He will heal as well, and join the campaign. You said he was injured. How badly?"

"No injury save death would be enough to keep Senden in Pevana if I am to march south."

"Excellent. Is that all?"

The image of Tomais' face in death and Eleni collapsed in grief flashed. Donari lowered his eyes. "Nothing you need concern yourself with."

"Then I won't."

The companionable silence born at the window lingered. Donari remembered, or perhaps only wished he did, another Roderran—an arrogant boy he once looked up to, and as often laughed at. They had been children once; and now they were men at odds, but joined by blood, and a purpose, even if that purpose was equally at odds.

"I was sorry to hear about the queen's latest miscarriage."

Roderran grunted. "As was I. They tell me it was a girl. I have girls enough, bastards all and useless as a gender where ruling is concerned. A son is what I need."

And then I become completely obsolete. Donari set those thoughts to rest. He was tired. His shoulder throbbed. And he had no more wit with which to banter this further with his hard-headed cousin. When Roderran's hand came to his shoulder, the bad one of course, and overlooked, he winced but did not cry out.

"The day's events were regrettable," he said almost gently. "But all is well now. No permanent harm done, and bit of an adventure, eh? It is not an entrance that will soon be forgotten."

"There is truth in that," Donari said. *Unless you are Tomais or Eleni Caralon.*

"Let us then put this behind us, and direct our efforts south, our forces under a single, redemptive purpose. You and your excellent cavalry will come with me to keep my flanks clear. I shall take all my malcontents with me on this adventure. Get me my victory and those restive fools with doubts will come around and we will spread my peace throughout the region."

So Casan and Corvale go unpunished, and I ride south against my will.

"Agreed," Donari murmured submissively. "You have but to command."

"I so command. Get you to a bed for a few hours. That shoulder looks uncomfortable." He gripped it harder, gave Donari a small shake. "I could use some rest myself. Council of lords this afternoon. Be there. Banquet later, I am told. Attend if you are able."

"As you wish, my king."

Donari left, shoulder throbbing and emotions muddled. He stumped down the hall toward his own rooms, a prisoner to policy rather than prince; and though his heart's desire was to check on Senden and Eleni, exhaustion and pain ruled his head. In his rooms, he fell face-first to his bed, and was asleep before his head hit the pillow.

Chapter 13: Pain and Preparations

DONARI STALKED DOWN the hall followed by two pages. The Council had been an agony. Two hours of official reports, peremptory demands and obsequious acceptance by all in attendance. Roderran presided over the affair like a man who knew beforehand all the moves on the board, rendering what took place a formality. The king reveled in a well-planned tirade, and while the tone and discourse made him want to vomit, Donari could not really blame him. He expected it, given the botched affair at the gates.

The Lord Prelate had overtly gloated over Donari's demotion and disfavor. The old man locked eyes with him and dared to smile, putting the truth to the rumors he and Senden had taken pains to chase. Sevire Anargi basked in Roderran's attention as the King *graciously* accepted the sum total of the man's wealth and influence. In short order the other merchant leaders followed suit. Donari sat there, silent and sore, through the whole charade.

He tallied up the cost as he neared his rooms. Nearly all of Pevana's shipping, an unrealistic number of wagons and draft animals were requisitioned for assembly when the weather improved enough to march. In the meantime, Pevana would live under a curfew policed by royal troops. Trained soldiers and all young men of age would enter the camps to train for war. Donari was outmaneuvered, outmanned and out of favor; it had been a most precise looting.

While his mind followed paths of recrimination, his feet took him beyond his own doors to the rooms where he had ordered the woman, Eleni Caralon, taken. He opened the door, advanced to the edge of the bed came to an abrupt halt, mesmerized by her unconscious form. Brow creased in sorrow's sleep, tears forcing themselves in a stream from tightly shut lids, Eleni was a mortal representation of Renia if ever Donari saw one. He thought she looked like a soul in retreat from life. Seeing her there, he knew his failure complete.

The little maid, Anlise, hovered near. He had her pull a chair over next to the bed and quietly dismissed her. Searching Eleni's face for some sign, some way to help her if he could, he felt rather than heard Senden's halting step come into the room.

"She has been like this all day, my lord," he said quietly.

Eleni moaned and pushed a hand out from underneath the covers. Her fingers found Donari's free hand and entwined within his own, griping briefly with an unconscious intensity that left Donari stunned. The action seemed to calm her, for her features relaxed, her grasp on his hand lessened, and her breathing calmed, but she did not let go. He bowed his head, assailed by guilt, painfully aware of the tragedy that now held his hand in sleep. Studying the softness of her fingertips, the long, shapely digits taught him more about the perils of power in the three minutes he held Eleni's hand than he had ever known in all those years playing at being Pevana's prince. The tears he smoothed away told him more about the effects of rule than King Roderran would have ever thought possible. It was a bitter, bitter knowledge. It left him with many questions begging for answers.

He half-turned his head to acknowledge Senden's presence. "You should be in bed, my friend."

"Says the one with his shoulder strapped in a sling. The potion wore off. The leg throbs a little. I won't lay abed with you stumbling about unattended and one armed. How is it?"

Donari smiled, thankful for the solidity of the man behind him. "It hurts but is already loosening. I left this sling on more for effect than need." He laughed softly. "I am one armed, you are one-legged; between us we almost make a man."

"Very amusing, my lord. How went the council?"

"Ill, oh, most ill, Senden, as I expected. Curfew, guarded streets, a fleet to prepare and forces to marshall. We are occupied more than allied. When the roads clear from this latest storm we go to war. We have a fortnight, maybe more, to heal you and I. Will you be ready?"

"Marching? No, but I will be able to sit a horse, my lord."

"Rest as much as you can force yourself, please. My official duties have been royally curtailed anyway. We will both have time on our hands to prepare."

"Don't let yourself get too bleak, my lord, we knew this would be difficult."

"Men will die, Senden, have already begun to die, for a false religion and vaunting ambition. Roderran risks everything with this invasion by sea and land."

"And?"

"And I don't know which will be worse: victory or defeat."

"Then we have our work cut out for us, my lord."

"Work? I march with the king, Senden, I and fifteen hundred of our people, as hostages to my loyalty and conduct. I see no options." He gently smoothed Eleni's brow. "Since the summer I thought always to preserve something, freedom to move, freedom to think, my people's peace."

"And you have done well."

"Says the man with one leg. Look at her, Senden, she will awake to desolation. All of us are maimed. Power," he spat, "power wounds everything." He fell silent, staring intently as yet another tear coursed down the young woman's face.

"I disagree," Senden said finally. "Power *is*. What really matters is who wields it and how."

"This is failure, Senden."

"Not just yet. Let's pray for rain, take our rest, and see what we can make of the time."

"Agreed." Donari nodded, and then he smiled. "How is it that one who dresses all in black can always see the brighter side of things?"

"Black is just a color, my lord."

Donari laughed, and the heavy atmosphere of the room lightened by a measure.

"Senden, my friend," he said, rising to leave. "Whatever would I do without you?"

"You'd manage."

"But not nearly as well. Come, we both need to rest."

They left Eleni's room and walked together down the hall, Senden's halting, thumping gait accentuating the dull ache in Donari's shoulder.

"Get to bed," Donari muttered at the door to his chambers. "You look rather pale. Off your feet, now. I've a feast to prepare for."

"And who shall protect you, should they make another try?"

Casan's smug confidence at council wormed its way to Donari's mind. "Roderran made my status quite clear in private," he said, "and at council. For the time being, I have nothing to fear of Byrnard Casan. He'd prefer me nearby to gloat over, in any case."

"And Corvale?"

"Is Casan's dog. He'll do as his Prelate commands. Roderran has deemed the Prelate untouchable."

"And then so too is Corvale." Senden blew a breath through his lips. "Tidy."

"Quite."

"You should still have a care, my lord."

Donari looked at his wounded advisor and friend and imagined the sleeping Eleni.

"I have many cares, Senden." He rubbed his shoulder. "But at least I will have good reason to sit out the dancing."

"My prince, you must be more—"

"Ease, Senden. I know what I must be. And you must rest. You've a little time before banquet. Consider it an order."

"Yes, my lord."

Senden opened Donari's door, stepped back and waited for him to enter. Donari shook his head, but complied. There was only so much ordering he could do, and still expect to be obeyed by the likes of Senden Arolli; and for that he was quite grateful.

* * *

Demona Anargi brushed her own hair, a rarity. The impulse to send down to Eleni Caralon's shop was quickly curtailed by the recalled horror of what happened at the gate square. A slight catch in her heart, a shake of her glorious head, and Demona set the poor woman's sorrow aside. As it were, she would have to make do with a gown she had, and that was sorrow enough.

She took extra care with her make-up. Despite the unpleasantness at his arrival, the king had ordered the plans for the reception-banquet to go forward. Pevanese society was nothing in comparison to this sudden elevation into such kingly audience; and he had noticed her. The cut of her gown, the low curtsey had caught his eye, just as she had meant them to. She ran her lovely fingers against her white throat, remembering the caress of his eyes. He was so tall, darkly handsome in his high, stern helm and commanding voice. The memory brought a rush of heat to her face, and dipped lower, to more appropriately inappropriate places. *Such a presence. So much power, so physically arresting. So different from Sevire's sniveling whine.* There had been a slight tension in the way the king took her hand, held it, and brought her up gracefully. She touched the spot on her hand where his lips had left their fiery, indelible imprint.

A disturbance downstairs interrupted her reverie. Sevire's clumping tread on the stairs accompanied his booming calls for wine and servants to prepare a bath. Despite having grown used to her husband's corpulent cruelty, the sound of his voice still gave her chills. She almost felt sorry for the young girl who would attend to setting Sevire's hair.

Brush handles leave welts.

Sevire threw open the doors to her room and waddled in, chortling and in good humor. Demona forced herself to smile his advancing reflection in her mirror and relax to receive his touch.

"Ah, my dear," Sevire wheezed. "Such a day this has been!" His sweaty hand rushed her left breast and she tilted her head to allow him to nuzzle her neck and quelled the shiver replacing the king's remembered heat.

"Did your council go well, my dear?" she said sweetly.

"Better than well, wife, much better!" Sevire squeezed her nipple, almost gently, and moved to the window. "Roderran has accepted my aide. Anargi ships will sport the king's banner when the move south comes. And Donari had to sit there, silent, and take it like the bitch he is! The chaos in the square only made it worse for him, but pleasant as that was, now it is time for the triumphant feast. Make yourself especially ravishing my dear."

"Always, for you, dearest." Demona pitched her voice high and compliant. Sevire was ever a fool for her deceptions. He prattled on.

"This spring will see me raised to the princely chair, my dear. I am sure of it. With the south tamed. The king will need my skills to set the trade."

Demona turned in her chair, let her robe slide from her shoulders to reveal her nakedness full, knowing how it would affect him. Sevire's jaw slackened. He rubbed at his manhood through his hose. Demona's lip twitched, but she did not smile.

How simple you are, you foolish man. How easily manipulated.

She trailed a finger along her pristine thigh, watched her husband's mind go blank, watched him lean forward, the momentum of his great bulk tilting him towards her. Demona pulled her robe closed before he could devour her.

"We mustn't, my darling. I would not want to weary you with my desires. You will need all your strength for tonight. The king must see you at your best." *Fat and foolish would suffice.*

Sevire fluttered, gave a last, near despairing look at the treasures obscured, and blinked away his lust. "You are right, my delectable darling," he said. "But after. . ."

A maid appeared at the doorway to announce Sevire's bath ready. He struggled to his feet and tottered out. Demona returned to her mirror, shuddered.

I need a man*, not a mountain of flesh.*

Reviving thoughts of the king, Demona took special care with her appearance. She applied her creams and colors and planned her assault on the banquet with the same care and attention Roderran gave to his plans for mobilization and invasion. Demona had not felt so alive in a long, long time.

Not since Talyior.

The thought of him sent her careening back to the passion of that sweaty, sexual summer. She stared at her reflection in the mirror; her brain awash in sensual memories. Almost unbidden, her hands stopped their actions and descended to lightly cup and squeeze each breast; the sheer fabric of her dressing gown creating an almost electric effect. Talyior had been a complicated delight but, in the end, no match for Sevire's jealousy. Roderran presented something altogether different. Power and immunity from Sevire's ways spiced his physical charms. She put away old memories in favor of new hopes. With Sevire simpering and Roderran lusting, the night loomed pregnant with possibilities.

Tonight I shall be royally fucked.

Her laughter, deep and throaty and uncharacteristically crude, excited her even more. She indulged in a few moments in sensual arousal, anticipating the night's possibilities, before setting in motion the realities.

An hour later she descended the stairs, a constellation of lace and jewels, as confident in her skills and appearance as any knight entering the jousting lists.

Donari resettled his sling and frowned out at the scene presented him in the ballroom. The charade of the banquet was anti-climactic given the disaster of the day. His injured shoulder allowed him to beg off making small talk with the merchant wives, their husbands and the northern lords and their officers. The room seemed full of embroidered emblems of houses major and minor, hair pinned to tower-like proportions, and roiling tincture of perfumes at war with each other for dominance.

Pity the consumptive in a place like this. But there aren't scents enough to hide evil's taint.

The room was a curious dichotomy all the same: the northern lords, freshly washed, dressed to impress, haughty with power and perceived control; and the Pevanese: a collection of anxious but curious faces, over-dressed but excited by the prospect of an audience with their king. Donari made only the major introductions of folk who had been missed down at the city gate.

The only thing that palliated the painful scene was the symphony of smells coming from the food brought out by the cooks. Once the king had been introduced to the various dishes, Donari's social duties for the evening were complete. Given his public censoring at the council, he doubted if much more would be required of him. He kept to his seat at the head table, picked at a plate of choice bits, and let the talk wash over him. He gave only the barest of comment, making sure to keep his face a pleasant mask

Food, chatter, muted music, everything seemed to be going smoothly, thank Renia—until, out of the corner of his eye, Donari saw the king's fork pause midway to his gaping mouth. He followed the direction of Roderran's gaze.

And saw Demona.

Luminous, unearthly, beauty personified. Even his loins stirred. She arrived on the arm of her painfully jovial, husband. His fat accentuated by her curvaceous form, his face like paste to her cream, Sevire's obvious and feeble attempt at composure failed miserably. He was defeated by the comic jiggling of his jowls, and the look of panic in his eyes the moment Roderran beheld his Demona.

Donari quirked an eyebrow, resettled in his seat to watch the show, and held up his glass for a page to refill. He took a sip, hiding a smirk before it became too obvious.

To the chaos looming, he toasted silently, and sipped again.

Roderran ate quickly and nearly silently, barely tasting the food while keeping a surreptitious eye on Demona. Donari noted her at a lower table, laughing gaily and eating sweetmeats and bits of fruit from Sevire's over-laden plate. Donari almost laughed out loud as he caught her taking clandestine glances at the King. Once, Donari thought they caught each other's eye, and Demona's hand fluttered to her breast to cover her alarm at Roderran's suddenly intense gaze.

Donari's humor faded. His life, the security of his city, and the lives of his people were at risk. The assembled military might of the kingdom flooded the city. People scurried about after power and advantage like mice over spilt grain. Life hung on the precipice of eventful days, but the rhythm in the room suggested a changed focus. Donari glanced at the king and saw there the look of a man who had made his dispositions satisfactorily, like a school boy completing an assignment, stuffing it into a satchel and moving on to the next task. Roderran had set in motion his plans for war and now launched a campaign for a different sort of conquest.

Truth can be a galling, bitter thing.

Donari found himself fascinated by the interplay of emotions on Roderran's face: Frustrating frown, desperate lust, cunning. Donari scanned the room; did anyone else see what he did? None of the faces that fell beneath his eye seemed to hold any recognition, save that of the Lord Prelate. The old man sat, smug and content in his chair at the other end of the head table like a cat who had dined well on illicit information.

Casan caught Donari's gaze and, before the prince could escape, the old man rose and moved over to sit at his side.

"It has come to my attention that you were injured in the unfortunate events of the morning," he said.

"My shoulder," Donari clipped. "Thank you for your *kind* concern."

"I have great concern for all children of the King's Theology. You must be in some considerable discomfort."

"I'll survive."

"Indeed." The Prelate elongated the word. Donari would not give him the satisfaction of his baleful glare. Byrnard continued, "One might assume your condition somehow appropriate given your mismanagement of the day."

"Is that a new tenet of the King's Theology? Renumeration for one's missteps?"

"Oh, I like that. I shall take it up with the king."

Donari cooled his temper with a sip from his cup. "Your man missed his aim."

"My prince!" A hand flew to his bony chest. "I am sure I do not know what you mean."

"Keep your charades, priest. I'm not well enough for parlor games."

Casan leaned closer. "You ruled your city for years as if you were well-acquainted with games."

"And bested you, as I recall."

"Temporarily, I will concede that to you." Casan leaned back again, chuckling softly. "But look around this room, my lord, and tell me I was truly bested. A winter's worth of planning all come together and wrapped up like a birthday present. Men. Ships." He gestured to Demona. "And more attractive treasures."

"I should have killed you last summer."

"Roderran would have, in your place," Casan replied coldly. "But you are not the man he is. You care too much, Prince Donari, and that is your greatest weakness. It will be your downfall with or without my assistance."

Donari raised his glass in mock salute and sat there at the end of the high table, physically and politically damaged. Casan and Roderran waxed powerful and in control of all the variables in play. The Prelate was right. He did care, perhaps more than he should; but it was not a weakness. It was his greatest strength.

Demona, Roderran, Sevire and the Prelate—*they* were weak, for their egos ruled them rather than the concerns of the greater good. In them he found much of what disgusted him most about people and politics. Individually they were an ethical sadness; together they were a disaster waiting to happen.

Now to avert that disaster or turn it to my advantage.

The King rose suddenly, drawing everyone's attention.

"Our thanks to our cousin, Prince Donari, and the efforts of his loyal subjects for this bounteous repast!" the king called out. All movement stilled at the sound of his voice. "Let us cast off the bleakness of the day and its troubling beginning! Musicians! Play. My lords and ladies, let us find our partners and repair to the lists!"

For a few minutes the hall resembled a disturbed ant hill as pages scurried about whisking plates, goblets and tables out of the way. The attendees milled about in the room's center, chattering and pairing up. Donari watched the king, accompanied by the dour Gaspire of Collum, advance on Sevire and Demona as they stood among the other merchant leaders and their wives. He took his glass off the table as pages made shift to remove it and sidled over to better observe the moment. Casan melted away toward the door.

"My good Sevire Anargi!" Roderran said, generously halting the attempts at genuflecting. "Nay, nay, no more of that! This is a party! Perhaps the last we shall have for some time. Let us not spoil the mood with formality. While the minstrel's gather, let us repeat our thanks to all of you, and especially Sevire, for the loan of your ships. Gaspire tells me they already fly our pennon. Well done!"

"One last matter of policy, before such a thing is cast off for the evening," continued the king. "I require all your captains and first mates to meet with Gaspire and Lord Tannen down at the docks, early, with you in attendance as well. I know it is an inconvenience, what with the music just about to start, but I am sure most of you will want to get back to your people to make sure that gets done. Besides, Sevire looks well done in. Are you well, fellow? Yes? No? We are agreed then. My apologies."

"But sire," Demona pouted. "Are we to leave then, too? But I so looked forward to the dancing." She included the other wives, generously, in her protest. "It has been such a long, cold winter, my king, please?" She reached a be-ringed finger decorously in supplication.

Roderran paused, as if noticing for the first time the crestfallen looks of the ladies, especially Demona. "Ah! How callous of me! I've upset the ladies, Gaspire! What can we do, sir?"

He swept up Demona's hand gallantly and led her a step away from her husband. Sevire blinked in surprised chagrin.

"My, my wife, sire?"

"Come, good Sevire," Roderran soothed, kissing Demona's hand and easing her to his side. "I would call it poor payment for all your good service if the night ends sadly for your lovely wife. Allow me to make amends with a dance or two."

Again, Sevire blinked, defeated, his bloodless face a pale piece of parchment, barren and desolate.

"But—" he began.

"But my loyal husband need have no fear for my safety," Demona finished for him. She waved her free hand like a butterfly at him in dismissal. "Who better to see to my needs," she said turning to Roderran, "than the king?"

The king bowed his head, accepting the charge. "Gentleman, if I were to personally vouch for their safety, would you allow the ladies to stay and enjoy themselves? Gaspire assures me there are officers aplenty to partner them. Let you send your carriages back in a few hours to collect them. I would take it as a boon above value, my friends. Count on it! We are agreed then? Ladies, I will expect a dance from all of you! You can each spare a spin to teach an old clutz like me, eh? Excellent, excellent! Gaspire will see you gentleman out. Remember, tomorrow an hour after dawn. Assemble on the quay outside of Anargi's warehouse. Now, ladies?" And to signal the end of the interview, Roderran offered his arm to Demona. "Mistress Demona, yes? Sevire, let me congratulate you on the peerless beauty of your wife." As he finished, the first notes welled from the musicians collected in the gallery. "Madam," he finished, keeping his voice conversant and normal. "Shall we?"

Donari faded back to a chair set against the wall as the group split up. The heads of household were ushered out the doors while a phalanx of northern lords and their officers advanced on the women to seek out partners for the first dance. He waited for an opportune moment to leave, reluctantly admiring Roderran's gambit and Demona's daring. Blunt yet decorous. Obvious yet subtle at the same time.

The king struck a masterful line as he led Demona through the forms. Donari paused in the door to survey the scene one last time, and he recalled one of his grandfather's favorite dictums: divide and conquer. He wondered how it might apply to the present. He did know one thing for certain.

By the time Demona spreads her legs to receive the king's first thrust, the conquest of Pevana will be complete.

Chapter 14: Sorrow and Salvation

ELENI WANDERED IN A LAND peopled by shadows. Images flashed before her sleeping eyes: her parent's faces swung in and out of focus, figures lurked on the edge of clarity; their features hinting at people she knew or had known. Sounds perplexed her, surrounding her with a cacophony of susurrations, spoken phrases that collected into almost-thoughts, vague echoes of cries and screams and rushing feet. And always, Tomais's ruined face falling away from her, his eyes fading to the ambivalence of death as they receded into the blackness. She wanted to scream his name, scream anything to spark a reaction, to call him back, but she had no voice in this place. She wandered lost through an indistinct landscape; no pathways formed themselves to her feet.

And then a wave of remorse washed over her, pushing her closer to the surface of herself so that she grew momentarily aware of her form in repose, the rise and fall of her breasts as she breathed, the soft touch of her hair caressing her forehead as she rocked slowly from side to side. Comprehension followed that awareness on a seminal level of what had happened to her, to Tomais, to their lives. Oh loss, crushing, crushing loss. Loss of light, of hope, dreams deferred now forever, sudden, irrevocable loss. *Tomais. Tomais.* His name became a litany repeated in darkness. She felt tears stream unchecked down her cheeks to wet the pillows and sheets, and as she wept the muscles of her mouth contorted back in an involuntary rictus; a tragic parody of a smile momentarily frozen as though in death like the desiccated corpses tomb-raiders found when they broke apart sarcophagi. And then the wave receded, and she fell back into the shadow world.

Guilt, Remorse, and Sorrow fought like jackals for the remains of her broken heart, snarling despair, whining, soulless screeching attended their unrestrained feast. So much hope. Plans. A future. *Tomais gone. Gone!* An intense cramp clutched deep within her, gut deep, womb deep. She felt the first tickle of liquid between her legs. *No, no, no! Renia! No!* She felt the blood rush from her face as the truth of what was happening took hold. *No, not now. A baby. Tomais.* She moaned; a visceral exhalation. Blood and tears flowed, leaching life away, leaving only emptiness behind. She half-heard voices raised in alarm, felt her body shifted, wet, warm clothes applied. Very nearly she left, drawn to follow the little soul now departed. She felt her spirit reach into the murk, the desire for Tomais and that other, little dream acting like a summons.

She tried to go and failed.

Brought up short as on a tether, she opened her eyes in a spasm's response to glimpse an unfamiliar ceiling. For a moment she lingered in now, blinked once, then light failed her again and she returned to the nothing that held no boundaries. *Tomais. Tomais. And the other. Gone.*

Eventually, her tears slowed then stopped altogether, and she sighed spent and weak from blood-loss and grief, but alive. She opened her eyes, accepted the ornate pattern painted on the ceiling, let its whirls lead her, gently, back to herself. She tested the air and smelt faint remnants of sweat and copper, managed to keep herself from a return to the dark and moved her legs on the sheets. Someone had cleansed her and changed her bedding. A moment passed, another. One breath, and then another, and a greater third. She achieved a semblance of balance between desolation and life. She lay there, quietly reliving the scenes of her life with Tomais, cataloging them and placing them in a spiritual box, safe and secure, defying sorrow's tide by focusing on the love.

Eleni Caralon returned to herself aided by the sure knowledge her husband would have wanted and expected her to. He believed she was the force behind their happiness; that her spirit could defy despair. Such faith always embarrassed Eleni, but now she understood how correct Tomais had been and loved him all the more for the memory. He gave her so much in their life together. Time held no power of definition. She would surmount this. As lost as she felt, Eleni knew she was not yet done. She had something yet to do. She knew she could face life without Tomais' solid, supportive ways. Tomais was still with her, tucked away deeply within.

The darkness receded a little, replaced with the promise of light. She had a sudden urge to find Senden Arolli, the Prince's eyes and ears, and ask for his help. From the dolphin sigil above the bedroom door, she surmised she lay in the Avedun Palace. Hope rushed through her, and she contemplated trying to get up to go in search. As she did so a vague image flashed to her of being lifted and held close and secure next to the faint echo of a steadily beating heart.

Then Prince Donari and Senden Arolli walked unannounced through the door, and suddenly it was not so strange at all.

She watched both men move cautiously towards the bed, concern on their faces. Senden, a bit more familiar to her than Donari, seemed weaker than she remembered. She watched him limp over to move a couple of chairs to the bedside. Despite the circumstances, seeing him lifted a weight off of her that intensified as the Prince settled into a chair, took her hand gently and kissed it.

"How is it with you, Mistress Caralon?" he asked.

She saw something akin to her own grief mirrored in Donari's eyes.

"My Lord," she whispered. "I think you know how it is with me. I know my husband is dead. I saw. I remember. How long have I been here?"

Donari took a deep breath and sighed. "You swooned in the square. I carried you here on my horse. You've been asleep for almost two days."

Eleni's face relaxed further, and a faint hint of color rose in her cheeks. "So, it was you. I remember. I—"

"Remember, what, lady?"

Eleni held back. *What do I remember, really?* As she confronted the memory, the rhythm of that heartbeat, the Prince's heartbeat, secreted itself deep within the empty space in her own.

"I remember being lifted," she responded. "That is all. My thanks, My Lord."

"None needed, madam. Because of your courage, I yet live. I am so very sorry about Tomais. It was a terrible accident."

"No accident, lord. Not completely. I saw the rider, Jaryd Corvale. It was him. If I am spared, I will kill him." *And not just for you, Tomais. For Kembril, the Maze-poor, all of them.* She saw the reaction on both their faces, but she knew she would do as she said if given the chance. "Corvale has much to answer for, my lord."

"Jaryd Corvale," the Prince said, shaking his head in empathy. "Yes, I saw him, too. I will exact recompense, Eleni, for both of us."

"Not if I get to him, first," interrupted Senden, smiling and sitting down in the other chair with a suppressed groan. "He and I have an appointment of long standing."

Donari flashed a smile at Senden's quip, and Eleni saw mirth slough away care. "Well, perhaps we should have a lottery to see who gets first chance at him. We could use the money from the ticket sales to rebuild some of the churches he's burnt!"

The two of them shared a chuckle that Eleni did not have it in her to match; theirs fell quickly into silence.

"Where is my husband's body? I need to see to him. He will need rights."

"He is with the Sisters of Renia," Donari responded quietly. "And they have seen to everything. I hope you will approve. He has been lovingly prepared. We were waiting for you to awake before . . . the end. Perhaps today, after you've eaten something? Senden and I would be honored to take you, and stand for Tomais."

"It would be a great honor, my lord. I am hungry, but I think I could get through this. With help."

Donari nodded. "Then we will call ourselves agreed," he said. "It is now somewhat before noon. I will have maids come and take care of your needs. I took the liberty of sending someone to your home for a few of your things. Eat. Gather yourself. We will see to your husband this afternoon. It is time."

"And afterwards, my lord? What—" But her voice cracked and words failed her.

Donari rose. "Afterwards," he said, his voice firm but sympathetic. "Afterwards we will see. There will be changes in Pevana, as I am sure you are aware, but I will not desert you, Eleni. You and I, we have things to do. If you are agreeable, you might wish to make use of these rooms for awhile. Going home; no one should be alone after such a loss."

Donari's sincerity brought more color to Eleni's cheeks. The specter of being alone in their home perplexed her. *So much change, so immediate, so final. How could one ever really prepare?* Everything at home bore Tomais' stamp, captured his presence in her life. She dreaded even seeing his work boots, carefully placed by the front door to avoid tracking mud across the floors. Their bed always smelled of him. Ache and exhaustion welled up again inside her. She managed to tamp down her emotions, to think logically.

I am not ready to face home. And yet, none of this will be real until I do.

"But, my lord," she said quietly. "I would not be alone. I have friends."

Donari rose and walked to the door that Senden held open for him. "I daresay you wouldn't," he said turning in the doorway. "I'll send for you in a few hours." And then he was gone.

A moment later, several maids bearing towels and basins of steaming water entered.

"My name is Anlise," said one, the youngest. "I'm so sorry for your loss, mistress."

"Thank you," Eleni responded flatly. Anlise helped her rise and undress.

"What you need is a good bath, lady. The priests tell us that water washes not just the body, but the soul."

"Priests? Renia's attendants in Pevana are women."

"Oh," squeaked the girl. "I meant The King's Theology priests, lady. I meant no offense." Eleni frowned. *Too many associations. Too close.* But the girl bobbed and smiled her to the bath, and she let it go.

Whether she wanted to or not, she rinsed away at least the physical portion of her grief, for her body felt more alive and alert afterwards. Water was a great reviver. When other servants entered with a steaming bowl of soup and a plate of bread and cheese, her body had to fight her spirit to be first in line for the spoon. Hesitant at first, by the time she finished she had put away her guilt and allowed herself to sink into the feeling of being clean and full. Her grief still throbbed, but she felt as if she had been granted a space to prepare herself to properly deal with it. Perhaps Tomais' spirit sent a final gift. The thought encouraged her.

By the time they brought her dress for the ceremony, she felt life pulling at her, sparked by a kind word, a gentle touch, and a heartbeat.

The Lord Prelate Byrnard Casan paced slowly down the hall from his rooms in the University library to his administrative office for an interview he hoped would be the last of its kind. His thoughts focused now on the fleet and troops it would carry for the assault on the southern coastal cities. He saw no further need of Jaryd Corvale's services. The man now served as part of Gaspire Amdoran's mounted force. Casan would not miss him. Corvale had a talent for petty cruelty but no affinity for the finer aspects of power politics. He would be better placed spurring a horse than crowding a deck. Casan looked forward to being quit of him.

The Prelate opened the door to his office to find Corvale already seated and making free with the wine. Casan would not miss that effrontery, either.

"Good afternoon, Cavalryman Corvale," he said, filling his own glass and seating himself at the desk. "The uniform suits you, nice and flashy, very direct one might say."

"My Lord Prelate, my thanks," Corvale responded, missing the insult. "I find I prefer direct action. Things go better when I do them myself." He paused. "Like today, though I understand it was not a total loss."

"Not total," the Prelate agreed. "The riot upset Roderran enough to discredit Donari. Much might still be accomplished on the road south if there were an enterprising person in the right place at the right time. There were regrettable injuries, however, and one death. Actually, barring killing our man, I'd say things ran out satisfactorily."

"Yes, about that death," Corvale said tentatively. "I think I know, now, why the effort might have failed."

The Lord Prelate paused, glass midway to his mouth. "I am listening."

"His name is, was Tomais Caralon, a capable leather-worker. I had some trade with him."

"I am aware. Go on."

"He has, *had* a wife, my lord. I have run into her several times before, recently, here at the library. She also had something to do with last summer's . . . events. She was with Arolli the night I sent the Maze up in flames. Him and those poets who caused such a stir. The one who was plucking Sevire's bitch and—"

Ambrose.

Casan held a hand up for silence, his far sharper mind racing. There were unsettling connections here. Images of those unsatisfactory days from last summer returned. Donari confronting him, secure, confident, always seeming one step ahead in the game. That poet, Ambrose, smirking after he recited that insulting, ridiculous poem.

"By the Light!" he snarled. "Donari made Caralon's wife a student here. The professors have been grumbling about her appointment and independence. But is she a student? Or Donari's spy reporting to Senden Arolli?"

Casan's gorge rose as he spoke. It seemed as if he still had unfinished business that reached back six months. Donari, Arolli, the two poets, and now the woman; all of them had upset his plans in some way.

They will not have the opportunity to do so again.

"I believe I have more deaths to arrange," Corvale said coldly.

"Yes, I thought you might at that."

"Donari may be safe for now, but there is the road south.

"He's safely weakened, yes, but still a nuisance better removed," finished Casan. "It is clear that this place needs to be purged! It is a nest of thinkers and spies. Roderran would do well to clean house thoroughly." *Besides, from what I saw last night, the king will get another heir.*

"Am I to make another try, my lord?"

"You will see to your new duties as a cavalry officer in his majesty's service, first," Casan answered. "You are to keep your eyes open for other opportunities that may present themselves as regards Senden Arolli and this woman. Look to it, but do it yourself. No more associates. If you can't do it alone, cleanly, then do not do it all."

"I see. Very good." Corvale's face took on an eager, hungry look the Prelate found particularly disgusting.

"Do you?" the Prelate responded icily. "You have become something of a bungler. But there it is. I am set to sail once the seas abate and the ships finish preparation. We part ways here, man."

"I will miss our talks and your wine."

"Then I will take the wine with me so you cannot steal it when I am gone."

Corvale tossed off his drink, headed for the door. Casan's last words halted him with his hand on the lever.

"Take great care, Donari has teeth yet. Yesterday got too messy."

Corvale chuckled. "Something clean, direct, bloody. It will be a pleasure." He slipped out the door.

Casan finished his wine in a far better frame of mind as Corvale's passage down the hall faded to silence.

Chapter 15: And Change

DEMONA ANARGI AWOKE in the rumpled remains of a ruined bed and rubbed the sore spot on her left buttock. Other places on her body also protested as she contemplated the ornate decoration gracing the ceiling of the room she shared the night previous with King Roderran. Dolphins played among waves frozen in mid-crest, the Avedun sigil of the Pevanese branch of the ruling family. Demona liked the colors, but she found the other sigil displayed in the room far more interesting.

She rolled on her side to face the King's banner, a great bear, uplifted on two feet with paws aggressively extended, hanging from the wall next the bed. *Odd how the sigils match the men they represent. A bear suits Roderran; it is more manly. And what a man!* She rolled onto her back and stretched, a delightful effect of passion bruises and dried love juices. She tried to remember when she had felt so sated, but she stopped when her thoughts ran back to Talyior. *No, not even then. That was in the past. This, last night, was Now and perhaps After.* Demona settled a pillow under her head and let possibility tantalize.

A peacock proud Sevire escorted her to the feast, his most precious bauble on display, dreams of a coronet adding a sweaty glow to his normally ghastly pallor, and lending volume to his yeasty, voluble laugh. And before the meal ended he and the other heads of households who sported attractive wives found themselves hustled out the door, dismissed, divested and forgotten. The look of cowed fury on Sevire's face as he shuffled off nearly paid for all the cruelties Demona ever received from him. She spared him the smallest glance before Roderran interposed himself, blocking out the past while taking her hand decorously and leading her to the present. *And so graceful despite his size. If he's a bear, then he's a dancing bear.*

Later, he showed her a different kind of dance. She massaged the mark he left on her behind once again and let the memory tease her back to sleep.

She heard the door open and close on the edge of a dream, sensed the rhythm of his heavy footfalls on the carpet, felt the bed give as he settled his weight next to her, his smell already familiar even after just one night. His hand caressed her flank, his lips kissed away the ache of the bruised flesh, replacing it with a different sort of ache that recalled last night's frenzy. He pressed himself against her, cupping her breasts, drawing her into his embrace with surprising gentleness. His beard tickled her neck as he brought his lips close to her ear.

"So sorry for the marks, lady," the king whispered, "but you were rather rough yourself. Such nails! I wonder what sort of crevasses you managed to carve into Sevire's back fat."

Demona turned her face, kissed her king once, shamelessly. "Never," she sighed. "I could never reach my arms around, even if I wanted to."

Roderran breathed a chuckle. "That explains much of last night, then, lady."

Demona reached up her hand and pulled Roderran's face close, kissed him again, drawing in more of the king's muted, morning flame.

"No," she breathed, releasing him. "It explains all of it. Sevire never took me for my pleasure, only his own, always."

"And I?"

She felt his interest and his manhood rising. She arched her back against him.

"Look at this bed, my Lord. Need you ask?"

Then his hands were upon her in earnest. Laughing, she rolled over and only gasped a little as he entered her from behind.

Free.

*   *   *

After, they lay in a tangle amongst the sheets and watched the rain drip down the panes of the large, southern windows. Outside the day progressed dismal. Great ranks of dark-grey clouds advanced across the view shedding rain like vapor, shrouding the ridges beneath a heavy, wet coverlet that spoke of flooding and delay. Demona never used to like the rain because it kept her indoors, trapped, forced to endure Sevire's company. She snuggled deeper into Roderran's chest.

"This rain delays me," the king murmured into her hair.

"I just decided I liked the rain. It means more time for this."

"Which has been amazing, my dear, but I should get you back to your husband."

Demona shuddered, snuggled even deeper into him. "Must you spoil the moment?"

"Don't you want to go home, where I trust most of the beds are still whole?"

Demona did not answer at first. The ecstasy seeing her husband's impotence was short-lived, as was a night in so kingly a bed. Faced with the reality of going back to Sevire brought the rain's chill leaching cold fear around her heart.

"I can't go home, my Lord," she answered finally. "He will not forgive this. He will kill me."

"Nonsense, my dear. Angari is a fat old fool but he is an ambitious one. He will—"

"Wait for you to leave Pevana," she said, more afraid of losing this chance than of interrupting a king. "You will march when these rains grant passage, then he will take his revenge."

"He wouldn't dare. The man has no spine."

"There is a spine in all that flesh," she told him. "He gave you his ships and his money. He expects other return for those that have nothing whatever to do with me. Minor indiscretions he can take care of. People who cross him tend to have accidents, or vanish without a trace. But this? This was far too visible, my Lord. He cannot do anything to *you*. And so he will do it to me. Unless he no longer has access to me."

Roderran stared at her in silence for a long, uncomfortable moment. Demona nearly wilted under the scrutiny of the king's dark eyes and creased brow. Roderran scowled and rolled away from her.

"Do not try to trap me, woman," he groused, reaching for his robe. "You've shared a king's bed. Others have been there before you."

Demona felt his words like a blow to her belly, but reached a hand, timorous and light, to touch one of the welts her nails had carved into Roderran's back.

"You are not the one trapped, my King. I am. By a cruel husband, by what passed in this bed."

Whether her words or the heat shooting through her fingertips, the king stiffened. Something primal passed from her to him, from him to her. Roderran spun about, his robe open and revealing his body like a frame. Demona took that finger, trailed it down the king's chest, drawing fire. She felt him rise to her touch and dared a smile. She grasped him, stroking, and leaned back, pulling him, ran a foot against his thigh, arched her hips to accept him. He loomed above her, breath quickening.

"Boriman's thunder possesses those thighs," he rasped. "Gods would vie to suckle at your breasts."

"I'd rather have a king."

Roderran ran his hands over her, grasping each breast possessively, pinching each nipple just to the edge of pain. She tightened her grip, sought to guide him into her, but he resisted, considering. Demona held on, but paused, waiting.

"Perhaps it *is* too soon to send you home," he said. "I will keep Sevire at my beck day and night so that he will not have time to wonder where you are. Perhaps his over-burdened heart will give out truly."

"And what of me? How long will you keep me at your beck?"

"Long enough, I imagine."

Vague, but enough to keep her alive, and sated, for the time being. Demona resumed her stroking. "And when you tire of me?"

"Tire of you? Ah, not likely, my dear. You've more moves than Tolimon's cat."

And more than even you imagine. Demona intensified her efforts, smirking when his eyes rolled back and he groaned.

"I cannot stay in bed all day, woman." He surprised her by rolling away. Demona noted this ability to stopper the springs of lust, tucked it away for future use. He pulled his robe closed and tied it tightly closed.

"I've a room full of generals, counselors and their ilk waiting for me. I've ordered a bath made ready, but you, my little bird, have kept me occupied too long to make use of it. Maybe later."

Demona swung out the bed to stand before him, challenging his control with her nakedness, with the diaphanous cascade of tresses shrouding her shoulders and breasts. "If I am a bird," she taunted, "then I am in need of more plucking."

Roderran surprised her again with a deep, sonorous rumble of laughter she felt between her legs. He grabbed her face, kissed her once, twice, and let her go. "Later," he said. "I shall pluck you when I have the time to do so royally. Now I must go."

Demona dropped onto the edge of the bed, careful not to slouch. She had accomplished enough for the moment, and determined to press that accomplishment later. He would take her as long as she found new and delicious ways of taking it. Her mind wandering to the bath he had drawn, the bath she had kept him from, brought a smile to her lips; and thus she missed the change in his demeanor, startling when he said, "Get dressed."

"My Lord?"

"You heard me, woman. Get dressed. The party dress from last evening will do nicely. It will remind them that a king takes what he wants."

"My Lord?" she repeated, reaching for the mess of fabric piled on the floor, but Roderran was already half-dressed. His tousled head appeared out of the neck of his shirt.

"Speed, woman, speed!" he laughed, moving to the side of the bed and pulling her to her feet. Picking up the dress she had been reaching for, he pushed it none-too gently into her arms. "Where is your head?"

"Forgive me, My Lord, but I don't understand."

"What is to understand? I'm taking you with me."

Demona's heart pounded. She clutched the dress to her breasts. "Where? Why?"

"To council. As to why, I will tell you so that you may understand." He pulled her closer, dress and all, squeezing her buttocks with both hands. "I want them to see you. And I want you to watch, to listen. They are *men*, Demona, your specialty."

The council meeting exceeded Demona's expectations. Within seconds of her entry on Roderran's arm, she sensed her effect. The most powerful nobles in the realm stood by their chairs as Roderran led her to the head of the table. All eyes locked on to her immediately with variations of interest, derision and insulted manhood. Though terrified, Demona flashed her best smile as she took her seat next the king. Life with Sevire was not without its useful lessons; a woman's best defense often lay in the carefully constructed illusion of happiness they presented to the world. She returned their stares with a false buoyancy she hoped they could not pierce.

She felt her way through the first moments, trying to piece together the threads of Roderran's intentions. After that initial scrutiny, and a series of hard questions from several lords, Demona receded into the background, and the rest of the event passed for her in a series of barely understood reports, calculations, and evaluations. She made the most of her obscurity, sensing that Roderran really did want her impressions of the warriors collected around the table. She had made a life out of observing Sevire's moods, working his urges and rages to her advantage whenever possible. Survival was a muse who lent creativity to the most desperate. And Demona watched the play of emotions around that table with desperate intensity. Her freedom from her past and the duration of her future depended upon it. She settled back in her chair, placed a proprietary hand boldly on Roderran's shoulder and trusted in her hard-earned experience with men to observe what she could. That they were all men, helped.

When the meeting finally broke up, Roderran led her back to his rooms. The bed had been repaired and a meal lay ready on a side table. Roderran poured for them himself.

"So, my thanks," he said. "You were wonderful."

"How?"

"You were a beautiful distraction. Put them off a little. I like them off. Makes them easier to deal with."

"They are hard men."

"I'm a hard king. We match. So, impressions?"

Demona sipped a moment before replying. No one ever asked her opinion. The novelty delighted her, made even more so that the first to do so would be the King of Perspa. She considered this new development in her world and realized she actually did have impressions.

"The Lord Prelate thinks I'm a piece of meat, Gaspire envies you and wants me, and Reegan of Sor-reel, well, my woman's ways tells me he might be a little different."

Roderran laughed outright at that. "Ha! The beauty speaks! You truly are amazing! Anything else?"

"They wonder about Prince Donari; I think they fear him. Gaspire had venom in his voice. He is not subtle. They wonder about your intentions for him."

Roderran waved the comment off. "Donari is none of your concern, or theirs. Gaspire does what I tell him to do, envious or otherwise."

"What next, my lord?"

Roderran popped a piece of cheese into his mouth, and fed her one, too.

"I think you might be more than a piece of meat. Casan is an old shriveled prick, but he knows how to plan a campaign! Ignore him. For now, you're mine."

Roderran's words stunned her.

"Excuse me, my lord, but I don't understand."

"You are useful, in so many ways."

Demona sensed she had passed some form of examination. She considered her station, a daydream removed from a daydream about freedom, and welcomed the beginnings of comprehension. After years of marriage buried underneath the layers of Sevire's abuse, the present blossomed for her like a breath of spring air that cleanses the sick room.

"What will my lord require?" she asked, but she could see the answer in his eyes even as she spoke.

"Eat, then take your rest. I have to be elsewhere. When I get back—"

"We have another go at breaking the bed?"

They took turns laughing and feeding each other.

Eleni Caralon did not cry as she witnessed her husband's burial. She managed to get through it with the blessed kindness of Prince Donari and Senden Arolli. Gania, one of Tomais's assistants, representatives from the Sisters of Renia, and the wife of their butcher were the only others to attend the ceremony. The small turnout did not disappoint her; she and Tomais both lost their parents young. They were all each other had, now halved. She found herself wishing the ceremony would pass more quickly. Open spaces made her feel vulnerable now, exposed. Not even the temple's grace worked to relieve her unease.

Eleni's essential pragmatism helped her get through it all without the emotional outcry churning deep within her. It would find a way out, in time. She dreaded returning to their home for fear, there, she would succumb.

For the present, she let Gania do the weeping for her.

When the final notes of the funeral dirge had been sung and the last candle lit, Eleni watched the attendants take her beloved away, and lower him into the space made ready adjacent to the temple. By Donari's decree, and though she protested, they placed Tomais in a plot reserved for members of the ruling family, yet another of his small, considerate kindnesses. Eleni wondered if her husband would enjoy the incongruity of being buried alongside a former prince of the royal family, and smiled to know that he would.

"These are changing times," Donari had said, his tone ever-kind and gentle. "I've had enough of the pain caused by class distinction. He will rest easily enough here. If any dare dispute it, they will answer to me."

Eleni let herself be ruled by his generosity. She stopped short, however, at his and Senden's gallant offer to escort her back home. They had other matters to deal with. She overheard their whispered conversation as they paced behind her; quiet mutterings of troop levies, fodder and materiel for the force they had to assemble once the king set a timetable for departure. In her opinion, they had already spent far too much of their time on her, even considering the circumstances.

Senden's limp grew more pronounced as they exited the graveyard. She felt drawn to both of them despite her grief, because of those circumstances, and those of the summer prior. Insight brought by reading Ambrose's verse came unbidden to mind: *changes, understanding the changes, that was the key.* But she would never have dreamed a change so drastic and fatal.

Donari insisted she take a carriage and several guards back to her home, and made her promise to do what she needed but return to her rooms at the palace afterwards. In the hollow space of her grief, seeing Tomais laid out had been so hard, his sudden concern and interest brought a little warmth. Accompanied by Gania and her well-meaning prattle, Eleni rattled down the hill to face her demons in better spirit that she expected.

She and Gania spent the afternoon organizing and setting aside things, taking frequent breaks to cry and laugh. As she feared, she sensed Tomais everywhere. She could not bring herself to touch his clothes. Gania packed them away in a closet. In the end, she stuffed most of her decent garments and all of her scholarly materials into two large bags. She put off Gania's offer of a room at her place. With Corvale still at large, risk remained, for both of them should she accept. Staying at the palace made sense. The few hours she had spent with the prince cemented that.

So kind. So human.

He made her feel less lonely than she might. Much as she loved Gania, Eleni shared a common bond with the prince, if slightly convoluted. He had given her the university; she had given him his life. In the process, they had both lost Tomais in ways both similar and disparate. Silently, so silently she barely admitted it to herself, Eleni Caralon had another motive for allying herself with Pevana's prince: without him, she could never hope to take her revenge upon Corvale.

Locking the door to the house brought a surge of relief and a tick of decision, making it easier to climb back into the carriage for the ride back to the Palace. As the carriage trundled up through the citadel gates, Eleni tested the term *widow* and found it just could not settle. Instead, she thought about asking Senden or Donari if she might find a place in their circle. She had talents beyond sewing and research. The dull ache of her grief drove all other thoughts away as unimportant. Without Tomais, her business and her studies seemed useless, part of a life she let lower into a grave. Events of great moment were fast approaching; she could feel it in the air. She wanted to be part of it, to see the days through, to whatever end. No longer a wife, she wondered if her days as a scholar were over as well.

If I avenge myself on Jaryd Corvale, I will call it a fair trade.

Eleni did not get the chance to ask, for she saw neither Senden nor Donari much over the next week. With Roderran's arrival the weather began to improve, as though Renia herself saw the inevitability of his ascension and relented of her tears.

The rains trickled out to occasional showers. The spring sun shone longer everyday thereafter, drying the roads south, sparking trees to bud and flowers to break through the mold. Activity in and around Pevana intensified. The harbor rang with the sound of palls on wood as the merchant fleet underwent alterations that would allow horses and siege machines transport. Every blacksmith shop and field forge rang with the sound of hammer on anvil as weapons were beaten out, armor adjusted and refurbished, spearheads cast and affixed to shafts.

Eleni spent long hours sitting in her open window bay, listening to the disturbing sounds. She found them oddly rhythmic and in keeping with the pulse of her sorrow, as though beating out a cadence of war and death to the world beyond the city walls. Drilling recommenced in the fields around the camps, and the Perspan host began to take shape.

She learned from Anlise, a young lady up on her gossip as well as catechism, the extent of those preparations. Roderran would lead over ten thousand men south. Another five thousand would sail with Casan and the fleet to assail the coastal towns. It was the largest assemblage of men and horses and shipping in the history of the realm. Eleni felt words stirring as she watched from her window seat. Below her the city fanned out, bisected by its main streets, connected by rooftops and square into a living, breathing thing. She began to understand the way Donari and Senden felt about their city. More than obligation, more than nobility; it was love. And what they loved lay supine and occupied by the trappings of violence, threatened as seriously as if some spirit-world horror, a spectral Corvale, held some metaphoric torch to its collective thatch.

Eleni began to write, drawn with growing certainty over the words flying off her pen to record what she saw. As she wrote the shade of Tomais relaxed its hold on her as though relinquishing her spirit to find its place again in life. She wrote feverishly for hours on end; her thoughts unrolling multi-directional at first, a running internal monologue that expressed the totality of all her jumbled sense impressions. And then she noticed a pattern forming in the words as if she crystallized all of the insight she thought she saw in the lines of Ambrose, Enmbron and the other Poets from Pevana's past. Those inferences, married to her heighten awareness of Donari's perspective, coalesced for her into a streaming line of truth that she began to follow, a literary hound on the scent of the sublime. And like a lost friend returned, the last lines ran together into a farewell verse:

Have neither fear nor care

For time cannot impair
My memories of you.
And though my days darken
In time there will be sun
To help me see them through
For you. . .

She never noticed darkness falling, nor the servants who lit candles and left food. She did not see Donari or Senden look in on her in wonderment and concern. She wrote until her hand cramped and then threw herself in bed to sleep, and in her sleep she dreamed of words and people and power and pain and all the passions to which man is subject. She dreamed she wandered a fantastic library whose books leaned over the shelves and whispered stories to her. Pages covered with words and images fell about her in a cascade of printed leaves, piling up about her knees as she rustled through the past.

And at the last turn she came face to face with Tomais, smiling, luminescent beneath a dolphin banner. In his hands he held a bound volume that he opened to reveal empty pages. He mouthed two silent words:

Fill it.

Then he stepped back and cupped his hands. Light filled that space, and Tomais held up the little soul of the child, of their hopes gone too soon. Together, father and babe bathed Eleni with love in farewell before fading, but the volume remained, hovering convincingly before her, spectrally unblemished for want of a pen.

Dolphin banner.

An empty book.

Piles of verse.

Pevana's soul, threatened.

Something lost, something found, something saved from the dark.

When she awoke with the dawn, she leapt out of bed and returned to her pile of papers, pen and ink bottle. She noticed her paper supply had been refurnished and that the ink bottle held a full measure of better quality ink than she normally used. She did not question the source but took up her tools oblivious to everything but the words that came to her in a long, steady stream.

She went on like this for a week, writing beyond exhaustion, and at the end of that period she collapsed into bed and slept, a long, dreamless, recuperative slumber that lasted almost a full day. The mid-morning sun on her face woke her up, blinking and flinching from the brightness. She pushed herself up on the pillows, and as her eyes cleared the blinding sunbeam she noticed Prince Donari sitting in the window bay, reading her manuscript by the morning sunlight.

Her movement broke Donari's concentration, and he turned to look at her, his face half in shadow but distinct and awash with suppressed emotion.

"My lord?" she asked tentatively in a hushed voice. "Those are just words—"

"Just words?" he interrupted, smiling deeply and waving the sheaf of papers slightly. "Not so, not so, something much more, I think. I remember those two poets you refer to, and one other, actually. He looked away and as if summoning a memory, recited quietly:

Dust,

Hangs in a sunbeam

That misses me and

Covers the torn pieces

Of all the promises you made.

I watch the particles collect,

Obliterating

All that was you in them

All that was light

All that was necessary

And important.

Now they are as shards

Rendered impotent

By a gray coverlet

That doesn't warm
But rather mocks
The memories. . .

Eleni felt the blood rush from her face as Donari's voice trailed off.

"I was there that night, last summer," he said. "I recall hearing poetry, but one in particular stayed with me. I remember the look on the face of the author as her husband read it to the room. There, I remember saying to myself as Senden and I made our way back to the palace, there is something of Pevana that would be worth any risk to save."

"But, but, how?" stuttered Eleni.

"How?" answered the Prince. "I do not know. I do not know why our fates seem so intertwined, Eleni. I am so sorry for your loss, but in reading this I feel like I, you, have found something, something of value."

"After Tomais, I thought I had lost everything of value."

"But your words here suggest something else."

"I don't quite know yet what it is, my lord, but I mean to find out."

"How can I help you, mistress?"

"You have already done so much for me."

"And yet, not nearly enough. However—" He waved the papers in his hand and gestured to the rest of the pile on the window seat. "—here lies the answer for both of us." He put the papers back on the pile, glanced out the window as though searching for words. "You say you've lost all you held valuable," he continued softly. "I bear some responsibility there. The servants tell me you have seemed adrift since the funeral." He placed a finger, pointedly on the pile of paper. "And then I read this."

He walked over to sit in the chair next the bed. Eleni felt a slight tingle begin at the base of her neck at his approach.

"I have need for a secretary," he said, smiling. "As it happens, my last one begged leave to enlist with my mounted troops. I share your fears, Eleni, and I believe we see things similarly. I want these days recorded. I want your observations. I need your poet's eye."

He locked eyes on hers, piercing, penetrating, as though he had come to a decision.

"And, mostly, I want you safe. Once we leave, I fear things will go ill for my adherents in Pevana. As ironic as it may sound, you might be better off coming with me when the army marches south."

"A woman, lord—*a poet*—on campaign?"

Donari smiled, a wry twist full of good humor. "Afraid of unseemly comments? Afraid of slowing us down? There will be nothing speedy about this army, Eleni. You will be taxed somewhat, but I suspect you will keep up. I am asking you to record not tote a spear in the charge."

He leaned forward, hands on knees, closer. "We are cut adrift, you and I, and beset by perils in all directions. I cannot recover your loss. But I can give you a purpose. Pevana needs us, Eleni. I feel as though we are at the tipping point here. I cannot explain it, but I think something awaits both of us in the south. I think we are tied together somehow, as though bound to see what ever it is through, together."

Eleni could not answer at first; having her own thoughts echoed so precisely unnerved her. She stood fearfully before an open door, sensed a profusion of confusion in Donari's words and in her reaction. It was so soon, after, but then what did time have to do with anything? She felt drawn to the words he could provide her and the power of his humanity.

"My lord, I. . ." she whispered. "I don't know what to say. Forgive me."

Donari smiled again, his face now sympathetic, understanding.

"Eleni Caralon," he said quietly, taking her hand, raising to his lips and softly, chastely kissing it. "It is I who should beg forgiveness. I hold myself responsible for your loss. My policies. My failures. This misadventure of the king's may cost deep. I saw this day coming and thought myself cynical enough not to rue the possibilities. And then I saw your face in sorrow and something in me leached away. In truth, we are orphans of a sort, we two. I am a prince but terribly out of favor. In seeing you, suddenly alone, so fair, I saw something for which I could persevere. Eleni, in the grand scheme we are both commoners supping at the table of our betters."

"But—"

"Eleni, there will be no *buts* between us." He gave her hand a gentle squeeze, and let it go. "The mind behind those words," he gestured behind him to the papers piled on the window seat, "that made those connections is no common mind. I have need of such a mind, especially when mine will be otherwise occupied." He rose from the bed and moved to the door, pausing with fingers on the handle.

"I am told we will leave in a fortnight, maybe a little longer. I hope you will come as my secretary. I promise I won't overwork you!" He laughed, and as he chuckled there in the doorway all the tension of the moment fled away. "But you don't need to give me an answer right now." He gestured to the papers on the table. "I can wait until you wear out another pen tip."

Eleni held her words for a moment, and then she laughed. She laughed out of a sudden realization that life, *life*, always held hope, that she could control herself and choose to live. She laughed because she saw opportunity without fear or contradiction that she could see through.

"There is no need to wait," she said after calming down enough to find words. "I have your answer. Yes, I will be your secretary. Thank you, my lord."

"Good! And is it I who should thank you. What's to come will doubtless make a great story." He graced her with a smile as he slipped out the door.

Eleni fell back onto the pillows, savoring the warmth of that smile, the chance at life, at words.

"A story," she whispered to herself. "But will it have a happy ending?"

Chapter 16: A Choice Given

DEMONA TUCKED THE TOWEL taught around her body and padded back from the bath she had just finished to the king's bedchamber. Several weeks of doing so made the path familiar to her. *Weeks and weeks!*

She checked herself often to make sure the whole time was not just a glamour. There had been a dream, repeated several times, wherein she awakened to Sevire's leering, wrathful face mouthing cruelties at her. She screamed herself awake once. Roderran calmed her then. She rather liked that.

She stood before the bed, combing out her hair, watching the king sleep. Roderran was a tempestuous man, bold, pompous, convinced of his own greatness, physically imposing and aggressive, both in council and in the bedroom. Demona luxuriated in the thrall of his power. He was a ruler determined to get what he wanted, and so she took care to make sure he kept on wanting her. She took no liberties with his patience, made sure she was ready for whatever he needed at all times, including risking saddle sores to her marvelous backside.

A docile beast was always ready for her to ride out wherever he wished for her to ride. Demona at first forced herself into the saddle and then surprised herself by taking to it quickly, gracefully. When Roderran took her along on his inspections, she found she enjoyed looking down on the world from horseback.

She let the towel fall as she climbed onto the bed. Roderran lay naked, chest rising and falling in slumber, strength at rest. They had taken turns exploring each other since that first night, and Demona knew some of the stories behind the scars that marred Roderran's otherwise magnificent physique. She knelt next to him, studying his face, the weave of his beard, the set of his jaw, in every way different

165

from Sevire's flaccid features, and infinitely more interesting, compelling, intoxicating. The flattery emboldened by a king's attention had changed tack in their weeks together. Demona was not simply flattered, but intrigued by the man beneath the crown. She liked and feared in ways she had never done with Sevire. She liked Sevire's wealth, but Roderran as a man. Demona feared displeasing her husband; she wanted to please the king.

She let the wet tips of her hair run along Roderran's stomach, blowing softly on his skin as she moved down to where his body already began to respond. With lips and tongue she teased him gently, eliciting a sleepy moan that awakened to words.

"Oh, but it is good to be king."

Demona giggled around her ministrations, felt his hands on her shoulders encouraging her, as she intensified her attentions. She paused when she felt tremors in his legs, rose and mounted him in a fluid motion, letting her hair cascade around her shoulders, her body flush with her efforts and her own desires. She held him there, at *that* point, placed her hands on his chest and rode him slowly, speaking with each downward grind of her matchless pelvis.

"Good . . . mor . . . ning . . . My . . . Lord. . ."

By the time she reached *Lord*, he lost control completely, and Demona hazarded a rare question.

"What's to become of me?"

"What?" he gasped, grabbing her waist and holding himself inside her.

"I said, what is to become of me? I've been watching the weather."

Roderran gave a last shudder and relaxed back into the pillows.

"We march within a week. Casan sails the day before we leave."

"And me?" Demona eased herself off of him and sat on her knees, waiting.

Roderran leaned on his elbow, facing her, and Demona noted an unexpected softness in his eyes. "We have choices to make."

"We?" His words surprised her. Even after weeks of dalliance and interaction, she had expected to have to plead to be taken along when the king marched.

"You, actually, I've already made mine." Again, a subtle change in his voice, a hint of appraisal, even humor.

"My Lord, I can't go home. I wasn't joking. Sevire will kill me."

"I know," he responded. "Although these scratches on my back suggest you might be able to deal with him yourself."

"Don't tease me. You know I want you, your fire. This," she gestured at the bed, "is only part of it, at least for me. But for you?"

She watched the emotions play out on his features as she waited for his answer. They echoed her own, a mix of desire, confusion, power and weakness.

"Demona, I will make no promise, and you know it. I don't have to. Women," and he paused as if confronting an unpleasant memory, "have been a disappointment to me. Until now."

"Then—"

"Then make your choice, woman. I go on campaign, but I hardly think it will be arduous. I'm not fond of cold skins in a tent. I want you to go with me. You wanted to be free of Sevire, of this place. The choice is yours."

Demona hesitated still, testing this new found gift. *A choice. My choice.* She let a breath go with a sigh and in that exhalation severed all ties to her old life.

"Here is my choice. I want to be with you, see the world, My Lord. I want to please you. I know I am no virtuous woman. The maids here whisper *harlot* under their breath when they come to shift the bedding. I own it freely, and I don't care."

"Virtue," Roderran mused, "I've never considered it, actually."

His words gave her courage. She fixed her eyes on the king's, holding them with every drop of it at her command. "I care nothing for marriage or virtue or propriety. I want free of him, of Sevire. I will go with you, Roderran."

The king's smile deepened then. He ran a finger down her jawline to brush against her lips, as if sealing the magic of her first, daring use of his given name.

"Then you better pack light, my dear."

A timid knock sounded at the door. Demona, naked and still flushed with passion, did not bother covering herself. The maid, Anlise, poked her head through, averted her eyes and said, "Forgive me, sire, but you asked to be wakened when the man you requested arrived. He is waiting for you in the parlor."

Roderran grabbed his robe and leapt from the bed. "Wait here," he said and crossed the room in two powerful strides, shutting the door behind him.

Demona let go a deep breath, and realized she was indeed breathless. One moment changing her life, the next dashing off, Roderran was nothing if not unpredictable.

He is taking you with him, she chastised herself. *Be grateful.*

But Demona slipped into her shift and sidled over to the door, putting her ear to the crease where she could just make out the beginning of a conversation even so.

"Your late master makes report of you," Roderran said. He spoke quietly, coldly, and Demona had to strain to hear. "He attests to your more covert talents; skills that might be put to better use with the land force rather than with the fleet. I've known of you, Corvale, and I need you to take care of a little matter for me."

Footsteps receded. The voices faded to an indistinct murmur cut off by a door opening and closing. . .

Sevire Anargi mopped the sweat from his brow with a towel as he struggled up the stairs, heading for his chambers. Full dark swarmed the night sky and the house was largely unlit save for lamps in the entry way and hallways. In fact, the place was practically empty except for a handful of house servants. The bulk of his folk were out seeing to the king's requests. The stream of orders that came spewing out of the palace once Roderran appropriated the Pevanese merchant fleet had kept Sevire, his chief lieutenants, ship captains and shore laborers running at a sprinter's pace to fulfill all the requests. For Sevire, each succeeding day dawned more bitter than the previous ended.

"Taken," he muttered as he gasped his way up the final steps. "I offered him my help out of loyalty, kindness and honor, and he takes them. My ships. My men! My *wife*! The cheek. The gall. How dare he? To *me*! Sevire Anargi!"

He cursed the day he had approached the Lord Prelate, but at the back of mind, so recessed that it enabled him to avoid confronting it, lurked the truth that it would have made no difference in the end. The king had always intended to take the Pevanese ships for his purpose. That thought swam to the forefront now as he reached, breathless, the landing of the second floor. He knew it then; accepted it in a fashion. It did not mitigate his helpless rage, but it did help a little to know that his Pevanese rivals in trade were in similar straits.

No, what caused his anger to swell like a threatening wave was the extended absence of his wife in the king's company. He could stomach the loss of wealth, but she, at once the least and most prized of his possessions, stood as the deepest betrayal. Nowhere else had Sevire devoted so much care and attention than in winning back control of Demona in the wake of last summer's crisis. And she was gone on a king's whim; bedded, no doubt, with laughter at his discomfort serving as sauce to the seduction. Whispers and suppressed laughter reached him within days.

And now she is gone three weeks!

The only thing that kept him from going insane with jealousy had been the need to keep pace with the king's demands. *Oh yes, I see it: keep Sevire busy so he would not be able to interfere. Royal bastard!* The insight just made the gall all the more bitter. He seethed as he stumped down the hall. The force with which he threw back the double doors was augmented by the fact that he knew he could do nothing—*nothing*!—about any of it.

He did not love Demona, and she did not love him. Not even her voluptuous form raised his passions. Power. Power raised his passion. Wealth was power. Power over her. Power over all. He retained his wealth, for the moment, but it dwindled as fast as his control. All for that rake wearing a crown.

The wound of this loss was an insufferable, bleeding ulcer made worse by the fact that Demona enjoyed it, the power of her sex, the power she robbed from him. Bad enough to lose to a man, but to a woman? A woman *he* had spent years subjugating until she was the exact toy he enjoyed playing with most. It made every corpulent fiber of his being ache.

Sevire had only one outlet for his pain: food. He paused, orienting himself in the room's half-light, and advanced to the table in the center laden with cold meats, pieces of roasted fowl, breads and cheeses piled high. He sat himself down, poured a huge measure of wine from the decanter and began chewing his way back to some semblance of himself. He stuffed his face with increasing portions and diversity, stilling the voices in his head by cramming food into their insubstantial mouths. Sweat began to pore anew from his face, dripping down to saturate his neck cloth and shirt front. He ate through the gathering darkness as the few candles in the room guttered and went out. He ate by feel, by texture, ravenous in his dismay. He ate until he lost himself in a sea of palliative grease.

"What in the—"

The knife blade pressed against his neck stopped him in mid-reach for his wine.

"Shut up you immense bag of wind." The voice was as cold as the face, dark and impassive, that swung into Sevire's view. He tried to lean away from the blade, but the man just shook his head, shifted the weapon so that the point pushed up underneath Sevire's many chins.

"Who are you," Sevire whined. His heart labored to keep up with his fear and beat a thumping defeat. His assailant smiled.

"Not that it matters, but the name's Corvale, Jaryd Corvale."

"What, why?"

"You've gone and upset the wrong people, friend. Not wise." Corvale sniffed, made a disgusted face. "Bah! You stink old man! When was the last time these rolls of yours last felt water?"

"Please, let me go. I have gold, jewels."

"And all very useful, I'm sure, for a man of your girth."

Sevire cringed when Corvale leaned closer and took another exploratory sniff.

"Yes, I have it now," he whispered. "I've known this smell. Anger. Sorrow. Fear. You get to know such things when you stick the blade in between the ribs. For one so fat, you smell empty to me."

"Please, have pity," Sevire wheezed. His heat labored anew, began to lurch out of rhythm.

"Have pity on you?" Corvale snarled, digging in the knife until the point pierced the flesh. "I'm not capable. Might have been, once, but if you kill enough people, it goes away. I find it more satisfying than stuffing myself with cold chicken."

Fear froze the words in Sevire's mouth. Blood trickled down his neck. Panic surged. He made a feeble effort to push his assailant away. Corvale grabbed the offending hand, slammed in on the table and pinned it to the wood with the knife.

White hot pain exploded, wrapped itself around Sevire's terror and squeezed. He stared at his abused appendage, opened his mouth and keened, high-pitched and at odds with his size. He gagged as Corvale grabbed his head and shoved something down his throat.

"Time to finish your meal, Anargi."

He tasted bread, thrashed from side, and tried to clear his lungs, to breathe. He felt Corvale's arm around his neck, more pressure on his throat, dimly aware of a long, thin loaf being shoved down his gullet. Frantic eyes locked on Corvale. His thrashing grew weak.

"Yes," Corvale breathed. "You've a lovely appetite. Why waste time with words, eh? You've forgotten to chew. Silly of you."

Sevire vomited against the barrier, a burning bitterness that faded with the light. A final, lumping heartbeat. Slackness. Stillness. The light failed. *Demona. . .*

Corvale waited until he was certain Sevire Anargi was dead. A schoolboy lesson about the evils of gluttony came to mind as he brushed crumbs off his shirt sleeve. He took a moment to sniff Sevire's unfinished goblet of wine. Impressed by the vintage, he downed a goodly swallow as a send off to his latest success. The moon, escaping a cloud, sent a pale beam in through the window, allowing Corvale a chance to take in the whole scene. What he saw pleased him. He took a moment to wipe the blood from Sevire's neck, a small affectation.

He left the old man his rings. The king paid better.

Chapter 17: South

THE FINAL WEEKS before the host moved south passed in blur for Eleni. Donari was seldom in the palace. She spent most of her time organizing her notes, talking with Senden and helping him with the paperwork that attended the formation of a cavalry corps and contingent of foot soldiers. At Senden's insistence she went with him to the Prince's stables to pick out a horse she could handle, and spend some hours in the saddle. She would be expected to keep with the column.

Senden's attention intimidated her until she realized it was how he dealt with his relative inactivity. His leg was slow to heal; the muscles refused to loosen up completely and when he tired, he walked with a pronounced limp. When with Donari, Eleni noticed he did his best to hide his infirmity. She saw the internal struggle he conducted with himself: pride against pain against pragmatism.

"Why do you work yourself so hard?" she asked after one of their riding sessions.

"I failed him once. Never again."

"You could never fail the prince, Senden."

He rubbed his wounded thigh.

"Neither of us labors under any delusions, you know," he said. "The king doesn't trust Donari, but he needs our cavalry and infantry to complete his columns. We expect to be used, and used up. Donari grieves for what will come. I'm sure the men know it, but they've been trained to follow orders."

"How can the king be so callous?"

"Because he is King and feels he can afford to be." Eleni could sense the disgust beneath Senden's curt tone.

"But who would want to follow such a man?"

"You've seen the northern Barons. They are a hard lot, all of them, and their immediate underlings reflect their hardness. They are ambitious to a man, dangerously so. And Gaspire Amdoran may be the worst of them. He and the others follow the king because he wins. He pummeled them into line beneath his banner with power and arrogance. As long as he wins they will support him. Look what has become of Pevana? We are being looted for men and material as surely as if we had revolted. Only the thinnest veneer of gentility separates the two. The king requires Donari to call for volunteers, to use our people's loyalty to him to enlist and leave their homes in the king's name. If Donari didn't agree to the game. . ."

"He could not afford to disagree."

"Yes, correct. If he openly disputed Roderran in letter or in Council, there would have been a bloodbath, and the result would have been the same."

"But neither you nor Donari, and others I suppose, would be alive, yes?"

"Quite right. That is the only thing that gives me hope, really. If Donari remains alive and viable, he might still be able to do something."

"Like what?"

Senden shrugged. "I don't know, Eleni, I don't know. Save some lives? Keep his honor intact? Keep his head? One thing is clear, however, whatever he tries he faces long odds." He pointed back toward the city gates. "Long odds, when set against people like that."

Eleni followed his gaze. The Lord Prelate's carriage had pulled up beside space where the lords Amdoran and Sor-reel had their tents. The two men stood by the carriage door talking to the occupant. Eleni saw a flash of red and Casan's pale, beaked face as he leaned forward. She felt instantly ill. The tension in her body irritated her mount and it sidled into Senden's, pressed against his still healing thigh and drew a gasp of pain.

"Senden, I'm so sorry!" she exclaimed, pulling at the reigns, trying inexpertly to calm her beast.

"It is nothing, Eleni. The real pain will come later, once those evil men set their campaign in motion. I'd almost give the leg to know for sure."

Eleni heard anguish in his voice, saw it echoed on his face as he stared at the group clustered around the Prelate's carriage. For the first time, she saw Senden as a real person, subject to weariness, sorrow, loss—just like herself. Tomais's absence swelled in her throat at the thought. Through the simulacrum of her personal devastation, she began to understand his, and through him, the devastating choices forced on Prince Donari.

"You love him, don't you," she asserted, curbing her horse to a standstill. "It's not just service with you. Gania said something to me once, back in the fall after the fire: *He's a fair-spoken man, our Prince. Too bad it took flames in the Maze for the people to see his care.* I think I begin to see it now."

Senden circled his around until they were face to face. "I never had a family of my own, mistress. He is my prince, my lord, and my closest friend. I have taught him and guarded him since he was a boy. I would give my life for him if necessary. I love him like the son I never had."

His words sent Eleni spinning down the maze of her own feelings about Donari, and she found them a jumbled mess, a confusion of fear, new grief, and empathy. She looked up at Senden and in his eyes and found there kindness and wisdom, and she felt his gaze intensify as if he willed her to understand.

"He needs you," she said with growing certainty. "He needs to know what he does is right. He needs folk to believe in him or else everything is lost. And he cannot ever let such things become public knowledge. He needs—"

"Yes, he needs me. He needs all of us. And, I suspect, he needs you, Eleni. He needs you to see, record, remember." Senden smiled and paused before finishing in a quiet voice. "Eleni Caralon, stand by him. I do not trust this leg of mine. I suspect it will fail at the test. He will need . . . support."

"I will," she whispered breathlessly. "I'm no warrior. I'm a poet."

"So is Donari." Senden turned his mount. "Come. We've an hour yet before we meet with him. Let us try the canter again. Hup, Hup!"

Eleni dutifully put spurs to her horse's flanks and followed him. The pounding rhythm of her horse's hooves on the turf kept pace with her jumbled, racing thoughts.

And then she encountered Demona in the hallway on the way to her rooms.

Demona looked stunning, as always, dressed for riding. The maid Anlise trailed behind her with hat and gloves. Eleni slowed and moved to the side to allow them passage, but Demona recognized her first.

"Eleni Caralon!" she squealed. "How pleasant! Anlise here told me you were attached to the prince. What was it, secretary or something?"

Everyone, including Eleni, knew about Demona and the king, as well as Sevire's unfortunate choking accident; fewer knew it for the murder it was. Since her husband's demise, Demona had taken to sweeping about the Avedun palace as if she were mistress to it as well. She created a bow-wave where ever she went, and Eleni had, until now, managed to avoid her. The more involved Eleni became in Donari's affairs, the more she understood the threats under which he moved. Demona was attached to the most powerful of them. In fact all of them, the Prelate, Corvale, the army growing outside the city walls were ultimately connected to Tomais's death. Just as Demona seemed well-acquainted with power, Eleni grew ever more familiar with danger. And because of what she knew, Eleni took pity on Demona.

"Demona, how nice to see you." She lowered her voice, stopped short of reaching for Demona's hand. "I heard about Sevire's . . . accident. I'm sorry for your loss."

Demona's cheerful bounce deflated, and she grew serious in turn. Patting Eleni's hand, she said, "And I was there when your poor Tomais . . . when he. . . Oh, Eleni I'm so sorry. It seems we share a loss. But you are looking well. Living in the palace seems to suit both of us."

Eleni grinned. *How very Demona.* And accepted the condolence as it was meant.

"It certainly seems to suit you! Rumor has it you claim the king's interest. Shall I congratulate you?"

"Please go on ahead, Anlise," Demona tossed over her shoulder. "I'll be with you in a minute. The king is," she continued when the girl turned the corner of the hallway, "an amazing man. He has been kind to me."

"Kind?"

"As kind as a king can be. He's strong, Eleni. And, as you say, I claim his *interest.*"

"He's dangerous."

"I was married to Sevire Anargi, mistress, do not speak to me about danger. All men are dangerous, but they are also simple. At least I'm not alone." She paused, bit her lip, repentant. "I'm sorry, that was unkind."

Eleni shook her head. "Demona, the king rides to war. Do you know what you are doing?"

"The *Prince* rides with him, Eleni. Do *you* know what you are doing?"

Eleni half-turned her cheek as if she had been struck.

"I'm learning to ride!' Demona continued, gushing. "I am going with the king when he marches. I'll be free, Eleni, free!"

"But this is war, Demona, mud, cold, blood, death, all of it."

"Yes. But at least I won't be here." She leaned in to touch a kiss to Eleni's cheek. "Renia's Grace watch over you, Eleni," she whispered, and hurried off after Anlise.

Eleni touched the place still sweetened by Demona's lips, the woman's words echoing between her ears.

Not here.

Not.

Here.

Her hand fell slowly. Donari's offer had come as a life-line, a gentle tug out of her despair, a path to purpose that might assuage the grief; but now Eleni saw the truth of it, given to her by a woman who would not know truth if it bit her shapely ankle.

It had all begun with Summer Festival, with words and a borrowed voice and courage. The fires had not burned it away, but fanned it hotter. This need in her, one she had almost let go for love, would have let go, if love had lingered.

I need to . . . to change. But, Renia help me, into what?

The fleet sailed an hour after dawn the day before the army was set to march. Eleni, Donari and Senden accompanied the king's retinue to the harbor walls to see them up anchor. Slowly, using sweeps at first, they crawled out beyond the headland. One by one Eleni watched as headsails were shaken out as the ships ran under the north coastal breeze. It all took the better part of an hour, but in the end all fifty ships, each one crammed full of men, disassembled siege engines, arms and supplies, weathered the point and moved off into the maritime haze. To Eleni they looked like a ghost fleet as they faded southwards out of sight, bringing to their destination the death and destruction of their kind, and giving to her the somber words:

> *On an airless day the ghost fleet sailed*
> *Full of shades and dreams*
> *'neath a sun strangely leached and paled*
> *Canvas filled with nightmare screams.*
> *And as they coasted tide swept shores*
> *Hope fled and pride decayed*
> *All who contested the spirit wars*
> *Fell battered and dismayed*
> *Before the bow wave of the Ghost Fleet. . .*

Roderran felt no such poignancy. When Casan's galley shook out its sail, he laughed in satisfaction, swept Demona into a waiting carriage, and left in search of breakfast. Donari stayed behind to review the Pevanese levies on his way back to the citadel. These he found drawn up in their lines near the harbor walls. They had been used to load and victual the fleet and ignored in the ceremonies on the quays. But that did not deter them from diving into their uniforms and making themselves presentable. Donari dismounted and walked the length of the first row, taking care to meet each man's eye as he passed.

To Eleni, waiting alongside Senden, the prince had the look of a man making penance for future sins. He walked steadily, paused to ask a question of share a word with a familiar face, kept his features open regardless of the cost. But what surprised Eleni were the looks on the faces of the men Donari inspected. To a man they returned the prince's scrutiny with respect and followed him with their eyes when he moved on down the line. Eleni fought down the tears that threatened from such an expression of trust and loyalty.

Donari finished and joined them to remount. Avarran stood by his stirrup, awaiting orders.

"Captain," Donari said, and his pitched his voice so that all could hear. "You have done wonders! I am pleased and impressed, and I am sure the king has taken note. We may face some bitter days ahead, friends, but we will see them through together."

"For Pevana and Prince Donari!" a voice from the rear shouted.

"Just tell us what you want us to do, lord, we're your men!"

"Huzzah for the Prince!"

Donari faced them again and let them go on for a moment before raising his hand for attention.

"My thanks, brothers! We fight for crown and country, but we also fight for each other and Pevana. Remember that!"

There was no calming them after that. Their shouts followed Donari, Eleni and Senden as they trotted back through the city gates.

The thrill of that moment stayed with Eleni as she followed. *With such men, he could be king, and Roderran knows it.*

She adjusted the folds of her cloak instinctively against the chilling thought.

That afternoon she watched as the companies of foot still quartered in the city marched out to the assembly camps. Like a grey serpentine they snaked down through the Land and Southern gates indistinct in their masses, banners waving, crowds lining the streets and cheering, although less than there might have been. Roderran's control of Pevana had not been gentle, despite all Donari's attempts to mitigate things. The Pevanese gave muted honor to the northern troops, reserving most of their good will for the local companies. These they cheered lustily, defiantly as they marched beneath their dolphin banners. No matter what lay ahead, the Pevanese took their pride with them. It seemed to Eleni as she watched from the citadel that the weak spring sun shone more brightly on them as they passed beneath the Land Gate arch and swung south. Such men would do their duty by the crown, but they would fight for Donari.

The scouts had been dispatched the day before. The cavalry wing commanded by Gaspire of Collum, which included the detestable Jaryd Corvale, had ridden out just ahead of the in-companies. She could still see them off in the distance, a dust enshrouded mass advancing down the west road, heading to take position on the western flank of the Perspan army. Eleni knew Donari's force of five hundred mounted men would leave the next day to pace the vanguard on its eastern flank. It was a position of honor, according to the king. Donari's troopers would screen the host from forces dispatched from the coastal towns and villages that aligned themselves with the city-states of Heriopolis and Teirne; and in the process face the brunt of any sorties from that direction.

The Prince asked Eleni and Senden to join him on the balcony outside his chambers that evening to share a glass of wine and discuss the attack plans. Eleni thought to take notes, but was surprised when they included her in the talk. The moon, sailing through a flotsam of broken clouds, alternated its muted light with their sips as the three of them contemplated the morrow.

"My friends," the Prince sighed, gently swirling the wine in his glass. "Roderran showed us a map tonight. He's meticulous when it comes to death, I'll grant him that. It was full of unit notes, rates of progress to be met, each column with its road. A cavalry wing on each flank. Three columns of foot soldiers, each assigned to a different track. A company in between all of them moving cross country to keep lines of communication."

"He seems to have been pretty thorough," Senden muttered.

"Oh yes, quite. I'd have expected nothing less from one schooled in campaigning by Byrnard Casan."

"And where are we?" Senden asked quietly.

"Where we thought, sadly, on the eastern flank, foot as advance guard. The bastard wants to bleed us." Eleni heard true resignation in his voice. "There are fifteen hundred Pevanese spearmen marching with Captain Avarran, equally divided at the head of each Perspan column. Roderran will not even let us fight as a united force."

"If you had any doubts, there's your answer," Senden said bitterly.

Donari snorted derisively. "I've never had any illusions, Senden. I'm supposed to take it as a compliment to my *skills* and the quality of my troops. Avarran has done a great job. They look sharp. He knows what is coming. How he kept it from his face . . . I don't think I could have managed it."

"Too good a job," retorted Senden, and again, Eleni noted the bitter tone. "The king must fear us to split our people up so."

"It does not make sense," Eleni offered, looking up from her notes.

Donari gestured to her glass. "Take a sip for truth, mistress. I'm afraid it makes perfect sense. As Senden mentioned, I *am* the heir, and not in good favor with the king or his people. My disapproval is well-known. Give me two thousand loyal troops and position on the flank, and I could make trouble if I were ambitious. I know Gaspire Amdoran thinks so. He seemed quite happy with the king's design. He keeps the right with nothing much to guard against except trees while we get a hundred leagues of potential sorties from the coast."

"So we bleed," added Senden, "as points to his spears and as a shield for his left. The honor of place leaves me under-whelmed."

Donari gave a wry chuckle. "There's nothing honorable in any of this, Senden, but we still have to see it through. I owe it to our people to fight alongside them, to somehow make their sacrifice worthy of the blood they will spill."

Eleni put down her pen and moved to the balcony railing to look south, the hills just visible under the light of a full moon as dark, threatening shapes. Donari joined her.

"I have never journeyed out of our valley, my lord," she offered. "I have seen your maps, but will it be so bad?"

"The hills are a jumbled mass of humps and ridges, shaped like a hand," he held his own up as an example, "their source the mountains to the east. We are in a bowl here, but once into the hills the land mass spreads out, tree-woven in the valleys for much of their length, bare on the flanks and crests; the abode of sheep and cut by mines and swift streams. The hills taper off into fingers of uplands that rise to rocky heights, largely pass-less, creating the valleys that serve the four city states. The ridges effectively isolate them. The majority of their trade with each other is seaborne. The largest and most prosperous valley leads down to Desopolis, ruled by Sylvanus Tamorgen."

"And he is a threat?"

Donari grinned into his cup. "Truth? No. Divided, the south is weak. Roderran has demanded treaties, trade advantages, all the things easily rejected. That was all pretense. We invade for glory, power, Roderran's ambitions, and to settle old scores. Plus, you've seen the northern lords at council. Warriors, all of them. The king needs to keep them exercised."

Eleni heard Senden's chair scrape and his halting tread. He joined them.

"So we get a hundred leagues of care and concern," he said, leaning his elbows on the railing. "If Casan succeeds on the coast, less trouble; if he fails, something much more difficult."

"And either way, people's homes will burn. Men will die," Eleni whispered.

"That is war," Donari concurred. "High words, banners, shining mail, none of those things can ever hide the truth." He swallowed off the last of his cup. "We should rest, friends, we ride in the morning."

That night, Eleni's pen flew across her pages as she sought to record everything she could. Two hours after dawn the next day she took to the saddle, riding in the van of Donari's column amongst the baggage train, escorted by two pages who served as guards and extra messengers. Donari rode at the column's head, a dusty shape, helmless but wearing light mail partially covered by his blue cloak worked with the Avedun crest. Eleni thought him proud and stern, war-like in his erect bearing despite his true feelings. The more Eleni observed the general trend of the Perspan nobility the more she began to see Donari as a man apart. Before she put down her pen, she reviewed all that she had set down. Most of the time she put a title at the head of her notes, but this time she placed it at the end: *A King's Gambit.*

It seemed fitting.

Chapter 18: Desopolis: A Proposal

LYVIA SAT ACROSS FROM the cleaned up but still battered and bruised Talyior and Devyn, who sat, drinks at their elbows, trying to take their ease under the scrutiny of Lyvia's father, Sylvanus Tamorgen, the Tyrant of Desopolis. Ergan leaned his immensity casually against the door to her father's private study, one of her favorite places. Three windows comprised the south wall, beneath which stood a desk piled with papers. As a child, she climbed the book-lined shelves built into the adjoining walls.

Talyior and Devyn appeared curious, yet guarded and followed Sylvanus intently as her father paced back and forth in silence. Lyvia proudly watched her father move. Sylvanus, tall and well-muscled, his hair tinged with silver, still retained the grace of an athlete and had a penetrating look to his eyes that many found daunting.

What are you up to, father?

He rarely paced. It gave too much away, he said. Only when he was truly preoccupied did such defenses get lax. Devyn and Talyior did not know that, and Talyior for one seemed intimidated by her father's prowling. Devyn, for the other, slumped in his chair as though in pain, but his eyes following her father back and forth, back and forth, spoke the truth. He watched. Warily.

Lyvia caught Talyior's eye and smiled, trying to break the tension. He returned it, grimacing behind a split lip that faded to caution when Lyvia's father ceased his pacing and sat down in front of them.

"You both look like you've run afoul of Borimon's temper." Sylvanus looked at each of them in turn. "But you seem to have come out of the experience well enough. It could have been worse. I apologize for the abuse of your intentions. I'll not insult your intelligence by interrogating you. We need to talk, all of us. Ergan, please see to it we are not disturbed."

Ergan bowed and left, closing the door behind him.

"Why were you attacked?" Sylvanus continued. "What is your real purpose here? Lyvia has her opinions. I still have questions."

"Why were we attacked?" Devyn barked, offended, insistent. "Who were those fools? One I know was the Priest called Bandle. I'd seen him before. The other idiot, Lyvia says he was a former suitor. What have we fallen into, my lord? What passes for normal in this city? I thought the Old Ways held poets in high esteem."

Lyvia froze, afraid and curious. No one ever dared take such tone with her father. Anger bloomed on Sylvanus's face as he looked from Devyn to Talyior, to her, and came to rest on Devyn.

"We do, and Lyvia assures me you are skilled, but do you expect me to believe you have no idea what is happening in the region?" he snapped. "You came south just ahead of it young man. That could look suspicious. Roderran of Perspa wants the whole peninsula. Your friend here spoke with my daughter of events that transpired in Gallina. My spies told me of certain temple burnings in Pevana last summer. Put all these facts together and tell me you have no idea why you were attacked!"

"I don't deny anything of what is happening in the north, but what has this to do with us being attacked? Being accused of spying?"

Her father leveled a glare. "I've made it my practice to make connections, have done it for nearly thirty years. Roderran is coming."

"Granted," Devyn responded. "And again, I ask, what do we have to do with all of that?"

"You have been accused of spying."

"We are no spies. We left Pevana *because* of those things. Gallina was an incident," he paused his jaw clenching, "that I only partly regret. It was personal. We don't look for trouble. Spies, we are not."

"We are musicians," offered Talyior, his voice still little shaky.

"Yes! And your music raised a reaction from certain elements working in my city that concern me. Why would they call you out?" Sylvanus fell silent, looking directly at Devyn, waiting. Devyn return her father's stare, brow furrowed and jaw still clenched, but Lyvia sensed a softening there.

"Perhaps they didn't like being reminded of their hypocrisy. Perhaps the Old Ways aren't as true here as I hoped. Perhaps—"

"And who are you to judge?" interrupted Sylvanus.

"Because of this," Devyn responded, slipping his sleeve up his forearm to reveal the scar he earned rescuing the offering bowl last summer. "I know a little something about hypocrisy. And I've had similar responses to my words from—" he paused.

"Yes? From whom, what?" Sylvanus urged. "Think, boy, out with it."

"From King's Theology priests." Devyn's features relaxed but the fire remained in his eyes. "I see it now. Bandle. He did not feel right to me. I thought he was just crazy, but he's one of Casan's, it fits. We were attacked to shut us up."

"But why should he wish you silent?"

"He bragged about being in control back there, after Tanli's, about information."

"And you just happened to fall into his hands? There must be more."

Devyn looked at Talyior, uneasily, with an expression of disgusted distaste.

"All those days, Tal, all that effort to avoid those people. And we run away, here, and they were waiting for us. Do you see it?"

Lyvia watched the comprehension sweep over Talyior's face. "The competition, the Maze fire, all those groups along the way. Casan sent word of us. Sevire Anargi. Ships. Very likely it was only a matter of time."

Devyn slumped back in his chair. "My arm, my poems, Talyior's affair with," he glanced at Lyvia, "You did tell her, right?"

"He did," Lyvia quipped, smiling to break the tension. "But he might have some more explaining to do. Go on."

"You know the north is coming. I suspect types like Bandle have been placed all up and down the coast to watch, to prepare the way. To keep any news from reaching the wrong ears. Perhaps Bandle thought we might try to warn you or something. Bandle spoke of *messages.*"

"And so the spies call the honest men false," Sylvanus scoffed. "It makes a sick sense, doesn't it? So this Bandle is Casan's creature. I know of the Lord Prelate Byrnard; that man has had an interesting career. Old, now, but no less dangerous. We have noted *missionaries* in the hills and along the coast. Sollust has been in Bandle's company since last summer, right about the time my Lyvia put him in his place. You two were unfortunate victims of several vendettas. I am sorry."

"I am sorry for *you*, my lord," Devyn said, sadly. "If such men are here, look to your temples. Flames will come."

Sylvanus rose to his feet, pushed thick fingers through the silver of his hair. "True words, young man, if what I have learned about King Roderran is true. Flames seem to spark when he acts. I know he is coming. If I do not stop Roderran's ambitions, more than temples will burn."

The resignation in his voice brought Lyvia to her feet. "Father," she whispered, hugging him. "You will."

Lyvia felt her father's arms tighten their embrace. "We have always enjoyed our independence from each other here in the south," he murmured over her head, "and it works against us now. We face long odds, perhaps impossible odds, but Roderran has not been secretive. We have had time to prepare."

"But is there enough will, here, to resist?" Devyn murmured.

Lyvia expected anger, but Sylvanus's answer came surprisingly gentle. "The Old Ways, here, may seem lazy and complacent to you, but that is because they are melded to the fabric of how we live. The roots are subtle and run deep. We are not a northern fief. Roderran does not know us. He wants to conquer, not unite. I will not let that happen." Sylvanus let go his embrace and Lyvia moved to Talyior's side and took his offered hand.

Her father looked at her, his eyes falling to where she grasped Talyior's hand, nodding as though accepting a reality.

"It's funny," he mused. "You spend half a lifetime anticipating change, but when it actually comes, it arrives quickly, catching you by surprise, like old age." He looked up, caught Lyvia's eye. "I've always been prepared to lose my city, and even though I've never officially claimed you, I never expected to lose you. It looks like both many happen. You ask what I intend. That depends on you three and one other."

"And who would that be, my lord?" Devyn asked.

"Prince Donari Avedun of Pevana."

"What? Why? What should a northern prince be so vital? " Devyn asked.

"Father, I don't understand completely," added Lyvia.

Sylvanus ignored her, kept his eyes fixed on Devyn

"Now we come to it," he said, scratching idly at his salt and pepper beard. "No more word dances." He pointed to Talyior and Devyn. "You need to choose."

"Choose what?" asked Talyior.

"Choose how?" added Devyn.

"You can choose to help me or keep yourselves apart from all of this. My daughter vouches for you, mostly on first impressions and instinct." He turned to her. "Are you sure of this one? Time for idles is gone, my dear."

For the first time since she was a little girl, Lyvia felt the full force of her father's personality focused on her. She had come to him with a suggestion, a thought only, that these two might be of use. But now, after spending time with Talyior and hearing the conviction in Devyn's voice, she knew what she felt was not just interest but emotion.

She realized she still held Talyior's hand. *Warm. Worried. Alive.* "Yes," she said, with growing certainty. "This is no idle. We haven't time. They are real."

Sylvanus gave her one last, hard look, then turned back to the other two.

"I give you a choice," he repeated, "to stay here, well-housed but guarded, until the end of whatever is to come, or offer me your service so that I may save what I can from the storm."

"Prisoners or soldiers," Devyn snorted. "Not much choice."

"That might be the most honest thing you've said yet, young man. I think, in the end, none of us have much choice in this matter. I have run out of time for choices. I must act, but I can see you both are tired. I can spare the rest of the night to think, but come morning, I must have a decision. Lyvia will conduct you to a room where you can rest, talk it out."

Devyn and Talyior rose to follow Lyvia. Devyn paused at the door.

"Why Donari?"

Lyvia's father had remained seated. Instead of looking back at Devyn, he stared out the window. It looked north. "A memory, perhaps, or a hope," he looked over his shoulder at Devyn, "of honor."

Devyn followed Talyior and Lyvia down the hall to a well-appointed room with several beds. He left them at the door and threw himself on the closest bed. Lyvia stood next to Talyior at the door.

"So, that was a bit different from *affluent audience*," he said.

Lyvia frowned. "I'm sorry. I thought I could help you, truly, but I also felt my father should talk to you. I didn't expect it to go like it did."

"But you aren't surprised," Devyn asserted, rolling over onto an elbow.

Lyvia let go of Talyior's hand. "No, I'm not surprised. But what you heard just now is true. The Perspans are coming. My father faces hard choices."

"And you?" Talyior asked. "Is this real, as you said?"

Lyvia smiled, moved close and kissed him. "I was curious in the boat, but I'm serious now. Rest now. Think. I'll come get you in the morning."

After she left, Talyior stood staring at the closed door.

"We should out of here," he said. "This is madness upon madness. We have no reason to get involved."

"Talyior," Devyn began, but Talyior cut him off.

"No, Dev . . . don't patronize me. Renia's Grace but she is amazing. Still, this is foolish. What have we to do with this war? We left Pevana because it became unhealthy. We can leave here for the same reason."

"And go where? Back north? Not for me. You've your family. Perhaps you should think about it. Me? I'm not so inclined, sorry. My home burned last summer. I've spent the months since trying to avoid the truth about my life, my people, and the dangers collecting against them. I'm through running away, Tal. I mean, I made my feeble protest in that festival last year thinking it was a fine, grand gesture, honoring my people's faith, honoring Kembril's memory."

"And you made sense, Dev, everyone heard it."

"But I didn't stop the flames, Tal. Don't you see? Casan's priests weren't sent home packing. They have spread. Gallina was a sign, Tal, that there is something left for me to do beyond poetics, beyond tweaking the egos and plans of fools like Casan and Roderran. This invasion Sylvanus speaks of is just more flames for me, Tal. I still see them in my dreams. Stones blackened, truth consumed. It's no good. If I can do something to stop all of it, maybe save lives. . ."

"But these are not your people!" Talyior interrupted.

Devyn smiled. His friend never dissembled. He had played with fire with Demona Anargi and received his own scars, but unlike Devyn, he had been able to move on.

"How does her hand feel?" he asked. The question startled Talyior.

"Amazing, perfect, hey! What do you mean?"

"Spend more time with Lyvia, and I think you will begin to see it," he said chuckling.

"Don't change the subject," Talyior growled. "We are talking about what *we* will do."

"I disagree, my friend, I think I know what I have to do. You are still running away from your family or maybe searching for your own. Lyvia is quite compelling."

"We've just met."

"That has never stopped you before, and you told her your life story."

"But this is different!"

"Exactly!" Devyn asserted, sitting up. "This is different. See, you understand it at least a little. I had a dream about Kembril soon after we came here. He urged me to go back. Now I know why."

"Don't spew poetry at me! Not now."

"Then how about some truth. Everything I have ever held true is threatened. I've had too much of flames. I miss Kembril. Sylvanus asked us to make a choice. I intend to help if I can."

"Then I will choose the same."

Devyn thought Talyior sounded relieved.

"Oh, such a hard choice for you!" he chuckled. "I don't think you really had a choice."

"She is, as you say, *compelling*. She scares me."

"And that would be a first, and another reason why I think your path is set, my friend. I envy you. I think this place needs you. A few days ago I was walking in one of the markets, still upset by my first encounter with that Bandle fellow, and I remember stopping by a stall of handwoven stuff. A young mother sat there crooning to her baby. I remember the words she sang clearly." He took a breath and began singing the words to a lullaby:

And sure you shall cry your tears
And sure you shall have your fears
For you are yet young at heart
And your life has yet to start.

And sure you shall find your way
And sure you shall have your day
For you are strong enough to last
Through the times that come to pass.

But until you set out upon your road

You shall have another to carry your load,
And when bad dreams lead you onto dismay
Grant that your Maman shall send them away.

For your Maman is always with you
And watches over you when you sleep.
For you are the promise your Maman
Has vowed to Renia's Grace to keep.

And so to sleep. . .

He let the last note fade. "Simple words but a complex sort of love," he said. "Worth the risk to preserve, I'd say."

The look on Talyior's face meant more to Devyn than the fact that, for perhaps the first time in all their days together, Talyior let him have the last word.

Lyvia doubled back to her father's study, thinking to at least say good night. The door was slightly ajar, and when she placed her hand on the handle to enter she paused. Her father and Ergan were talking.

"They are spies, if I say they are, and heroes if I decide otherwise, Ergan. I'm marching out with two thirds of my troops in a few days time. We will be swamped by Roderran's host if what the scouts tell me is true. But this Devyn might be a way to Donari that Roderran will not expect. These two have a history with the prince. If I can separate Prince Donari, make him think about power, then we have a chance. If he is the man I think he is, I even the odds."

"That is a slender thread, my lord. And if the Prince is not the man you think he is?"

"Then I fall fighting with my men. I bleed Roderran down and hope you can save what is left of this city and our people."

"My place is at your side, lord."

"Coast watchers tell me there is a fleet sailing south as well. This city will be attacked, one way or another. I want it defended by the best warrior and the best mind I have."

"Best mind?"

Sylvanus gave a small laugh. "I meant no offense, Ergan. I mean to recognize Lyvia and name her regent when I march. The two of you will defend the city."

Her father's declaration illicited an involuntary gasp. Instantly, the door open to reveal a startled, frowning Sylvanus. Lyvia froze, watched the run of emotions cross his face, pride, frustration, remorse, fear. She waited. His features softened to a sardonic grin.

"What, couldn't reach your usual hiding place?" He drew her into the room, held her hands, the grin faded to an intent, somber look.

"Lyvia," he sighed. "I have not been a good father to you. We have been through all this, I know, but I want you to know how proud I am of you. When I leave this time, I may not come back. I will go before the council today and claim you for my own true daughter and name you regent, along with Ergan, for the rule and defense of the city in my absence. I'm sorry to take your freedom, but like this war, I have no choice."

"The greybeards will laugh at me, father, you can't."

"The people love you, Lyvia, why do you think I have let you grow so wild? Did you think it was because I didn't care?"

"At first, yes, I thought as much, but later I learned otherwise, but still—"

"When the arrows fly, the greybeards as you call them will scurry for doors to lock and holes to hide in, but the people will look to you, my dear, because they know you."

Lyvia felt a moment's swell of pride, but anger surged along with it.

"So I am and have always been part of your calculations? Have you no conscience?"

Her father eyes showed the smile he kept off his face.

"I have ruled as I have seen fit, Lyvia. I have made choices along the way. That does not mean I have slept well. Those who rule cannot always abide a conscience. Remember that when you come to the chair."

"If."

The smile became genuine, finally. "You sound so much like your mother when you do that. Yes, *if,* small word, many variables. *If* these two young men are what you and I think they are, and *if* I can bring Roderran to battle in favorable circumstances, and *if* Donari proves biddable, then we might come out of this alive."

"That's a lot of *ifs.*"

"In uncertain times, *if* dominates *when.* But enough of that. This Talyior, he reeks of honesty. And you like him, yes?"

"Yes, I like his hope," Lyvia responded. "He's different, kind."

"And good looking."

Lyvia blushed. "Father, is this the time for such talk?"

Her father laughed gently and took her into his arms, something that rarely happened during her early years, repeated for the second time in an hour. Lyvia accepted the embrace, surprised at how much she wanted it.

"I thought so," her father murmured. "At least you and this Talyior will have a little time together. Show him our people, Lyv."

"Father," Lyvia breathed into his chest. Sylvanus tightened his embrace.

"Time," he sighed, letting her go. "I've wasted most of mine. Make sure you use what you have left to better purpose."

"Father, you can't talk like this."

He moved to the door. "No, Lyv, I'm just being honest, probably for the first time in my life."

The morning sun rose bright over eastern headland, sending a beam through the corner window of Sylvanus's study to lighten an otherwise dark interview. Devyn and Talyior, looking better for the time alone, sat in their chairs as before. Sylvanus leaned back against his desk, studying them. Lyvia sat in her father's chair at the desk with a stack of reports she had been reading. She looked at Talyior, taking heart from his intent expression.

"So," Sylvanus began. "I can see you've rested. Have you considered?"

Devyn answered for them. "You gave us a choice to help or to stay as hostages. Is there a difference?"

"There is a great difference, young man. When I said I needed your help, I meant it."

"What can we do? As Talyior said last night, we are just musicians."

"Don't dissemble. I'm not without my intuitions. I think you understand what we face."

"What makes you think we can do anything?" Devyn asked. "What makes you think we would want to?"

Lyvia's father pointed a finger at the poet and matched him word for word, tone for tone. "Because you are a young idealist. You stuck your blade through a King's Theology Priest in Gallina to shut him up because you didn't like how he went about his business. I think you have a role to play because agents of my enemies tried to kill you and your friend. I think you may have hidden qualities that I might put to use. In fact, now I am certain of it."

"Poor choice by you, then," Devyn said quietly.

"That remains to be seen," Sylvanus responded. "I'm going to roll the bones and tell you everything. I don't think you'll betray me. Besides," he grinned, "You are unarmed and Ergan is just outside the door."

"I have held the rule here for more than thirty years," her father continued, settling into a chair. "I've outlasted all of my southern rivals, and kept the north at arm's length in the bargain. We in the south may lack unity, but at least we don't prey on each other. I've no respect for kings who war on their own people, and both Roderran and his father made it a practice of their rule.

"I once sat across the table from Donari's grandfather, a hard man but wise, that one, and he had his grandson with him. Barely fifteen, maybe, a stripling with darting eyes. He seemed different to me even then. Young, but astute, I judged. Well-made but not a physical beast like his uncle and cousin. In fact, I think Donari's family had a different cast to it than the fools who mounted the northern throne. I realize now that difference contributed to the peace we enjoyed here. The grandfather had no southern ambitions, and the grandson seemed to carry on with the same ambivalence. I have heard he's a bit soft."

"No," Devyn interrupted. "Prince Donari is not soft."

"He's a good man," added Talyior with feeling. "He is the reason why Dev and I still live. Last night was not the first time our words have placed us in danger. He's, he's—"

"Much, much more than he appears," Devyn finished. "I doubted him once. Saw the surface as the substance. Blamed him for our people's loss of faith. I was wrong."

Sylvanus nodded, and Lyvia could tell what he heard reassured him.

"I risk everything on that assumption," he said. "Roderran and his trumped up faith, this *King's Theology*, are nothing but naked ambition draped in red arrogance."

Lyvia turned to Devyn, whose face had grown pale beneath its bruises.

"Kembril said much the same thing," he whispered.

"Your father?" Sylvanus asked.

"No, as good as, I suppose. A poet and my teacher. He saved me from the streets. Casan's thugs burned him in the fires of last summer. Your words reminded me of him."

"We heard about those fires," Lyvia said. "Old Ways temples, the homes of the poor."

"And they call it *reform,*" scoffed her father. "And they call me *tyrant*, absurd."

Everyone fell silent in a moment of decision. Talyior sat next to her, lost in his own thoughts, rubbing his temple. Devyn stared at the carpet, hands clasped before him, tense as though reliving bleak memories. Her father leaned back and waited in forced passivity, but his jaw worked beneath his beard. The need to speak drove Lyvia's voice.

"I have a question. Why such concern about this Prince Donari?"

Devyn looked up as she spoke, and then to Sylvanus.

"You think Prince Donari is the key," he asserted.

"I'm counting on it."

"Why?"

"Because I intend to make him King."

Devyn laughed, a burst of ill-mirth. "You're mad."

"Mad enough to lie to my people, to convince them to fight Roderran, bleed him, make his arrogance as costly as possible. And all for a fool's hope that his cousin is a better man and will see his way to words rather than blood, to peace in the end."

"Can you send your people to death on such a flimsy hope?" Talyior asked. "That's treason."

"I'm told such behavior comes with being a tyrant. Win or lose, I have doomed my people to life under a northern scepter. All I can hope for is to ensure the right head is wearing it."

Again silence fell over the room. Lyvia understood how much it cost her father to speak as he did. He proposed taking on the guilt of leading their people to war on false pretenses. To the uninitiated, such actions would seem callous and indifferent, but Lyvia knew better. *He has to win to lose, and in the losing, save.* She rose, walked over to him and hugged him tightly for a long moment. A tear slipped down her cheek. Sylvanus returned her embrace with a father's intensity. No words. Decision waited.

Devyn's voice, quiet but clear, broke the moment:

And to the field they all came
Treachery rather than honor the game
War and peace, risked equally the same
If all there lost and all there won,
Who would be to blame?

"So," he asked, rising. "What will you do? Spring must have reached the northern reaches by now. Roderran might be on the march already."

"He is. My watchers report his lead elements nearing the hills. They sighted Donari's banner. They are coming."

"And how will you get word to Donari?"

"I'm sending you."

Devyn stared then stumbled back to his chair, hand to temple. "I knew it," he muttered. "I knew it all along."

"What do you mean, Dev?" Talyior asked.

"I had a dream, that first night here. Kembril's shade came to me. Told me to go back. At first I thought it was for revenge on Corvale, but now I see it more clearly. This is crazy, but I'll do it."

"Who said war was sane?" Sylvanus asked quietly. "I think you will do this for me, Devyn, because of your lost mentor, because you have met the prince and because I have no one else to send."

"I'll go," Talyior blurted. "I'll do it. We'll both go."

"No, Talyior," Lyvia said, beating her father in rejecting the idea. As soon as Devyn agreed to the proposition, she knew what would come next. Suddenly, she did not feel quite her father's equal. "That won't do."

"Listen to her, young man, she understands it now," Sylvanus urged.

"So I'm a hostage?" Talyior's voice rose with the beginning of real anger. "You must be joking!"

"I do this alone, Tal," Devyn said firmly. "Lord Sylvanus, my friend stays. He does not have the stake in this that I do. I want him safe."

"I'm not a piece of baggage!" Talyior objected, standing. "How can you let him go alone?"

Sylvanus ignored him. "Done," he growled. "He stays for surety of your good effort and as a favor to my daughter. As for safety, none of us will be safe."

"And if we fail?" Devyn asked.

"Then it won't matter," Sylvanus responded, "because we'll all be dead."

Chapter 19: Departures. . .

WHEN NO ONE ANSWERED her knock, Lyvia carefully opened the door to the room Talyior and Devyn shared. They had returned there after their interview with her father to wait for more instructions, eat and rest. Devyn was gone. Talyior lay on the bed deeply asleep. Lyvia glided to the side of the bed and stood for a moment watching the gentle rise and fall of his chest, his slack features, eyes moving beneath their lids chasing dreams. He looked innocent. Her father was correct; Talyior possessed a physical honesty hard to miss once pointed out. Lyvia understood why she found him so attractive. She had never met anyone even remotely close to him. Sollust Megare, that unpleasant memory, was night to Talyior's day.

She bent and placed a finger softly on his lips, lingering there, eyes closed, as if she could share his dream. Colors, faces, images of towers bathed by sunlight or perhaps encased in flames flashed behind her lids. From the depths of his slumber, Talyior's lips responded to hers, moving, pressing, exploring. She broke away reluctantly. His eyes, wide awake and bright-blue, stared back at her.

"Are you real?" he asked.

"I don't know. Am I?"

"I've heard dreams can be powerful things. I dreamed of you, and here you are."

She brushed her finger along his lips as he spoke. *So, very, nice.* "What else were you dreaming of? Besides me?"

"You. And another woman I once knew, before."

She curled a fingernail gently under his chin, the flicker of jealousy replaced by interest. He had been honest with her, after all.

"Demona?"

He nodded. "You. Her. People, places I've known. My father. Your father. Flames. All jumbled. And in the end, Devyn. Devyn *leaving*." He came up on his elbows, looked around. "He's gone."

"He might be with my father. You've slept a good part of the day away. Spend the rest of it with me. Let Devyn do what he must."

"So you can be my jailor?"

"And if I was?"

He made to pull her down on him. "Nice jail."

"No!" she refused, pulling away. "I'm not your guard. Never think that, Talyior."

"Devyn goes on your father's fool's errand. I stay here for surety. Wanted or not, Lyvia, I'm a prisoner."

"Only if you think that way. Come, let me show you my city. If you are going to stay, you might as well get to know your prison."

His brow smoothed. "I'm not sure what to think, Lyvia, but you make staying behind easier to take."

"I know. I used to think I was always a half-step ahead of my father, but he's working all of us here. I'm sorry about most if it, but not about what I said last night. I meant it. This is different, Talyior."

"*This* is dangerous, but I feel it, too." He reached a hand to run it through her hair, a liberty that spoke more than the words he used. He gently pulled her down and kissed her, a chaste touching that lengthened into something more communicative.

Lyvia felt something inside her give away. Her father had finally claimed her, and would soon march to war. Her city faced an uncertain future. Everything was terminal. She decided to follow her father's advice. *No time to waste, not even on innocence.*

"Likewise. Come, I had the kitchen pack us a basket."

She took him on a tour of the city as she saw it. They meandered among folk at market, looked into shops she frequented, and stopped and chatted with people. Lyvia had done so all her life, but this day was different. Talyior's presence changed everything, as did her new status. There were speculative glances, outright questions, and she could tell Talyior felt the weight of the evaluation. And yet he carried himself confidently, and when he took her arm in his, she sensed a change in the people's reaction.

Lyvia knew that intensity came from her father sending out the call to assemble the columns that would march north. The people buzzed with the news and the change in their wonted practice, but Lyvia saw acceptance, too, and that included Talyior and the genuine, solid feel of his hand in hers. In taking him about the streets and squares, Lyvia wove his presence among the familiar things in her life. By the time they reached the outer defenses of the harbor forts, the pattern felt complete.

The end of the day saw them watching the sunset from one of the northern tower's seaward crenellations, munching on cold roast chicken, bread and cheese. Except for making sure the guards had a bite and some of the cider, they ignored them completely in favor of the stars that came out at full dark. Under their watchful silence, they talked quietly, continuing the learning begun in earnest with that morning's first embrace.

"Thank you," Lyvia sighed, settling more comfortably against the curving tongue of the battlement, "for a lovely day. I can't explain it clearly, but I felt as though I were seeing this place and all those people for the first time after a long, long absence."

"The birth of legitimacy," Talyior joked.

"No, I'm serious. I felt different," she insisted. "It went beyond my father's action. They have always been my people in ways no blood relation can touch. No, today was special, and sad, in a way."

"How so?"

"It was special because I was happy showing it to you, and I could tell you understood. Uncanny, but right, somehow."

"Lyvia, nothing about this is ordinary."

"I know, and that is why it was also sad because I know it might all go away. I grew up thinking I didn't need anything, mother or father, I was in control. I always had the freedom of this place, of these people, and I thought that would be enough. And yet—"

Talyior reached over and took her hand in his. "And?" he asked gently.

She looked down at his hand, weighing its substantiality melded with her own, marveling as her fingers responded to his touch.

"And in the space of days, I find you, I find I have always needed a father, and I find I want to keep my world about me in the worst way. And here I sit, picking gristle out of my teeth, aware that as a woman there is little I can do to save anything. It's not fair."

"Life is not fair; life just is."

She sighed. "I'm not sniveling. All this maturity drivel is new to me. Right now part of me wants to wrap myself in my own illusions."

Talyior shifted behind her, took her gingerly into his arms. "I don't have any illusions to hand," he whispered. "But will this do?"

She relaxed back against his chest, sighing. "So this *is* better, but still—"

"But nothing," he said, confidently, tightening his embrace. "I have learned more about you in these hours than I ever would have thought possible under other circumstances. Your people love you, look to you, need to see you happy. Your father may rule the city, but you rule the people's hearts. And mine."

She made to shift around at his words, but he kept her still, and his kiss on the back of her head sent a thrill down her neck to her heart.

"Perhaps the nearness of peril makes things more poignant," he continued. "Or maybe I'm just a silly poet who sees romance in danger. I don't know for sure. But I have been in thrall since you stopped in front of me on the pier and asked me to go fishing! And I know you care for me, and that both of us are more perplexed than we would like to admit. Lyvia, neither of us are innocents. I think we both know this is no dalliance."

"So, what are you suggesting?"

"That we take each hour fate grants us from here and live it. I am done running away from my life. If chance grants us time, I intend to spend it with you. And if you don't want me, I'm sure you would tell me. And I would loose my arms from around you like this." And he slowly opened them to allow her to move.

She laughed gently, and re-wrapped them around her. "I think I could stay like this all night," she whispered.

"But what about your poor guards?"

"Bad luck of the draw?"

"What happened to, *they are my people*?"

She scowled good-naturedly, caught in the web of her own ethics. "Oh, fine! I suppose we should take pity on them and return to the palace."

Hand in hand, they walked back followed dutifully by their pair of tired but bemused guards.

Devyn studied the map spread out before him on the table. It presented a detailed rendering of the topography of the main valley that ran back from the coast and the walls of Desopolis to the slopes of the highlands to the north. Devyn recalled his impressions of that region from his and Talyior's traverse of it on their journey to Desopolis. Closer to Gallina, woods shadowed the river and road that meandered back and forth through the center. These thinned as the valley opened lower down. Small streams cut their tributary channels into the hills to the west and east. Several towns along them served the farms and mines that fed Desopolis and provided its mineral wealth. The northernmost was Gallina, where he and Talyior had their misadventure with the militant missionaries.

He would leave that night. Sylvanus had made it plain delay would not serve. His bruises from Bandle's assault still ached, but he would have to ease his hurts as best he could in the saddle.

He heard footsteps behind him, coming closer. The sure tread of his gait announced the tyrant of Desopolis before Devyn turned to look. Then Sylvanus stood beside him, scrutinizing the map. He pointed to the dense mass of the highlands.

"They will split up into large columns for the march through the northern regions," Sylvanus said. "The roads coming out of the Pevanese plain are unimproved, a product of the weakness of our trade with each other, sadly. Perhaps if we exchanged more than spies and illicit goods, they would have been better."

"To make invasion even easier?" Devyn asked.

"Or perhaps with better roads and better understanding, no need for invasion at all."

Devyn looked at him sidelong. "Do you really believe that?"

Sylvanus chuckled. "No, not really. Especially not with Roderran as king."

"Which is why I am going."

Sylvanus nodded, still studying the map. "Yes, which is why you are going." He pointed to a place which showed a ford to the river that cut the valley. "Here is where you should leave the rode and climb up the eastern slopes. The land is tree-woven and the shoulders of the range form a small escarpment. You should be able to ride undetected until you reach level to the lands around Gallina. Also, climbing gets you above certain places I do not want you to see, and what you do not know cannot be forced out of you."

"I see."

"I'm sure you do. Devyn, I risk everything with this campaign and your journey. But if you should get captured by the wrong sort, well, too much knowledge could kill you."

"If I come from the south, will it matter?"

Sylvanus smiled, conceding the point. "Perhaps, but I would like to think I at least tried to have a care for your safety as much as I am able."

Devyn laughed, a bitter sound, quickly squelched. "Which means, of course, that you are unable."

"True," and with the word Sylvanus turned to look Devyn in the eyes. "So please make use of all those skills that got you this far."

"I will. And, though I do this partially to help you, I do have my own reasons for going, too, my lord."

"Care to share those reasons?"

"I feel called to the task. This seems like it fits with a pattern I am meant to follow. I have unfinished business in the north. Something tells me I may encounter him."

"Him? Revenge? Who is the unfortunate fellow? Should I be worried about your commitment?"

"Roderran leads those who burned my life," Devyn responded, turning once again to the map. "And you already have surety of me, remember?"

Sylvanus frowned but nodded agreement. "Your friend will be well looked after, if I read my daughter correctly."

"He likes it here. Lyvia has captured him more completely already than any bonds you might have place on him. He needs this. I need the other. Revenge, as you say."

"Then so be it. Have you any other questions? There is no moon, and I will pull the guards at the north gate. Make good time, but spare your mount. You may require speed later in the hills. I will march out in three days. Time only matters if and when you get close, but things will go well or ill within a fortnight at the most. I suspect Donari will be on the flank. That is where I would put him. I have several Pevanese dams in my stables. He will be with cavalry; I am sure of it. Roderran is not too much the fool in matters military. Look for the Prince on the east flank, and may Renia's tears sustain you."

"Is there to be a letter? How will I convince the prince?"

"There will be no letter. Too risky. You know my mind in this. At the very least, Donari must be made to hold back, to think. No letter. Besides, you are a poet. I know you will find the words."

Devyn sighed. "Words, you say. Weak tools."

Sylvanus grinned. "In the hands of the unlearned or unskilled, perhaps, but remember what response you words have had heretofore. The right words, spoken at the right time by the right person can have more power than any sword."

"*May Renia's tears wash us clean,*" Devyn said, quoting the first line of an old prayer.

"*And sustain us in our hour of need,*" finished Sylvanus. "Luck to you, poet."

The benediction felt genuine. "And you, lord," Devyn whispered, "and you."

Sylvanus left, the sound of his booted feet on the tiles tapping away into silence. Devyn continued to stare at the map as though he could animate it to show him his future. So much depended on what happened over that ground. Lines on a page, like words to the poet, held warrant and risk. He made a motion with his hand as though shaking and rolling dice. He followed the imaginary tumble and nodded, once, satisfied by the result.

Devyn rode slowly, nearly blind in the full dark beneath a sliver-moon and stars. Their pale light, that worked such eldritch magic on lovers, served no useful purpose for him and mocked his effort and made him feel even more alone. The rush of putting spurs to horse at the city gate had long since faded. Now he forced himself to slow down and keep his seat on his horse, still skittish over his stranger's touch despite his skills and gentle command. He could barely make out the road's edge, and the dark reduced him to a bouncing clutter hardly the stuff of a secret, desperate mission. Actually, he found the slow pace a blessing, for everything up to that point had gone incomprehensibly fast.

Like how he had gone from wondering poet to oath-bound spy.

It was enough to drive a man to distraction, and that did not help keep him on the road. He slowed even further, curbing his mount to a gentle rolling walk; if death awaited him at journey's end he saw no reason to rush.

One day passed, then two. Though his pace remained slow, his mind raced ahead, and he knew better than to attempt restraining it. He huddled over a small fire that fluttered and stuttered at the whim of a cold northern breeze whistling through the jumble of rocks where he had set his camp. Stars swam through oceans of cloud to peer down at him in his extremity. The image of his task hung before him, lit by the fitful flames of his campfire, mocking his presumption.

I am insane. So many variables to this. Avoid Desopolisan troops, avoid Roderran's scouts, find Prince Donari, convince him I'm no traitor, but that the only way to save anything is if he turns traitor himself. Mad. Mad Mad.

Weariness taxed him. He doubted himself. He knew he would rest a few more hours and then continue on before first light. The contradiction of his situation taunted him: a coward driven by vanity to pursue heroism, a poet in search of a perfect line that still might be used to write the ending to a tragedy.

"Renia help me," he muttered to the flames. "This is a fool's errand. What was I thinking?" His better sense took over about the same time the fire's warmth reached his bones. He entered willingly into this folly thinking to save something precious at the risk of his own—as he had done before, running into a burning temple.

Chapter 20: Perspan Army: Donari and Eleni

PRINCE DONARI SHIFTED HIS WEIGHT in the saddle, looking for a way to ease the twisted knot that throbbed painfully in the small of his back above his left hip. He came from a family of horsemen; part of the Avedun power in Pevana in the early years came from the quality of their horse herds and horsemanship. Life as a ruling figure, despite his irreverence, meant certain skills and muscles atrophied. In the weeks of their march south, his skills returned to him, but his rump hurt. The Princely Chair did not condition the muscles in the lower body.

But Donari's aching backside fell to a small irritation when compared to the larger issues he faced. His force, charged with keeping the army's left flank clear, had borne the brunt of the harassment thus far. Harassing raids from small, poorly armed detachments lacking insignia or badge struck at them from wooded slope and rocky defile and forced caution however light the casualties. Donari found it exasperating that such irregular troops, hastily assembled hillmen, shepherds and miners, could so easily influence their progress.

He urged his mount up a rise to the crest of the low hill his men cleared earlier. Senden and the rest of his escort followed him. He dismounted and reached for the water bag from his saddle. Senden dismounted as well and limped over, rubbing his thigh. His motion disconcerted Donari. It had been over a month since the wound, and Senden had yet to regain his wonted mobility.

Donari drank and proffered the bag. Senden took it wordlessly, nodding his thanks.

"It's quiet," Donari said, and gestured to the lands east and south. "This hill is well-placed. I don't understand why it is undefended. Look there," he pointed. "See those tracks? They come from Teirne and Heriopolis and join the north-south path just below us. This could be a strong place at need. A tower would command a wide view."

"I'm surprised it wasn't held against us," Senden replied, handing the bag back. "Fifty archers could cause some trouble from up here. This has been all too easy."

"I agree. You've seen the gear they have left behind. Poor stuff taken all around." Donari turned to the west, a jumble of tree covered hills and bumps alternated with rocky areas breaking the symmetry like jagged basaltic moles. The Perspan force in three columns, with the king's the centermost, inched its way underneath that canopy, each column led by a contingent of Pevanese spearmen. Donari spied smoke lifting up through the trees from three different but roughly parallel locations.

"Roderran continues to take it slow," he muttered. "For a man whose career was made by being brutally decisive, he seems overly careful."

"He does have Demona."

Donari snorted. "Wouldn't that be perfect? Lose momentum by easy marches just to diddle one's mistress. *That* actually makes sense. If my men weren't dying while he plowed the bitch, I wouldn't mind."

"You never had a choice, my lord."

"I know. That makes it even worse. Too much sniveling about it brings obvious doubts. Open rebellion means failure because we are too divided this way. I cannot but do as I am bid. I hate the death I have seen so far, Senden. If I were better placed—"

"You would see the wisdom, despite the pain to our people, of being patient. Roderran was reckless to do this, Donari. He and his folk expect success, dominance. Anything short of it—" Senden paused, turning to look back east.

"Anything short of what?" Donari asked. Senden pointed.

"Teirne is burning."

Donari turned and realized what he thought at first was a grey cloud oozing above the land eastward had darkened into an angry column rising into the sky. He swung south to where Heriopolis should lay and saw nothing, yet.

"That explains much," he said. "Casan must be having it his way, judging by the size of that smokey pillar."

"That also explain why we have not seen more opposition here."

"Yes, and not likely to see more until we reach further south, closer to Desopolis. All we will see from that direction will be refugees."

"They could still prove troublesome."

"We will leave a company here when we move on. I'll send word to Roderran for a covering force to come here. Who knows, maybe the news of Casan's success will lighten his sentence on us. I'd love for some of my own people here at my back."

"But you doubt that will be the case."

Donari's answering laugh held more bitterness than mirth.

"That leg of yours has spoiled your sense of humor, Senden." He lost his smile. "You are too much about. Your limp grows worse, my friend. You need to take as much rest as you can."

"I won't let you do everything alone, my lord."

"Call it another price I pay for my failure. We will camp here tonight. Get back to the column and set others to making arrangements. Don't think I haven't noticed you and Eleni hovering. One or the other of you always seems to have an eye on me."

"Loyalty?"

"And much appreciated, but I can manage to do things for myself."

"Like take an ill-made arrow unawares."

"Look around you, Senden. You've been efficient. Now, off with you. Ride a wagon back."

Donari watched Senden limp away. A mix of emotions contested for his mood. His men had done well on the march. The reports Avarran sent to him spoke of casualties countered by a strong spirit within the ranks. His men knew how the wind blew. Senden taxed himself unduly, and Eleni had become such a fixture within the camp that no one questioned her near constant attendance at his fire or at meetings with squad leaders. Donari had much to be proud of despite the difficult situation he and his people faced. He walked back to his horse. It had wandered off in search of grass and how stood near the east summit framed by the symbol of Teirne's fall. *But there is still death and flames; I've had enough of both.*

He remounted with a little difficulty; his shoulder still not quite right even now. When he was most tired it showed weakness, and yet he tempered any personal misgivings by remembering Senden's limp and committed himself to the idea of doing more in the days ahead.

He rode back to meet the column, catching sight of Eleni walking her horse alongside a wagon piled high with tent canvas and poles. She wore a large hat, a response to Donari's joke about her blond hair providing an easy target, and an old mottled green and brown cloak he insisted provided better cover than her own. The sight of her down there, steady and uncomplaining, brought a smile to his lips.

On the road into the hills, she seemed to comport herself well enough, kept out of the way, took notes as required. But things changed after that first attack. In the chaos, he caught her looking about her, face pale and contorted in a fashion that reminded Donari of the moments her husband met his fate. Amongst the shouting, and rushing she stood there frozen, stunned by the sudden change. He lost her when more troopers rushed up to provide cover; the need to see to stabilizing the situation took all his attention. He found her later by accident when he visited the wounded. The face she raised to him was no less pale than before, but held a difference in the eyes; a more determined carriage as that of one who had faced down a bad memory and come out of the experience shaken but undeterred. Donari decided that, in finding her own way to be of use, Eleni had formed her own defiance of grief.

As time passed, Donari realized Eleni Caralon was more than just useful; she was essential. Her presence at first caused a few raised eyebrows from amongst the men, but after that first blooding they quickly accepted her. Her role as his secretary helped. What began as an empathetic gesture in Pevana progressed to something that felt natural and correct, even on the war-trail. A week into the hills, she began sharing moments at the fire with Senden and himself as they went over the day's events and plans for the morrow. By the time they reached their present position, she had become a fixture in the rhythm of the column.

Donari rode down the slope frustrated by how slow and helpless he felt. He took it upon himself to see to the horse lines and the trooper's comforts before giving thought to his own. Dark was spreading down the hill by the time he grabbed a camp chair and set it close to the fire. Senden sat there with his ailing leg stretched out. Eleni sat across the fire wrapped in a blanket. Donari grabbed a stick and practically threw it on the fire. The shower of sparks startled Eleni and brought a cynical laugh from Senden.

"That's it, punish the coals!" Senden barked, moving his leg out of the way of a glowing ember.

"I'd like to punish Roderran," Donari huffed, slumping back into his chair. "We crawl here, take losses, and to what purpose?"

"To bleed along with our people leading his columns?" Senden asked.

Donari followed Senden's question into the coals, searching for an answer amid the pulsing, glowing mass. Nothing came. Then Eleni spoke, quietly yet with growing conviction.

"The king is goading you," she said. "The bleeding is only part of it. He wants you to make a mistake."

The wisdom of her comment snapped Donari's attention, and he stared at her face, calm, bathed yellow-red by firelight, for a pregnant moment as he considered her suggestion.

"Mistake?"

"He still fears you, my lord. He doesn't fear what we march toward. You, he knows or thinks he knows. I watched him in council before we marched. Every time I would look up from my notes, I received the impression that no matter who the king addressed, half an eye was always concerned with you. You and Senden mentioned neglect back then, but I think otherwise."

"I know he doubts me. I have not been subtle."

"True, my lord," she replied. "But you have not yet grown desperate. He pushes you and our people, hoping you will do or say something that will justify a royal response."

"And you come by this, how?"

Eleni gestured to her bag of notes and papers hanging from her tent pole.

"From your gift to me, my lord. My studies. My record of these days. The soul of Pevana, as recorded by her poets, has always been somewhat independent. Perhaps too much so for types like Casan and the king to bear. Among the last bits I discovered were words from a noble mind with questions, concerns, attitude."

Donari froze like a charlatan exposed, thoughts spinning back along his own span to those days when he played at subterfuge with words.

"I wondered who that last poet was," Eleni whispered. "Now I know."

Donari experienced a thrill at her words, a release as in acceptance without cost of the truth.

"When?"

"Death opened my eyes, I think. Tomais. That poor trooper from that first attack and the other graves we've left behind on the way. Your face, lord, each time, such pain. Such anger."

"And what would you tell that poet?" he asked.

"Take the pain, have the patience Senden advises, and wait for Roderran to make his mistake first."

Donari shifted in his chair and realized she was right. During the course of their march the three of them seemed to find each other increasingly during the lulls between actions, sharing the solace of flames, processing notes, taking stock, a tri-partite weave of calm. But this time her words charged a different atmosphere. Donari looked at her with new eyes, traced the line of her jaw and the set of her lips as she returned his scrutiny. The firelight reflected in her eyes passed to and through him to burn away all pretense. For the space of a handful of heartbeats, Donari was no prince and Eleni no widow, but rather man and woman.

A bit of wood popping in the fine brought him back from the precipice, and he let the moment pass; but the residue, a disturbing confusion of duty and suppressed desire, remained.

Donari blinked, realized true dark had fallen. Senden stirred, further breaking the spell.

"I think I'll go check the sentries," he muttered, making shift to rise.

"No," Donari ordered, forestalling him. "I will see to it. I want you off your feet till morning at least." He tossed some more wood on the coals and rose with the flames.

"I will leave you to your notes, mistress. And thank you."

"For what, my lord?"

"For reminding me of someone I used to be. I miss that person. Good night."

Eleni stared at the prince's retreating form, thoughts awash with confusion and care. She glanced at Senden, but he had returned his attention to the magic of the coals and flames.

Questions. Suddenly. Questions.

She grabbed her pen and pad and began scratching away at the day's impressions. Divergent thoughts accompanied her writing, a collection of the objective and subjective that intertwined, wove back and forth like a cat through her legs, insistent, demanding attention. Frustration claimed her and she crumpled the page she had been working on, tossed it into the fire. The ink added a moment's blue tint to the flames before all fell to ash lifted by the heat to float away. The action brought her no peace; even with the evidence gone, thoughts remained. She brought her eyes back to the fire to see Senden looking at her over the dancing flames.

"That's rare," he said. "You are not one to waste paper. Bad thoughts?"

She shook her head. "Senden, I am lost."

Senden smiled kindly in the half-light. "And as you have always done, you chase words around the page to find your way?"

"Yes, but this time," she sighed, gestured at the fire, "this time nothing makes sense."

Senden rubbed his leg and chuckled. "Eleni, if anyone can make sense of any of these days, you can."

"But the prince, just before he left. . ."

"You can't remind a man of his basic humanity and expect no response. You asked me how I felt about him before. I only gave you half an answer. I love and follow Donari because of the man he is. And more than the princely circlet, the name, or the authority he wields, Donari is the man who wrote those lines you found in your research. He has a true spirit, lady, that the present trials threaten. You say you are lost; so is he."

"How can I help him?"

He laughed and stood. "Just being here among us helps, Eleni. You give us something other than death and mud to think about." He moved by her seat, placed a companionable hand on her shoulder. "You follow words to express how you feel, mistress, perhaps you should take a moment to feel first and let emotions find their own words."

He bent down and retrieved her pad from where she had dropped it in her frustration and held it out to her. "Feel. Follow. Fill it."

His words stunned Eleni. She felt him place the pad in her nerveless fingers and heard his halting gait fade away in the darkness. She stared at the fire. Flames danced before her; their heat leached beyond the walls of her fear and slowly untied the bonds she had placed on her emotions. She felt the strain leave her face; the muscles of her cheeks and neck relaxed. As if in response impressions of words began to well up like tears from deep within her, a wave of realization rushing upwards, raw, unintelligible, overwhelming. They swam before her like nuances of understanding and whispered to her mind's ear of permission long denied. She imagined watching herself dip the pen into the ink bottle and begin writing, and when the first marks appeared on the paper she returned, like a breath suspended, to herself, to follow the pen's progress and marvel at what she wrote:

You play upon me as a master plays the pipe
Unconscious joy
The intangibles of art
All jumbled in the runs along the stops.
Knowing yourself you play me
So I may find my way
To you.
I see you there
Regal in your intentions
Having a care
For my protestations
Of fear
Of coming too close
Too near
To you
To save myself.

In my darkness you are
The Harpist of Light
And you show me
How stars
Speak to us
Of Truth.
And like a youth
Lost and orphaned
By Fate's fatal blows
I am besieged
By questions
And buffeted
By destiny's winds
That rip the sails
Of my sanity

Abandoning me to
The ignorant vanity
Of my expectation
Of Love
From
You.

But if hope is eternal,
Ephemeral
And sublime,
Then I will trust you,
Harpist of Light,
To play me the way
To Hope and Grace
To one day
Touch
Your face

A tear splashing on the paper brought her out of her reverie, spent and bemused. The fire had died down to embers. She looked at her paper, saw the words she had placed there and understood the truth of them. She ran a finger down the pad, felt them, an echo of a spiritual presence with sentiments unalterable even were she to make a conscious effort to change them. Even if she threw the paper into the fire as she had done previous, the effect of the words would remain as a constant goad to her timidity and a call to risk life.

The glowing embers mesmerized her to sleep.

Donari returned with a few extra pieces of wood for the fire and noticed her there, slumped over in her chair, ink well, pen and pad forgotten on the ground next to her. He looked at her for long moments in the growing light as the faggots ignited. Nearly stupid with fatigue, bed called to him, but the fall of her hair and the line of her cheek held him. *The man I was.* Gently, tenderly he picked her up and took her over into her tent and laid her down on her cot, covering her with the cloak he had given her. She sighed once but did not awaken. He returned to the fire, gathered up her writing materials and looked around for her satchel. A gust of wind caused the fire to flame brighter, and he noticed the writing. He read the lines, looked back at her tent, and wept.

Chapter 21: Roderran and Demona

DEMONA'S BACK ACHED but she decided it ached a little less intensely than yesterday. Hours on horseback, regardless of the slow pace, still took their cost. The pain was as nothing compared to the dross that her life had been married to Sevire Anargi.

Oh, Sevire. She pursed her lips. Roderran's coldness regarding her husband's death reminded her more of the man himself than she liked. *I did it for you,* he had protested, and that did make her feel a little better. Combined with the freedom the end result gave her sparked her beyond recriminations, as well as a time of unrestrained passion between them. Demona buried any lingering guilt felt faster than the servants could inter Sevire's corpulent corpse. She had worn black for the day, and that had been enough.

More than Sevire deserved.

Roderran, for his part, kept her nicely occupied.

Life on the road with an army was unlike anything Demona might have imagined, if ever she might have imagined such a thing. So much energized manhood thrilled her, and she could not help likening the march to a sexual encounter. They met opposition as the host penetrated the hills, initially fierce but after a first push things eased considerably. Those first camps had been lively affairs as the companies adjusted to the change. No more training. Real blood. Real screams. The effect came to Demona through the fabric of Roderran's tent as a faint, orgasmic echo.

The rhythm of the march quickly settled down to a crawling pace, much to Demona's pleasure. Each day held just enough time ahorse, just enough new ground to observe and marvel over and a safe, early camp. Even through imperfect weather, she daily sloughed off the remains of her city-bred life, adjusting along with the army to her new pattern. The action certainly motivated Roderran's ingenuity. The man had interesting ideas of how one might otherwise use a saddle.

Eleni's caution about mud had been the only hardship Demona found almost too much to endure. There *was* mud. Everywhere. Copious amounts attached itself to her gear, coated the hemline of her skirts, weighed her down and made her feel grimy. But she had consoled herself quickly that mud dried and could be brushed away, unlike the unwanted attentions of a fat, sweating, brutish husband. Soon, it began to remind her of days long forgotten when one measured happiness by the amount of ooze one could squish between one's six-year-old toes. Mud had become an analogy, a manifestation of her deviant behavior as a Pevanese socialite. It washed easily, erotically away in her nightly soakings shared in the tub Roderran had ordered carted along for their use. Yes, Demona liked mud. She might even love it; though it did, now and then, make her think of Eleni Caralon.

They had not talked again after that chance hallway encounter, but Demona saw her several times accompanying Prince Donari to meetings prior to the march. She knew Eleni rode in Donari's company; and without the benefit of a kingly tub. Widows, the two of them; one in sorrow and one in joy. Eleni's loss had been true, deep. Small, nearly silent parts of Demona almost envied the woman's grief. Thankfully, such thoughts dissipated quickly in the face of her more immediate interactions. Roderran filled her in so many ways.

She trotted now several lengths behind the king as he finished his inspection of that night's perimeter. He seemed to draw strength from his horse and made his dispositions with a decisiveness that never failed to excite her. The sound of his voice snapping orders worked on her like a love bite; especially because she knew that when he finished there would be different orders directed at her.

Roderran drew rein finally before his tents and dismounted. The lords Reegan and Gaspire stayed mounted. Roderran took Demona into his arms and kissed her hard, holding her against him as he tossed off his orders to the two lords. "Wipe the grime off, gentlemen," he rasped. "Be back here when you are through."

To Demona he said, ""Bath. I left orders. It should be ready."

Demona wriggled in his arms, teasing him before disengaging. She turned to enter the tent but paused at the opening when Gaspire chuffed disdain.

"How long will you be, my lord?"

The hints of jealousy noticed first back in Pevana lingered in his half-cast glance her way. Demona returned his look boldly. Gaspire had long ceased to intimidate her; especially when she was around the king. Roderran laughed, scooped mud off his boot and threw it at Gaspire who sidled his horse to avoid it.

"Shut your mouth, Amdoran!" the king chortled. "I've seen the doxy you've got cutting your meat. Make sure she doesn't cut something else in your sleep! Back here in an hour."

Demona entered and let the tent-flap fall, slightly muffling the voices outside.

"Ouch!" Lord Reegan barked. "A hit there, Gaspire!"

"Shut it, Reegan, or I'll shut it for you."

"And waste your hour? Bad planning, that."

Roderran's voice interrupted them. "Both of you stifle and get going. I said an hour. No more. We have things to discuss."

"With her there?" Again, Gaspire's voice, and this time Demona felt a moment's unease.

"Mistress Demona will attend at her leisure, Amdoran. Besides, she's less apt to gossip than the trollop who listens to your nightly mutterings. Leave off. Next time I won't throw mud."

She hurried through the curtain separating Roderran's sleeping space from the rest of the tent, out of her clothes, and stepped into the steaming tub as Roderran entered. She made sure to slip into the water slowly, letting him see her. She liked the effect, for Roderran stopped, his second riding glove half-off, to watch the objects of his pleasure slip beneath the water.

"An hour?" Demona asked, sighing as she settled back, arms on the rim.

"Maybe we'll keep them waiting," Roderran husked. "It'll serve Gaspire right for getting testy."

"He doesn't like me."

"That is because, as you said back in Pevana, he wants you and cannot have you. You drive men to distraction, my dear."

"Do I distract you, my lord?"

"*Some* men," he amended. "Gaspire amuses me when you work him. That's one reason why I keep you close. He is all for a mad rush to battle in the south. He sees spies behind every tree. Doubtless he thinks you keep a notepad in your cleavage and messenger birds in your baggage."

"Can you be so sure I don't?"

Roderran finished pulling off the glove.

"Quite sure," he replied. "But there is always room for closer inspection."

Roderran removed the rest of his clothes, taking care to place them on a frame for drying. Demona found that habit an interesting contrast. In other things he seemed impulsive, like with her, but he took special care with his gear. Beneath the crown, outside of the man and lover, Roderran was first and foremost a warrior. He walked to the tub naked, and she returned his earlier scrutiny.

"Delicious," she cooed.

"As are you, my dear." He slipped in and reached for the brush. "Turns?"

From the look in Roderran's eye, Demona thought Gaspire and Reegan might be waiting quite awhile longer than that hour.

The light of candles serving as paperweights illuminated the large map Roderran unrolled on the table. Demona leaned forward to take a closer look. She had seen few maps in her time, and this one held special interest for her that likely differed from the king and the lords Gaspire and Reegan. To them, the map showed their progress through the hills and what they could expect if they met battle once they spilled down from the heights. Demona was interest mostly in how long this riding idle might last before things got really serious.

She ignored the scowl Gaspire gave her from across the table, smiled sweetly at Reegan and pointed to where the king had placed and apple core.

"So, my lord king," she said, pitching her voice at its most beguiling. "This is where we are, yes?" She ran a bejeweled finger down a foot-long inked line to where it ended next to a square with the words, *Gallina* next to it. "And this is where we are going? How nice! And you say there are mines there? How long will it take us? I'd love to see how a mine works."

Roderran took her hand in his, removed it from the table, kissed it and placed it softly back on the table out of the way. Gaspire coughed, his frustration obvious enough to satisfy her.

"We would be there in a week if we would stop inching our way along, my lord," he grumbled, waving his cup in company with his words. Wine sloshed over the rim to splash a red-purple stain next to a spot where three lines intersected.

"Patience!" Roderran snapped. "And have a care with that wine! It's my favorite. And wipe that stain away. This map came from some of Casan's missionaries. I'm told it is quite accurate, and I don't want your slops confusing things."

Gaspire drained what remained and placed the vessel, pointedly, at the end of the map on top a larger square marked *Desopolis*.

"The way there is clear, sire, and I'm sure Sylvanus will have plenty of wine waiting for us, *if we get there before he drinks all of it!*"

Roderran slammed both hands on the table and thrust his head forward. Demona saved one candle from over turning as the king raged at Gaspire.

"Do not bait me, my lord! You know my reasons! We want open battle! I do not want a siege!"

"But Casan's fleet—"

"Has managed to burn Teirne, but that is the last word we had! I do not want Heriopolis left to support Sylvanus. He is mine! Understand? Casan is to burn his way down the coast. I want Sylvanus out in the open. He won't be able to deal with Casan's force and our own at the same time."

Demona looked from face to face around the table. For a moment Gaspire held up against the king's ire, but rank and power won out in the end and he sat back down.

"So you have told us," he said, his tone just wide of sullen. "But how can we be sure?"

"Because I am going to burn Gallina and every hamlet south of it to draw him out. He will have to risk a battle. He won't know where Casan is, but the smoke we raise will tell him how close we are. I don't want a siege. Too messy. A siege for Sylvanus means defeat. He'll take the risk."

"So we traipse along."

"For another week."

"And Donari?" Lord Reegan asked.

Roderran sat back down with a satisfied expression. "And Prince Donari covers our left flank and bleeds, while his people clear our front and bleed, and so I exact payment on all accounts."

Gaspire smiled, and Demona thought it a cruel, wine-stained slit half hidden by the man's beard.

"And I thought for a moment there you had lost your nerve," he sneered. "Just what our cousin deserves, if you ask me."

"I did not ask," Roderran returned coldly. "And you have ridden the war trail with me long enough to know better than to think something like that. I never let anything go unaccounted for, not even slips of the tongue from my fief-lords. Remember that."

Demona wisely kept back in her seat, the tension palpable as the table fell silent. Lord Reegan broke the mood by reaching and pouring another measure into Gaspire's cup.

"Well now," he offered. "Seems like things are clear again. Drink up, Lord Amdoran, and try not to spill this time!" He poured likewise for Demona and the king before gesturing at the map.

"You say a week gets us to Gallina. Those will be easy marches then. If we have the time, I can see no reason to rush things. Let the Pevanese do our work for us. We will come to the field fresh and in good order. Does my lord have any other instructions?"

"Push out the Pevanese further down the trail tonight. Let them have a few cold camps. You remind me that I haven't exacted payment enough. Make sure word leaks out to our cousin. Let it trouble his mischievous little dreams for the next few days."

Demona let the king trace the fingers of her hand as he talked, and his motion and words made her question how she should feel. Those Roderran *bled* were her people, even if she had never really thought about being Pevanese. Hearing Donari disparaged, and his men calculated against so coldly did not seem right.

And yet his touch trumps all of that. It was his hand that freed me from Sevire and Pevana's walls.

Demona leaned deeper into her chair, shifted a little to calm a slight lurch in her stomach, and let her eyes wander along with her thoughts, to the map, to the stain of wine barely, yet still there at that crossroads, to the mine earlier mentioned. The men's voices washed over her, muted and garbled. If Donari was mentioned again, she did not notice.

The march progressed, the weather improved, the hills grew higher and then began to fall away as the host crested the low passes and began to filter into the uplands of the valley that ran down to the sea where Desopolis hugged the coast. Demona began to see graves alongside the track as she rode with the king's escort. The sight set off gurgling tremors in her gut. She began to sense a different sort of tension in the column as riders appeared from time to time on lathered horses. Demona overheard reports of increased pressure on the forward elements. Wagons of wounded dressed in Pevanese blue trundled by them on the way to the rear. Roderran waxed ebullient and irascible by degrees depending on the news he received. Demona quickly learned to check the look of the messengers that arrived. The ones that came from the west, from Gaspire, rode easily, delivered terse messages of progress and departed just as quickly. The ones from the east, from Donari, rode lathered horses, sported bloody bandages and delivered rushed information in aggrieved tones. The only word from the three main columns were those wagons of wounded.

Curiosity drove her to stop Roderran's cupbearer as he passed on an errand.

"Boy, what does all the rushing about mean? What news of the king?"

"We come close to Gallina," he said. "Lord Gaspire has flushed some archers from the heights to his flank. Lord Donari has crested the rises that lead down to Teirne and Heriopolis. There has been fighting there and to our front, weak resistance and easily pushed aside. The cowards fall back. These southerners make poor warriors."

"Poor? Then why these wagons of wounded men, and that line of graves under those trees?"

The boy's flush fell at her question. "This is war, lady, but the southerners won't face us. Most of our losses come from arrow fire in ambuscade and man traps set amid the trees. The king's ire grows as the Pevanese turn cautious. He has sent word forward to Avarran, the Pevanese captain to increase the pace now." The boy gestured to the graves. "I heard the king say those men fell because the Pevanese lack fire in their movements."

Demona recalled Roderran's comments to Gaspire and Reegan. *And so there is blood. My people die, but are they my people?*

The boy dashed off, and Demona straightened in the saddle, fingers tightening on the reins, the daydream of this war march falling fast to darker truths. She saw movement and death everywhere she looked. Young men she might have flirted with in the streets of Pevana now lay tucked in roadside graves; her own freedom bought with blood.

Her unease deepened through the day and into evening. She sent Dyna, one of the less objectionable camp followers whose aid she had enlisted, to look in on the little mare that Roderran chose for her use. Dyna was long in returning and the king was off with his aides, leaving Demona to her own impatient devices. A rumble of hooves outside, drove her to her feet and out the flap in hopes it was the king returned, but instead she found Lord Gaspire riding into camp, a small escort in tow. He drew up short before her. Demona had to step back to avoid his restive mount's hooves.

"Where is the King?" he demanded.

"He rode off with Reegan some time ago." Demona did not like Gaspire's look. It was even darker than usual. Baiting him was one of the things she took great pleasure in, but now, caution seemed the better choice.

"When will he return?"

"I don't know. He does not tell me everything."

"I find that hard to believe," he sneered, dismounting. "What with your assets so ready to hand. I'm sure more than sweat passes beneath the skins."

"You've an over-active imagination, my lord."

"And you are a strumpet far out of her station." Gaspire came closer, and Demona forced herself to stand her ground despite the sudden churning in her stomach.

"You forget yourself, my lord," she said, mustering her dignity. "The king will not be pleased."

Gaspire scoffed. "I know myself, lady, and you can tell the king what you like. In the end, your charms serve only a small purpose. What will you do when he grows tired of you? He needs my cavalry and my loyalty more than he needs your charms."

Despite his insults, the lust in Gaspire's eyes betrayed him. Demona relaxed. *I am not without my own weapons.* And yet the queasiness increased and she placed a hand involuntarily on her belly, motioning with the other to a servant standing near the tent opening.

"Wine for Lord Amdoran, please." She turned back, recovered. "You may wait, if you wish."

Gaspire handed his reigns to a dark faced trooper who looked vaguely familiar to Demona.

"Walk him a little," Gaspire barked. "And see to water and fodder for us. Find someone and send a wagon to our people. We need grain." His escort moved off. He took the cup the servant offered and drank deeply, draining it in one drought. "And I will wait." He returned the cup. "Set me up a chair by the fire there, fool, and bring me something to eat." He turned back to Demona. "Will you sit, mistress, and give me the *pleasure* of your company?"

227

"Much as that would please me, my lord, I think not." Demona stepped aside to allow him entrance. "I'm off to see to my horse. I find her better company than most these days."

Gaspire laughed as he ducked into the tent, murmuring words she chose to ignore.

Demona strode off to the horse lines, ignoring the dust that hung in the air, preferring it and her horse to Gaspire's derision. She found no sign of Dyna, but spent a precious few minutes gentling her mare. The beast's soft ruckling soothed her jumbled nerves, helped her ignore the twisting in her stomach, and gave her courage to return to her tent even if it meant facing Gaspire again. Trying to retrace her steps, she found herself passing between unfamiliar tents and came face to face with Dyna, pressed up against a wagon by the dark-faced trooper Gaspire had sent for grain.

". . .what else is a camp whore good for, eh? And I haven't had a woman since Pevana."

"Leave off me!"

"I'll be quick if you'd just shut your mouth and. . ."

"Stop it this instant!" Demona snapped. "Get your hands off my maid, fool!"

The man did not startle. He barely turned his head to the sound of her voice. Even at a distance, she could smell the wine on his breath. He let off his fumbling with Dyna's skirts but kept his grip on her.

"Well then," he sneered. "If it isn't the merry widow."

"I said let her go."

"Or?"

"Or I will have a word with Lord Amdoran."

"Tell him whatever you like. He is not who I answer to."

"Then perhaps I should go straight to the king."

The man snarled and thrust Dyna away from him. She crumpled to the ground, whimpering. Demona stepped forward to help her to her feet. Dyna had bruises already beginning to redden on her arms and what looked like teeth marks on one cheek. Her bodice had a broken tie as though she had been grabbed harshly from behind. Demona put Dyna behind her, but the string of oaths she summoned died stillborn, quelled by the off look in the man's eyes. She backed away a step, stomach clenching. *That face. I know that face.*

The man came close, a cruel sneer slipping over his features.

"Tell the king he owes me for services already rendered, and cold camps with an ungenerous master is no proper payment. In fact, the way I figure it you owe me something yourself, Mistress *Anargi*." The way he emphasized her name sent a chill down Demona's spine.

"I owe you nothing, cur, but I will make you answer for this insolence."

The man raised a hand menacingly as though to strike her. Demona recoiled and Dyna whimpered behind her shoulder. The man laughed coldly, dropped his hand.

"*Insolence*," he mocked. "Careful, bitch, or I will give *you* the same *answer* I gave your husband." The man backed away, still laughing. "Service, lady, only service! That's all anyone ever requires of Jaryd Corvale. No thanks, no, never that, just orders and proud words from cunts like you. Keep your scrawny slut, bitch. I'm done with this mess. I've another *service* left it seems, and I'm done waiting to perform it. Tell Lord Amdoran or the king what you like. I'm off."

He turned on his heel, gathered up the reins of his horse tethered on the wagon trace, mounted and swept off, showering the two women with dirt and dust. The shock of the moment settled again in Demona's stomach as she struggled to calm herself and Dyna.

Corvale. Pevana. The banquet. That dark face next to the Lord Prelate. The finals. That voice in the palace.

Comprehension flooded over her like ill water released all at once from a dam.

Sevire!

A sudden remorse, combined with a tenfold rise in her queasiness bent her vomiting over a wagon wheel. She had felt almost nothing for her husband's death—until she came face to face with his killer. Her gut clenched again, a deeper, primal wrench that set spots dancing before her eyes. She emptied herself, expelling memory, present fear and rage all in the same motion.

Sevire. And as his name rose unbidden to her mind she recalled similar pains, once, long ago, before she grew brave enough to seek precautions. Her stomach rebelled a third time, burning bile, burning certainty, burning change. She hung on desperately to the wheel, fought to right her senses, did a fast calculation as the nausea receded. She felt Dyna's hands on her shoulders helping her to straighten.

First horror, then hope.

"Are you unwell, mistress?" Dyna asked.

"Renia's Grace," Demona whispered. "I'm pregnant."

Chapter 22: Two Moments of Crisis

SYLVANUS TAMORGEN SAT HIS HORSE stoically as the last of the nearly two thousand spearmen marched out the land gate of the city. Even as he acknowledged the salutes of his men, Sylvanus's thoughts winged northwards to consider Devyn Ambrose's location, now three days into his desperate mission. Sylvanus urged his mount to a canter and doubled the column, and with each pounding length his doubts grew. By the time he reached the column's head his mood had turned bleak, despite the sun that shone down on his banner and the martial pride of his domain.

If Devyn failed, if Sylvanus's gambit with Prince Donari Avedun of Pevana played out ill, then he marched his people and himself to bitter defeat and futile death. He did not worry overmuch for himself, but he grieved for his people and especially his daughter. She deserved so much more than her life had given her. He conjured an image of her when they parted, standing next to Talyior at the top of the palace steps. Pride and fear, unwept tears and strength roiled her expression. Sylvanus knew in that moment he had left off acknowledging her for far too long. Policy had kept them strangers in many ways. Though he acted now out of love for her and the future she symbolized, that did not make the parting any less bitter.

As he plodded along with his escort, he thought also of Talyior. Newcomer, almost a stranger, he had returned Sylvanus's farewells with a mix of hope and curiosity. His status as a pawn, and the intense affection he bore Lyvia conflicted him in ways that showed in his expression, in his movements, whether he knew it or not. Sylvanus had not overlooked the possessive, almost taunting way the poet's arm draped Lyvia's shoulders as he waved that farewell.

Young love.

231

The notion nudged at the bleakness. He had loved once, lost and found the progeny of that love, and now marched under a double purpose. His city deserved a chance at peace, and his daughter and her new young man deserved a chance at love. He tested a word then, mouthed it silently around his tongue, *grandfather*. He liked the shape of it in his mind, and wondered how it would sound if he were granted the grace to say it aloud.

His horse clattered over a bridge that spanned one of the tributary streams that fed the Lyranden, and the sound jarred Sylvanus into the present. He looked back down the column and the road behind. Desopolis now lay hidden by a fold in the hills. The sea lingered as a blue line against the horizon.

Such risk I take, and leave my daughter to bear the price.

There would surely come a seaborne attack; all reports and rumors pointed to it. But to stay behind walls invited certain defeat. And the thought of defeat brought the bleakness flooding back, dispersing all colors of fond hopes and dreams of the future, replacing them with an internal coverlet of gray tinged with black and rumors of the indefinite.

Sylvanus grabbed the pommel of his sword, looking for something solid with which to dispel his dark mood, but even the well oiled metal, polished to rival the spring sun above, failed. He set his horse to pace on, riding into ill humor and a battle he knew he could not win.

The only illusions Sylvanus kept were the ones that let him hide his growing dismay from his people as the need to arm and organize grew more acute. The tone of the missives Roderran sent turned aggressive several years ago, prompting Sylvanus to send men north to listen at tavern benches and beneath windows. And then the red tide of reform swept down the coast burning temples and spawning irritating missionary groups. The signs all pointed to invasion. The restive north needed to express its will on the sleepy south, and so Sylvanus lied and trained his few to contest as they could against the many.

He walked among them each night when they made camp beside the river, playing the role of the confident, determined leader. He found the deceit dismayingly easy; the habits and craft of thirty year's rule slipping into his manner like an actor's mask. He told himself it did not matter much in the end, these last little lies. If Devyn failed, they would all die anyway. No one would be left to sing of them in the fashion of the Old Ways. Glory in defeat only happened if some identity of the vanquished remained to recall. That was the real lesson in the flames of Pevana last summer. There would be no glory here with a northern victory; there would be change irrevocable, an end to familiar things.

Great gambits required great sacrifice, and so Sylvanus walked among his men, touching, laughing, saluting, and silently offering them and himself up for the wager.

The smoke of burning Teirne and Heriopolis framed their fifth day's march, affecting the mood in the ranks. Sylvanus chose to ignore the signs and kept them going at a tiring pace, keeping them too busy cursing his hurry to consider the evil in those twin portents. It worked until the afternoon, when an additional pillar of smoke rose in the hills to their front. Gallina burned. However small and backward, Gallina was theirs and they reacted to its loss. Sylvanus expected anger, some dismay, but he confessed himself surprised by the stiffening resolve.

His men marched faster.

The refugees met them in the afternoon.

Fear-strained faces clustered about Sylvanus and his officers. Many asked for succor, others for revenge, a few asked for weapons. One who passed for their leader, an aging miner with wild, white hair and the still impressive remains of a blacksmith's forearms, spoke of a small force determined to defend the main hill town of Gallina.

"The fools there would not leave," he grated, holding on to Sylvanus's stirrup. "Wooden walls, a few spears. They stood no chance."

"But they were brave," Sylvanus responded. "They may have delayed them." The lie tasted bitter as he spoke, for he had sent those men there, the only sizable group he had committed to the highlands to harry and entice Roderran out from the hills. Sylvanus wanted some flames and wounds there at the apex to at least give the appearance of stiffening resistance.

"They died, and the town still burned. What good was that, my lord?" The old miner let go Sylvanus's stirrup with a dismissive gesture. "What good was any of it?"

Sylvanus let the stream of people ease the old miner away. He forced himself to look at faces as they passed. The sadness and destitution, the fear and the panic he saw made him feel older with every northward step his horse took even though he had held age at bay far longer than other men. He let a small sigh escape, recalling awakening tired that morning, a dispiriting revelation of mortality.

On the tenth day out from Desopolis, his army reached a place where the valley narrowed between a wood buttressed by small hills, mere bumps thrust out in some ancient time from the ridges that framed the land. They were not imposing rises, but they broke the sweep of the valley and provided his army a small chance to control an enemy massed to their front. They did not, however, provide protection from cavalry; especially it they were attacked from both flanks. Sylvanus had got to where he needed to be. When he retired to his tents to sleep after setting his men digging, he thought of his daughter, but his final thoughts went out to Devyn along with a prayer.

Renia, grant your grace, and more than grace—luck.

Devyn held his horse's nose to keep it silent as the file of archers passed below him. This was the third such group he had encountered on his northward trek. Mindful of Sylvanus's warning, the need to avoid contact with anyone until he found Donari slowed Devyn's pace, and he feared he lost too much time trying to work his away around the forces Sylvanus set in motion. He tried to keep to the upper reaches of the ridge slopes, skirting along at line where forest gave way to rock, but ravines and scree periodically cut the largely trackless way. He often had to double back to find a way around, and in those times he had to move to his left, down-slope, to pick his way carefully to keep from running up against Sylvanus's bands.

He stood now screened by undergrowth, watching the group he let pass make camp. The western hills had already pierced the sun's orb, throwing the valley floor into lengthening shadows. Up there on the eastern slopes, the light loitered. Devyn contemplated moving on, the need now to find and convince Prince Donari of Sylvanus's intention a constant thrum, and yet he knew he lacked information. He backed away carefully and made his way back up hill to where he left his horse hobbled and tied to a low branch. He checked his knots, made sure there were oats within reach and settled himself against a tree trunk to wait for nightfall. The sun, once pierced, plunged quickly beyond the horizon and soon the light began to fail altogether. From below his hiding place, sounds of men taking their ease filtered up through the trees along with the smell of meat roasting on spits. After a week's worth of cold fare and forced solitude, the sounds and smells drew at him and reminded him of the friend he missed and the absurdity of the task he so willingly accepted.

The idea of missing Talyior surprised him. A year ago, he laughed at loneliness as only a survivor of the Maze could. But all that changed over a chance meeting and three days of adventure. Now he realized how much he depended on Talyior's cheerful nature to balance his own darkness. He grinned at his own admission and counted himself lucky; the orphan often had to take what sense of family he could find. Part of him envied Talyior his new attraction for Sylvanus's daughter, and he decided Lyvia was probably a match for his friend. He looked up and spied the first star winking at him, communicating some celestial knowledge he accepted with a soft, silent chuckle.

"Ah, there it is," he whispered. "I am still the orphan. Alone, I am called. Talyior needed to stay. I'm still wandering the Maze."

He fell silent, testing the sounds below as they quieted. He laid aside his sword and unlaced his spurs.

"And the only way out of it is forward."

He took off his cloak and hat and slipped down slope like an elemental, as silent as the exhalation of time. He slithered in between the watchers and crept to within earshot of one of the fires.

"We are close. Probably no more fires after tonight."

"The boys won't like it."

"They don't have to. Let them get a little hot over it; they'll fight better."

Devyn froze. In the firelight, two figures were talking and Devyn took them for officers taking their ease before retiring. He closed his eyes for concentration and calmed his breathing to better hear their words.

"No word from Desopolis since we were sent out," groused one of them.

"And not likely to get any now, either," said the other.

"Asten came back this afternoon. The others are in place."

"And about time, too, the northerners are getting closer. We should link up tomorrow as planned. Maybe we can sting them."

"Pinpricks and run away. When I was down with Tarley yesterday, he said their host had almost cleared the hills before Gallina. It's vast. We will need to do more than sting our bunch."

"Tarley is an old woman. I wouldn't waste my time listening to him."

"I didn't. I listened to the wagon of wounded I met on the road back. The rest of their fellows stayed behind in Gallina."

"This is a bad business. Bastards."

"Sylvanus is coming behind. We will cross them yet. Let us do our part, at least."

"Yes, we can do that, at least. Asten said the Pevanese have moved down ahead of the main force. If we make good time tomorrow, I know of a place where we can take their lead groups."

"Yes! I know the place! That might work. I'll roust the boys early. We'll have to push it hard."

"I'll send word to Tarley before first light. With both of us there, we might have an easier time of it. You're sure we can make it?"

"Absolutely, we can be there by mid-morning, get set, and take them with the sun at our backs. It's perfect."

"Then it is off to the blankets for us then. Wake me when you change the watch."

Devyn opened his eyes and took a deeper, tentative breath. As he suspected, he was close. If he were to win through, it would have to be tomorrow. He eased back away from the camp and made his way back uphill. The night grew chill, but the words he overheard struck that chill even deeper. Prince Donari faced ambush by the next afternoon, but Devyn could do next to nothing about it. Almost everything depended on timing. He cursed under his breath as he gathered his things and freed his mount. Of all the actors in this nightmare play, he was the one who knew the most but faced the crisis of having to do the least.

He walked his horse, not trusting the terrain in the dark, and turned his curses partly back on Sylvanus himself. The closer Devyn got to the looming conflict, the more lives he saw advancing innocently to their deaths. The whole thing was a cruel, cruel game with too many moral ambiguities for comfort. None of it was fair to any of the players. Devyn began to understand how much the affair cost Sylvanus.

Despite leaving early, Devyn chose not to risk the path the southern archers used. By mid-morning they caught up with him and he paced himself parallel with them as best he could over the rough ground. He crested a small rise and risked being skylined to get a decent look at the lands about him. The valley spread out below, bisected by the Lyranden River. Southwards, he made out the serpentine line of Sylvanus's march. The sun glinted off spear heads and shields creating the illusion that a host of diamonds rather than too few men marching northward. Devyn followed the line of the road to where it passed between two small ridges that swelled into the valley from the east and west ranges. The land narrowed there, and just on the edge of sight a bridge spanned the channel. Devyn remembered crossing that bridge less than a day's ride from Gallina.

He smelled the smoke before he saw it. North, and west, plumes reaching skyward from the coast. Teirne and Heriopolis were burning. Battle in earnest had commenced inland and on the coast. Devyn froze. Images of Kembril, Corvale, Donari, Talyior and the mysterious Senden Arolli swam through his thoughts, wove in between the smoke plumes and the progress of Sylvanus's column to knit a weird tartan of intention.

No time. No choice.

The rhythm of his poem last summer in Pevana came back to him; a first throw in a crazed dice game with Fate. Then he had felt words would be enough, an eloquent protest against the rising dark, but now he understood otherwise. It was not enough just to protest if those against whom one protested ignored it. Sometimes something more was required, something definite and committed. Kembril knew it then and still allowed Devyn his youthful invective and dalliance with the power in art. But war demanded weapons more physical, real risk to spice the gods to pay attention. One had to act to give the grace to one's thoughts. To try. To die, maybe. Nothing less would suffice. Words that had run through his head crystallized to the rhythm of his horse's pace, and like a final grace before the plunge into chaos, they formed themselves into lines that he whispered to the world:

At the mid-point between night and day
Spinning black and white into grey
The poet searches in his lonely way
For the most compelling words to say
To move the world to rise above
The debris that's the product of
Too many lies, not enough love;
Too much the hawk and not the dove.
Caught between the councilor and clown
Amid caustic words and alliances down
The poor weep with hardly a sound
For justice rarely wears a crown.

He took the thrill he felt along his neck as a spiritual stroke from Kembril. He ran them over again in his mind, committing them to memory, vowing one day, if he survived the storm, to give them the voice and music they deserved.

He came back to himself, aware of his exposure on the slope.

"Justice, what a farce," he muttered, spurring on to get under better cover. "The only way to get any is to see this thing through." The ground before him leveled for a space. He urged his horse to more speed, committed, now, like never before. *Ready or not, Prince Donari, here I come.*

Chapter 23: Desopolis: Hope Besieged

LYVIA SAT UNEASILY in her father's chair, flanked by Ergan and Talyior, and scowled at the group of old men arrayed before her; all that remained of the city council. Several had marched with Sylvanus, others had chosen to flee once word came clear of the threats the city faced. Those who remained were a mix of the loyal, old and avaricious. She surveyed them now and felt certain she could count at least several who sought to take advantage of her father's absence and the time's disjoint. She wondered how many of them had already tried to communicate with the enemy fleet that had burned Teirne and rumor said neared Heriopolis.

Ships sailed fully laden with stored goods, several of the great houses on the slope above the harbor now stood empty, their owners seeking the questionable safety of the sea in an effort to avoid what they saw coming. The cowards took with them their personal galleys that Sylvanus had counted on for part of the city's defenses. Lyvia had been powerless to stop them. The flood of departure began as soon as Sylvanus's column passed from view. Many folk took what they could and marched out the land gate heading for dubious sanctuary in the hills westward. Folk spoke of trying to make it to Eadne farther down the coast. Lyvia thought them foolish. The way was hard, the people unguarded, and Eadne was still connected to the sea. If Desopolis fell, they would find no peace in Eadne.

"Lady Lyvia, if you please." Jorian Malri, a balding septuagenarian and one of the city's leading shipping magnates stepped forward, urged by his comrades. Most of the man's ships were now coasting west and south out of harm's way.

"Speak, Malri." *Before I have you beheaded. Or whipped. Or at least pilloried.*

"We ask you to consider what we are to do. Lord Sylvanus gone. You recognized so quickly, and though we rejoice at your fortune, you can hardly expect us to accept you without question."

Lyvia almost snorted her derision. "Really? I know you are old, Jorian, but surely you cannot be surprised at my father's actions. You've known me and my parentage. Your grandson made a play for my favors when I was still a child. And you have *questions?* I have *questions* of my own, sir. Where are your galleys? Surely, one with your experience would understand that a coastal city's best defense is the ships she can man and send out to confront her enemies?"

Jorian bridled under her attack, waved his hands in frustration and made a feeble remonstrance. "My lady, you must understand, so much confusion, sudden orders, how—"

"I understand that my father left me as regent to defend this city and hours after he marches half of your brothers left. Again, where are your ships, sir?"

"I had to think of my goods, mistress."

"Regent. When I was a bastard, I was *mistress*. Now I am *Lady Tamorgen*. See that you and your fellows behind you remember that. And where do you think you will sell your goods if this city falls? Have you no loyalty? Those missing seem to have made their choice. How will you choose? Our people need us, sir. Some of you have sons marching with my father. What will you? We must make a defense here to keep something for our men to come home to."

The older man's defiance wilted under her attack, and by the time she finished he was nodding as though satisfied of what he had heard. He looked to his fellows to include them in his response. Grey and balding heads bobbed up and down, singularly and in groups as the crisis passed.

"My lady, I cannot speak for those now gone. But we here see our place. Command us."

Lyvia took up a paper, scanned it quickly and shoved it across the table to Jorian Malri. "Check this, please, for accuracy." As the man read what was on it, she addressed the rest. "Malri has a list of those now gone, let it be known that all are now outlawed and banished from Desopolis. All those families owned is now claimed by the city."

Malri coughed, breaking her rhythm. "My Lady?" he asked. "This last name."

"There is no mistake, Malri."

"But my sister's family?"

Lyvia included all of them in her sweeping response. "House Megare, as Malri has pointed out, was among the first to flee. Recent events—" and she glanced at Talyior, "—have implicated them with northern elements."

"And this young man with you, with his northern voice, as rumor puts it," Malri asked. "What is his role in this?"

Lyvia kept her eyes fixed on her questioner. "He and his friend, since you seem to know so much, have come with warning. They serve." She leaned forward, thrusting the full force of her personality at her listeners. "Gentlemen! Such times as we face require all to make choices. My father has chosen to fight; we can do no less. You ask for my command: stand. We've force left in the city to man the walls at need. Prepare as best you can with food and supplies at need. Our sister cities to the west and north are burned or at risk. You *cannot* shirk here. Flight is no surety. Our city, our faith, our people require courage . Grant me all you have, or else I will have Ergan take it."

That left them mumbling as they retreated from the hall. Lyvia did not like the sound of her own voice, but she knew what she requested of them was the right thing to do. They had to hold the city if they could. Her father's great risk, callous on the surface, required she maintain the theater. Men would die. Life would change. Now, as never before, she understood the cost of rule her father had borne for thirty years. The week in his place left her exhausted and gasping, terse and terrified beneath her bravado. As she rose to leave, she reached for Talyior's hand, finding something there of warmth and solidity.

So new, those feelings, and yet maybe they were the only things worth fighting for. If all else lay subject to chance, maybe love provided the only viable reason.

She dismissed Ergan to set about collecting what shipping still remained in the harbor and to find weapons and orders for what levies her tirade might produce. She and Talyior walked together down the hall to their rooms.

"Thank you," Lyvia said, giving his hand a slight squeeze.

"For what?"

"For not running away." His answering pressure reassured her.

"Well, I am a hostage."

She turned, reached up and kissed him. "And if you were free?"

"I think I'd still stay. Although seeing you in there just now, makes me wonder."

She wrapped her arm in his and continued down the hall.

"I'm sorry. That was necessary, but I didn't enjoy it much."

"Liar."

She laughed. "Fine! I did, a little. They've been pestering me all week, testing me. None of them would ever question my father. I needed to show them I mean to rule. If we survive all this, I will have to. Still want to stay?"

"Like I said, I am a hostage, in more ways than one. You are amazing, Lyvia, and you scare me, but I'm done with running away. Sitting there today, watching them snivel at you and stare at me, I realized Devyn was right. We have been running since last summer. I've been running since before I went to Pevana; away from family, my fears, from making any real decisions about the kind of man I want to be. Those old men don't frighten me as much as the thought of losing whatever this is between you and me."

"What is this between us, do you think?"

He surprised her by kissing her in turn. "We can lie about it if we wish," he whispered. "But I'd rather not, even though I know I'm out of my depth."

"Time," she started. "I wish—"

"Doesn't really matter now," he finished.

She kissed him again and this time let her lips linger against his, drawing and giving power by degrees, mindful of the tasks that awaited her but unwilling to break this moment, this indefinable, true moment, perhaps the first such moment in her life. She kissed him again and found all the answers she needed.

The first refugees from Heriopolis began arriving the next day. Lyvia and Talyior took a carriage down to the harbor battlements and stood watching a ragtag flotilla under sail or creeping under oars struggle to clear the headland. Folk had spied smoke rising in the distance a few days before, and that led them to expect the collection of craft that bobbed and beat its way into the inner harbor. Once those first reached shore, word spread like wild fire. Perspan forces led by the Lord Prelate Byrnard Casan had sacked and burned both cities, sweeping away the defenses easily before falling to raping and pillaging, slaughtering thousands. The few who managed to get away gathered around Lyvia and her escort, begging for sanctuary. Lyvia listened, appalled at what she heard and spoke with a quiet assurance that worked magic on the haggard mob. Most had fled with nothing but their lives; they were exhausted, famished and terrified. Lyvia calmed them and ordered servants from the various temples to take them in charge. They formed a forlorn column several hundred strong as they trudged off toward the succor offered by the religious way-houses

"Those poor people!" she said, in a mixture of empathy and anger. "None of them were warriors. Women, children, helpless, how they managed to get their craft here at all is a miracle. I can't imagine. The flames, the fighting. . ."

Lyvia bit her lip to silence her own voice. She looked sidelong at Talyior, who had seen a city in flames before. The blazing Maze burned away part of Pevana's soul; perhaps a part of his. Only a sudden downpour had saved the rest.

"People do what they must in order to survive," he responded at last. "They always will."

Lyvia started to reach for him, but her attention was taken by a man who had been securing one of the boats and missed leaving with the others. He limped toward them—older, grey hair in his temples, his skin tanned and leathery, the deep wrinkles on his face partially obscured by an eye patch and its attendant bindings. As the man drew near, Talyior stiffened beside her. She glanced over, took in the sudden pallor, and stared anew at the man drawing closer.

"What is it?" she asked.

"An old, old friend," he murmured, "bringing with him an old, old life."

"Talyior, lad?" the man wheezed, stopping before them and reaching up a hand in tentative greeting. "Is that you?"

"Espan! Renia's Grace, Espan!" Talyior choked, stepping forward to embrace the old man. Lyvia stood stunned, questions forming on her lips that Talyior forestalled by turning and presenting the old man to her.

"Lyvia Tamorgen. This is Espan Gale, my father's head foreman."

Lyvia stared in wonder and concern as the old man, sagging against Talyior, sketched an attempted bow.

"Lady Tamorgen," he said, and Lyvia could hear the exhaustion in his voice.

Lyvia nodded acceptance of the courtesy and moved to help Talyior.

"Espan," Talyior asked quietly. "How do you come here, now, in this fashion? Why aren't you with my father? No, wait. Let's get you settled first."

Together Lyvia and Talyior assisted Espan down the pier to the carriage. As they rode back up to the palace, Talyior supported the older man with an arm around his shoulders. He turned a pale, stricken face to Lyvia.

"So thin," he said to her. "I remember him with broad, muscular shoulders gained from heaving heavy carpet rolls about. Now, his shoulder blades cut through the cloth under my hand. Espan," he asked quietly. "What has happened to you?"

"Ah, now, this is much, much better, lad, than bobbing about in a skiff with frightened, ignorant folk." He sighed and let his head fallback. "It was all I could do to keep us from sinking."

"Did you come from Heliopolis?" Lyvia asked.

"I wasn't in the city when they stormed it, lady. I was just down the coast looking into some potential cargo. I heard they attacked Teirne and Heriopolis at the same time. I saw some of Sevire's ships in the group that pushed into the harbor. They were full of King Roderran's men. They overwhelmed the city's guard on the quay. And when they finished there, the real killing began. I snuck in through the gates in the chaos."

"Risky," Talyior murmured.

"I had mates in there."

"Why were you there?" Talyior pressed. "I don't recall my father having business this far south down the coast."

Lyvai saw Espan stiffen, close his eyes, and take a deep breath and hold it for a moment before letting it go in a long, tired wheeze.

"Oh, lad," he whispered. "I don't know how to tell you."

"Tell me what? Why were you there? Why weren't you with your ship?"

"My ship . . . ha . . . I have no ship. In fact, I was looking for a new ship when the city was attacked."

"What do you mean?"

"When I left you, that day, you never returned home. I heard about it later. Pretty bold boy. I have to admit. I didn't know you had it in you."

"What about home?" Talyior continued. Lyvia heard a different tone in his voice then, fearful, angry. "No, I never went back, didn't see the need, considering he cut me off, remember? What are you trying not to tell me?"

Espan pinched his eyes shut and cleared his throat before continuing. "Lad, Talyior. I'm sorry, but your father is dead, and your mother and sister, all of them. Fire. I sailed in to the harbor at Hallar Port while the smoke was still rising. That was back in early October."

Lyvia watched what color remained in Talyior's face drain away at the news. He stared forward, his expression awash in conflicting emotions.

"Talyior, what—" Lyvia began.

"I did not part well with my father when I left," Talyior explained. "But I always intended to return home, successful and matured, to make amends. Home," he choked and blinked back tears. "And now it seems I've been homeless and an orphan for five months. I should have gone back."

"Don't blame yourself, lad," Espan wheezed. "It wouldn't have made any difference."

"I'm not blaming myself," Talyior said. "But I could have at least buried them."

"I saw to it."

"My father's holdings?"

"Stuff in Pevana also went up in flames. The ships? All claimed by the crown. In fact, one of them was in the bunch that took Heliopolis."

Tears teased Lyvia's eyes. "I'm so sorry, Talyior." She reached out a hand to touch his knee, felt there the tension she saw griping his jaw. He looked at her, lips pursed, eyes beginning to flame. He removed his arm from around Espan, stared straight ahead, breath quickening.

"So, then," he said, his voice gathering force as anger welled up inside him. "My family, our business, our ships, all those *events*." And as he said the word he nearly spat with fury. "All of them were no accident. Yes?"

Espan groaned, nodded his head. "No accident, none of them."

"Right. Murder and theft, then. Who?" Talyior's voice grew cold as grief and wrath warred for control. Again, the change alarmed Lyvia and she sat back, waiting for it.

"Who do you think?" Espan responded.

"Sevire Anargi?"

Espan nodded his head again. Then, his news delivered, weakness took him and he slumped further.

"Yes," he rasped, his voice betraying his hurt and anger. "Sevire, who else, at least for the Pevana fire. Bastard. Your parents, sister, his work, too, I think."

Lyvia's own tears came then to match the old man's that now wetted Talyior's shoulder. Lyvia understood grief suspended, the cost of long silence; that had been her own life up until a week ago.

"No, Espan. This is my fault, all of it. Father, mother, little Kendry. My sister," he said to Lyvia by way of explanation. "Sevire Anargi had them all killed to avenge his embarrassment. The affair with Demona. I practically killed my family with my selfish behavior." He stared forward then, and Lyvia could only imagine the connections he made. A dark look passed over his face as though he had found a way to bundle his rage and grief into a tight little package. When he spoke, his words communicated purpose.

"I'll kill him," he said tight-lipped. "I'll walk right into his house and slice him slowly, carefully, into a thousand little pieces, and I'll save his heart for last."

"No need," interrupted Espan.

"What do you mean *no need*?"

"He's already dead. Killed at table. It is said he choked on some bread just before the fleet sailed south about three weeks ago. And what's more, Demona's gone off with the king."

"What?"

"It's true, the tart left Sevire when the king showed up in Pevana. Spent the whole time before this mess began in the palace. You've been outdone, lad."

Lyvia looked closely at Talyior to gauge his reaction. She had spent her whole life privy to the connections and intrigues of power. Espan's off-hand account made a pattern for her: dalliance, wealth, power. It seemed death followed this Demona like a shadow. She could tell Talyior did not make the same connection. Once again, she found herself drawn to his unusual innocence. The world around him plotted, lied, manipulated, and yet he took himself to task for things gone way beyond his control. Despite his sorrow, she found herself smiling a little, for he truly was the first honest man she had ever known.

The carriage trundled up the slope to the palace. Espan, his ill news delivered, sagged into half consciousness against Talyior's shoulder. Talyior stared out at the passing streets, silent and fuming. Lyvia wisely held her tongue.

By the time they reached the palace courtyard, a darkness had settled over Talyior's brow. The hand that helped her down had a different feel to it than from before. Tense. Suppressed. But his voice came strangely calm.

"So be it," he vowed. "Revenge on Sevire might be denied me, but there are others. I see it now, how things connect. Devyn saw it sooner. Sevire, Roderran, Casan, string pullers. Filth, all of them. I'll make them pay." He kissed Lyvia's hand. "By living."

Servants came and carried Espan inside and placed him in bed. Lyvia led him to his chambers where he cast himself onto the bed half swooning in sorrow. She sat by his side until sleep finally claimed him. Ergan came to get her with news from the refugees that supported Espan's tale.

The refugees brought the conflict surging behind them. Watchers on the headland sent word the topmasts of the Perspan fleet were visible on the horizon. War had come to Desopolis, and Lyvia would have to help Ergan see to its defense.

Chapter 24: Battle and Betrayal. . .

EMONA'S QUEASINESS SUBSIDED by the time the king returned to his tents. She made a gallant effort to maintain a cheerful, accustomed face and manor despite her uneasiness. She knew the signs; she had made sure to lose the two babies Sevire managed to start in her early on in their marriage. Thereafter she always took pains to send a trusted servant to find the necessary herbs. In the rush of attaching herself to Roderran, she forgot about those precautions, and she existed moment by moment now unsure how he would react if she told him. It was still early, but already she could feel her body changing, fear and joy at war within.

To bear a king's child, maybe even a son. . .

The thrill working through her equally at odds, Demona's thoughts leapt to the future. The king made no secret of dismissing the Queen, and everyone knew it was because she could not bear; there was even talk that she had recently lost yet another, sparking Roderran's ire and sending him off to make war to assuage his manhood. If Demona were to bring the child to term, Roderran would be pleased, grateful, proud. She would have honor, status, power, perhaps even a crown. The possibilities spread before her like a laden banquet table. These thoughts made her feel different. She checked herself in a hand-mirror, positive she *looked* different.

Sevire never noticed, thank Renia. But will Roderran? Do I want him to?

He did not that day, or the next; midway through a late night rumble in the skins later that night, when Demona hung at fever-point of pleasure, as Roderran thrust away, he halted abruptly and brought his face down close to hers.

"What is it?" he demanded, and Demona recoiled inwardly at his tone even as she sought a return to the rhythm they had been making.

"What is what?"

"Don't evade, Demona. I don't think that is your strongest talent."

"What do you mean, my lord?"

"And don't call me *my lord* in bed. We are past that, you and I."

"I'm still not sure what you ask, my lor—"

"You're different."

"Well, Dyna found some early flowers and put the sepals and petals in my bath water this afternoon."

Roderran laughed. "No! Woman, no flower can mask what I am smelling. I've got your scent, my dear, and this *feels* different."

Demona let her hands fall away from the king's back, mind racing.

"I'm sorry, my lord. I don't know what to say."

"How about the truth? I realize I am king, supposedly blind to anything but my own needs. Most of the time I am and happily so, but, woman, you've swamped me since I first held your hand in that gate square. How long now? Two months?"

"And a little more."

She watched his face slacken in thought, the glow from the brazier near their sleeping place giving his eyes an eldritch, red cast. Hope and fear contested in her womb, waiting. Then his eyes cleared to look deeply into her eyes.

"And a little *more?*" he asked. "Demona are you—"

Hope prevailed.

"Yes, I believe I am."

A smile ghosted across his lips. A knot untied itself in her mind, and purpose tingled her skin. All tension flowed away, evaporated like their after-love sweat. Demona risked touching his cheek, hand trembling, and grew bolder when he did not flinch away.

"I'm sorry," she whispered. "I didn't know how to tell you, or if I even should."

He rolled off her and cupped her face, unusually tender, and kissed her slowly.

"I wonder if it happened that first night? That was an epic battle, lady! Nothing but a son could come from such fire."

Demona let him cradle her, and this, too, seemed new and dangerous because it was the first time they had lain thus.

Demona calmed her rushing pulse as she fought to gain control of herself, her thoughts and her hopes. Contentment frightened her; it had merely heretofore been a physical lassitude after sex, or a temporary joy over a new dress or bauble. This was different. She brought Roderran's face down and returned his kiss, and the touch of their lips brought a single tear from the corner of Demona's eye. Despite the circumstances, in spite of the cold, the damp, the official hardness of the king, Demona understood what it meant to be happy.

"Dare I assume you are pleased?" she asked, brushing his lips as she spoke.

"You may assume." He kissed her back. Demona's heart fluttered.

"Bastard-born or not, I hope it is a boy."

Roderran lifted his head. The gleam in his eyes thrilled and frightened her. "You will not use that word for my son again," he said. "Do you understand me?"

"I—I understand."

"Nothing but a lion shall come from our loins, mark it. The world will change with this campaign, my lady, then we will make right this child's status. If it be a son, Demona. If it be a son, I will be very pleased, indeed."

Roderran trailed his hand over her breasts as he spoke, tracing their fullness and down to stop at her belly and the new life growing there. Peace wrapped itself around her racing thoughts and warmed them to calm. As she slipped into slumber, caressed by Roderran's slow, even pulse, she realized she had never done so before, not ever, not even with Talyior. She slept and dreamed of family for the first time, an explorer carefully pushing into unknown, virgin territory.

*   *   *

Roderran made no secret of her condition when his captains came two days later to meet and prepare for the first real assault of the campaign. The host had finally reached the fields before the mining town of Gallina. Scouts had come back with word that it was defended, though Demona was made to understand its defenses were rudimentary and posed little concern. She sat back away from the table where Lord Gaspire, Reegan and their under-commanders took council with the king. Most offered combinations of genuine and guarded congratulations; Gaspire kept silent at first and fixed her with a naked, contemplative stare before adding his own. Demona returned his glare with genuine boldness.

Yes, lord, I am not without weapons. And now you know it!

Her boldness lingered until the next day, when Roderran took her along with him and his escort to scout the approaches to the town. He stopped at the poor camp of the re-assembled Pevanese. Even to her untutored eye, Demona could see the sad state of most of the footmen. Roderran's ploy to use them as spear points for his columns had worked. Many of them sported bloody bandages. There were several newly dug graves off to the side. Men collected at Roderran's approach, moved more slowly than normal into ranks and attention, echoing, Demona thought, the somewhat sullen look of their captain, Avarran Tandari, a man of high enough rank to have been known to her in Pevana.

Roderran noticed the altered Pevanese atmosphere, too; she could tell by the way he stiffened in the saddle, the way he thrust his jaw forward, growling silently, as he paced his horse in front of the foremost ranks, stopping abruptly next to Avarran, who still held a shovel in his hands.

"Graves, captain?" Roderran questioned. "So close to your tents? Unseemly, and you stoop to digging? I'd think that a fit job for lesser men."

"I ordered them to their deaths, sire, I felt it my duty to bury them."

"Just these?"

Avarran held up his hands, and Demona could see the cracked blisters and calluses he proudly bore.

"No, my lord," he said. "All of them. As you can see, I have been busy."

"Do not be impertinent, sir!" Roderran's voice gave sound to the umbrage in his body. "You are one of my officers, not a mud grubber."

Avarran dropped his hands and bowed, deeply, using his spade to ease his return upright.

"I am sorry, my king. I forgot myself in my weariness. We have had some hard grubbing through the mud." He waved a hand at the troops behind, a blue sea of Pevanese uniforms universally mud-caked, tattered and disheveled. Something caught in Demona's throat—a gasp, or a sigh.

Such a difference between these and Roderran's northern troops.

"And you have done your *duty*, Captain Avarran," the king returned, then turned his attention to the weary troops. "We have made a good march through these infernal hills. My thanks for your hard service, men of Pevana! But look!" He jutted a finger at Gallina's makeshift defenses. "I want those walls down, and there are several hours of daylight left. Gather your companies and make test of their resolve!"

Roderran swung his horse around and so missed the incredulous look Avarran gave him; but Demona did not. She thought she saw fire in the Avarran's eyes, but whatever complaint he might have made fizzled.

"Yes, my lord," he answered, bowing. "My men are but just now reunited with their fellows. We are tired, hungry and hurt from our good *service* in your name, but we will make a test of their walls if the King so orders."

"I do so order, Captain Avarran. My thanks for your good service remain, though I do not like your tone or carriage. Both will be forgiven if you take those walls! Now, off with you!" He rounded his horse impressively and spurred away.

A far cry from the tender man he was when I told him of his child, Demona thought, and stilled her hand before it could move to her still-flat abdomen. Instead, she watched, a woman no better than a camp follower, and just as invisible to tired men. Guilt perched on her shoulder as Avarran marshalled his tired troops. She felt the stirrings in her stomach again, a lurching awareness to go along with the queasiness.

"He's killing us!" she heard a man grumble.

"Why us? Always?" another added. Others took up the tone of dissent. Demona feared to stay and hear more, feared to go and draw their attention. Avarran's snapped command brought startled her to action. His eyes fixed on her, he bellowed, "Why us, you say? Because we are the men of Pevana, Prince Donari's men, and the best in the king's service!"

"Then we deserve a rest!" someone shouted, but Avarran shouted over him. "And let those northern doxy-boys grab the credit for taking the walls after all our hard work? No, friends, he's doing us a favor."

The scowls turned to smiles as he spoke. Around him men began straightening their gear and adjusting shield straps and hefting spears. Avarran looked away, but Demona still felt the heft of his words as powerful as his glare.

"Right," he continued. "Let's show those northern lads and these southrons what Pevanese men are made of. Archers! Fill in behind the first ranks and pick at those faces above the gate. We won't even need to fashion ladders. At a steady jog now, go!"

Nearly six hundred men lopped off toward the defenses of Gallina. Demona did not watch them go. She urged her horse to follow after the king—*the King. Roderran. Father of my child. The man who saved me from Sevire*—shaken to the core.

More than two hundred of those men did not make it back.

Roderran ordered a general assault.

Half the host stormed the town. The southerners sold their lives dearly; it took three rushes to surmount the defenses and overwhelm the garrison. The defenders shot every bolt and threw every spear they possessed. The Perspans absorbed the blows and forced their way in through the breaches.

High on a hill overlooking the ravaged town, Demona shivered despite the noonday sun.

"What will happen to them?" she asked. Roderran barely looked her way, his attention on the battle below.

"Run like rats if they are smart, but Gaspire is to the south to snatch up those who do. As for any others, let them form shields in the town square and fight to the last for all I care. I have no need for prisoners. Ah, there!" He pointed to where smoke had begun to billow. "That is what I want! A nice big pillar of smoke and flames!" He turned to a messenger. "Get down there and find Reegan. Tell him to burn everything that doesn't look like it might be useful later. I want a blaze big enough for Casan to be able to see it from the sea. Let the old bastard know we are here and having success."

The roadside graves did not prepare Demona for her first, close look at men in battle. She fiddled with the rings on her fingers to avoid watching. She struggled to keep the image of her child, Roderran's child, uppermost in her mind to drown out the disturbing screams, the clash of metal, the flames' roar. She tried to convince herself the embers of Gallina dying were just rubies reflecting candle light. She reached back to find some of the defenses of her former self but only gained a half-measure.

Donari scowled at the two missives he raised up to the last of the sunlight to read. The left hand held Avarran's sad report of their state after taking Gallina. Anger imbedded every terse line; not even the official language they had agreed to use lest Roderran's spies intercept their messages, could disguise the rage behind the words. As he read Avarran's report, Donari's own anger swelled to a hot fury; so many of his men sacrificed to Roderran's spite, condemned souls goaded to the fore to take the enemy spears down with their bodies. So many good men; young fellows whose spirits had refused to break. They deserved so much better. Avarran claimed pride in their behavior, but Donari could not bring himself to match it. He felt his failure intimately in the description of the dead and wounded. He passed Avarran's report over to Eleni to record in her log.

He watched the expression on her face change from worry to sorrow as she read.

"He reports more than those words suggest, Eleni," he said quietly through tight jaws. "Almost all the army's casualties during the march have come from our people. Damn Roderran. He wastes good men to no purpose. Two hundred in a vain assault on pitiful fortifications! Unsupported! It is criminal. I have failed them. Us."

Senden sat across the fire from them and coughed to gain his Prince's attention.

"My lord, Donari, you have walked this ground already. What choice did you have? Roderran had held all the variables since we marched. Avarran has done well to preserve what he has. The king can have no complaint, surely?"

Donari answered by hefting the right-hand letter that had come from Roderran on the heels of Avarran's message. "Hear the words of our most puissant lord and king," he said disgustedly as he read the letter aloud.

"To our most Royal cousin, greetings. Your request for a covering force to be detached to the northeast is denied as being both inexpedient and unnecessary. In truth, sir, we marvel at your tone for it seems timid, almost reluctant and, thus, out of character. You will cull such troops as you feel fit to cover those passes from your available troopers. None will be spared from the direct assault down the valley toward Desopolis that we are now preparing. Gaspire has been ordered to push down the west flank a days ride ahead to clear passage for our arms. We wish you to do the same with what force you have to hand. Spare no effort here, cousin. Such is my royal command. I expect to hear from you within two days."

He finished reading, but when Eleni reached out to take the paper Donari crumpled it and tossed it onto the pile of bracken and twigs that had been gathered for their evening fire. "No, mistress, this is not worth recording. Let it serve as the tinder it is. He beards me, this cousin-king of mine. He weakens us further and in the next sentence extends our column dangerously out in front of the main body. If we get attacked in earnest, we will stand unsupported. His gall is amazing."

"But not surprising," finished Senden. He rose to stretch his leg. Donari noted how he favored it and frowned.

"Agreed," Donari replied. "He is just staying in character. I am not surprised, but I have to do something." He shook his head, lost and embittered by the knowledge. "But I cannot yet see what. We must follow these foolish orders, or Avarran and his men will pay even more dearly. I am sure of it."

"Orders, my lord?" asked Senden.

"Find this messenger. Tell him we will do our king's bidding or words to that effect. I'll not waste ink on a written response. Then get him out of our camp." He paused. "And chat with our squad leaders. I want two companies, along with any lightly wounded who can still serve, to double back to that hillside from two days ago."

"That won't leave us much over two hundred for our purpose. Dangerous."

"Like you so rightly said just a minute ago, my friend, we have no choice. What we have will have to serve. At least we won't be burdened with some of the wagons and the wounded. They are better off well out of the way if things grow desperate."

Senden limped off, passing close by Eleni, who caught Donari's eye as the Prince followed his friend's halting progress.

"And am I to go with them, my lord?" she asked.

Donari did not answer her at first. He wondered if she could trace the interplay of emotions on his face and in his eyes.

"It might be wise, I suppose, Eleni," he said ruefully. "But I will not order it. Perhaps I am as profligate with my friends as Roderran is with my men, but I confess that I want you near at least for awhile yet. We are close, very close to real battle. Keep your wits about you, and if things should go ill, then I expect you to take to horse and save yourself."

"My lord," she protested, but he cut her off with a small gesture. His features softened as he recalled the words he had read from her journal. *The will and the grace, to one day touch your face.*

"I know, Eleni," he said gently. "But I leave you to choose." He rose to go, touching her shoulder in passing. "Forgive me if I sound harsh, Eleni, I've seen too many fall. I begin to wonder if I am worthy of anyone's loyalty."

He left, wrapped in a spiritual darkness that defied the light of the setting sun, to go grieve for those lost and those still to be lost.

Donari rode alongside Senden with their lead company, moving through a wooded area. They were a full day ahead of the main host as ordered. Behind them, their remaining company rode guard on the supply train and its collection of small wagons and pack animals. They had reduced the number of wagons as the tracks they followed narrowed. Streams cut across their path infrequently, and so it was well that Donari had ordered all unnecessary items to go with the covering force.

Donari's horse stumbled and skid on a loose rock as the descent steepened. The path trended to the right and west. Trees began to close in around them. He looked ahead to where the ground grew more level. He gestured, turning in the saddle.

"Senden," he said. "I do not like the looks of this ground. It is too close here. Get forward and fan a few scouts to our flanks. The ground evens out ahead from the look of it. Better yet, dismount a few men and let them ghost alongside our column."

"We've seen nothing for two days, Donari."

"True, and all the more reason for caution now. The smoke from Gallina will have been seen. And as you said, Roderran has us pushed forward."

"I will see to it."

"I will be right behind you." He urged his horse out of the way as Senden spurred on down the path.

An uneasy expectation grew on him. The wood contained the normal animal sounds that stilled at their approach, but he felt his skin prickle as though he were in the sights of some hidden archer.

He looked behind him. The slope had created a gap as the mounted men picked their way down the sloped path, and his force had become loosely strung. He moved on, reached the more level ground. Ahead, Senden and his men passed through a small clearing created by the intersection of their track and another descending from the hills above. The sun dappled the ground about, seeming brighter at the crossroads. Senden's horse passed under the shadows of the trees that encircled the clearing, and into the trap awaiting them.

Arrows rained down from the slopes above and up from the boughs below. Donari heard the screams and the war cries; he heard Senden's authoritative bellow. He spurred his mount forward, into the fray, but the horse stumbled and fell forward when four arrows buried themselves in its chest, launching Donari over its withers. He landed with an armored crunch that left him stunned and breathless. Chaos bloomed all around him. His guard recoiled from the attack and fell back to regroup around their fallen Prince.

Donari struggled to regain his breath surrounded by a sea of thrashing feet and limbs hazed by dust. He managed to get one knee under him before Senden clattered up, dismounted and shouldered his way through the guard to help Donari to his feet.

"Remind me never to doubt your intuition," he shouted.

"How many down?" he asked, unsheathing his sword, ignoring the throb in his shoulder.

"The squad ahead took a volley at short range. Not good." From behind the shield of Senden's horse, Donari made a quick scan. Arrows still flew. Men and horses were down. Then the arrow-fire slackened, replaced by the sound of new voices raised in southern war cries. Spearmen in Desopolisan livery struck, swarmed.

"Ware that, Senden! Take the left!" Donari shouted, then to his men, "Form line! Form line!"

Donari grabbed a fallen shield rallied his line to the right. Time became a madness of spear points thunking against bucklers and blades crashing, metal sliding along metal. Men fell to either side of Donari, reducing his world to the space immediately in front of him. He fought for his life, and the lives of those near him. He fell into the rhythm of parry, thrust, shield up, gauge it, swing it, do not over extend the arm, balance, power and control. Watch the enemy's eyes.

With every blow to his borrowed shield, his shoulder screamed. Sweat blurred his already blurring vision. Sound became buzzing insects in his ears. Light narrowed. . .

"Donari!" Senden's voice brought him back. He struggled against the hands of his own men trying to lift him bodily into a saddle. Someone forced his foot into a stirrup.

"Stop fighting, my lord! Get to the rear, while there is a lull! You can do no more here!"

Donari's wavering consciousness rebelled, but his mouth would not work. Light began to narrow again. He saw Senden toss the reins of his mount to a mounted trooper. "Get the Prince out of here, now!"

"Wait!" Donari managed, and only when his horse did not canter off did he realize his men had listened. He reached down and grabbed Senden's shoulder. He said not a word, and did not have to. Friends of such long association needed no words. A glance held. A smile returned. Then Senden said, "Go."

This time, his voice issued no command. His horse jolted into motion, and it was all he had left in him to hang on.

Senden watched the Prince ride out of sight before turning back the remains of the company. His leg throbbed. He refused the need to rub at it. The brief lull that allowed him to see to Donari was already regaining momentum. He could feel it building like a storm. There was no time for pain.

"Form line! Shields up!" he shouted. "Let's not make it easy for them."

The southern force rushed in from all sides, crashing into the half-formed defensive line. Men fell. All semblance of order disappeared. His men were hopelessly outnumbered. Cut off. Senden fought to hold his position. His leg grew weaker by the minute. More men fell around him. *So few left!* He blocked a blow and returned it with a thrust that struck home, and spun about to seek out another and felt the overburdened muscle in his leg tear. He fell just as a spear point reached over his shield rim to take him in the shoulder. Another blow struck his helm. The sounds of battle rose to that pitch-point of triumph; not for his men, for the enemy. His vision clouded. Nausea clenched his throat. Senden fought for consciousness. He tried to focus on the blue sky above the clearing, but could not see it for the black spots in the way. Battlesounds moved beyond him back up the path. Sounds of renewed conflict came to him as an indistinct turmoil. He tried to look back, but his head, weighted by blows and failure, defeated him. He lay still. Sound reached him through his disembodied senses.

Laughter.

Then silence.

Senden lay amid the dust and the fallen. The world stopped spinning when the natural sounds of the wood returned. He blinked away the lingering spots, managed to raise his head, and found he was alone. Struggling to an elbow, he gasped as he got his good leg underneath him and managed to get himself upright. The spear wound to his shoulder sent white-hot waves of agony shooting down his left arm. His right leg would not hold his weight. He leaned on his sword, breathing heavily, and looked about him. No more sounds of battle behind. Failure. *Donari!*

A lone figure detached itself from the shadows on the edge of the crossroads and moved cautiously into the light. Senden brought his blade up, squinting. Fatigue and pain blurred his vision, but he knew that figure. He knew the man. He raised his blade higher.

"You are a bit far from your master's side, aren't you, Corvale?"

"Not a lover of the sea, myself. I prefer hard earth beneath my boots." Corvale took in the carnage, shaking his head at the scope of it. "Your leadership skills seem to have failed you, Arolli."

Corvale's eyes flicked past him as though measuring their isolation.

"You know," he continued. "You have a maddening habit of always getting in my way. Did you have to slap the horse? I had your precious Donari sighted down the length of the straightest arrow in my quiver, and there you go acting all appropriate and getting him out of range. Tolimon's balls, man, how can you stand being so damned noble all the time? I should have gutted you back in Pevana."

Despite his agony, Senden managed a small smile.

"And perhaps I should have killed you that night in the rain. Renia knows you deserved it."

"My victims get what's coming to them. People who get in my way pay for it, in blood if I'm lucky."

"Did Sevire Anargi get in your way?" he asked.

"A favor for my king.

"Truth? Surprising. But what of Tomais Caralon?"

"Who? Oh, the saddle-maker! That was my horse, actually, but no tragedy. Word has it his wife is with Donari. Nice bit of stuff, that, eh? When I take down your Prince, I intend to give her my complete attention."

Senden raised his sword. "You are a madman, Corvale."

Jaryd raised his blade and advanced smiling. "Maybe," he sneered. "But in a minute your opinion won't matter."

The first blow sent tremors up Senden's arm but it did not fail him. Corvale chuckled, walked a slow and steady perimeter Senden half shuffled to follow.

"And what'll you do when I'm behind you, eh, Arolli? You going to spin on that gimp-leg? About now I bet you're sorry you took those blows meant for your Prince, eh? Where is he? Safe and away, while you are left here to face me, alone?"

Senden balanced, raised his blade, tensed for the blow, but Corvale sidled back around and around, his sword coming up and striking in a blur Senden felt like a punch in his gut. Heat bloomed, spread like blood—*was* blood. He slumped to his knees, sliding off Corvale's blade as he did so.

"Give my best to Caralon when you see him."

Jaryd raised his sword for the third, final thrust. Senden would not look away even if he could not see more than shadows.

He had heard peace overcame a warrior so close to death, but Senden Arolli felt no such thing. Anger. And sorrow. And regret. Jaryd Corvale was not worthy of his blood, but he would have it. Senden felt no more pain, only this rising fury. He heard its whisper as it passed by his ear, as he fell the rest of the way to the ground, and the ring of metal on metal that came as a vague, musical note from behind a black curtain.

Devyn Ambrose had been forced to witness the whole attack and could do nothing to change its outcome lest the whole gamble unravel. He rode up through the trees behind the force as it assembled for the attack. He tied his horse off in a dense grove growing in a culvert and crept down to a vantage point above and behind the main part of southern force. He had seen the Pevanese colors coming down the track and cursed in frustration. *So desperately close...*

He recognized Senden and Donari immediately and watched in growing dismay as the ambush occurred. It took everything he had to keep himself from rushing down and warning them. His spirits lifted when he saw Donari spur out of the melee to safety, but then watched in horror as the survivors all went down singly and in groups until Senden went down under a hail of blows. He sat frozen to his hiding place as the attackers reorganized themselves and moved on up the forest path after the prince.

Long moments passed in indecision. Should he go on and try to find the prince? Then he noticed Arolli sitting up and struggling to his feet among the fallen. Movement off to the southern edge of the clearing drew his eye. A single figure, leading a horse walked slowly into the afternoon sunlight. *Jaryd Corvale.*

Devyn felt himself rise as if his body were controlled by another, unseen force; all thought of finding Donari forgotten. He scrambled to his feet and threw himself full pelt down the slope.

Devyn lost sight of the clearing in his mad dash. He rushed, leaping over bodies and horse carcasses, to the center of the crossroads. He drew his blade in a flourish while the two before him traded a first pass. Then Senden missed his block, took a thrust to the abdomen, and slumped to the ground. Devyn leaped, swinging his blade wildly to deflect Corvale's final lunge while lowering his off shoulder to take the larger man in his exposed ribs. The blow sent both of them sprawling.

Corvale recovered quickly. Devyn saw the recognition in the man's eyes. Corvale laughed, seemingly pleased at the chance to settle two old scores at the same time. He attacked savagely, punctuating each cruelly aimed blow with a phrase.

"Why is it . . . that I just can't . . . get quit . . . of all you . . . meddling . . . fools! You! . . . little scribbler turd!" He sent Devyn falling backward over a body and paused to get his breath, looking quickly about. "So, where is your doxy-boyfriend? Let's make this reunion complete, shall we? Come, up with you, boy. I want you to get the full treatment of this edge here . . . see it? That's Arolli's blood there, cub, and yours is about to join it."

"Renia has a place for heroes like Senden Arolli," Devyn said, quickly regaining his feet and side-stepping.

"Where's your Renia now," Corvale sneered. "I'll tell you where she is. Your weepy goddess is getting it up the ass from the King's Sun God! Not the same sort of tears there, eh?"

Devyn did not respond, eyed more open ground to the left, and kept moving.

Corvale followed him, eyes white with the killing joy. "All of you fools just can't seem to see how the world goes. Arolli. Done. That old cripple from the Maze, what did the gravestone read? Edri? Done. I pissed on it before I left. A bit much for a dirty cripple, I think."

Devyn had never heard about the honor bestowed on his old mentor. Wrath and sorrow combined to turn his sinews into steel, and he attacked Corvale with more than skill. Fate guided his blade's point. Grief lent power to the thrusts. Corvale retreated, and Devyn sensed his confusion.

"You're an adept killer but no swordsman, Corvale. Murder by stealth and flames, that's all you've got." Devyn deflected a wild blow. "And it's not enough, now."

A wrist flick sent Corvale's sword flying through the air still grasped in the man's right hand. "That is for Renia's Temple," he rasped. Blood spouted from the stump, showered Corvale's face. He screamed in shock and pain. Another flick sliced through Corvale's throat. "And that is for Senden Arolli," he continued. Blood flowed around the fingers of Corvale's left hand as he coughed and staggered backward, gurgling, eyes already dulling. Devyn's last blow sent his head flying through the air in a bloody arc. The headless trunk fell in a crimson heap at Devyn's feet. "And that," he finished, "is for my master, Kembril Edri, may Renia wash him pure in peace."

Devyn cleaned his blade on Corvale's light cloak and hurried back to where Senden lay and found him barely conscious. Devyn pushed up Senden's mail and ripped open the undershirt to check the wound. Blood pulsed from the rent in the flesh with every breath. Devyn looked up to find Senden looking at him, a trace of a smile gracing his ashen face.

"Reunion. . ." he coughed. "That may have been Corvale's best line." He swallowed with difficulty. "Well met, Devyn Ambrose. From where . . . ah . . . I see there is a tale here that I will miss. I always felt we might meet again." He gestured feebly. "This wasn't what I had in mind." He coughed again and blood dotted his lips.

Devyn took his neck cloth and pressed it against Senden's wound. Senden grimaced, pushed away Devyn's hand.

"Not much use," he whispered.

Devyn sat back on his knee. "Stay," he urged. "I need to get to Prince Donari."

Senden waved a hand back up the path. "Back there, if he still lives." Another cough. More blood. He gripped Devyn's arm intensely as with his last strength.

"Find him. Save him."

"That is what Sylvanus sent me here to do."

Senden's face clouded in pain and confusion. "Sylv . . . what?"

"I am to make Donari an offer."

Senden smiled at that. Perhaps it was the grace granted those near death, for he looked as though he understood what Devyn meant.

"Sneaky bastard." He coughed again and blood flowed from his mouth. There were no more breaths. Devyn closed Senden's eyes and knelt there, calling on every god and goddess he could remember to take the soul of Senden Arolli into the grace his loyalty and honor so richly deserved.

He was still praying when Donari returned with the rest of his troopers.

Chapter 25: Lost and Found

DONARI AND HIS RELIEF COMPANY came cautiously into the clearing. All dead. All but one kneeling by one of the fallen. The prince drew rein. The man rose, hands up in surrender. Several troopers took him by the arms and held him fast. He did not struggle, but waited for Donari to dismount. Recognition flooded his brain, sending waves through him.

"I know you, poet," he said. "But how, where. . . ?" And then he saw Senden's body. All color left his face. "Oh, Senden," he moaned. "Dearest of friends. . ." He knelt, too shocked even for tears, to examine the slack features, the bled out death wound. Remorse rose in him like a great wave of darkness, and he froze over Senden's corpse, hand on his friend's already cooling brow and gave himself up to grief. A tear came then, but only one.

All the years of their friendship passed before his mind's eye. So much shared toil, shared joys, the lessons of rule, his subtle hand guarding his young adventures, tempering his darker moments. Laughter. Plans. Pride.

"Oh, my friend," he whispered. "You deserved better than," he glanced around with unfocused eyes, "this obscure, petty death. May Renia wash you clean. Ask her to save some for me." He gave Senden's shoulder a gentle squeeze, hoping that, even as his friend's spirit sped on its way to the afterlife, he might hear that last request and so meet the goddess laughing. He pressed his hands to his eyes and lost himself again in darkness.

Other riders arrived. The sounds of bodies being moved came vaguely to him. A gentle touch on his shoulder brought him back to Eleni's stricken face, tears already beginning to flow, her other hand covering her mouth as though she were trying to stifle despair's rictus. She fell to her knees beside Donari, and he felt her hand snake in to grasp his. He returned her grasp, lending what strength he could, putting his arm around her shoulders as she sagged against him.

"Oh, my lord, I'm so sorry. Senden—" Her breath seeped as warmth through his ring mail and the fabric beneath to pierce his own darkness.

"The fault is mine alone, mistress," he murmured into her hair. "And he died well. See that we live as well for recompense."

Shuddering sobs took her then, and he held her while they ran their course. He took stock of the area. Men awaited his orders. Devyn Ambrose still stood grasped and guarded off to one side. He helped Eleni to rise. The afternoon sun dappled the area with shadows and beams of dust-filled light, a mockery of peace.

Fitting that only the dead can ever have the real thing.

He motioned for men to come take Senden's body.

"Clean him up as best as you can," he said quietly. "Bury him here, in the path, wrapped tightly, mind! If we survive this insanity, we will return and take him home. Detail a squad to bury our dead. They should finish by the time the train gets here." He checked the sun's position. "We will camp down the trail a ways." He turned to Eleni. "Mistress, will you help with the wounded?" Still ashen-faced, Eleni nodded and moved off to comply.

Donari turned back to the men clustered about him. "Listen, all of you!" He raised his voice to command their attention. "Note how this was done! My fault! Look at those badges! These were regular troops not skulkers from the mines and hills. We are close, then, I feel it. Ware and watch this night. Send. . ." His voice nearly broke, grew thick with emotion. "Senden will expect us to respond well. So let us do so."

He turned to consider Devyn. "And you," he rasped. "Like a specter you appear out of the air. Explain yourself."

"My lord, I am sorry about Senden Arolli," Devyn said. "I arrived too late to stop Corvale—"

"Corvale? Jaryd Corvale? What do you mean?"

Devyn pointed to the battered and bloodied head. Donari's frown deepened in anger and confusion.

"Corvale? With southerners? This is a riddle."

"No riddle, my lord. Corvale came after the southerners left. Senden had been badly wounded. He hadn't stood a chance. I took vengeance for him, and for others."

Donari shook his head in disbelief. "Corvale had unfinished business with me. Senden saved me twice, then."

"I would suspect so, my lord."

"*Arrived* you said. From where?"

"I was sent, my lord, from Sylvanus of Desopolis to find you."

Donari gave Devyn an incredulous look. "Poet to spy? Assassin? No, you haven't the look. Messenger? What would Sylvanus of Desopolis have to say to me that he need kill my people to deliver?"

"The force that attacked you had no knowledge of my mission, lord. I traveled alone and unseen from the city under Sylvanus's orders."

"How did you know where to find me?"

"I didn't. Sylvanus guessed you would be placed on Roderran's left. It was a fool's hope, lord. Perhaps there is a force directing us, I don't know, but it seems that hope was granted. I found you."

"For what reason?" Donari searched the poet's face, saw there indecision, caution and fear. He pressed further. "Come, man, be clear with me! The tyrant set these men to kill my people, and you come as a messenger? Ambrose, they killed Senden! What are you about, sir?"

"I do not know all of Sylvanus's mind, my lord," Devyn responded. "But he could not tell his folk anything. He needs them to fight. If they knew of the risk I represent—"

"You speak in riddles, poet."

"My lord, I have ridden in silence all this time. My words are for you alone."

Donari heard truth in Ambrose's tone and gestured for the troopers to release Devyn, leaving the two of them alone in the middle of the clearing.

"What is this *risk* you speak of?" Donari demanded. "What message?"

"Sylvanus of Desopolis wants to surrender, and offers his fealty and the loyalty of his people . . . to you, my lord."

Donari recoiled at the words. "He's mad! He would betray his folk?"

Devyn shook his head no. "I said much the same thing a week ago. But I do not think he is mad. And I do not think he betrays anything. He has marched since I left. He intends to fight no matter the odds. As he put it, 'Any victory Roderran wins will be bitter.' I think he seeks to save what he can, my lord."

Devyn's words stirred memories of disturbingly similar words between Senden and himself. Donari paused, sifted, doubted, too quickly put to the test absent his best advisor.

"My enemy councils me to treachery. How can it be other than madness?"

"But is he *your* enemy, lord? I remember last summer. Flames in the Maze. I've seen the smoke from the coast and Gallina. What price peace? Sylvanus will fight Roderran, and lose, unless—"

"Unless?" Donari interrupted. "Dangerous ideas, Ambrose."

"Sylvanus cannot win, but he will fight to lose . . . to the right man."

Donari looked at Devyn for a long, silent moment. *Is this treachery? Or is it a fool's hope for peace?* The question pervaded his thoughts like the after-effect of an epic poem. Senden's face in life loomed before his mind's eye, nodding affirmation, and he had his answer.

"Very good," he said decisively. "I need to hear more of this. We will talk tonight. For what its worth, Ambrose, I believe you. Absurd though the whole thing seems at first, I believe you."

He looked again at Corvale's head; someone had rolled it next to his corpse. "And I thank you for trying to save Senden. And for taking care of that irritation." He nudged the head with his foot. "He has caused much grief to me and those close to me."

"I, too, had cause, my lord."

"The Maze fire, Edri. Yes, young man, I remember. There is much to this, it would seem. I assume you've a horse?"

Devyn gestured to the slope above. "Tethered in some trees."

"Get it and return quickly. Two of my men will accompany you. We make camp down that track soon. My men will bring you to me."

He turned to go paused when Devyn shifted in front of him and bent to one knee.

"My lord, take my service. Let me honor Senden Arolli's memory. He saved me, too, more than once."

"How many masters can you serve, poet?"

"A poet from Pevana need ask?"

Donari managed a smile at the bold reply. "Madness, and yet I will consider it," Donari replied. "Hurry, we have much to discuss and little time."

Devyn rose and bowed formally. Donari watched him and his guards slip up through the trees then turned to deal with Senden's interment. Men had washed most of the blood away and wrapped all but the face in blankets. Eleni stood by the newly dug grave. Donari joined her and motioned for men to finish and lower the body.

"The earth may be a measure more full," he said to his friend, reaching down to help push soil in. "But my world is empty."

"Renia's grace," Eleni whispered.

"Wash him pure," finished Donari. "Rest now, friend. I will return and get you home."

True night fell while Donari picked at Devyn's astounding tale. They sat on camp stools around a fire with Eleni taking care to take down every detail. A season's worth of wandering and words only to end up attacked for northern politics in a southern alehouse. An audience with the enemy his folk marched to defeat. A romance begun between the friend left behind and the tyrant's bastard daughter. An offer to commit treason for a higher good; an offer that bent both ways. Attached to the offer came the caveat of fealty and allegiance; an open invitation to rebel against his blood relation and sworn lord, a relation and lord he had vowed to kill if given the chance.

To even consider the veracity of what Devyn told him seemed foolish, but nearly a month watching his folk bleed for a greedy, vengeful king had abused his sense of propriety. He recalled his frustration after the council of war in Pevana; so reduced in status afterwards that he despaired effecting anything on his people's behalf. And yet the absurd offer created an opportunity to do something.

Senden would have called it heroic; a gambit worthy of a king. But to break faith went against all of Donari's instincts. He had spent his adult lifetime controlling his reactions, finding ways to navigate between conflicting perils to mitigate risks, minimize the cost of keeping his and his people's options open. And now Sylvanus's offer and Senden's death informed him he had run out of space and time. He had to choose.

He stared now at the flames after dismissing Eleni and Devyn to their rest, searching amid the coals for certainty. Everything about Devyn spoke of truth and integrity. Donari remembered last summer, too. Devyn's presence felt like a summons to make amends for not acting more directly during those dark days. The young man's offer of fealty came as a gift but one with dire consequences.

The night grew chill around him. The glowing coals led him down memories. Deep into his personal darkness he found much to place against his account. Senden's loss struck hard now. He felt like an appendage had been sliced off, like a twin who had lost its sibling; where once there had been a shared universe now silence reigned in a grey nothing. He took himself to task, recalled how ill he had used his most important friend and how uncomplaining that friend had been. *Senden was more prince than I.* Black despair swallowed him. He wept, quietly, for a long time.

When his own tears finally ran out, he rose to go in search of sleep. As he passed Eleni's tent he heard her sobs. How hard it must have been for her to see Senden laid out for burial; in little more than a month, she had lost two of the most important people in her life. He placed a hand on the flap, unsure about disturbing her grief.

"Eleni?" he asked tentatively. "Are you all right? Is there anything I can do?"

She opened the tent flap. Even in the faint fire-light, Donari could see her swollen eyes and cheeks still wet with tears. She stared up at him in silence, her eyes searching his, intent, desperate, wanting, lonely, confused, consumed by conflicting emotions, desires, needs. She backed into the tent, drawing him in with her. They stood thus, a moment suspended, half-shadow, half-real, a spell in search of glamour's final word to melt the barrier between them. Donari embraced her wordlessly, a gentle, timid enfolding. She began weeping again, and as she wept she whispered words into his chest that pierced his heart.

"I miss him, Donari. I'm so afraid. First Tomais, and now Senden. Why do all those I love perish? What have I done? He was so kind, so wise."

Donari groaned and held her tighter, but she resisted comfort, insistent, and words came out of her in a rush.

"He talked about you . . . so much love there. So well-deserved. So cherished. When I saw him, I . . . I am sorry, lord, but I thought first of you. Your people need you. I need . . . you. Losing Senden hurts so much. I do not know what I will do if I lose you."

"Eleni, heart, please," he began but she pushed away wiping away her tears.

"I'm sorry to burden you, my lord. You have lost him too, a dear friend, yes, but your greatest advisor. My grief belongs only to me. You must think me foolish."

"No, Eleni, never, never think it."

"Senden loved you, and he showed me how our people love you."

Donari swallowed a sob, held her, again. "Eleni, I don't deserve such—"

She leaned away in his arms, searched his eyes. "Seeing him laying there," she said. "I finally had to realize how much I, too, love you."

Her words mesmerized. Lost in that trance, Donari took her face in his hands, bent his lips to hers and kissed her long and tenderly. The movement of their lips and the slickness of their tears created a cosmic friction that burned away any barriers of blood or station.

They were suddenly and simply two souls confronting the enormity of their loss; each of them searching for a way to fill the void so recently created. And Donari understood the danger of that kiss for Eleni. She stood at the edge of desolation, fragile, tenuous, and only the steady pressure of his lips on hers kept her from the fall. And only her obvious need of him kept him from sorrow's pit.

His hands moved to cup the small of her back. She reached up to touch his jaw line; her gentle touch shredding the layers of responsibility and protracted grief that had so characterized his days. Donari marveled at how his body responded to hers through their clothing. She clasped him tight, insistent, trying to push bodily into him. Donari found himself whispering nonsensical words as his lips moved over hers. And she seemed to respond in kind as though breathing in those syllables gave her volition.

They parted only to explore laces and buttons. Donari felt Eleni shiver when his hand brushed her breast as he loosened the ties to her blouse. She let the garment slip off her shoulders to join her skirt and stood before him naked in the half-light. For Donari, it seemed as if he saw her for the first time; her body a newly discovered poem. He felt himself rising as she undid the clasp to his belt, felt her hands whisper across his chest, her fingers reading the contours of his body like a blind man touches another's face.

He lay her down on the sleeping skins, both of them heedless of the spring chill. He kissed her mouth, her neck, and sucked both nipples into rigid attention that brought gasps. Her hands entwined in his hair, drew him back to her lips, his body into her body all a-rush of rhythm and wordless breathing. Donari felt the cold chill that had clutched his heart since seeing Senden's body, ease, melt away in the heat of their physical union. He marveled at her power as she matched him, grew momentarily afraid when he sensed the depths of her loss. But then it was too late for the mind; his body took over as did hers and there was nothing left but to fill up the emptiness.

Her finger gently tracing his ear, her breath warm on his cheek brought him back to time and an altered world. Nothing could ever be the same. He brought his face up to hers, searched for a word in her eyes.

"Change," he said.

She kissed him. "Hope," she whispered.

For the rest of that long night Donari made love to her slowly, easily, drawing and giving power and comfort, composing love's defense to keep sorrow at bay.

Chapter 26: Decision at Desopolis

LYVIA TAMORGEN HURRIED DOWN THE HALL to Talyior's rooms. It had been two days since Espan and the other refugees from Heliopolis arrived at the quay, and watchers on the headland now reported seeing sails cresting the horizon, heading straight for Desopolis. Old salts gauged the distance and sent word to Lyvia that the city had two, maybe three days before the Perspan fleet arrived.

The news sparked a fresh exodus from the city, but only from the land gate. Lyvia ordered the barrier chain raised in the harbor to keep what craft that remained available. The panic seemed to infect even the stones of the city buildings. Folk gathered at the palace gates with questions and fears. Lyvia had called a meeting, and set Ergan to gathering what council members, officers and troops remained in the city; enough, he assured her to put up a spirited defense.

She swept into Talyior's room without bothering to knock to find him sitting in the window seat, playing a guitar. He looked up at her approach, smiled his easy smile, and Lyvia's jangled nerves calmed.

"I found this in the corner," he said, strumming softly. "Very nice. Makes me miss my own, but this one is better."

"If we survive what's coming, you can keep it."

Her words vanquished his grin.

"News?"

"The Perspan fleet."

"Soon?"

"Too soon, but maybe it's better this way. No time to waste energy in worry."

"What can I do?" he asked, rising and putting the guitar aside.

"Hold me, kiss me, tell me everything will be all right," She sighed dramatically, fluttering her eyelashes, and Talyior's smile returned. He took her into his arms.

"Gladly, but—?"

"But that's really not very helpful, is it. How about your voice? Ergan wants to plan a defense."

"I'm not sure what I can add."

"Your Espan is in no condition to attend. At the least, you can verify his story and add some perspective."

"Will they listen?"

"I'll make them. I'm feeling my way through this, Talyior. Having you helped me the first time."

They entered the council chamber to find a handful of civic leaders, Ergan and several others officers seated around the long table. Lyvia acknowledged them with a nod, and got right to it.

"You've all heard. They come for us, now," she said, leaning over the table. "Our fate is tied to what happens with our people in the north. I say we fight and save something for them to return home to. I want to *do* something. Sitting behind our chain and manning the battlements is not going to save our city. I want ideas."

Silence.

Some of the older men at the table had been part of the deputation that questioned her right to rule even after Sylvanus acknowledged her. They now had the look of cowed men too enfeebled to even flee even if they still retained the means. She turned to Ergan, huge and solid, who returned her stare with disconcerting stolidity.

"Lady Lyvia," he said. "Our walls are not insignificant, and we have men enough to man them. What more should we do? Let them come and waste themselves against our defenses."

His words set off a groundswell of reaction as others around the table began chiming in, adding their querulous voices to his.

"Let them come to us!'

"I'll not risk any more than I already have!"

"To attack would be a waste of lives!"

The recrimination bounced back and forth across the table until it grew impossible to tell one voice from another. Lyvia sat down in digust as the noise rose, intensified by the fears of old men more inclined to consider profit margins than the need to act to preserve freedom. The insight steadied her. They had made their careers finding ways around the policies of power. They were used to different kinds of risks. Lyvia drew breath to try and shout them down, but then thought better of it. Instead, she sat back in her chair and watched their faces redden, veins distended. Empty words. Empty minds.

Sheep waiting to be shorn and slaughtered. Money has made them dull.

Eventually, the clamor subsided as one by one they either ran out of breath or realized that no one else was listening. Lyvia sat stone-faced and waited.

Ergan broke the silence. "My lady, we cannot meet them bow on. We've too few ships. We could not afford the loss of any crews that would have to sail them. There were burned hulks outside of Teirne and Heriopolis, drowned masses floating in the swell. We cannot waste lives to no effect. We cannot sally."

"So we wait passively, let them come unopposed?"

"Prudence, lady," wheezed the oldest of the merchants there.

"Did all of our courage march north with my father?"

Again, silence. Lyvia felt Talyior shift next to her.

"Fire," he said, tentative at first as all eyes turned to him. "My father's old foreman, Espan, survived the sack of Heriopolis. He described the flames. We've all seen the column of smoke. Casan has a fondness for fires when he's the one setting them." His voice gained conviction. "When I was a child, Espan always used to tell me sailors feared fire the most. You could use fireships, vessels crammed with flammable material. Well aimed, you could cause great confusion. Turn their weapon against them. You say you only have a few galleys. A few is all you'd need. Burn them first before they burn us."

"Us?" the old man asked.

Lyvia took hold of Talyior's hand, and he seemed to take confidence from her gesture.

"I have an interest in survival, hostage or not," he responded. "I know some of you question my place here. My friend rides north for Sylvanus. He took the risk, so will I. I have a certain knowledge of flames, gentlemen."

"But they are your people," the old man sneered. "Your accent gives you away, boy."

"There are those in that fleet I hold responsible for the deaths of all my *people,* sir. All that I hold close—" He raised Lyvia's hand still clasped in his. "—is here, now, and I will fight for it. Will you?"

Talyior brought their hands down, let hers go, and settled back in his chair. Scanning the faces around the table, Lyvia saw speculation and guarded hope. She paused at Ergan.

"Can we spare men enough for these, *fireships*?"

Ergan's features relaxed into a feral smile. "Absolutely, my lady. And we've storehouses full of materials whose owners, now gone, will surely not miss."

Hope gobbled up the last of the doubt. Conversation about the table grew more vigorous. Lyvia leaned closer to Talyior.

"Well, you *are* full of surprises. That was more than I expected. You meant that bit about fighting?"

"I can use a blade," he said. "And I have some knowledge of boats."

Lyvia chuckled. "I've seen you at the oars, *minimal knowledge.* Ergan!" she cried, quelling the table talk. "I will leave it to you to select what ships we will use. And gentlemen, by your tone, I assume you agree to the effort? Yes? Then no more talk about whose ships, please? I consider them weapons for our use. I'd rather they burn on the open sea than tied up to a dock. Ergan, how long?"

"We will start immediately, my lady. We will only need small crews and keep one vessel clear to recover those who sail the fireships. We can leave with tonight's tide and use the land breeze to come up to them before dawn."

"Done," she said, rising to leave. "I will join you," she paused, looked at Talyior. "*We* will join you at the appointed hour."

"Lyvia?" asked Ergan.

"I told my father I would fight for our city. I am going."

She motioned Talyior to follow her and swept out of the room.

"Thank you," she said as they paced back toward Talyior's chambers. "You shocked them. You didn't have to go and volunteer. If you think I am going to let you risk your life on one of those fireships, you're mad."

Talyior laughed off her protests. "And why are you going? Honor?"

"Responsibility."

"Which is why I have to go, too. I don't want to disappoint your father. Besides, what if neither of us makes it back to check on the other? Won't matter much would it?"

"That is not funny. How can you joke about this?"

She felt his hand smooth hers. "I know, Lyvia," he said, leaning in and dropping his voice. "Listen, I have nothing in the north that claims me. No family. No home. Just you and the way I feel. I want to stay, and I need to do something to prove myself. If I am to be anything to you, I need to become something to them. Did you see the looks from those old men at the council? Before I piped up they were sizing me up for a doxy boy, Lyvia's new plaything, a worthless scribbler of foreign verse."

"But not after."

"No," he agreed. "Not after. But I saw similar looks from your people during our times out together these last days. Doubt. Questions. But they know you, Lyvia. It is pretty obvious they love you."

"Those old men don't. They see my father's hand in this."

"Those old men don't matter. Not now. You've got their ships. The people have already granted you far more power."

Lyvia stopped. "I'm afraid of failing them," she said.

"You will save them."

"How can you be so sure?"

"I just am."

*　*　*

They shared a light meal in Talyior's room as the sun set. The messengers came requesting her attention to other matters, and she left him to take what rest he could before full night. Her tasks kept her some time, and when she finally broke free she found sleep impossible. The bed felt too big to hold her thoughts.

And such thoughts.

Images of her father and the lands through which he and his men marched, interspersed with black ships manned by men of evil aspect, flashed around scenes of Desopolis, her people at market, the sun on the garden below her room, and running through everything Talyior's face, strangely helmed, eyes searching for something.

Her.

Waking, Lyvia judged it past midnight. She rose, felt for her robe in the darkness, wrapped it loosely around her, slipped down the hallway, an emotional shadow among shadows. Soundlessly, she opened Talyior's door and moved to the foot of his bed. She could just make out his silhouette rolling over at her approach.

"Talyior, are you asleep?"

"No, not even close."

"Are you frightened?"

"Are you?"

"Yes, terribly. Do still intend to do this?"

"We've been over that already," he responded. "Besides, I gave my word, and I'll not go back on it."

There followed a long moment of silence. Lyvia could hear his breathing. Neither of them moved.

"Lyvia, what is it?" he asked.

Certainty.

She shrugged off the robe, let her night dress slip down her shoulders, the silky fabric sliding off her hips like water, and climbed into bed with him. He accepted her without question as she pressed her naked body against his. Her lips found his by instinct and feel. She kissed him slowly, softly, penetrating, assertive. She felt his body respond, his hands move along her back, stop; he drew back for breath.

"Lyvia, why now?"

She kissed him again.

"I'm giving us both a reason to come back."

Lyvia swayed with the motion of the relief galley's rolling deck as it sailed behind the rest of the fireships. The tide's flood and a following wind sped them toward where they expected to find the Perspan fleet. Heavy clouds masked the moonlight, deepening their cover. Ergan wanted them placed to the windward of the approaches to Desopolis. The experienced sailors among them assured Lyvia that the Perspans could not approach from the north. They would have to sail across the wind, slowed by the land breeze until the tide turned and the breeze with it to aide their attack. Ergan hoped to use the last of the wind to come up to them just before dawn. The watchers on the headlands had reported the Perspans sailed with running lamps to keep formation. Ergan counted on that over-confidence to point their fireships.

She kept her eyes fixed on the light winking from the stern of the ship in front of them. Talyior helmed that particular vessel. The memory of their final hours together before sailing kept her company. That and the words he whispered into her ear on the dock during their last embrace.

"No secrets, Lyvia. Only two women have ever come to my bed unlooked for. The first time had been *goodbye*, but the second time, you, that was a promise."

He kissed her and wiped the tears from her cheeks, laughing gently. "No tears, either," he finished. "Don't worry, I can swim." And then he was gone and by the time they cleared the harbor he was a heartbeat connected to her by swinging lamplight.

Time passed slowly for Lyvia until a line of second lights appeared ahead; the signal that the Perspan fleet had been sighted. The bobbing lights before her swung onto a new tack, and then she saw the glow for herself. They were heading directly for a cluster of lights to the southwest. The sound of oars being put to use came to her across the water. The lights aboard the fireships spread apart as they targeted and built up speed. Lyvia looked behind. Dawn was still just a rumor on the horizon.

The first galley's sudden eruption into full flame caught her off guard. The light cast by that first craft served to illuminate the Perspan fleet, and Lyvia could see they would hit the enemy ships in mid-tack. The first plunged into the midst of the lead Perspan squadron. Its sudden appearance threw the Perspans into confusion. Ships collided trying to avoid the flames. One by one the Desopolisan crews set light to their ships and thrust them into the Perspan columns.

The scene flickered into horror and chaos as the fireships spread their flames among the Perspan vessels. Grapnals bound ships together in burning embrace. Shadow figures in skiffs rowed away from the tempest. The lurid glow illuminated Talyior's vessel. Men rushed about the deck, used oars to sheer off and avoid already burning craft. She shouted to Ergan and pointed. He swung the tiller over and followed in Talyior's wake. Lyvia's heart pounded in her throat. As the light of the flames grew, she could see Taylior's ship had lost its escape boat.

Ergan steered as close as he dared. Lyvia recoiled from the heat. Around her flames rose to greet the dawn, accompanied by the screams of men caught in the maelstrom. Ships collided, flames spread. Men and ships died. Talyior's vessel crunched into a group of three larger Perspan galleys. Immediately, flames leaped into the rigging and within seconds all were alight. Lyvia fought the urge to scream as Talyior's men retreated to the stern to find their boat gone. Men leaped one by one over the side. She rushed to the rail, heart in her throat, tried to make out Talyior in the bobbing group, then spied a last figure balancing on the taffrail. As the flames licked around the after part of the deck, he dove over the side. Lyvia knew in her core it was Talyior.

Ergan shouted an order. Oars backed. Men rushed to throw lines to the shadows swimming toward them. Willing hands hauled heroes aboard. Lyvia went among them searching faces turned macabre by reflected firelight. No Talyior. She ignored their smiling, exultant faces, scanned the dark, dancing water. No Talyior. Ergan ordered men to the oars, the ship gathered way. Panic seized Lyvia. She turned to scream at Ergan to wait and came face to face with a dripping, exuberant Talyior.

"Looking for me?"

Lyvia threw herself at him. His lips tasted like salt and joy. Someone put a blanket around them, but Lyvia hardly noticed. Nothing mattered in that moment but that he was there. She broke away, wrapped the blanket closer around him.

"My whole life, I think."

"So, do you think I did enough?"

Men moved by them, congratulating him, making ribald comments to her. She kissed him again.

"Much more than enough," she said.

She led him to the stern. Behind them the sea was dotted with burning, smoldering ships; the light from the flames making the water dance with tints of red and yellow. Lyvia counted over twenty vessels. The surviving Perspan galleys plied oars, regrouping as shadows to the southwest. The destruction, the screams passing out of earshot yet lingering in her head, appalled Lyvia in ways she had not prepared herself for.

This is war. I didn't know. Renia help me, I didn't know.

"Terrible," she breathed. "So much death. What it must have cost you."

"Those men are not my people," he soothed. "They were led here by Casan. Good men die from the mistakes of their betters. They came. We made them pay. That is all there is to it."

"Do you think Casan—"

He shook his head. "No, look at those other ships. There's order there. They may delay to pick up survivors. We have bought some time, at least."

Ergan joined them. "We have stung them," he rumbled. "An expensive effort for us, to be sure, but I wish we had a dozen more ships. I'd set light to them myself if they could bring as good a result as that." He gestured at the carnage dropping astern. "They will rejoice at this back home."

"Home?" Talyior asked. "Is that where I am going?"

Lyvia took his face in her hands, forcing him to look at her.

"After last night, and now this, and you have to ask?" She kissed him before he could respond. She felt Ergan's heavy tread retreat and heard the taunts rising anew from the men collected in the waist, but she did not care. Talyior swept her up in his arms and returned the kiss, heedless and accepting.

"Fine," he whispered when he finally released her. "No more questions."

"Let's go home," Lyvia said.

"Yes, *home.*"

He said *home* like a man planting a seed in hope's rich soil; at least that is how it sounded to Lyvia Tamorgen in this first light of a new and glorious day. She hugged his midsection, and together they stood watching the burning wreckage drop further astern. The wind shifted to their quarter and crew raised the sail to catch the freshening breeze.

Home. We'll have a day, maybe. Talyior returned her embrace. *Time enough.*

The mid-day sun illuminated their passage over the inner harbor cable, and they coasted in to tie up at the quay. Folk met them there to rejoice at their news, but the mirth faded and sobered as they realized what they would next face. Still, it was a victory of sorts. Folks crowded around Lyvia and Talyior as they walked to their carriage.

Lyvia gave them what words she could, touched outstretched hands, tried to project a confidence she did not altogether feel.

"We have done what we could," she told them. "But they still come. Take heart, good people, that we have stout walls. My father will expect us to do our utmost."

The rest of that day passed oddly normal. What folk remained went about their business or at least the shadow of their business. Ergan set about completing preparations for the city's defense. Talyior and Lyvia spent much of the time together. Lyvia felt the need to be out among her people, ignoring Ergan's orders to stay safely guarded in the palace. Everywhere she and Talyior went she gave versions of her earlier comments. Folk smiled in appreciation, but she could tell their fears still grew. By evening, people retreated to their homes or the city's temples to pray. All grew still, silent, expectant.

By the next morning, bells sounding from the harbor defenses alerted the populace to their present peril. The remains of the Perspan fleet filled the sea lanes before Desopolis, effectively closing all egress from the harbor. Sails and hulls filled the horizon from headland to headland. Lyvia watched their approach from palace walls. She recalled the flaming hulks from the night before and questioned their success, for the fleet spanning the gulf before the city seemed to crowd the area like beggars at a bread-line. Talyior joined her, munching on a roll.

"The people will be afraid," Lyvia said, gesturing out to sea.

"They should be," Talyior responded around a mouthful. "We hurt them, but we did not defeat them." He paused to swallow. "I know what I saw, what we caused. This might daunt the common folk, but you and I know there are holes in that host of canvas."

"Can we win?"

"You know your people better than I do."

"Our people."

"And will *our* people fight?"

Lyvia did not bother to answer. She knew they would fight. Both harbor forts were manned, the chain barring the inner harbor had been raised and locked. Hope of victory was another thing, however. She had heard desperate screams in the dark last night; she did not want the scene repeated in the city squares. If the chain failed, they had little hope, but that, too, she kept to herself. Playing the part of the ruler made her feel like she was trapped in some crazed story, forced to watch scenes unfold, waiting for her cue and helpless to change the plot.

"You are the poet," she said finally. "Will this be worth a song?"

"If we lose, then there won't be anyone to hear."

She glanced up at him, saw the emotion behind his carefully composed features, and any doubts she might still have harbored about him faded away.

"Then we better win," she said. She looked beyond him to the approach of two pages she had earlier tasked. "Ah, here they are."

"What's this?" Talyior asked.

She had one of the pages hold up his burden. It was a shirt of ring mail, and the other held a light helm.

"Let the guitar replace the one you lost at Tanli's," Lyvia said. "You earned these with the fireships. Appropriate, really. Both the mail and the guitar belonged to my father."

Talyior accepted the mail shirt. "Music, mail, and you; I am deeply in your father's debt."

"And it will take you a lifetime to pay it all back, I assure you."

"Well then," he responded, lacing up the ties. "As you said, we'd better win."

A bell sounding from the north tower sent them hurrying to the parapet.

Talyior pointed. "There, look! The Perspans come."

The wind blew fresh from the sea in that hour, and the Perspan fleet took advantage of it to advance shoreward. Three of the largest galleys separated themselves from the van and surged ahead, and when the headland broke the breeze double oar ranks snaked out ports and bit into the bay's placid waters.

"They make a try against the harbor chain," Lyvia said grimly.

She forced herself watch the Perspan galleys approach. If the chain held, they would wreck themselves by tearing out their hulls, effectively blocking any other ships from forcing the harbor mouth. It was a risk that, if successful would mean hot work all those gathered to defend the shore. She could see men gathering at the quay, heard their shouts as the galleys neared the chain. Missiles from the towers arched through the sky to splash harmlessly alongside all three vessels.

Just before the lead boat struck the chain, Lyvia thought she saw its bows rise slightly. The two boats on either side followed suit, as though all three were subject to some sort of rogue swell. All three crashed into the barrier, slowed, then rose to crest and pass along its top. Their combined weight defeated the cable. It sank beneath the surface. The pins anchoring it to the northern tower failed, snapping with an audible crack. Lyvia's skin grew chill as, with the barrier down, the rest of the fleet followed, spreading out to seek landing places within the harbor. The shout from the Desopolisans forming line on the quay came to Lyvia a combination of defiance and despair.

The battle for Desopolis began on the quay and along the beaches and streets of the shoreline. Perspan troops leaped from the lead ships as they crashed alongside the quay and rushed the Desopolisan troops gathered there. Lyvia tensed for the concussion, felt it despite the distance, watched as men fanned out along the wharf to engage the Perspan troops massing there. Other Perspan craft spewed men who swiftly advanced to cut off the harbor forts. The scene looked like a melee of chaos and defeat. It had taken just a few moments, and yet it seemed as if a giant wave swept away the city's defenses. Lyvia cursed. She could do nothing from her vantage but watch as her city died.

Bitter tears threatened. She blinked once, twice, dispelled them, looked with clearer eyes at the scene below and the struggle developing. Instinct led her eyes to the square that opened off the quay where she first kissed Talyior a lifetime ago.

"It is there," she shouted to Talyior, pointing. "We must hold there! All the shoreward streets exit into the square." She pushed away from the battlement. "If we break there—"

"The city falls. Yes, I see it!" Talyior cried, pointing in his turn. "But, see how your people stand, Lyvia?"

And Lyvia did see. Though they were twice outnumbered by Perspan attackers, the enemy could only bring an equal number to the battering on the quay. As long as the Desopolisans kept them from the square, they could hold them indefinitely. The war cries of desperate men and the din of battle froze her. She could only watch.

Men screamed and died. Sword and spear blades beat against shields or rang against shaft in a sick symphony of death. Arrows and spears rose and fell like waves. The fight on the quay turned into a bloody attritional horror as men fought and fell, cursed and slipped, and struggled to remain upright in the press.

Beside her, Talyior grunted and drew his sword.

"This is no good," he said. "I feel less than useless, standing here and watching." He turned to leave, but Lyvia grabbed his arm.

"Don't leave me."

And it seemed to her that Talyior heard the deeper meaning behind her plea. He took her off hand in his, kissed it.

"I'm done running away," he said. "I have to go."

"Not alone."

She hurried by him to forestall his protest.

"But what of your father? Ergan?"

"Father isn't here and Ergan is busy. Neither of them ever succeeded in keeping me caged. You won't, either. This is my city. I will fight for it."

"But—"

She turned, grabbed his face with both her hands, and kissed him.

"If we are to have a life together," she whispered. "You are going to have to stop trying to protect me. Together, remember?" She smiled, let him go and walked to the set of doors that led off the battlements. A guard stood to attention as she approached. She stopped, slipped a knife from its sheath on his belt. Turning back to Talyior, she brandished the blade. "Let's go make the bastards pay for spoiling our plans."

She swept through the doors and down the stairs, Talyior and the guard following in her wake. Another guard met her in the courtyard.

"My lady?" he asked.

"How many of you did Ergan leave?"

"A handful, lady, for your protection."

"Then if you want to do your duty, you'd better collect them and follow me."

She paused at the gate, considered waiting for horses or a carriage, then dismissed the idea and plunged out and down, heading for the din of battle below. Talyior caught up with her in the street.

"I'd say this is madness, but you are armed. Not worth the risk."

She smiled despite the moment. "Perhaps the first smart move you've made."

Folk streamed by them on their way to the harbor. A few recognized her, called out warnings, some followed. By the time she reached the square, she had a small column attending her. Her group fanned out around her and Talyior, separating them from the rearmost ranks of the defenders.

The din was terrible. Death was palpable throughout the area. The pounding, grinding Perspan assault pushed the Desopolisan's back until their thinning numbers stepped onto the cobblestones of the square. Lyvia sensed a shift in the mass of defenders to her front. Cries of alarm came from either side of the square as Perspan forces rolled up the defenders. Soon the remnants were afflicted on three sides. Lyvia looked for some sign of Ergan but could make nothing of the sea of swarming, fighting, falling men. She tightened her grip on her purloined knife. Talyior joined her, sword drawn and ready at need. Lyvia realized too late that she had been foolish.

We are too few. We cannot hold.

The battle slowed for Lyvia then, and with other senses she understood it had reached that tipping point when pressure interacted with courage, exhaustion and despair to set in motion victory or defeat. The Perspan flankers crashed through the right hand defenders to spill out to form up in the square. At the same instant, the defenders at the quay saw their hold on its narrow front eliminated as their line was pushed back and out into the wider space beyond. The Perspans raised a shout, for they sensed victory in the ragged fight that ensued. Men bled and died where they fought, others slunk away out of fear, making for the roads back up the hill and the hope of escape through the land gate.

Lyvia's guard from the palace linked shields around them. Their group fought and slipped sideways over the square. Their discipline was just enough to give their attackers pause and in that pause many of them died. In frustration and despair, Lyvia hurled her knife into the press and took a tall, helmeted Perspan in the throat.

They almost made it out of the square but were finally hemmed in by a press of foes on all sides. Lyvia shrunk next to Talyior. His sword danced, thrusting over the shoulders of Lyvia's guard at faces and exposed arms and legs of the attackers. His sword tip dripped blood. Lyvia felt a tightness in her chest watching Talyior move, a growing desperation as he fought against what she sensed as the inevitable. They would fall here gutted like fish. Remorse contested with fear, but still she would not let herself give in. To lose all that she had so recently found--unthinkable. She felt the line waver as more guardsmen fell. It would not be long now. Talyior stepped back from a sword thrust and scooped her into the fold of his free arm.

"Lyvia, if we give here you must run. Get yourself out of this if you can," he gasped, forcing her behind him, fighting and moving backward. His blade etched a pointed defense to the fore, keeping any that ventured close at bay. They were near the opening of the street that ran up hill toward Tanli's. Almost they cleared the area, and then a fresh roar came out from the northern edge of the square. Lyvia looked that direction and saw a familiar face.

Ergan and his force had won through to them.

And then the real slaughter began.

The pressure in front of Lyvia and Talyior eased as Ergan's force took the Perspans in mid-career, exulting after breaking the Desopolisan formation like a ship's prow slicing through water. Ergan's assault cut right through the confused and ill-led Perspan ranks, clearing the near half of the square with their first rush. The Perspans were swept away. Many forced their way back on to the causeway and made haste to retreat to the safety of the galleys tethered down its length. Within minutes, the area around Lyvia and Talyior emptied of living foes. Like an illumination, Lyvia realized Talyior had been correct when he said they had hurt the Perspans with the fire ship attack. The intensity of the attack had come not from confidence in numbers, but as a desperate attempt to mask its real weakness.

The change in fortune worked like a quick-silver, banishing Lyvia's fear. Talyior shouted victory along with the others. Lyvia stood rooted as Talyior moved off with the others in pursuit. Some of the Perspan ships managed to cast off from the quay, but men rushed by Lyvia with buckets of rags soaked in flammable spirits. Men took up discarded bows, scavenged arrows, wrapped sopping rags around points. Someone struck a spark to the bucket. Within moments shafts arced through the air to plunge into the piled sail-canvas of the nearest Perspan vessels, setting several alight with others desperately trying to back water with their skeleton crews to get out of range. Lyvia could see that some ships would escape, but the action doomed the bulk of the Perspan attack force to death or capture. The defenders exulted in their sudden victory.

Lyvia turned to look for Talyior and share the joy, the move abruptly curtailed as someone grabbed her from behind. She drew breath to scream, but a grimy hand clamped on her mouth and stifled her. She lost her balance as her attacker began backing away from the quay, dragging her bodily through the square.

"Now then, mistress," Sollust Megare breathed foully into her ear. "Battle's done, maybe, but we are not finished. Not by half."

The sound of Sollust's ill-remembered voice froze Lyvia. In the rush of new emotions with Talyior and the conflict's crisis, she had forgotten about Megare.

"Sollust," she cursed. "Did your papa leave you behind? Did the rats tire of you and kick you out of their hole?"

Sollust did not respond. His scraggly beard ground against her cheek as he forced her backwards, away from the roil of victory. He stank. She wondered where he might have hidden himself since the failed kidnapping. He took his hand from her mouth, but replaced it with a knife-blade pressed against her throat. Lyvia suppressed a scream. She picked out Talyior in the press, willed him to turn around and see. Megare tightened his grip on her mid-section and continued forcing her backward. Lyvia swallowed her rage and fear and disgust against Sollust's knife edge and calmed herself. She fixed Talyior in her vision, drank in the image of him. *So close. Renia, help me.*

Talyior turned, smiling, to look for her. Lyvia's heart pulsed once, twice, slowing time.

Then he saw her. His smile froze. Talyior did not hesitate. He unsheathed his sword and advanced purposely toward the struggling pair, each step punctuated by a quickening beat of Lyvia's heart as hope returned with time.

Megare forced her back two more steps, and for Lyvia the world became a space populated by three. All else retreated unimportant, uninvolved, meaningless against the rasp of Megare's beard, the stench of his breath, the pressure of his blade against her neck and Talyior's resolute advance.

"That is far enough," snarled Sollust. Beyond Talyior, the survivors of the battle had yet to notice the drama unfolding behind them.

"Enough of that, now." Sollust drew the blade across her throat, but did not cut her. Chuckling madly, he forced Lyvia to take another step. Sweat dripped from Sollust's lank locks; dirt clung to him like shame.

"Sollust, don't be a fool," she said. "There is no way out."

Sollust grabbed her arm, bent it cruelly behind her back. Lyvia grimaced but mastered her pain. "You say you love me. If you do, if you care, then let me go."

Sollust spat at Talyior and in the same motion planted a wet, sweaty kiss on Lyvia's cheek. "Don't worry, Lyvie," he sneered. "Your Sully's going to get you out of this. Even if you think you've got yourself a new doxy-boy. Stay put you!" He placed the knife point under Lyvia's jaw in response to Talyior's continued advance. "Leave off and clear our way or the lady bleeds!"

Talyior froze but kept his blade unsheathed. Behind him, Lyvia could see her few surviving guards fanning out around them. Sullust's threat stopped their motion.

"Leave well enough alone, friends!" Talyior said loud enough so all could hear. "Master Sollust and I have a standing argument. Please, leave him to me. Lyvia," he continued more quietly. "Have I told you how much I care for you? Our life begins here, today, Lyvia, as soon as I deal with this piece of trash."

As he spoke he waved his sword point before Sollust's face as though he were a carnival magician seeking to mesmerize a subject.

"Talyior," she whispered, but Sollust pushed his knife blade up, slightly piercing the skin so that Lyvia gasped and flinched, reducing her to silence. Blood dripped down her neck.

"Brave words, fool," Sollust jeered. "But you will not take her. I should have killed you when I had the chance."

Despite the pain in her arm, Lyvia let herself go half-limp, leaning her weight against Sollust's chest as Talyior edged a half foot closer.

"You should have," Talyior said. His eyes flickered from Sollust to her. "But you didn't and now you smell like dung and cowardice."

"Weak insults, poet."

Talyior edged a step closer. "Let her go, Sollust. Look around you. The Perspans are beaten. You've no way out."

"I don't give a horse turd about the northern scum," Sollust grated. "All I want I have, now, in spite of you."

"Rather unromantic to hold a knife to the one you profess to love, isn't it? Let her go. I see you have a blade. I'll give you a chance to draw it, fairly. Let you and I see this thing through, yes?"

Sollust spat again, adjusted his grip on Lyvia's arm, but he stopped moving backward. "I am not a fool," he snarled. "She and I leave together or she and I both die here."

Talyior edged another step closer. "Oh, but you are a fool, Sollust, and what is more you know it, too. You've been a fool for longer than you can remember; in love with a woman too intelligent for you; a disappointment to your father. I have been a fool and a disappointment, too, in my way. But no longer."

"Tal. . ." began Lyvia, but he shook his head slightly and slipped a half-step closer.

Sollust coughed. Spittle hung from his lip. "I hate you," he muttered. He forced Lyvia back another step, hit an offset cobblestone and stumbled. His knife blade slipped an inch away from Lyvia's neck. She turned her face slightly.

Talyior lunged. His sword point whispered by, missed her cheek by an inch, and took Sollust in his right eye. Blood splurted down Lyvia's neck as the point pierced the orb and continued deeper into Sollust's skull where it skewered the brain and then punched through the back of his head. Lyvia swung away as his grip slackened, fell forward into Talyior's embrace, and looked back. Sollust tottered, face frozen in a silent rictus, no breath for a final scream. He crumpled to the ground with a metallic twang.

"My fencing master would have been proud," Talyior whispered. Lyvia buried her response in the hollow of his neck.

Ergan marshaled the surviving Perspans in a group on the quay. They made a dispirited mass with their ships reduced to burning hulks behind them. Smoke clouded the area, but Lyvia could still make several galleys collected just outside the harbor. While Ergan and his men collected weapons, those ships set oars in motion and crabbed out beyond the headland. Once clear, they set canvas and sailed east and north and were soon lost to sight.

"Victory," Ergan announced during a pause. "But dearly bought."

Lyvia could see the truth of it. Bodies littered the square and docks or floated in the shallows. Most of the survivors on both sides sported wounds.

"We need to get word to father" she said. "He must know of this."

"Agreed," Ergan responded. "But we can't spare enough men to make a difference for him. Besides, they couldn't get there in time."

"I think the news would be more use than spears, Ergan. A small group, mounted, would cover the distance well enough."

"I will see to it."

"No," Lyvia interrupted. "I will. You've enough to do."

"But, my lady, you can't be thinking of going yourself?"

Lyvia just smiled, turned on her heel, and swept off toward the palace. Talyior and the remnants of her guard followed in her wake.

Chapter 27: The Battle at Lyranden Bridge: Donari's Dilemma

ELENI WOKE UP, alone, to the sounds of the men breaking camp. She reached for Donari, but all she grasped were the memories of last night and her clothes. She did not know whether she should be embarrassed or proud of herself and decided she was a little of both. Strangely, she felt no shame. What happened was right somehow, natural. *Change. Hope.* Senden's death was a blow to both of them and last night's intensity only partly assuaged the pain. Senden's death reminded her how much she had side-stepped truth and guilt since Pevana. *Hope. Change.*

She tied the laces to her bodice, sighed as she shoved her feet into her boots. The busy sounds outside her tent echoed the roiling emotions coursing through her. Devyn Ambrose's reappearance only added to the chaos inside her mind.

Am I fated to always crunch against the misadventures of men?

Tomais dead, Senden newly buried, Devyn just returned with dangerous intent. . .

. . .and Donari.

His hands, his lips, his eyes, his smell in sleep. She had thought herself empty until she sensed the gulf within his need last night. They had fallen into each other like drowning victims, clutching at their rescuers and in the cataclysm had woven a net that kept them both from the deeper darkness. She squared her shoulders and pulled back the tent flap half-expecting to see Donari but found instead Devyn Ambrose sitting on a camp stool at the fire and nursing a cup of something steaming. Eleni sat next to him. A cook's helper hurried over with a roll and a cup of what turned out to be weak tea.

298

Devyn graced her with a tentative smile. "Good morning, Mistress Caralon. It has been a long time since that rainstorm last summer."

Eleni studied him over the rim of her cup and remembered that night, their sodden conversation, Corvale. And yet she knew she had some advantage over him in this second meeting. She had studied Ambrose's words all winter and still had them, along with Talyior Enmbron's, tied in a bundle in her baggage. Those months had left Eleni changed; she could see the changes in him, too. Weathered, tired, ill at ease given his surprise presence in the Pevanese camp, and yet Eleni thought his eyes retained a hint of the conviction she read in his verse.

"Good morning to you, Devyn Ambrose," she responded. "And thank you."

"You are welcome," he said; an eyebrow quirked. "For what are you thanking me, exactly?"

Eleni sipped at the weak tea, for once wishing for something stronger. Her lip trembled. "You killed Corvale. He killed my husband. Thank you for avenging him, even if you did not know."

"Tomais? Dead?" The fury flared momentarily then subsided. Devyn sighed, his shoulders slumping. "I am sorry. I came looking for the Prince, but found an old argument. It is finished. You are very welcome, for what that is worth. Had I known, I'd have added one more thrust for your husband."

"Jaryd Corvale is dead, one thrust more or no. The world is a better place for that."

"And would be an even better place if I'd gotten to him a few moments sooner. Senden did not deserve to die by that miscreant's sword."

Eleni swallowed her too-hot tea to ease the clench in her throat.

"Senden knew what he was about. At least you were there to hear his last words. If you would, I'd like them for my notes."

"Of course."

A silence fell, one that was both comforting and uncomfortable. "Senden truly was a good man," Eleni said. "He was kind to me . . . and Tomais."

"He saved my life, twice, and I could not return the favor. That doesn't seem fair."

"None of this is fair, Devyn. None of us would be here if *fair* had any place in Roderran's councils."

Devyn tossed the dregs from his cup onto the coals. He did not look at her when he asked, "What will Donari do now, do you think? About the offer I bring from Sylvanus?"

Eleni sipped at the tea, cooler now, and soothing. Donari would have asked Senden his council, but there was no Senden to go to now. He was on his own.

"I don't know that Donari has any choice," she said finally, staring into the coals. "Going on as he has been is certain death down to a man, and yet to join force with the host that has been killing his people for over a month seems absurd."

"I know. Sylvanus knew, too."

"Which is why he sent you." She looked up at him. "Any other man, save perhaps Talyior, would have been dragged off as a liar. But you are a poet of Pevana, Devyn Ambrose, and the prince has heard your truth before."

"And you believe that will convince him?"

"I wish I could say." *Senden could have.* She swallowed the lump in her throat, rose to her feet. "This whole affair reeks of ego and madness, lies and half-truths, lives spent for policy. I'm sick of all this double-dealing. The tyrant's offer means more men will die, Devyn. How can Donari trust? If he does nothing, and Roderran still wins the day, the king will kill him for a traitor. Donari must either become king or die."

"Sylvanus only wants him to hold back."

"Which only makes it worse for the prince. To stand by while good men die for bad leadership, hardly what one looks for in a king."

"Sylvanus pays the same price Donari does, mistress. Sacrificing good men for to save more good people is a ruler's burden. They are both men of honor."

"Honor," Eleni scoffed. "Tell that to Senden, and all the others who now lay in the ground. You saw the smoke. Tell it to those lost in Teirne, Heriopolis, and Gallina. The cost is high, Devyn."

"I'm no soldier, mistress, but I think Senden would understand. Soldiers sacrifice themselves to save others. And yes, the cost is high."

Devyn looked away, his jaw clenched; and Eleni remembered.

"Of course, you know about that cost, Devyn Ambrose." She sat down again. Closer this time. "Did you know we buried your Kembril in the place where the tree once stood?"

Devyn nodded. "Corvale taunted me with the information. Honor." He breathed the word. "I thought I knew the meaning of the word. But when I killed one of Casan's priests in Gallina, I felt no remorse. I should have. It all connects. All of this."

"And yet you still say there is honor in the tyrant's offer?"

Devyn straightened, looked her squarely in the eye. "I would stake my life on it."

"You already have."

She patted his knee, rose again and left him to find Donari. Without Senden, he was truly on his own with this decision, unless. . .

My role here has changed, all in one terrible, beautiful night.

Eleni wrapped the thought around her, taking solace in her new emotions, and made her way through the camp. She found him sitting on a rock, staring down at the valley floor below. The slope before Donari ran gently down to meet the swell of the terrain. A small stream, nearly a river, bisected the valley flats in a sinuous line that sparkled in the morning sunlight. On the far side, some miles away, a large hillock reared its mass from the eastern ridge. A battlemented fortress frowned from its summit. A road ran alongside the stream, crossing at one point over a small bridge, a pastoral scene. New growth gloamed green over the whole region. Eleni stopped alongside Donari's perch, stared ahead, taking in the scene and kept her silence, waiting.

"I meant to be there when you woke," Donari murmured. He sat on his rock like a mountain king. "Word came just before dawn. We move this morning. The southerners have come to the fields below. Roderran intends a battle today. And this—" he finished, sweeping his hand in an arc, "—is the field."

In the new morning light it looked peaceful. She looked closer, half-expecting to see herds cropping the grass, but nothing animal moved. Instead she saw raw earth, newly turned and tossed into the shape of rough redoubts and barriers. There were vague hints that the turf had been disturbed to the flanks and in front. She picked out pennons and the glint of spearheads catching the sun.

"Sylvanus?"

"Yes," Donari replied. "He will be here, if Devyn is correct." He slid down the rock to stand next to her. "This is a cruel business, Eleni. I need Senden. I miss him."

"As do I, my prince."

He looked at her, pragmatic even as he fought to process what the day might hold for him, for all of them.

"I am sorry, Eleni, for not—"

"Prince Donari, please—"

"No, let me finish. Last night was no small matter. Much may be lost today, Eleni, but last night I found, something, a reason," he touched a stray hair near her brow, "you."

She fought against the urge to drop her head. Not now. Not ever again. *Change.*

"I've no regrets, my lord, for what I said, what I, we, did."

He looked at her searchingly. "Neither do I, lady. Now is not the time or place for regrets. I feel I am a poor vessel for love, but I *felt* you last night, Eleni. *Hope,* you said." He looked down at the valley below. "What little I have you've given me. Thank you."

Eleni hesitated, wanting to say more, wanting surety, but she realized weakness would not serve. She let the moment pass. If they survived the day, there would be time for deeper truth.

"I cannot replace Senden, my lord. I cannot advise you as he would. What will you do?"

Donari leaned back against the rock and returned his gaze to the scene below. He nodded to the north to where the road snaked down from the hills about Gallina. A column of footmen marched, flanked by horsemen, heading for the bridge over the river.

"I have a choice to make," Donari answered. "Now that he is done bleeding us, Roderran will take the lead. He wants as much glory for his crown as possible. Gaspire must be pleased. I see his colors at the head of the cavalry. He will head for the ford below the bridge."

"But if the King orders you not to take part, doesn't that make your choice for you?"

Donari did not answer at first. He stared intently at the valley floor, and when he spoke, Eleni noticed a different timbre to his voice.

"That would seem to be the case, Eleni. Easy absolution. And men die. I've been thinking about that since I left you. And I have been remembering how much I have to my account. Flames in my city. I let others take their risks, used their words for my own policies. Tomais. Kembril Edri. All those graves along the path." He laughed derisively at himself. "I cut such a fine figure here, safely out of the way, while others fight my battles for me. I have to trust a tyrant's word for a chance at peace!"

"You cannot be so hard on yourself, my lord."

"I've been trying to see through Sylvanus's plan, Eleni, and all I get is shadow. He means to fight, but he's given Roderran the bridge and ford. The ground is open. He has defenses, but hardly sufficient to blunt what comes."

"Devyn said Sylvanus wanted you to wait."

"On trust? Honor suggests otherwise. Nothing can ever be the same now, Eleni. No matter the outcome of what's developing down there. All I can hope is that from this darkness a brighter light comes."

Donari's words sounded familiar. She cocked her head, and the Prince smiled.

"Like I said, I have been remembering." He fixed his eyes on her and recited the rest of the verse.

Though the funeral barge of hope slips beneath the waves
And riot and ruin become the order of our days
I will pray, though Fate's numbers add to irregular sums
That from this present darkness a brighter light comes.

Eleni found it hard to breathe as Donari fell silent, took her hand, and raised it to his lips.

"Eleni Caralon, I will treasure last night," he said. "And if a crown comes to me today, I will wear it and be the poet-king. Senden would expect no less. I can *do* no less." He released her hand and turned back to the view. "May Renia grant me courage. I cannot falter now. Stay with me, please."

Eleni reached up and took Donari's face in her hands and kissed him as his men filed out from the trees to take up their positions on the slope.

Courage.

She focused all her senses on the friction and symmetry of her lips on his, unafraid, unabashed, unrestrained. She kissed Donari like she wished she had kissed Tomais on that last day, and if this were to be the day where her world ended then she would face it unrepentant.

She felt Donari's arm encircle her waist as he matched her ardor, and Eleni understood the night previous had been no accident born of sorrow, no treason to remembered vows or a falling away from pride or place.

It was love.

The sounds of trumpets in the valley below forced them apart, and hand in hand Eleni and Donari stood to watch the day's drama unfold.

"Shall I send for my pad and pen?" Eleni asked.

"No need for words today, Eleni. If we fail, who will read them? We watch."

"When will this begin?" she asked.

"Roderran will give the word any moment now. Massed troops to the fore, archers on the flanks and behind to lay covering fire, shields up till the front ranks get close enough, then a charge. Once the King breaks through, Gaspire's horse will exploit the gap. It is going to be bloody. Renia's Grace, what is the fool doing?"

"What? Where?"

Donari pointed. Gaspire's mounted force, marshaled in their squadrons, began moving forward at the walk, then like water spilling over a dam the whole mass gathered pace and in short order became a thundering mass of armor and spears. The ground trembled, and the sound came to Eleni like the distant report of an avalanche.

Demona, dressed and hatted for riding, walked alongside Roderran toward a small group that included the Lords Reegan and Gaspire. Off to the side, grooms waited to bring forward mounts. They assembled on a rise above the road that led down to the small span bridge over the river maps labeled *Lyranden*. Demona looked south and considered the slender channel barely worthy of its name.

She paused with the king to watch as troops marched by their vantage point, high spirited and confident. After more than a month spent trudging through sodden hills, they looked forward to crushing the forces arrayed before them behind temporary earthworks. Demona thought the king's men terribly martial and strong; she almost pitied the poor rabble waiting to receive their attentions. She dared to let herself wander in reverie for a moment and imagined them passing before her in review, dipping their spear tips and flags to Roderran, his queen and the newborn heir she held up for their adoration.

Roderran's harsh laugh snapped her daydream.

"Look at them!" he roared, slapping Lord Reegan on the back. "You've done well, sir! See how the light glances off their shields. Fresh and ready for it. Excellent!"

Lord Reegan bowed at the compliment, and then to her as if in afterthought. "They are most ready, sire. May I have your leave to see to their order once they cross the bridge?"

"Please! I will be there directly." Roderran took Demona's elbow and led her over to her horse. Gaspire Amdoran stumped up, spurs ringing.

"My King, mistress," he said, and here, too, even more pointedly, Demona sensed the grudging acknowledgement in Gaspire's swift, sneering smile. "I'll bring Sylvanus's pennon back to you as a gift."

"Ha! Well said, Amdoran!" Roderran barked. "We'll use it to line the child's bedding."

Demona studied Gaspire's face as the import of the kings words dawned on him. She felt one part pleased at the surprise and yet another disturbed at the quick, calculating expression. Demona thought he hid both well with a near-gracious bow.

"Then all the more reason for victory, my king. I'll be off to set my company in motion."

"Do so. Wait for my signal, Amdoran, none of your reckless tricks now."

Gaspire mounted with practiced ease and spurred off, laughing, with a flourish of his gauntleted hand. The king watched him ride off, took a proffered cup, and turned back to Demona.

"I've time yet for a last sip. Call it a toast to fortune," he touched her stomach, "and the future. You are feeling better?"

Demona forced a smile. She had awakened queasy when the king's pages came to arm him. More proof that she was, indeed, with child. She managed to suppress the rebellion in her stomach as they helped Roderran don his resplendent mail. The black helm with its mounted battle-crown set off his dark eyes, their irises seeming to radiate flames as the battle lust took over his other sensibilities. The effect helped Demona minimize her visible discomfort. She answered him now with good will and hand placed protectively over his on her belly to remind him his question had two answers.

"I am well enough, my lord, to wish you glory and fortune today."

She meant it, too, for the results of the day would determine everything for her. More than glory, more than conquered cities and lands were at stake that morning. Her future and that of her unborn child, Roderran's child, hung in the balance. Demona's pulse quickened, and not just over the kiss the king gave her before mounting his war horse. She felt like one of Fate's dice tumbling in the cup.

"I've set some trusted men to guard you," Roderran said, leaning down from his saddle. "You can watch the slaughter from here well enough. They are weakly placed, no matter the dirt Sylvanus has piled. He could have given battle further north with better chance. He's an old fool, and now he will pay the price for it." He reached down and cupped her chin delicately, despite the rough leather glove. For a second the flames receded from his eyes, replaced by a hint of tenderness. "We'll share a glass and a bath when I return. Take care of my son."

Then the flames of glory madness returned and he, too, spurred off to meet destiny.

A page brought a camp chair and placed it so she could sit and view the field. Several miles away from her vantage point the raw, turned earth of the southern breastworks stared back at her, stretched between two rises above the river. To the west, the stream ran up against a basaltic massif, an outlier of the ridgeline that ran south to the sea. Even Demona, despite her untutored eye, could see there was no passage on that side of the river. Roderran would have to go through those earthworks to gain the victory. At this distance all shapes were blurred, but she tried to imagine what Sylvanus would look like. She pictured a hairy, stronger but barbaric version of Sevire and convinced herself that the king and his men were right to have such confidence.

A page offered a cup of wine mixed with warm water. She sipped on the tonic and settled back to enjoy the show. She followed Roderran's progress across the bridge and on up to pass through the ranks to the front of the host. Movement from the right near the banks of the river drew her attention. One of her guards saw it too and cursed.

"What is Lord Amdoran doing?" she asked.

"Gaspire is going, early. He wants all the glory for himself. See?" The man pointed, accusing. "They charge. Fool!"

Demona did not quite understand but followed the man's gesture. Gaspire's squadrons had indeed leaped forward, a surging mass gathering pace. Her guard ran off, shouting anger and surprise. Others around her took up the call. Demona looked at the rush of northern horseflesh with uncertainty; her watered wine cooled, forgotten, in her hand.

"Gaspire was always too ambitious for trust," Donari said, moving over to mount his horse. "He's gone too soon."

Eleni still stared at Gaspire's charge as it gained momentum. The northern cavalry came on as a great wedge pointed at the left angle of the low earthworks. Eleni took thought then to go find her own mount, but when she turned to hurry off she found Devyn trotting down from the trees with her mare in tow already saddled. He tossed her the reigns, and she managed to mount smoothly. Donari brought his horse closer.

"It has begun, Devyn Ambrose, do you still think Sylvanus of Desopolis a true man?" He spoke with a rasp that suggested tension rather than anger. Devyn eased his horse by hers to respond.

"He will see us here, lord, and he will know. What happens below is now his affair. But think of this: even if he is false, you rest here with the high ground and what will likely be the only unified force left on the field. He must be asking the same question of you, Prince Donari. Are you true?"

Donari leaned over, face to face with Devyn Ambrose.

"Now *that* was spoken like the young poet I remember. Let us watch and see."

Eleni shifted in her saddle as all those on the slope concentrated on the events quickening below. Gaspire's charge reached a point three bow shots from the southerners. Eleni made out the sound of their war cries; fighting men around her tensed for the collision.

The hand of Tolimon struck the Perspans, as though the mischevious god himself poked a celestial stick at the legs of the horses, and rents began to appear in the thundering formation. Eleni gasped and others in the group on the slope took up the reaction as more and more ripples of upset began to show in the charge below. Donari shouted, pointing *behind* Gaspire's force where irregularly placed pits now revealed themselves filled up with broken and struggling riders and mounts.

Eleni swung her gaze back to the head of the formation. Gaspire's pennon still flew and the charge kept its momentum, reformed and swept up the gentle rise to within a bow shot of the ramparts. Another set of pits claimed more horses and riders before they could swerve away or rein back. The foremost ranks faltered, were pushed in by the rearmost crashing unheeding into them. Those hidden pits reduced over a thousand of Perspa's finest cavalry to a milling, broken mass. The survivors stumbled to the foot of the lefthand rampart.

Southern spearmen and bowmen showered Gaspire's bleeding remnants with missiles. More men and beasts fell, others tried to spur forward to get at their tormentors but were flung from the saddle, and still others shied away but arrows found those as well. Riderless horses screamed and kicked. Dismounted riders ran about seeking shelter from the onslaught, fell back on foot or grasped the stirrups of their fellows who dragged them back to safety.

Eleni looked to Donari. His face had lost all its color, but he kept his jaw clamped shut and stared at the terrible waste of life, a supplicant forced to accept the biting criticism from an unfair judge. She could sense something building there.

He raised his hand. Eleni felt sure he would sound the charge in spite of his earlier decision. She could hear the men nearby cursing and shouting, asking for the word.

He's going to do it. He can't help himself.

"Donari!" she screamed, and the higher tone of her woman's voice managed to cut through the noise and he turned to her. "Are you true?"

She waited, every heartbeat a reverberation beating against uncertainty, hope and fear. Donari stared at her during those heartbeats, hand still upheld. The noise around him subsided as more and more men saw his hesitation.

"Eleni Caralon," Donari said quietly. "The gods and men may damn me for a coward, but I will live this day and all the rest of my days with you."

He brought his hand back down to rest on his sword hilt and stayed. Eleni looked back down the slope. The survivors of Gaspire's charge bled back away from the enemy ramparts as the foremost ranks of Roderran's massed footsoldiers shouted their defiance and advanced at the run toward the killing zone.

"Renia's Grace," she whispered, turning to Devyn. "Will this ever end?"

"Mistress," he responded. "It has only just begun."

Eleni had to fight down the urge to vomit. She sidled her mount over next to Donari's and forced herself to watch. And what she saw convinced her of the cruelty of pride and ambition, the terrible cost of folly married to restless, immature power.

Pits also took the lead rows of rushing spearmen and archers attempting to get to the fore to loose a volley, and again the pattern appeared haphazard but the effect universal. Roderran's men slowed, shuffled to the side to avoid exposed traps and in the movement lines became confused, commands mixed and lost their unity. The pace of the onslaught slowed almost immediately to a picking crawl as the lead rows used their spears and sword points to test the ground for more hidden barriers, and all the while, Sylvanus's men poured shaft after shaft into their ranks with devastating effect. Many of Roderran's troops had tossed away their shields in their haste, and that foolishness now cost them as they faced front, nearly defenseless against the arrows of their foes.

Eleni cringed as the arrow fire decimated the Perspan ranks time and time again. They surged to the foot of the low, earthen wall only to come up against a solid line of spears and shields. She marveled at their senseless bravery in the face of butchery at its most martial.

Donari walked his horse forward, slowly, his eyes focused on the carnage as if summoned to observe the final tragedy closer, as if making final payment on a debt of soul-like proportions. She followed and, looking right and left, saw that the rest of the Pevanese advanced as well. No charge this. They paced down the hill with measured tread.

Eleni could not see how the Perspans could stand, but one group in the center withstood the Desopolisan bolts better than others. Here, men had kept their wits and their shields about them, and some of them formed a safe barrier protecting King Roderran as he exhorted his men to further efforts. Eleni thought she could make out his crowned helm and marveled that his presence. Those who could collected to him, men sacrificed themselves to pass their shields forward. Slowly, in the midst of the protracted agony of the Desopolisan response, Roderran redressed his line and regained control of the situation.

Eleni wished now that she had her pen and pad. She scanned the field. The Perspan losses had been immense. In the distance, the sad remnants of the cavalry wing attempted to reform near the bridge to cover any possible retreat. But the issue in front of the ramparts remained in doubt, for despite their horrific bloodying, the Perspans still outnumbered Sylvanus's force. That force now rolled forward once again along the entire front, for men enough yet lived for their numbers to take the day. Eleni saw now the resplendent figure of the King. He gestured back up the slope towards Donari's group, as though heartening his men and making a sort of signal for the Pevanese to come and join the fray.

Donari spurred a step forward, hesitated a single heartbeat, and lost the opportunity beyond recall; Sylvanus's entire force roared defiance and rushed down to fully engage the Perspans at the foot of the small ditch fronting their defenses. The distance between the two forces may have been fifty feet, but in that space Sylvanus's spearmen were able to muster enough energy to slam the Perspans back with loss.

Within minutes the melee became general. Lines dissolved into groups of desperate men fighting, slipping and falling in the mud of the churned earth. Banners waved and fell, only to be swept up anew as men rallied to the colors. Donari slumped in his saddle. Behind him, strangely, his men stood to arms or sat their mounts in silence. No one urged him to order an attack. They knew. Roderran's cruelty had taught them too well.

As they drew closer, Eleni made out a large warrior with a high helm lead a press of well-armed swordsmen against the group protecting Roderran. The two groups crashed together, the sound of their collision rising above the general din caused by the other conflicts. In the space created, Roderran and the large warrior Eleni assumed was Sylvanus faced each other with shields up and swords singing.

Donari spurred his horse forward to walk down the slope, and the others followed. Eleni the recorder, the historian, not the widow or the lover easily kept pace with Donari as members of his guard swept by them to test the ground to their front for the same sort of traps that had so disrupted Roderran's effort. Halfway down, they found the first of them.

The discovery did not surprise Donari. He gave Eleni a rueful smile and motioned her to follow his as he picked his way through the maze of pits.

"So much for complete trust," he said grimly. "Let us see this out, mistress."

Without her pad and pen, Eleni set herself to observe minutely. Behind her the Pevanese fell into a single column that serpentined down the final meters. Before them the battle reached its penultimate moment. Sylvanus and Roderran came together in the middle of the melee. The fighting slowed around them, the cessation moving outward like the rings on a pond disturbed by a pebble. Within a short time, the only two men left fighting were the two leaders standing toe to toe, trading momentous two-handed blows with their great-swords.

Their blows rang ever louder in the growing silence of the men around them. This was a combat of leaders, king and tyrant, and all stood by, their immediate quarrels forgotten in the knowledge that how that fight went would answer the larger questions. The power of the duel between the two leaders allowed Eleni, Devyn, Donari and some of his guard to pick their way through the mass and arrive at the edge of the scene. So intent were all there that none marked the appearance of a woman amid the ruins of blood and mud.

Roderran rained blows down, seeking to drive the other man into the mud through brute force. And yet the older man seemed able to deflect the blows without taking serious hurt. Roderran struck out twice for every single return blow from Sylvanus but with almost nothing to show for them. The king's attack weakened, almost imperceptible at first, but Roderran refused to fall back. His breath came in gasping heaves as he raised his blade and swung. Both had marked the other with slight wounds, minor cuts and gouges to mail from deflected blows. But now Sylvanus began to attack in earnest. He took Roderran's last desperate flurry with hardly a backward step before swinging wide and taking the king in a sweeping cut to the side. The mail withstood the blow, but Eleni heard bones crunch. Roderran groaned but kept his feet, managed to deflect yet another thrust and raised his own blade for one final effort.

His footing betrayed him. He slipped in bloody mud and fell slightly forward with the force of his aborted blow. His exposed neck gave target to Sylvanus' sweeping sword. It took him just below his jaw bone in a bloody spew of phlegm and life as it ripped through Roderran's throat.

Eleni stared, seized by the sudden finality of the moment. *There is nothing of glory here.* Sylvanus's death blow was but the final cut in a day of butchery.

King Roderran II of Perspa gurgled once and crashed to the ground, dead before he finished falling.

Silence.

No cheers from the victorious southerners; no cries of dismay from the Perspans. From her vantage she could see a stream of the surviving northern footmen flowing away from the field, tossing shields and weapons for speed, heading for the dubious safety of the bridge and the lands beyond. No one chased them. All within sight of Roderran's cooling corpse stiffened along with him.

313

From the edge of the scene, victorious southerners started cheering. Men beat swords against shields and brandished spears, the noise swelled like love unlooked for, but Sylvanus's ringing voice brought an end to all such activity.

"Stand! Stand men of the north and south!" he yelled. He climbed partway back up the slope so that he could see over the heads of those around him. "Stand! No more! This is no victory. Look around you. See the dead and dying? We may yet march home to a burned and desecrated city. Think of Gallina, Teirne and Heriopolis. No, this is no victory save that those of us left alive can now take council for the future. Let this end here, now. Men of the north! Your king is dead. Stand and face judgment."

Sylvanus took off his helm, and Eleni could see the exhaustion in his face, in the way he fought against weariness to stand erect and draw breath to speak. And such a voice! A trumpet sounding clear in a narrow mountain valley. Eleni scanned the mob, Donari and Devyn; all eyes fixed on the victorious Tyrant of Desopolis. Eleni recalled Donari's question to Devyn back up the slope and thought she knew the answer.

Sylvanus slammed his sword into the dirt next to him. Men who had moments before been locked in mortal combat now stood side by side to listen. Standing amid the mud and the blood, the dead and the dying, after a day of folly and loss, to listen, finally, to words of wisdom and life seemed otherworldly.

"Here me now," Sylvanus called out, more quietly, but with no less force. "Let this be done. Now. You have tried us and found us equal to the challenge. Even if you take Desopolis with your fleet, and that is no sure thing, then how would you rule? The man who led you to this pass is dead, a casualty of his own ambition to invade and dominate. He failed. He burned half this land. What need to burn the rest?"

He paused to scan the faces of those around him, and Eleni felt the pull of his personality, the will of his eyes daring each man to look him in the eye and see the truth in his expression. He held them for a long moment, and then he looked to Donari.

"But do *we* need to fail?" he asked. "Must we continue to slay each other for ambition? Plunder? Faith? What answer do we make for the children dead in Gallina? What answer do we make for the fallen here? All these, I freely add to my account. I, Sylvanus Tamorgen of Desopolis, take responsibility here for all my lies! As Roderran misled his people, so I, too, my own. I lay this suffering at my feet, brothers, and ask your forgiveness."

He raised a gloved hand to still the swell of protest from his people.

"I seek no conquest!" he cried. "I seek an end to protracted sorrow. North and south, free peoples both, should they be united through war only? Do we gain from domination? I say we lose more than life, more than *freedom*. We lose hope. I choose otherwise."

He wrenched his blade free of the mud and walked down the slope, deliberately, heading towards Donari, who had dismounted to receive him. Eleni, Devyn and the rest of Donari's guard did the same. Eleni moved to stand next to the prince. She touched his arm and felt the tension there; the tautness of an over-wound spring. His face had that deathly pallor that comes when one faces one's deadliest fear. And Eleni knew then what Donari feared the most: responsibility and failure. She slipped her arm around his waist and hugged him. He turned his livid eyes to her. She smiled, and certainty lent her some of Renia's Grace.

"Be true," she whispered. He blinked once. Distant. Twice. Closer. At a third, Eleni saw his eyes return to focus. She let him go, and stepped back.

Sylvanus paused next to Roderran's body and bent to take up the king's battle circlet half-buried in the dirt and notched where it turned the blow that broke it off the king's helm. Sylvanus shook it free of grime and held it aloft for all to see.

"Hear me! Men of the north and south! We have got so much so wrong, for so long. Let us get this right! I say we need peace. We need trade not spears, life not death, nor hate. Though some will mock me for saying so, by Renia's Tears we need love. We need a King for *all* of us."

Sylvanus let his last words linger then stepped up to Donari and placed the circlet in the prince's nerveless hand, proclaiming in his loudest voice.

"Here is Roderran's heir! Prince Donari Avedun of Pevana! I here swear fealty to him and his house for my people, and the south!" And he knelt before Donari, offering him the gore splattered hilt of his sword.

Donari stared, shocked that Sylvanus had actually carried out what Devyn said he would. Slowly, as if dream-struck, he reached out his hand but stopped short of laying his hands on the sword grip.

"Are you sure you know what you are doing?" he managed to mutter.

Sylvanus looked up at him and Eleni noted a glint in his eyes and a ghost of a smile pushing through the blood and dirt in his beard.

"Not entirely. At least I'm paying for all my crimes," he said quietly.

"But you won. There were pits on the slope. Meant for me?"

Sylvanus gave a small shrug. "An afterthought for contingencies."

"What are you?" Donari asked, his voice growing more astounded. Eleni echoed his wonder, intrigued by this strange, victorious yet gracious man.

Sylvanus actually laughed a little. "I am a man who doesn't want to be king."

Donari took the hilts. "Then what do you want?" he asked.

"Peace, and for *you* to be king," Sylvanus responded. "And I want to be a grandfather."

Donari smiled then and grasped the hilts firmly. "Then I accept your fealty," he said. "Let us make this a kingdom of peace."

He slipped the crown over his helm and turned to look over the sea of recent combatants all kneeling in unison.

Eleni noted a tremble in the hand Donari raised in acknowledgement. He swung a face transformed by joy yet tempered by wisdom back to her and put a hand to his helm in wonder.

"Eleni," he said. "It fits!"

*   *   *

Demona watched her world end from her vantage point above the bridge. The king's charge sent a thrill through those around her. There were cheers, cries of wonder at the grandness of it all that turned to questions and expressions of dismay as the advance stalled and the missiles came and the losses became visible even to those a mile away. Demona did not see Roderran fall, but she felt his death blow as a punch to her womb. She doubled over and vomited on the grass, and when the spasm finally passed she looked out on a scene of rout and dismay.

A rabble rolled toward the bridge, leaderless and urged on by fear and defeat. Single horsemen raced by on the road below. Men jammed the bridge span, fell or were pushed over its railing. Other desperate souls flung themselves into the river and tried to wade or swim across. In minutes the space under the arch was choked with drowned men and horses.

The swelling noise from the valley floor chased the remnants over the bridge and soon a clattering, jittering mob stretched out along the road. Gaspire Amdoran of Collum reigned in his foam flecked beast before her. He had lost his helm and Demona thought he had a look in his eyes that spoke of flight.

"What news, my lord?" she asked.

Gaspire looked at her incredulously before sneering. "Have you ears? Listen!" The sound of Donari's name swelled and struck like the lash of a whip. Gaspire curbed his mount and stared back at the scene before the southern ramparts. A page brought Demona's horse to her and helped her mount before running off to join the stream of stragglers making their way to and through the camp. She turned angry, fearful eyes to Gaspire.

"Two thirds of my men are lost," he snarled. "Treachery and cowardice! And your precious Roderran is dead, lady."

"There's many say you mistimed your charge, lord."

Gaspire recoiled at the accusation. He leaned over, shook his fist and grated through clenched teeth.

"Glory is for those who take it. I'll not ask to be invited to the party. Sylvanus fought without honor, and Roderran was a fool! Take note of your place, strumpet. What is to become of you now?"

"Whatever I need to do," she said firmly. "For the King's child." She placed her free hand on her abdomen.

Gaspire saw the gesture and reached over to grab her hand, twisting it harshly.

"So it is true? No lie?" he asked.

Demona nodded her head slowly. "Yes, I bear the king's child, and I suggest you take care, or when he's old enough I'll make sure he takes your head."

A sly look stole over Gaspire's face then, and he smiled. He softened his grip and raised her hand to his lips.

"Well, then, my lady," he said. "I suggest it is in your best interests to come with us."

"And I suggest it is in *your* best interests to see to my comfort and safety."

Gaspire chuckled, accepting the point and released her hand. Turning in the saddle, he shouted for his officers.

"Send a detail through the camp," he said as they clattered up. "We will need food and fodder for a fast ride. Cull the lame horses, organize remounts, and catch up with us."

"What of the wounded and the rest?" one asked, gesturing back down toward the bridge where the fugitives from the debacle still streamed across, a desperate line of blown and terrified men, weaponless, armorless.

"Leave them," Gaspire snarled. "They are done. Gather up as much of the horse as you can and follow. We will take the central road beyond Gallina. Our wounded must take their chances with the *new* king." He glanced back to the battlefield and its rising chorus of celebration. "We are finished here. Let us get Roderran's lady, and his child, to safety. Come, mistress, northwards."

Taking hold of her reins, he turned her horse and put spurs to his own, heading back up the road. Demona followed after a last backward look. A tear welled from her eye, a single admission of allegiance and sorrow. Then she set spurs to her horse determined to make the most of her dubious safety and uncertain future.

Eleni found her pad and pen and took hurried notes as Donari mounted to the camp chair placed at the top of the earthworks. One by one Sylvanus's officers, followed by the mass of the Pevanese led by Avarran, swore oaths of fealty to Donari. At the base of the slope, men had cleaned Roderran's corpse as best they could and laid him out honorably, his sword upon his chest, making it necessary to pass by the former king to pledge their oaths to the new.

Donari looked up from accepting Avarran's fealty. Eleni followed his gaze and saw a group of horsemen in the distance spur away. Sylvanus stood next to her and took in the long column of fugitives still crowding the bridge.

"Shall I send a force to round them up?" he asked.

Donari hesitated. "They are a defeated rabble, but that actually makes them more dangerous. They will suffer in the hills. Most will not make it back to their homes. Though they deny me fealty, they are still my people. Do what you can to save them."

"And what of that mounted group?" Eleni asked. She could see Gaspire's banner at its head.

Donari stood, watched as Gaspire's remnant disappeared beyond a fold in the hills.

"Gaspire could be a problem," he said. "But I doubt he will try and hold Pevana against me."

"Why?" Eleni asked.

He turned, met her eyes, then Devyn's and Sylvanus.

"Roderran's last missive had other news than insults," he said sadly. "Something I kept from you, Eleni. The king's mistress, Demona Anargi, is pregnant with his child. His note informed me I no longer had to worry about being his heir." He gave a wry smile. "So I guess that makes me a usurper in his mind. Given the tenor of the day, that almost seems appropriate."

"But your claim is legitimate!" Sylvanus barked.

"And what role has logic played in all of this?" He looked at Eleni, and it seemed he asked her a different question.

"You have my oath, and that of my people," Sylvanus asserted. "We will round the stragglers up, put them to work rebuilding Gallina, and then send them home. But if what you imply is true, then that mounted column will be another problem, however."

Donari shook his head ruefully.

"We have much to do, and too few hands to do it. Let Gaspire go for now. I would rather honor our dead than chase that lie." He raised his voice and all in earshot stopped what they were doing. "We must clean up our tragic mess! Let all who can work together without rancor. On your oaths let there be peace among us!"

His word sent groups comprised of men from both armies to lay the fallen into the pits Sylvanus's men had dug for their destruction. Eleni trailed behind as Donari, with Sylvanus and Avarran, toured the area, identifying the nobles who had fallen. Eleni wrote them down in an ever growing list. In addition to Roderran, most of the northern nobles or their sons and heirs perished in the battle. *So much death.* If Gaspire won back to his home in the north, he would find it mostly leaderless. Many noble houses would now pass to lesser sons or fail altogether.

Donari stopped near one of the pits.

"Was all this necessary?" he asked Sylvanus.

Sylvanus grimaced in remorse. "I had to fight," he said. "To get to Roderran, I had to go through all of them. I will pay for it. I don't think Renia has enough tears to wash clean my sin. I have much on my account."

Donari's words from that morning returned to her then. *And I have been remembering how much I have to my account. Flames in my city. I let others take their risks, used their words for my own policies.*

Eleni looked at both men now and realized they shared many qualities. The older man's face held true sorrow, time dearly bought that no spoken apology could ever assuage. And the younger man, helmed and crowned, whose brow suggested, moment by moment, that he understood the truth of his task and the awful responsibilities it entailed.

"I think I understand," Donari said. "But why me?"

Sylvanus turned and looked him in the eye for a long moment, silent, intent, searching. Donari faced him, undaunted. They stood thus until Sylvanus smiled, and stepped back into a full, formal bow.

"My lord . . . and liege," he said quietly. "Perhaps I acted out of the memory of a fifteen year old boy with sharp eyes, or maybe I acted out of hope," and he turned his head to include Devyn in his comment. "Or perhaps I was swayed by the words of a poet's tale, well told and true."

"You presumed much on little," Donari asserted.

"How else do you think I survived so long? Experience is its own short cut."

"I've done the same, in my own way. And so you chose."

Sylvanus smiled. "And so I chose," he agreed. "And chose well, my King. For me, the thing came easy. I know how hard it must have been for you."

Before Donari could respond, there was a disturbance from over near the road, and a small group of horsemen galloped up to them on lathered, exhausted mounts. Eleni recognized Talyior Enmbron but not the slim, young blond woman who dismounted alongside him and flew into Sylvanus's arms.

"My daughter, Lyvia" he told them. "And seemingly with news or else she would not be here when I ordered her to stay in the city." He released her. "Take a knee to your new king, my dear; your young man, too. Then you may tell us of home."

"Roderran's fleet made a try at the city, and failed," she gushed. "Ergan has the survivors chained in captured galleys. The remnants, led by Byrnard Casan, have sailed north and east."

"We have ridden like madmen for two days to bring the news and what help we had to hand," Talyior added.

Sylvanus laughed. "You bring my daughter to a battlefield?"

Talyior frowned. "I could not keep her away, my lord, from any of it!"

Sylvanus's laugh deepened, and Eleni and the others found themselves joining him as though sucked along by mirth's undertow. Such a glad noise on a day of change and sorrow; it spread like relief through the survivors.

Eleni drew a circle on her pad. She would need no other words to better describe the moment. Somehow it seemed fitting that, from unlooked-for paths, through trials traumatic and personal, she, Talyior and Devyn should find themselves together on Fate's foreign field. She sent a silent thanks to the Goddess Renia. Tomorrow would dawn in peace.

But hours still remained of that day, and when the laughter ran its course, Donari asked, "Casan's ships. How many?"

Lyvia answered. "No more than a handful, most likely with barely enough crew to work them."

"They could go anywhere, or back to Pevana, but the winds?"

Sylvanus considered for a moment. "Will not be in their favor."

"Then we will finish here and leave at first light. Avarran!" He called over his shoulder. "See to forming a flying column to return to Pevana. Food, remounts, set the men to cull what they can. Then take command of our forces, marshal them, help with this task, and then march north afterwards." He turned back to Sylvanus. "And you?"

Sylvanus bowed in gratitude. "Give me two months," he said. "I need to see to things, explain myself to my people and collect representatives from the other cities. With your permission, I will free Casan's men we hold as prisoners and set them to cleaning up their mess. Teirne and Heliopolis will need attention, and I could use the men. In two months, I will sail with them and embassies from the cities into Pevana's harbor. And then we shall make this a kingdom of Peace."

"On your word?"

"On my oath."

"Done."

Eleni retired to her tent in the early evening exhausted by the day's events. Men worked until true dark burying the dead, dressing the wounded, piling weapons. Donari moved about in a swarm of people. He had no time and, perhaps, no need of her. Talyior and Devyn came once to check on her. She met Lyvia and saw right away that Talyior would not be returning north. They shared an hour of talk while darkness fell, comparing their stories and speculating about the future. A season's worth of repair at least awaited Sylvanus in the south. Turmoil and questions of his right to the crown awaited Donari in the north. The impressions and the talk left her feeling empty. She went to her bed the same way she awakened that morning—alone.

A trooper woke her at dawn with a cup of tea and some warm stirrabout. Outside her tent men made their breakfast while others walked the horses to warm them up for the ride. Eleni looked for Donari in the half light and found him off to the side deep in conversation with Sylvanus. A screen of guards kept the curious away. Eleni decided not to wait and instead went to pack some of her things and ensure her horse was saddled and ready.

An hour later Eleni mounted her horse and drew up beside Devyn Ambrose. Behind them a hundred troopers with extra pack animals and a score of remounts awaited Donari's signal to ride. Donari exited from his tent along with Sylvanus, and the two men clasped hands before Donari swung into the saddle. Sylvanus turned to leave, but paused when he came to Devyn and the two men shook hands. Once again, Eleni found herself impressed by the older man.

Here is a man who could have been king.

"Thank you, my lord," Devyn said quietly. "For trusting me. I will trust you, as well. I hope your folk will listen to you."

Sylvanus looked up at him, eye brow arched inquisitively. "They will listen or we all lose in the end. Peace needs trust. I think I chose well, twice," he said. "Safe journey to you, Devyn Ambrose."

Sylvanus' last words struck the poet in Eleni, and perhaps the historian as well. As he walked away, she reached into her saddle bag for her pad and, balancing the inkpot as best she could, dipped and began making quick notes.

She looked up when Donari sidled his horse next to hers. He leaned over and gently removed the tablet, read what she had written. Then he laughed, a quiet welling of mirth mixed with responsibility. Eleni studied him, her mind a confusion of love and intimidation, aware of their closeness, but even more aware of the distance created by that golden circlet attached to his helm.

King. King Donari.

Eleni's mare trembled beneath her knees at the closeness of Donari's stallion, or perhaps they were her own. She could not tell. Blood rushed to her cheeks. Love and battle, shared sorrow and turmoil, a shared bed. All passed before her like evidence presented in a court, and she knew herself guilty of hope, of need, of desires close but questionable no matter what Donari told her yesterday. They returned to Pevana, but to different worlds, and the sorrow of that struck her like Minuet's arrows.

"What is this?" he asked, raising the tablet higher.

"Donari, my lord, my king. . ." She tried taking the tablet back from him. He held it out of her reach. "My notes . . . Sylvanus said something that I. . ." She steadied her voice, despite the heaviness of her heart. Sitting taller in her saddle, she swiped the tablet from him. "It is my job to tell the story of these days, my lord. I am your historian."

"No," he said. "You are not."

"I'm not?"

"You are much, much more," he said softly, "than just my historian."

He leaned over and kissed her. Their restive mounts did not deter him, and after a moment, did not deter Eleni either. Her tremors faded in the touch of his lips on hers.

"I have had enough of this story for the moment. Come love," he whispered, his lips brushing hers again. "Let's go home and start a new story. *Our* story."

About the Author

Photo credit: Grace Eide-Gabriel

Mark Nelson is a career educator and for the last twenty-two years has been teaching composition and literature at a small high school located in the rain shadow of the Cascade Mountains in eastern Washington State. He is happily married to his best friend and fellow educator and together they have raised three beautiful daughters and one semi-retired cat. Words, music, food and parenting permeate his life and serve as a constant source for inspiration, challenge and reward. To temper such unremitting joy, Mark plays golf: an addiction that provides a healthy dose of humility.

His first book, *The Poets of Pevana*, was released in 2012 to critical acclaim.

Also from Mark Nelson, his companion book *The Poets of Pevana*.

Look for these fantastic fantasies from Hadley Rille Books